An International Bestseller
A *New York Times* Bestseller
A *USA Today* Bestseller

"A magnificent and tenderly crafted novel that brings Eden's journey to a fitting and honest close. Smith's sequel is an empathetic and unflinching look at the journey through trauma to a place of healing and hope."

—Kathleen Glasgow, #1 *New York Times* bestselling author of *Girl in Pieces* and *The Agathas*

"*The Way I Am Now* is an absolute stunner of a sequel: a brave, complex journey of healing, relationships, and life after trauma. A tender, vulnerable, and hopeful book that probes the intricate depths of human emotion."

—Laurie Elizabeth Flynn, author of *The Girls Are All So Nice Here* and *All Eyes on Her*

"Amber Smith has a way of holding our hearts so even the hardest things seem possible. With *The Way I Am Now*, she shows us that the potential of love and healing, no matter how messy, is already, and always, inside us."

—Amy Reed, author of *The Nowhere Girls*

"I could not put it down—a moving and powerful portrayal of trauma, love, and hope."

—Alyssa Sheinmel, *New York Times* bestselling author of *A Danger to Herself and Others*

"Highlights with painful honesty the process of moving forward following trauma."

—*Kirkus Reviews*

THE WAY I AM NOW

ALSO BY AMBER SMITH

The Way I Used to Be

The Last to Let Go

Something Like Gravity

Code Name: Serendipity

THE

AMBER SMITH

WAY

Margaret K. McElderry Books

I AM

New York London Toronto Sydney New Delhi

NOW

This book contains material which some readers may find distressing, including discussions of sexual and physical assault, rape, and suicide.

MARGARET K. McELDERRY BOOKS
An imprint of Simon & Schuster Children's Publishing Division
1230 Avenue of the Americas, New York, New York 10020

Cover design by Debra Sfetsios-Conover

Simon & Schuster: Celebrating 100 Years of Publishing in 2024
For information about special discounts for bulk purchases, please contact Simon & Schuster Special Sales at 1-866-506-1949 or business@simonandschuster.com.
The Simon & Schuster Speakers Bureau can bring authors to your live event. For more information or to book an event, contact the Simon & Schuster Speakers Bureau at 1-866-248-3049 or visit our website at www.simonspeakers.com.
Also available in a Margaret K. McElderry Books hardcover edition
Interior design by Debra Sfetsios-Conover
The text for this book was set in Minion Pro.
Manufactured in the United States of America
First Margaret K. McElderry Books paperback edition November 2024
10 9 8 7 6 5 4 3
The Library of Congress has cataloged the hardcover edition as follows:
Names: Smith, Amber, 1982– author. | Smith, Amber, 1982– Way I was
Title: The way I am now / Amber Smith.
Description: First edition. | New York : Margaret K. McElderry Books, 2023. | Audience: Ages 14 up. | Audience: Grades 10–12. | Summary: Eden and Josh reunite as Eden's rape case goes to trial, testing the strength of their relationship amidst the challenges of college life and Eden's pursuit of justice.
Identifiers: LCCN 2023019628 (print) | LCCN 2023019629 (ebook) | ISBN 9781665947107 (hardcover) | ISBN 9781665947114 (pbk) | ISBN 9781665947121 (ebook)
Subjects: CYAC: Interpersonal relations—Fiction. | Dating—Fiction. | Trials—Fiction. | Emotional problems—Fiction. | LCGFT: Novels.
Classification: LCC PZ7.1.S595 Wav 2023 (print) | LCC PZ7.1.S595 (ebook) | DDC [Fic]—dc23
LC record available at https://lccn.loc.gov/2023019628
LC ebook record available at https://lccn.loc.gov/2023019629

For us.

For all of us—messy and imperfect—

daring to wish, to hope, to heal.

A NOTE FROM THE AUTHOR

Dear Reader,

When I first wrote *The Way I Used to Be* more than a decade ago, I hadn't planned for anyone ever to read it. I wasn't sure I would be able to share something so personal with the world. I was just writing it for myself, to work through my own thoughts and feelings as a survivor, as well as someone who has known many other survivors of violence and abuse. But when I began tentatively sharing what I'd written with a few close friends, it became clear that this story was bigger than me. And I started to hope it could contribute something meaningful to the wider conversation.

I always had my own private thoughts about what happens to Eden after the story ends. But when I wrote my final draft in early 2015 I couldn't bring myself to write an ending I didn't believe in my heart could really happen. And I also couldn't bear to give Eden an ending that was anything less than she deserved. So I left the story off with a hope, a wish.

Eden's story is many things, but at its core it's about finding your voice, and in writing it, I found mine. In the years since, I have seen the courage and bravery of so many people during the #MeToo Movement, refusing to be silenced, fighting to gain even a modicum of justice. Countless readers have also reached out, confiding in me the solace they found from seeing their stories reflected in Eden's. Empowered by their voices, I continued to work through themes of love and hate, violence, and justice in my subsequent books. However, Eden has always been in the back of my mind. Ideas would creep up unexpectedly and tap me on the shoulder, whisper in my ear, refusing to go away. At last, fortified by your strength and vulnerability, the next chapter to Eden's story—a new beginning—finally seems possible.

With Love, Amber

PART ONE

April

EDEN

I'm disappearing again. It starts at the edges, my extremities blurring. Fingers and toes go staticky and numb with no warning at all. I grip the edge of the bathroom sink and try to hold myself up, but my hands won't work. My arms are weak. And now my knees want to buckle too.

Next, it's my heart, pumping fast and jagged.

I try to take a breath.

Lungs are cement, heavy and stiff.

I never should have agreed to this. Not yet. Too soon.

I swipe my hand across the steamy mirror, and my reflection fogs over too quickly. I choke on a laugh or a sob, I can't tell which, because I really am disappearing. Literally, figuratively, and every way in between. I'm almost gone. Closing my eyes tightly, I try to locate one thought—just one—the thing she said to do when this happens.

Count five things you can see. I open my eyes. Toothbrushes in the ceramic holder. One. Okay, it's okay. Two: my phone, there on the counter, lighting up with a series of texts. Three: a glass of water, blistered with condensation. Four: the amber prescription bottle full of pills I'm trying so hard not to need. I look down at my hands, still not right. That's five.

Four things you can feel. Water dripping off my hair and down my back, over my shoulders. Smooth tiles slippery under my feet. Starchy towel wrapped around my damp body. The porcelain sink, cool and hard against the palms of my tingling hands.

Three sounds. The exhaust fan whirring, the shallow huff and gasp of my breathing getting faster, and a knock on the bathroom door.

Two smells. Peaches and cream shampoo. Eucalyptus body wash.

One taste. Stinging mint mouthwash with notes of lingering vomit underneath, making me gag all over again. I swallow hard.

"Fuck's sake," I hiss, swiping the mirror again. This time with both hands, one over the other, scrubbing at the glass. I refuse to give in to this. Not tonight. I clench my fingers into fists until I can feel my knuckles crack. I inhale, too sharply, and finally manage to get some air into my body. "You're okay," I exhale. "I'm okay," I lie.

I'm staring down into the black circle of the drain as my eyes drift back over to the bottle. Fine. I twist the cap in my useless hands and let one chalky tablet tumble into my palm. I swallow it, I swallow it good. And then I down the entire glass of water in one gulp, letting tiny rivulets stream out of the corners of my mouth, down my neck, not even bothering to wipe them away.

"Edy?" It's my mom, knocking on the door again. "Everything all right? Mara's here to pick you up."

"Yeah, I—" My breath catches on the word. "I'm almost ready."

JOSH

It's been four months since I've been back. Four months since I've seen my parents. Four months since the fight with my dad. Four months since I was here in my room. I've been home only a couple of hours, haven't even seen my dad yet, and already I feel like I'm suffocating.

I slouch down and let my head sink into the pillows, and as I close my eyes, I swear I can smell her for just a moment. Because the last time I was here, she was here next to me, in my bed, no more secrets between us. And as I turn my head, I bring the pillow to my face and breathe in deeper this time.

My phone vibrates in my hand. It's Dominic, my roommate, who practically packed my bag and dragged me out of our apartment and into his car to come home this week. I had to come home sometime.

His text says I'm serious. be ready in 10 . . . and don't even think about bailing

I start to respond, but now that my phone is in my hand and Eden is on my mind again, I find our texts instead, my last three still sitting there unanswered. I haven't looked at them in a while, but I keep rereading them now, trying to figure out what I said wrong. I'd seen the article about his arrest. I asked her how she was handling it all. Reminded her that I was her friend. Told her I was here if she needed anything. I checked in a couple of days later, then again the next week. I even called and left a voice mail.

The last thing I wrote to her was should I be worried?

She didn't respond and I didn't want to push. Now months have passed, and this is where we are. I type out a simple hey and stare at the word, those three letters daring me to press send.

My bedroom door creaks open with two sharp knocks, followed by a pause and one more. My dad. "Josh?" he says. "You're home."

"Yep." I delete the word quickly and set my phone facedown on the bed. "What's up?"

"Nothing, I—I just, uh, wanted to say hi." He shoves his hands deep into the pockets of his jeans, his eyes clear and focused as he looks at me. "I didn't see your car outside."

"Yeah, Dominic drove us home," I explain, feeling my guard lower, just enough to let my anger start to rise inside me.

"Oh," he says, nodding.

I pick my phone back up; hope he takes the hint.

"Actually, if you have a minute, I've really wanted to talk to you. About the last time you were home. Look, I know I wasn't there for you when you were dealing with . . ." He pauses, searching for the rest of a sentence I suspect also isn't there.

I watch him closely, waiting to see if he actually remembers what it was I was dealing with the last time I was home. I make a bet with myself while I wait: If he remembers even a fragment of what happened four months ago, I'll stay in tonight. I'll talk with him like he wants. I'll tell him I forgive him, and I might even mean it.

"You know," he starts again, "when you were dealing with all that."

"What is this, making amends?" I ask. "Step nine already? *Again*," I mutter under my breath.

"No," he says, wincing softly. "It's not that, Josh."

I sigh and set my phone back down. "Dad, I'm sorry," I tell him, even though I'm *not* sorry. But I don't need him breaking his sobriety again just because I took a cheap shot, either. "Shit, I just—"

"No, it's okay, Joshie." He holds his hands out in front of his chest and shakes his head, just taking it. "It's all right. I deserved that." He backs up a couple of steps until he can hold on to my doorframe like he needs something to lean on. He opens his mouth to say something else, but the doorbell interrupts him. I can hear my mom downstairs now too, talking to Dominic.

"I don't know why I said that." I try to apologize again. "I'm sorry."

It's fine, he mouths to me, then turns toward the hallway, greeting Dominic like the picture-perfect father he sometimes really is. "Dominic DiCarlo in the flesh! Good season for you, I hear." What he doesn't say is how *my* season has been shit—he doesn't need to say it, we all know. "Keeping this one in line, I'm sure," he adds in that good-natured way of his.

"You know it," Dominic jokes, shaking my dad's outstretched hand. "Someone's gotta keep him in line." He's all cheerful until he sees me, taking off my hat and trying to smooth the wrinkles in my shirt. "Man, you're not ready at all."

EDEN

My hands are steady now as they reach for the door handle. Steady as I flip down the visor in Mara's car and swipe mascara over my lashes. Steady as Steve climbs into the seat next to me and interlaces his fingers with mine, smiling sweetly as he says, "Hey, I missed you."

My heart has slowed now that the medicine found its way into my bloodstream. Even though I know it's not a real calm, I guess it's enough for me to do this for my friends. To be out and acting normal for one last night before I drop another bomb on them. And so I lie and say, "Me too."

Mara's boyfriend, Cameron, slams the passenger-side door as he gets in. He kisses Mara and then glances back at me and says, "We're probably gonna miss the opening act now."

"We will not," Steve responds in my place, then leans toward me and kisses my bare shoulder. "I'm glad you decided to come."

"Yeah, me too," I repeat, feeling like I should mean it.

"It's about time you got out again," he says.

"That's what I told her, Steve," Mara chimes in, all smiles.

"Think of tonight as a new beginning," he continues. "You'll be back in school on Monday, and then we have the last couple of months of our senior year to enjoy. Finally. We've earned it!"

"Hell yeah, we have," Cameron agrees.

They act like I'm recovering from a bad flu or something. Like now that I'm not keeping secrets, things can magically go back to normal, whatever normal used to be. As if finishing senior year is not the last thing on my mind right now. Or maybe they're right, and I should just try to ignore all the rest of the shit and be a regular teenager for the next two months while I still can.

"Cameron," I hear myself call above the music, and they all turn to look at me. "We bought the tickets for the headliner, anyway, right? So if we're late, it's still gonna be okay."

Not that I care much about either, but I owed them a little enthusiasm.

He rolls his eyes and turns back around, muttering, "You mean *I* bought the tickets." Cameron is the only one not pretending, not suddenly being nice to me just because of everything that happened, and I feel strangely grateful for that. "You can pay me back anytime, by the way."

Our bickering somehow makes Mara smile, and Steve holds my hand too tightly, both taking this all as a good sign that I still have some fight in me. I clear my throat, preparing to give them the disclaimer my therapist helped me work out during my session this week.

"So, guys, um," I begin. "I just wanted to say . . . You know it's been a while since I've been around a lot of people, and I might, like, get anxious or—"

"It's okay," Steve interrupts, pulling me closer. "Don't worry, we'll be there."

"Okay, it's just that I might need to take a break and get some air for a few minutes, or something. And if I do, it's not a big deal and I'm okay, so I don't want anyone to worry or feel like we have to leave or anything like that." It didn't come out as smoothly as I'd practiced, but I said what I needed to say. Boundaries.

Now his nervous puppy eyes are back on me. And Mara squints at me in the rearview mirror.

"I mean, I might not. It's hard to say," I add so they'll stop looking at me like that. "Or I could just get really drunk and we'll all have a great fucking time."

"*Edy*," Mara scolds at the same time Steve is shouting, "No!"

"Joking," I say with a smile. It's also been four months since I've done anything bad. Though my therapist would tell me to replace bad with "unhealthy." I haven't done any drinking or guys or smoking of any substances at all. I'm still not sure how taking these pills when I get overwhelmed is any different from the other *unhealthy* stuff. Not sure who decides what's good and what's bad. But I'm doing it anyway, following these rules, because I want to get better, be better. I really do.

Walking up from the parking lot, we pass a group of college kids with drinks in their hands, hanging out around this old wooden picnic table that looks like it's being partially held up by the concrete walls of the building. Their cigarette smoke calls to me as we walk by, and I watch them laughing and spilling their drinks. If Steve weren't holding on to my hand so tightly, if things weren't different now, I'd imagine myself drifting toward them, finding an easy space to fit for the night.

But things *are* different now; that kind of easy doesn't seem to exist for me anymore.

At the door we're each issued a neon-pink UNDER 21 wristband that the guy puts on me, grazing the inside of my wrist as he does so. I know it's nothing, but I already feel somehow violated by that small touch, yet also strangely numb to it.

It's too tight, the wristband. I tug on it to see if there's any give, but they're the paper kind that you can't tear off or squeeze over your wrist.

Mara doesn't seem bothered by hers at all, so I try to forget it.

Music's thumping from the speakers. Everywhere I look people are drinking, laughing, shouting. Someone bumps into me, and I know, I know my body should be feeling something about all this. That old shock of adrenaline, heart racing, breath quickening. But there's nothing. Except for that disappearing feeling again, except this time it doesn't kick off a panic attack. It just makes me feel like part of me isn't really here. And I'm suddenly unsure if I can trust myself to even know whether I'm safe or not with that part of me dormant.

This time I hold on to Steve's hand tighter as he leads us closer to the stage. Mara takes my other hand, and when I look back at Cameron holding hers, I'm reminded of kindergarten recess, little kids forming a human chain to walk across the street to get to the playground. I hate that I need this now.

"You good?" Mara says, close to my ear, as bodies start to pack in around us.

I nod.

And I am. Sort of. Through the first set of the opening band, I'm good. I even let myself sway a little. Not dance or jump or move my hips or close my eyes and touch my boyfriend the way Mara is doing that makes it look so easy. It's different, chemically, the absence of alcohol, the presence of this medication clouding my head instead.

By the time the band—Steve's favorite band, the one we came to see—takes the stage, I feel myself emerging again. Softly at first. There's that familiar jagged heartbeat in my chest and my breathing comes undone and messy, the bass reverberating in my skull. "It's okay," I whisper, unable to hear my own voice in my head over the music. I let go of Steve's hand. My palms are getting sweaty. And I'm suddenly very aware of every part of my body that's touching other people's bodies as they bump up against me.

I look around now, too quickly, taking in everything I missed when we arrived, all at once. I spot our school colors; a varsity jacket catches the lights from the stage. I immediately get a sinking feeling in the pit of my stomach—I don't know why I hadn't counted on seeing people from school tonight. We're here, after all. But then I see him in clips, flashes, his head back, laughing. Jock Guy. One of Josh's old friends.

No. I'm imagining things. I close my eyes for a second. Reset.

But when I open them, he's still there. It's definitely Jock Guy. The one who found me at my locker that day after school. The one who chased me down the hall. The one who wanted to scare me, wanted me to pay for my brother beating Josh up. I face the front, look at the stage. It's now. Not then. But I can't help myself; I look over again. Close my eyes again. Hear his voice again in my ear. *I hear you're real dirty.*

My head is pounding now.

I clear my throat, or try to. "Steve!" I yell, but he can't hear me. I place my hand on his shoulder, and he looks down at me. I cup my hands around my mouth, and he leans in. I'm practically shouting in his ear. "I'm gonna step out."

"What?" he yells.

I point toward the exit.

"You all right?" he shouts.

I nod. "Yeah, I just feel weird."

"What?" he yells again.

"Headache," I shout back.

"Want me to come?"

I shake my head. "Stay, really."

He looks back and forth between me and the band. "You sure?"

"Yes, it's just a headache." But I'm not sure he hears.

Mara notices me leaving and grabs my arm. She's saying something I can't make out.

"It's just a headache," I tell her. "I'll be back."

She opens her mouth to argue and grabs hold of my other arm now, so we're face-to-face, but unexpectedly, thankfully, Cameron is the one to gently touch her wrist, making her let go of me. He nods at me and keeps Mara there.

I squeeze through openings in the crush of bodies, holding

my breath as I struggle against the current. My head is pounding harder now, in time with the music but out of sync with my footsteps, setting me off-balance, the music rattling my chest. I finally make my way through the worst of it, bouncing like a pinball as I fight my way past the line of people still waiting to get in.

I hear my name, I think, over all the voices and music spilling through the doors.

Outside, I go straight for the parking lot, and now I know for sure he's calling my name. Steve always wants to be some kind of Prince Charming, but if he's the prince, I'm just another fucking Cinderella, my magic pills having worn away, the spell broken. I'm in rags, the ball raging on without me. And I don't belong here anymore; I never did. I know already, as I try to catch my breath, the cool air hitting the sweat on my face and neck, there's no way I'm going to be able to go back in there.

I tilt my head skyward and breathe in deeply, close my eyes as I exhale slowly. In and out. In and out, just like my therapist showed me. There's a soft tap at the back of my arm. "I said I'm fine, Steve, really." I spin around. "It's just a head . . . ache."

JOSH

Dominic keeps complaining about how long it's taking to get in, how much of the show we've already missed. He's texting with our friends inside—*his* friends mostly these days. "They're saving us spots near the back," he tells me. When I don't respond, he adds, "Stop."

"Stop what?"

"I can feel you brooding from here." He glances up from his phone at me, the briefest exchange. "Stop it."

"Sorry, I just don't get what the big deal is with this band," I tell him, pretending my mood is over me not being into the concert instead of because of things with my dad. "So, they were kinda famous for a minute in the early aughts." I shrug.

"And they're from *here*," he emphasizes. "Have some hometown pride, you ingrate."

I shake my head because I know he doesn't really care either. That's not the reason we're here, at this concert, or here, back home. He's meeting up with someone—the same someone he's been texting this whole time—but won't just tell me that's the reason he wanted me here.

"At this rate, we'll miss the concert altogether," he mutters, "so you might get your wish after all."

"Well, we wouldn't have been so late if you didn't make me change my clothes."

"You're welcome for not letting you out of the house like that." He scoffs and looks at me, finally putting his phone in his pocket. "Sometimes you're so straight, you don't even know how lucky you are to have me."

He reaches up to try to fix my hair, but I push his hand away. "Seriously?"

"You have residual hat hair, man!" He's laughing as he reaches for me again. I dodge him and ram right into someone.

"Sorry, excuse me," I say, turning just in time to see the side of her face rushing past. I turn back to Dominic. "Was that . . . ?"

"Who?" Dominic asks.

I look again. She's moving fast toward the parking lot. The hair is different, but it's her walk for sure, the way she's holding her arms crossed tight to her chest. "Eden?" I call, but there's no way she could hear me in this crowd. "Listen," I tell Dominic. "I'll be right back."

"Josh, don't," he says, clamping his hand on my shoulder, no playfulness in his voice anymore. "Come on, we're almost in—"

"Yeah, I know," I tell him, already stepping out of the line. "But just give me a minute, all right?"

"Josh!" I hear him yell behind me.

My heart is pounding as I jog after this girl who may or may not be her. She's walking so fast, then stops abruptly.

I finally catch up to her, standing still in the parking lot. "Eden?" I say quieter now. I reach out, my fingers touch her arm. And I know it's her before she even turns around because my body memorized hers in relation to mine so long ago.

She's saying something about having a headache as she spins to look at me.

"It *is* you," I say stupidly.

Her mouth opens, pausing for a second before she smiles. She doesn't even say anything; she just steps forward, right into me, her head tucking perfectly under my chin as it always did. I don't know why it surprises me so much when it feels so natural, like what else would we be doing besides holding on to each other like this? Her lungs expand like she's breathing me in, and I bury my face in her hair—only for a second, I tell myself. She smells so sweet and clean, like some kind of fruit. She mumbles my name into my shirt, and I realize I've forgotten how good it feels to hear her say my name. As I place my arms around her, my fingertips touch the bare skin of her arms. It's so familiar, comforting, I could stay like this. But she pulls away just a little, her hands resting at my waist as she looks up at me.

"You're literally the last person I thought I would run into tonight," she says, still smiling.

As much as I've been worried and upset and depressed over everything that happened, I can't help but smile back. "Literally the last?" I repeat. "Okay, ouch."

She laughs then, and it's the best sound in the world. "Well, you know what I mean."

"Yeah, I do." She lets go of me and crosses her arms again as she steps away. I put my hands in my pockets. "I'm not as cool as you are. I get it."

"As cool as *me*?" she repeats, this little lilt to her voice. "Yeah, right. No, I meant what are you doing in town? Shouldn't you be at school?"

"Spring break."

"Oh." She looks around and tips her head in the direction of the line. "Do you need to get back or—"

"No," I say too quickly.

"I mean, if you wanted to—" she says, just as I'm saying, "We could—"

"Sorry," we both say at the same time, interrupting each other.

She gestures to a wooden picnic table around the corner of the building. I follow alongside her and take her all in. She's maybe put on a little weight since I've seen her last, a little softer somehow, stronger, and God, she looks stunning in the streetlight. Her face and her hair—her everything. In all the years I've known her, I realize I've never seen her like this, wearing a sleeveless shirt and jean shorts, her feet in sandals. We were always cold months, fall or winter. Seeing her bare arms and bare legs, her painted toenails—parts of her I've only known in the context of my bedroom—makes me long for the cold again. I try not to let her catch me staring. She does, though.

But instead of calling me on it, she just looks down at her feet and says, "So, you're on spring break and you decide to come *here* of all places? Boringville, USA?"

"Hey, I told you, Eden, I'm a pretty boring guy."

She gives my shoulder this playful little shove, which makes me want to wrap my arms around her again.

We reach the table, and as I sit down on the bench, she steps up to sit on the tabletop, her legs so close to me. I have the strongest urge to lean forward and kiss her knees, run my hands along her thighs, lay my head in her lap.

God, I need to stop my brain from going there. What is wrong with me? Need to stop it right now. So I promptly step up too and sit on the table next to her.

"Is this awkward?" she asks.

"No," I lie. "Not at all."

"Really? Because I'm weirdly nervous to see you. Happy," she adds, her hands fidgeting with the hem of her shirt. "But nervous."

"Don't be," I tell her, even though I can barely get the words out with my heart pulsing in my throat like this. For me it's not nervousness; it's more that every nerve ending seems to be coming alive in her presence, all at once. She looks at me like she always has. Like she really sees me, and for the first time since the last time we were together, I realize I don't feel quite so lost. And because it's always so easy to talk to her, too easy to tell her my thoughts exactly as I'm thinking them, no filter, I force my mouth to say something else, instead of those things.

"You cut your hair."

She runs her hand through her hair, pushing it back away from her face. "Yes, I'm reinventing myself." She makes a noise somewhere between a cough and a laugh and rolls her eyes. "Or whatever."

"I like it."

She tips her head forward and smiles in this shy way she only ever does—*did*—when I would try to compliment her, and her hair falls forward into her face. I reach out and tuck a strand back behind her ear like I've done so many times, my fingers brushing against her cheek. And it's not until she looks up at me that I remember I can't do that anymore. "Sorry. Reflex or something. Sorry," I repeat.

"It's okay. You can touch me," she says, and my heart again, in my throat, mutes me. "I—I mean, we're friends now, right?"

I nod, still unable to speak. It's a lot easier to just be friends with her when we're not sitting next to each other like this.

She clears her throat and turns her whole body toward me, looking at me straight-on. Now she reaches out, her fingers barely touching my hair near my forehead before she trails the back of her hand along the side of my face. There's a part of me that so wants to lean into her touch.

"Your hair is longer," she says. "And you're growing a beard."

Now I'm the one smiling, all shy and awkward. "Well, I'm not intentionally growing a beard; it's just stubble."

"Okay, stubble, then," she says, smiling now as she seems to consider something. "I like it. Yeah. It's very, um, *College Josh*," she adds in a deeper voice.

I laugh, and so does she, and all that tension between us just sort of melts away. I know I'm staring at her for too long again, but I can't help it. This is all killing me. In the best way.

"What?" she asks.

I have to force myself to look away, shaking my head. "Nothing."

"Then what's all this grinning and sighing about?" she asks, drawing a circle in the air with her finger as she points at me.

"No, nothing. It's just that whenever I think about you, I somehow always forget how funny you can be." Usually, when I think of her, I'm only thinking about how sad she can get and how worried I am about her. But then I'm around her and I remember almost immediately that for all her darkness, she can be just as bright, too. I bite my lip to keep myself from saying all that out loud. Because these aren't the kinds of things you say to a girl you used to be in love with, while you're sitting on top of an old picnic table behind a graffitied building while drunk people randomly walk by, with a smelly rock show banging on in the background.

"You think about me?" she asks, suddenly serious.

"You know I do."

There's a silence, and I let it sit there between us because she *has* to know that I think about her. How could she even ask me that?

For once, she's the one to break the silence. "I wanted to text you back, you know," she says, like she's reading my thoughts. "I should have."

"Why didn't you?"

"It just felt like there was too much to say, or . . ." She trails off. "Too much to say in a text, anyway."

"You can always call me."

"Oh, definitely too much to say in a phone call," she adds, and even though I'm not really sure what that means, I also think I kind of understand anyway.

"I thought you might be mad at me," I admit.

"What? Why?" she bursts out, her voice high. "How could I be mad at *you*? You're—" She stops herself.

"I'm what?"

"You . . . ," she begins, but stops again and takes in a breath. "You're the best person I know. It would be impossible to be mad at you, especially when you haven't done anything wrong."

But that's the thing, I'm not sure anymore that I didn't do anything wrong. "I don't know, I worried that you might be not just mad at me, but sad or, like, disappointed in me."

"What are you talking about?"

"You know, the last time we saw each other."

She's shaking her head slowly like she really doesn't know. She's going to make me say it. "How I kissed you," I finally announce. "I thought about it later—a lot, actually. And under the circumstances, with everything that was going on, that was probably the last thing you needed. And then everything I said to you. Given the situation, it was pretty messed up, not to mention just the worst, stupid, terrible timing, and I thought maybe I made you feel uncomf—"

"Wait, wait, stop," she interrupts. "I thought *I* kissed you."

I don't know what to say. I think back to my room, four months ago, and it's suddenly a blur of hands and mouths and exhaustion and desperation and emotions running high, higher than ever, and now I'm kind of not sure who kissed who, who reached for who first.

But her laugh interrupts my thoughts. It's loud and sharp and clear. "And here I was feeling like the inappropriate one."

"Inappropriate?" I laugh too. "Why?"

"Kissing you after you explicitly told me you had a girlfriend—a serious girlfriend," she adds, using my own stupid words against me. "Could've saved myself some shame spiraling if I'd known you were to blame this whole time."

She's joking around, I know, but that word. *Shame.* Her voice sort of snags on it, like a thorn. It's not a casual word you use if it's not really there under the surface. So, I know this isn't the time to confess the whole truth about my girlfriend—*ex*-girlfriend—or that we broke up that night, *because* of that night.

"All my fault," I say instead, laughing along with her. "I take full responsibility."

There's a chorus of cheering from the crowd on the other side of this wall, but there couldn't be anything more exciting going on inside than what's going on out here right now.

"Well, fuck, Josh." She throws her hands up. "This is just classic us all over again, isn't it?"

Classic us. I hate that I love the way that sounds.

EDEN

It all feels foreign to my body, the laughing, the lightness. It's making me jittery but in a pleasant, slightly overcaffeinated way. To be with him again, sitting here talking, it feels like I must be making it up—making *him* up—dreaming or hallucinating or something. Because there's nothing I needed more tonight than this, with Josh. And God, how I'm not used to getting what I need.

"So, you seem good, Eden," he says, but his smile is fading.

"Yeah." I nod, but I can't quite make myself meet his eyes. "Mm-hmm." Nodding, nodding.

"You *seem* good," he repeats, and I sense it's more a question than an observation, but I'm not ready to let go of the lightness yet.

"So you've said." I try to keep up this banter that we're so good at, but he studies me, squinting like he's trying to see something in the distance, except he's looking into my eyes. I focus on my hands and not him.

"Come on," he says softly.

"What?"

"Are you good, though?" he finally asks.

I shrug. "I mean, sure. I—I'm doing better, I think. I'm not doing a bunch of crazy shit anymore, so there's that." And I hope he knows that by "crazy shit," I mean I'm not getting trashed and sleeping around with strangers anymore. "Oh, and I quit smoking," I add.

"Really?" He smiles. "Congratulations. I'm impressed."

"Thank you. It sucks."

"That's not really what I meant, though," he says. "I meant, how are *you*? Like, are you okay?"

"It's not like I really have a choice to not be okay. But I'm trying to be b-better," I stutter. Jesus. It's not a hard question, but I can't seem to answer it.

"Yeah, but how are you *actually* doing?"

He's going to make me say it.

"What? I'm not okay, Josh," I blurt out, almost yelling, but then I rein it in. "Sorry. But yeah, I'm not. Okay?"

"Okay," he says gently. "No, I'm not trying to argue. It's just that you know you don't ever have to pretend with me. That's all I'm saying."

"I'm not pretending anything with you," I tell him. "You're the only person I don't pretend with, so . . ." Not finishing that sentence.

He opens his mouth as if he's about to say something more, but then he suddenly shifts toward me. I think, for a fraction of a second, he's leaning in to kiss me. My heart starts racing. But then he reaches to take his phone out of his back pocket. As he looks at the screen, all I can think is that I would've kissed him back—again, always. Even with Steve just inside. Even with Josh's girlfriend existing somewhere. I would have.

"Someone missing you?" I ask, really hoping that someone is not the girlfriend—that he's not about to leave me to go be with her instead, even though he should. "Do you need to go?"

Please say no.

He glances up at me while he taps out a message. "No. I'm just letting my friend know I'm out here." He sets his phone facedown on the table now and looks at me with those eyes that have held me captive since I fell into them in a stupid study hall on my first day of tenth grade and have never quite managed to climb my way out. "What about you?"

"What about me?" I ask, unable to even remember what we were talking about.

"Is someone missing you in there?"

"I highly doubt it." I tilt my phone toward me so I can see the screen. Nothing yet. I set it facedown next to Josh's phone. "I told them I needed some air. It was getting kind of claustrophobic in there, and the music was giving me a headache." I decide to leave out the part about spotting Jock Guy. It would be too tempting to tell him the whole story of what happened that day, and I need to focus right now—focus *on* right now—soak in as much of this as I can, while I can. "I'm not much fun these days, I guess," I conclude with a shrug.

He keeps watching me as I talk and then reaches out. "Here, can I see?" he asks, gesturing to my hand.

I let him cradle my hand in his, carefully positioning his thumb and forefinger where my thumb and forefinger meet, pinching that fleshy part.

"It's a pressure-point thing," he explains, pressing down harder. "Supposed to help with headaches. My mom used to do this for me when I was a kid."

I close my eyes because this suddenly feels too intense, too much intimacy and realness, too much everything. I can't take it. I feel my throat closing up, my eyes burning. I could cry right now if I let myself, and I'm not even sure why. But I won't. I won't.

"That doesn't hurt too much, does it?" he asks, easing up for a moment.

I shake my head, but I can't open my eyes yet.

"You sure?"

I nod.

He presses down again, silently.

It's the opposite of disappearing. Like I'm more here than I've ever been anywhere at any time in my whole life. It's all the rest of it that's disappearing now, not me. After several more seconds, he lets go. Takes my other hand and does the same thing. As he releases the pressure, I take a deep breath, open my eyes, and look at him again. He's still watching me so closely.

"How does your head feel now?"

Do I even have a head anymore? I think. Because all I feel is the spot where his hands are touching mine. *And this is exactly why I never texted you back*, I want to tell him. But that wouldn't be fair, considering all the very unfair things I've already done to him. It's not his fault he makes the pain go away or the world disappear.

"Better," I tell him. "Thank you."

We're sort of lazily gazing into each other's eyes, and as I feel myself kind of swaying to the muffled music on the other side of this wall and I wonder if we're both not saying the same thing, one of our phones vibrates.

"Is that you or me?" he asks, picking up his phone, and I'm grateful for the disruption. "Must be yours."

Steve: do u need me?

I write back, no, I'm good

He texts back right away: u sure?

Yes.

"Everything cool?" Josh asks. "I don't want to keep you—well, I mean, I do, actually. But I won't. If you have to get back."

"No. I'm not going back in." I set my phone down again and tug at my wristband. "I didn't really want to come in the first place . . . but I'm glad I did." I don't think I'm flirting; I'm just being honest. I think.

"So am I."

"Are you sure you don't have to get back to your friends?" I ask him.

"I honestly keep forgetting the reason I was here to begin with. But I guess you kind of have that effect on me in general."

But *he* might be flirting.

"I don't know how to take that," I say. "I'm not sure that's a good thing."

He shrugs. "Feels good to me."

The way he's looking at me, my God, I can't breathe. I laugh involuntarily because it's the only way I'm going to be able to get air in my lungs.

"Why are you laughing?" he asks, but he's almost laughing too. "I'm being serious."

"I know," I tell him. "I am too."

He nods and seems to understand this is getting to be too much for me because he clears his throat and sits up a little straighter, changing the subject, if there was one. "So, you're almost to graduation?"

"Yeah. Um, sort of."

"Sort of?"

"I mean, yes, I'm graduating, but I'm actually not in school right now. Physically, I mean. I've been doing everything online."

But I don't tell him why I'm not physically in school. How I had a total meltdown my first week back from winter break—some kid ran into me in the cafeteria line, only I didn't realize that was all that was happening. It felt like more. It felt like I was being attacked. And I just reacted, kicked him in the shin and threw my tray of food at him. Of all the things to spontaneously do, I don't know why I did *that*. But I did. And then I ran, backed myself into the corner of the cafeteria, sank to the floor, and started hyperventilating in front of everyone. Even the teachers seemed too afraid to approach me. But Steve was there. He helped me to the nurse's office, waited with me until my mom came to pick me up.

My eyes refocus now. On Josh staring at me, concern creasing his forehead the longer I go without speaking.

I shake my head, shake off the memory, keep talking as if I didn't just space out. "Um, I'm thinking about not going back for the rest of the year, maybe getting a jump start on community college while I finish up. Try to, I don't know, figure out what I'm going to do with my life."

"No pressure or anything," he says, that crooked smile of his making an appearance.

"Right?" I try to laugh, but it sounds hollow. He nods in this understanding way, like he gets why none of the colleges I applied to have accepted me. "I really fucked up my grades these past couple of years," I explain anyway.

"That's not really your fault."

I shrug. "It kind of is. I barely studied for the SATs. And then I made a mad rush to submit a bunch of crappy applications to random colleges right before the deadline in February. Hail Mary sort of thing. But . . ."

"Haven't heard anything yet?" he asks.

"No, I've heard."

"Hey, there's nothing wrong with community college, you know?"

"I know." I sigh. "So anyway, that's the plan, at least for the moment. Finish up online and hope my friends forgive me for not coming back. I mean, it's just easier this way."

"Which part?"

"School, I guess. It's easy doing school online and it's . . ." I realize I haven't actually articulated what the problem is, not out loud, to anyone else, anyway. "It's hard there. It's hard to *be* there. I think some people kind of know something's going on with the whole arrest and trial thing and that somehow I'm involved. They're not *supposed* to know about me and Mandy. Amanda, I mean. That's his sister. But fucking small stupid town. People talk.

It's just hard, you know?" I can hear my voice trembling, and now he looks at me like I'm going to break or something. I shrug like I can shake it all off.

"Yeah." He nods. "That makes sense."

"Thank you."

"Why are you thanking me?"

"I don't know, sometimes I doubt myself. And I think maybe I should be better, grateful, over it, or something. Like, I don't think my friends really get it. I don't think it makes sense to them, so it's just . . . *validating*," I say, pulling out one of my therapist's favorite words.

"Well, they know, right?" he asks. "Your friends know what happened to you?"

That lump in my throat is instantly there again. I swallow hard. "They do; it's just I'm not sure they get why I'm still not . . ." Jesus, I can't complete a goddamn sentence.

"Okay?" he finishes for me.

I nod, and now there's no hiding it. I feel my cheeks getting red and my eyes getting full and my blood getting hot under my skin. He reaches out and touches my shoulder, then my cheek, and that pushes me right over the edge.

"Josh," I groan, pushing his hand away from my face. "I don't want to be messy tonight." But I'm folding myself into his open arms anyway. I'm wrapping one hand around his shoulder, the other pressed to his chest. It's like he said earlier, a reflex. A habit, a good habit I so want to fall back into. I'm closing my eyes, cheek against his neck, feeling his voice vibrating.

"It's all right," he's saying. "You can be messy. I don't mind."

In this tiny, delicate space between us, I realize the wild rattling of my heart isn't because it's shattering. It's because this is the best, the strongest, my heart has felt in months. As I open my mouth to tell him that, my lips brush against his collarbone, and I let them linger there a second too long. I hope he doesn't feel my open mouth on his skin. But he must, because then his hand is on my cheek again, trailing down my neck, and if I open my eyes, I won't stop myself and I don't think he will, either, and God, why does it always come to this, why is it never the right time for us?

"I'm fine," I say as I pull away. "I'm fine. Really." I don't know if I'm trying to convince myself or him.

"Okay," he whispers, letting me float out of his reach.

"I'm really not as fragile as I seem right now, I want you to know. I'm not sure why I'm being so emotional." I finally dare myself to look at him again now that I'm back in my spot across from him, my side of the invisible line I've just drawn on the table, arm's distance between us. "I mean, I sort of do," I say before I can stop myself.

"You do what?"

"Know why I'm emotional," I answer, but even as the words come out of my mouth, I'm not sure what I'm going to tell him, how much of which truth.

"Why?" he asks, then quickly adds, "Not that you need a reason or anything."

You. You're the reason.

But I don't say that.

"We heard from the DA earlier this week," I begin, instead. "Me and Amanda and Gen—Gennifer, I guess, is her name. His girlfriend. Or ex-girlfriend. Gennifer with a G, that's pretty much all I know about her, but . . ." I ramble, stumbling through the words, not sure I really want to be talking about this with him.

"So there's news about the trial, or . . . ?" he asks hesitantly.

"Yes and no," I tell him. "This hearing thing we were supposed to have this spring just got pushed back, so now it might not happen until the summer or fall, even." I still have the text from DA Silverman sitting there on my phone, unanswered, along with the voice mail from our court-appointed advocate from the women's center, Lane, telling me she was available if I needed to talk about it. I look up at him, realizing I've stopped in the middle of the story.

"I'm sorry," he says, like he really means it.

"I guess Kev—" But my mouth won't let me finish; I have to clear my throat before continuing. "He has this fancy new legal team that's representing him now." I take a breath, look down at my lap, trying to squeeze the wristband over my hand.

He reaches out and places his hand over mine. "That doesn't change what he did," he says, and I stop messing with the stupid wristband and take his hand; I know I'm holding on too tightly, but he doesn't seem to mind.

"I'm just starting to wonder if any of this is ever going to happen." I glance up at him. "If this was all even worth it."

"Don't say that. It's worth it," he insists, giving my hand this small, reassuring squeeze.

I nod, but I make myself let go of his hand because I'm going to have to sooner or later.

There's a brief silence between us. He looks down, then out at the parking lot, like he's trying to think of something to say. "Where did he get money for a fancy lawyer, anyway?" he finally says. "Not his parents—they wouldn't, not with his sister being . . ." He trails off, not finishing, but some part of me really wants to know what he was going to say.

Not with his sister being . . . what, his *victim*? Is that what he was going to say? I wonder. Does he think of Gennifer as his victim too? Do *I*? And what about me—am I his victim?

"No, not his parents," I finally answer—now's not the time to try to navigate that ongoing victim-slash-survivor tennis match that's constantly bouncing from one side of my brain to the other. Their parents are on Amanda's side, which still seems pretty miraculous to me, knowing the gravitational pull of Kevin.

"It's some rich university alumni guy—or guys—who are backing him, just waiting to induct him into some kind of Look What We Can Get Away with Hall of Fame." I try to laugh at my bad joke, pause to catch my breath, to reel in my emotions a little. "I don't really know. It all has something to do with fucking basketball and—" But I stop myself, immediately place my hand over my mouth. Sometimes I forget he's part of that whole world too. "Sorry, I didn't mean—"

"Don't, you're right," he interrupts, shaking his head. "No, I get it. Fucking basketball," he repeats, somehow with more contempt and bitterness in his voice than even I had.

"I didn't mean, like, *all* of basketball is bad. Or that sports are evil or anything. Just . . . just this part."

"Yeah," he says, his voice tight, narrowing his eyes as he stares off. "The part where they can't have their team's name tarnished. Their legacy, their image," he scoffs, air-quoting with his fingers, like he's heard these phrases too many times before. "I'm sorry, this shit just makes me . . ." But he doesn't finish that sentence either. He sighs and rubs the back of his neck, like he might be just as emotional about this whole thing as I am.

"Okay, let's talk about that instead. Let's talk about *you*. Please, really. Please."

"Me?" he asks, lifting his shoulder in a half shrug, shaking his head. "No, I don't want to talk about me."

"You always let me talk about myself way too much."

"Well, there's nothing going on with me."

"Yes, there is."

He looks at me like I've startled him. "Why do you say that?"

I'm not really sure why I said that, but his response tells me I'm right. We're interrupted before I can try to answer. People suddenly pour out the doors in droves, shouting and stampeding and disrupting all this sensitive air protecting us in the bubble we've created.

"It can't be over, already," Josh says, picking up his phone to look at the time.

I look at mine too. "How is it after eleven?"

And then I see the series of texts sitting there.

Steve: hey r u coming back?

Mara: are you ok

Steve: getting worried now. you OK?

Steve: will u pls respond

Mara: steve is freaking out

Mara: I kinda am too btw

Steve: where are you???

"Shit, they're looking for me," I tell Josh as I type out a message but then delete it, unable to decide who will be more understanding, Mara or Steve. "I'm sorry; I wanted to keep talking."

"No, it's okay," he says, squinting at his phone for a moment before pocketing it again. "I think I'm in trouble with my friends too."

"You can blame me," I tell him.

He just smiles, shakes his head. "Never."

People are beginning to congregate around our table now, edging us out. "I guess we should go," Josh says as he hops off the table and holds his hand out for me to take.

I step down from the bench onto the pavement, still holding his hand as I turn and walk right into Steve.

JOSH

This guy is standing way too close. I'm about to tell him to back off, but then I recognize something in the look on his face as his eyes flash between me and Eden, then down at our hands. She lets go too fast.

I recognize the look because it must be mirroring my own.

"Oh," I say out loud, my brain processing what's happening way too slowly.

He says he's been looking for her, and as she steps away from me, he puts his arm around her shoulder like he's claiming her. *Mine*, his eyes tell me.

"Um, Josh, this is Steve," Eden says. "Steve, you probably remember Josh—he went to school with us."

"No," the guy—*Steve*—says.

Another girl walks up and puts her hand on Eden's other shoulder. I recognize her; I met her once. "Oh my God," she says as she recognizes me too.

Eden steps away from Steve. Takes her friend's arm instead. "I don't know if you remember—"

"Josh, yeah, of course. Hey."

"Hi, it's Mara, isn't it?" I manage to say.

"Yes," she answers, smiling. "Good memory." Then she lets go of Eden's arm and pulls another guy forward, who raises a hand to wave at me. "This is my boyfriend, Cameron."

"Oh, yeah." I don't know how I'm continuing to speak and breathe when she's so close now and she's about to be far and I don't know when I'll see her again. "I think we had a class together, didn't we? Bio or—"

"Chem lab," he corrects me with a nod.

"Right," I answer, but it's hard to focus because I'm watching her twisting her arms together, her fingers wrapping around one another so tight, and I can feel how uncomfortable she is. This guy, *Steve*, grabs her hand, separating it from her own grip, and he's staring me down like he wants a fight. I can feel it radiating off him, seeping into my skin.

Behind them, I see Dominic walking toward us through the crowd. As he gets closer, he's shaking his head and he's holding his arms in the air. "You missed the whole thing!" he shouts. And because he has this deep, bellowing voice and towers over the entire crowd, everyone turns to stare.

As he comes to stand next to me and sees what's happening, he gives me a look—an *I told you so* mixed with sympathy.

"Dominic," I say, thankful to have something to say. "This is—"

"Eden," he finishes, so cheerful he doesn't give a hint at his true feelings about her—or rather, about *me* and her. "So good to finally meet you."

"Oh," she says, surprised, I guess, that he knows who she is. But she offers him a quick smile and a nod. "You too."

I continue the introductions. "And this is Mara, Cameron, and . . ." I meet Steve's eye, and I know it's a dick move, but he's the one holding her hand right now. "I'm sorry, remind me?"

He clenches his jaw. "Steve," he hisses.

"Right. Steve."

Dominic takes over, making conversation about school, the concert, normal things. Easy, like it always is for him. I stare at my feet because if I look at her again, I'm afraid I'll say something dramatic and stupid, like, *This guy, really, Eden? You're gonna leave with this guy? This guy who's clearly jealous and possessive and angry*—but my thoughts suddenly stall out midstream—unless it's me. Maybe *I'm* the one who's clearly jealous and possessive and angry.

When I look up at her again, her mouth is open slightly, and I want her to say something, anything, to let me know what she's thinking, to let me know what *I* should be thinking. Because I thought, for a minute there, *maybe*. But now I watch her take a breath, and just when I'm sure she's about to speak, she's interrupted by the rest of the people we were supposed to be meeting up with. A bunch of guys from the old team, some girls I vaguely recognize from our graduating class. They're all yelling and waving their arms, shouting for us. Eden glances over at them, and I can see her physically turn inward, making herself smaller, and this time when she looks at me again, it feels like it's from such an immense distance that it would be impossible to even hear each other if we tried to talk again.

"There's this after-party," Dominic tells them, gesturing to the crowd of people clearly eager for us to move along. "You all are welcome to join."

Steve speaks up, seemingly for the whole group. "We have plans already."

Mara chimes in. "But thanks."

"No worries," Dominic says, clapping me on the shoulder, snapping me out of it. "Ready?"

I nod, even though I couldn't be less ready.

"Eden?" I manage. "Let's . . ." *Go. Try again. Run away.*

"Let's catch up soon," she finishes for me. And I want to believe so badly that there's some deeper meaning in her words, some secret message that I'm not the only one looking for secret messages. As I watch the two of them walking away, there's too much happening, and it's like we're being separated from each other by these opposing currents, carrying us away, losing each other in some kind of devastating natural disaster.

Eden looks back at me like she might turn around and come running to me after all. Steve looks back then, too, a warning. She faces ahead again and doesn't look back this time.

"So, that was the infamous Eden, huh?" Dominic asks.

But I can't quite find my voice again until she's out of sight. My heart sinks into my stomach, and as I watch her disappear, I have the urge to run after her, the fear gripping me like it had the last time we parted in December. When I stood on my front steps and watched her walk away, not knowing whether I would see her again.

"Hey." Dominic nudges my arm with his elbow. "You cool? Wanna ditch these guys?" He tilts his head in the direction of our old friends. "We can do something else. Really, it's only gonna be drinking and doing stupid shit like always. I can leave it."

"No," I finally say. "Come on, I'm not making you miss this."

He turns his head to the side and squints at me, trying not to grin.

"What?" I shake my head. "I'm not that oblivious. Your secret admirer's going to be here tonight, no?" I ask him. I think his name's Luke, and I only know that much because D slyly asked me once if I remembered him from school. I didn't—he was a year behind us. But I know he's the real reason Dominic wanted to come home. They've been talking online, although Dominic has been weirdly quiet about it—and ever since we got to college, he hasn't been quiet about anything. "It's that guy, Luke, right?"

"Aren't you sneaky and perceptive," he answers.

"It's the only reason I can think of that you'd insist on coming home this week."

Dominic laughs and sighs. "I think I might be *his* secret admirer, though."

"Oh," I say. "Like he's not out, you mean?"

"It's unclear."

I nod. "Well, drinking and doing stupid shit sounds fantastic right about now."

"Okay, that's the spirit!" he says, too enthusiastically. "Let's go."

As we approach our old friends, they welcome me back into the fold with open arms and pats on the back and cheers and shoves.

One of the girls—I think she says her name is Hannah—introduces herself as I'm passing her and looks at me like I'm supposed to be hitting on her. My mouth is suddenly filled with this bitter taste that makes me feel nauseous.

It's going to be a long, stupid night.

EDEN

The drive to the all-night diner is unbearable. Steve sits all the way on the opposite side of the back seat, staring through the window. Mara and Cameron keep glancing back at us uncomfortably.

"God, I'm starving," Mara says, trying to break the awkwardness. "I hope it's not packed."

No one responds.

Cameron and Mara exchange a look, and then Cameron adds, "Dude, that second set was sick, wasn't it?"

Nothing.

We pass through two traffic lights, and he's still pouting, fuming, acting like I did something wrong.

"Will you say something?" I finally ask.

Steve turns to me now, looking at me for the first time. "You can't just disappear like that."

But I am, I think. I'm disappearing all the time. I'm disappearing right now. That's all I ever do when I'm with you. But what I say is: "I didn't disappear. I had to get out of there, and I told you that."

He shakes his head like I'm not making sense.

"What?" I demand.

His eyes flick up to the front seat, and then he turns toward me, inching closer. "Did you plan to meet up with him tonight?"

"You're actually asking me that?" I say, more than loud enough for them to hear too.

"Well, you can't blame me if that all felt just a little familiar," he says, still talking low, as if he doesn't want to embarrass *me* in front of our friends.

It takes me a second to rewind all my sins of the past couple of years until I land on the memory he must be referencing. "Oh, so you wanna go there? Okay, let's."

That night is fuzzy, but I remember the highlights: We were at a dorm party, me, Mara, Cameron, and Steve. Mara had been pressuring me to give Steve a chance. But his sweetness as he talked to me in the crowded hall grew increasingly offensive the more I drank. Like he still thought I was the innocent little band geek he was friends with freshman year. And so I sent him off to get me another drink and hooked up with the first guy who looked at me. Until my brother showed up for some reason—those details are lost—and we had a screaming match in front of everyone. I was exceedingly drunk and terribly mean to everyone, I am told. When I relayed the story to my therapist, she said this sounded like my rock bottom. I can only hope that's true.

"Edy?" Mara says from the front seat. "I'm sure he didn't mean it like that. Right, Steve?"

I ignore her because he definitely meant it like that. "You do realize we weren't even together when that happened, right?"

"Fine, never mind." He grabs my hand. I snatch it away. "Forget I said anything."

"Tonight, which is what we're *actually* talking about," I say, trying to keep my voice from shaking. "Josh saw me running out, and he came after me to see if I was okay."

"You told me not to come," he argues. "You said you were okay!"

"Obviously I wasn't okay." How does Josh know I'm not okay, but Steve—the one I see all the time, the one I'm supposedly in a relationship with—doesn't? "You know that I'm having these anxiety attacks, which make me feel like I'm actually fucking dying, by the way, and that I wasn't going to be able to make it through that fucking concert. And you pressured me to go anyway, and now you—"

He starts laughing but not in a ha-ha-funny way; in an angry, I-have-the-moral-high-ground way that makes me want to open the door and jump out of the moving vehicle just to not be sitting next to him anymore.

"What's so funny?"

"You still didn't answer the question."

"And I'm not going to!"

"Guys!" Mara shouts. "I'm trying to drive, and you're giving me middle-school flashbacks of my parents' pre-divorce fighting."

"Yeah, can you take it a little easy there?" Cameron says, and I'm about to argue with him until I realize he's talking to Steve—for once not blaming everything on me.

The car is silent until we tumble into the parking lot over the potholes that threaten to tear Mara's old brown Buick apart. She pulls into a free spot and slams the car into park, then turns around and says, "We're going in and getting a table. You two can stay out here and fight or fuck or whatever you need to do. Either way, I'm going to order a banana split. Lock the car up when you're done." She tosses the keys onto the back seat, and they go in, leaving us here.

"So, I guess we're fighting," Steve says as if he didn't start it.

"Well, we're not doing the other thing."

"Right." He scoffs. "Why am I not surprised?"

"What does that mean?"

"You know."

"No, I don't."

"Come on, it's not like I'm some frat bro all hard up for sex, but—" He stops midsentence.

"So, wait, I'm confused. Is the problem that I'm *too* slutty or not slutty enough for you?"

"Never mind, you're just twisting what I'm saying."

"No, I just want to make sure I get it right, *Stephen*," I add, using his full name like I used to when we were just friends. "Is this because I didn't want to give you a blowjob the other day?"

"God, do you have to say it like that?" he whisper-shouts.

"Because you know you asked me at the worst possible time, right? When I was trying to have a serious conversation with you about coming back to school."

"I know, and I said I was sorry. But it's not just that." He rolls his eyes at me and sighs. "Why do I feel like you were more interested in me before we were together?"

I bite my lip, try to keep myself from smiling or laughing, or worse. Because I could hurt him if I wanted to. I could tell him the truth, which is that I was never all that interested in him. But I'm trying to be good. Trying to be happy in my relationship with the age-appropriate boy who my best friend pushed onto me because she thinks he's the nicest guy we know. The truth is, he was just there. And I was just there too, trying so hard to be normal, thinking maybe he was the way.

"Before we were together," I begin, still deciding how honest I can afford to be, "I was interested in fucking anyone with a pulse, so . . ."

"Nice." He gets out of the car, leans in, looks at me, and says, "That's great, thank you very much." Then slams the door in my face. *Too honest.* I grab Mara's keys and follow him to the edge of the parking lot, where he's standing with his back to me.

"Steve!" I yell, marching over to him. "Look, I meant that as, like, do you really want me to be acting the way I was before we were together?"

He swings around so fast that I have to fight the urge to shield myself. "Did you have sex with him?" he blurts out.

"Are you serious? We were only talking!"

"Not tonight," he snaps. "I mean, *have* you had sex with him?"

"Why?"

"Because he was looking at you like . . ." He clenches his fists as he turns to one side and then the other, like he's searching for words he's dropped on the pavement.

"Like what?"

His face twists in disgust as he starts again. "Like he . . ." And I decide I don't want to know what he was looking at me like, anyway, because it's pointless to know something like that.

"Like he was concerned?" I finish.

"And *I* wasn't concerned? I was texting you all night, Edy!" he shouts.

"All right, I'm sorry, I know. Please, Steve, I don't want to be fighting."

"I don't either." There's a silence, and when he starts talking again, he's quieter. "It's just—he was holding your hand."

"He was helping me down from the table. And we were just talking. We're friends. That's what friends do."

He shakes his head as if the things I'm saying don't even matter and cuts his eyes to me like he thinks he's catching me in a lie. At this rate, maybe I should've just kissed Josh like I really wanted to—significant others be damned.

"But you used to be together, right?" he asks.

"He's my friend," I repeat, more firmly.

He looks down at his hands, then back up at me, squinting.

"He's my friend *now*. And he's helped me a lot, and he's really kind, and you were a total jackass to him."

"I know I was!" he shouts. "But he was being a jackass too."

"No, he wasn't."

He scoffs and shakes his head. "You just didn't see it," he says, dismissing me.

I hate when he gets mad—it's dizzying and scary and makes me want to be small and back down. It makes me feel weak, which scares me more than anything else. "You know I didn't plan to run into him there, don't you?" I finally say, giving up the last shred of self-respect I was clinging to.

"I know," he admits.

"Then why are you being like this?"

He turns his head and looks at me like I'm an idiot. "You know, I do realize that you're a ten and I'm like, what, a three," he says, softer now, more like his usual self. "On a good day."

"What?" I laugh. "I'm not a—"

"And that fucking guy. *Miller*," he mutters, knowing his name after all. "I mean, Jesus, could he be any taller?"

"Wait, so you're really just . . . jealous?"

He shrugs and nods, his cheeks darkening, embarrassed now.

"And that's why you're being mean and insulting me?"

"I'm sorry." He extends one arm toward me and taps the fingers of my right hand with his left. "I really am. It's just that, I don't know, ever since we've been together, I feel really insecure. Like you're gonna realize you're way out of my league and—"

"That's not even—" I try to interrupt, but he interrupts me right back.

"No, I'm serious. I feel like it's only a matter of time before I'm gonna lose you to someone just like him."

I reach for his hand now, and he pulls me into a hug.

"You don't need to be worried about that," I tell him. Because it wouldn't be someone *like* Josh—there's no one like Josh—it would *be* Josh.

He tilts my chin up as he looks at me, and I can't tell what he's really thinking, but he leans down and presses his lips against mine. He wraps his arms around me again and says "I'm sorry" one more time.

I should tell him it's okay. Not because it is, but more in the spirit of making up. I can't force myself to do it, though, not when I can close my eyes and still feel Josh's arms around me.

"Will you stay over tonight?" he mumbles into my hair before pulling away to look at me. "My dad's at his girlfriend's house. You could tell your mom you're sleeping at Mara's."

All I want to do is go home, flop onto the couch, and fall asleep with the TV on. But before I can even think of a response or an excuse, he continues.

"It's just—I feel like we haven't had any alone time lately. We're always with Mara and Cam. You know I love them, but I miss just us."

"I'll text Vanessa—I mean my mom," I correct myself. Trying to get back into the habit. My therapist says it will be good for me to start calling my parents Mom and Dad, that eventually I'll start feeling like we're family again.

We walk in and I spot Mara and Cameron in a booth near the kitchen. I send Steve over and signal to Mara that I'm going to go to the bathroom. When I get inside, I lean against the sink and wait for her. "A little tense out there," Mara says.

"Just a little," I agree. "Honestly, did I do anything that wrong?"

"No—I mean, no, but . . . ," Mara hesitates, hoisting her bag up on the counter. "It was kinda scary when you weren't texting back, but Steve was definitely being a little agro jerk. Which is bizarre, because he's like the king of calm."

"Not always," I mutter. Didn't she remember that day in the

hall four months ago when he told me off in front of everyone in our study hall? He called me a bitch, which was fair enough, but then he also called me a slut, and no matter how many times he's apologized for both, I don't think I've quite forgiven him for that one. "I can't believe he brought up that stupid party."

Mara's lips twist, and she sucks in a breath, hissing. "Yeah, that was a pretty low blow. I guess even big, sweet teddy bears like Steve can be assholes sometimes."

"Teddy bears are still bears," I say, but she doesn't seem to give my statement much thought as she leans forward to wipe the mascara smudges from under her eyes. I'll have to remember that one for my therapist; she's great about making me feel smart and insightful.

Mara meets my eyes in the mirror. "So, Joshua Miller," she says—a question, a statement, a command, an exclamation.

"So." I inhale deeply, suddenly unable to catch my breath. "Him. Yeah."

"*Joshhhh*." She draws out the word, torturing me, and then she smiles in this mischievous way. "Apparently he just keeps getting more and more attractive, huh?"

"Oh, really?" I ask her, though I can't seem to wipe the smirk off my face. "Jesus, don't tell Steve that. Speaking of, I thought you were Team Steve all the way."

"I am, but . . . *damn*." She fans herself with her hand like one of those Southern belles in black-and-white movies. "Who knew he could rock the scruffy look?"

I shake my head, ignoring her eternal fake lusting after Josh, and examine myself in the mirror, thankful I'd at least taken a shower today. "It was weird seeing him."

"Makes sense," she mumbles as she presses her ruby lipstick to her upper lip. "It's been a while since you saw him." And then her bottom lip. "A lot's happened."

"No, but that's the thing. It was weird that it *wasn't* weird. Like, after the initial awkwardness, we just kind of picked up where we left off and . . ." I stop myself before I say something too true. Like how I've been on pause these past months while my life has just been moving on without me, and tonight, with him, it was like being unpaused, feeling what it's like to be alive again, even if only for a little while.

Mara turns around to face me now. "And what?"

I unscrew the top of her tiny expensive pot of lip gloss and dip my ring finger in, dab it against my lips instead of answering, admitting that I've been thinking about him way too much ever since I started seeing Steve, comparing everything he does—and doesn't do—to Josh.

"You wanna go there again, don't you? And by there, I mean the whole Josh . . . *thing*."

"The whole Josh thing?" I ask, almost laughing. "What's that?"

"You know, the whole steamy-secret-Joshua-Miller-yumminess-passion thing?" she adds, with an exaggerated shiver through her whole body.

"Okay, one: you're ridiculous. And two: even if I did, it doesn't matter." I shrug and toss her lip gloss back into her purse. "Josh has a girlfriend."

Mara laughs with her head thrown back and then says, "And Steve has a girlfriend, too, don't forget!"

A waitress comes into the bathroom, probably checking to

make sure we're not doing lines in here or something. "Shut up," I mutter under my breath. "Obviously, that too."

As we move toward the door, Mara stops short and turns around to face me again. "I'm Team Edy, by the way," she says. And she looks at me more seriously than she has in a while—she's avoided too much seriousness with me ever since I told her what happened. I think she's trying to keep my spirits up, but sometimes I miss this look.

She gives my hand a little shake. "You know that, right?"

JOSH

I can feel Dominic staring at me the whole car ride. "Do we need a code word or something?" he finally asks as he parks next to the other cars in the lot behind the football field.

"Code word? What are you talking about?"

"If you need to leave."

"Why would I need to leave?"

"The whole seeing-your-ex thing," he says, as if that should be obvious.

"I told you I'm fine."

"Yeah, and I know you too well to believe that."

I go to open my door, and he locks it. "Do I need a code word for you to let me out of this car?"

"It's me you're talking to," he says. He gives me that look he's given me so many times this semester when I'm on the verge of screwing something up. "Can you at least admit you're not fine?"

"Okay," I relent. "Did it suck seeing her with that dickhead guy? Sure. But we're friends; it's not like we made some kind of promise to each other or anything."

"I'm just gonna say one thing, and then I'll shut my mouth, all right?"

I sigh. "Fine. All right."

"She seemed like a nice girl and all. Cute, I grant you. You know, I'm sure she's not purposely trying to be an agent of sheer fucking chaos in your life. But—"

"All right," I interrupt. "Don't push it."

"I'm just saying maybe seeing her with another guy isn't such a bad thing. You can finally move on."

"Move on?" I laugh. "I *have* moved on."

"Yeah, okay." He squints at me, raising one eyebrow in his signature you're-full-of-shit look. "I'm just saying you can stop carrying this weird torch you have for her. You're gonna set yourself on fire with it."

"I've told you before, it's not like that with us," I tell him again.

"I mean, she *is* still in high school," he continues anyway.

"I know that, D!" I snap at him. "And again, we're just friends."

"Maybe, but I still feel like she's been stringing you along, and meanwhile you—"

"That's not it," I interrupt him. "She's not doing that, Dominic. Not at all."

"And *meanwhile*," he says, louder, talking over me. "You've literally blown up your whole damn life over her and she's with someone else. I just wanna make sure you see it—that's not cool."

"It's not like that," I repeat. "None of that stuff was her fault."

"Oh, it's not her fault you broke up with Bella and wound up on my doorstep without a place to live?"

"No. And, technically, Bella broke up with me."

"Right, okay, so then I guess it's not Eden's fault you spent all of winter break in a black hole, missed one of our most important games of the season, and almost got kicked off the team after you spent one day with her? One day," he emphasizes, holding up his index finger to make his point, even though the point he's making couldn't be farther from reality.

"I didn't—" But I stop myself because it's better if everyone keeps thinking I just didn't show up to the game, instead of what really happened. "That wasn't because of her."

"So, it's just a coincidence you haven't dated anyone since then? I mean, you never even tried to fix things with Bella—who, by the way, was a very solid person we all really liked."

"Look, I appreciate you caring, but I just can't keep talking about it or . . ." *I'll say something I shouldn't.* "I'm fine. Okay? I promise. Can that please be good enough for you?"

He sighs but then nods once and presses the button to unlock the doors. Pops the trunk. We get out of the car, carrying the six-packs we picked up on the way to this stupid impromptu reunion, and we cut across the field, past the giant outline of our old mascot against the brick wall of the bleachers.

That's when Dominic says, "Oh! How 'bout 'eagle'? For the code word."

"Working 'eagle' into a conversation won't sound conspicuous at all."

"The code word could be conspicuous," he says, laughing.

"Fifty percent chance no one'll know what that means."

He got a smile out of me. "You're mean," I tell him, and as I look ahead, I can see cell phone flashlights dancing up in the bleachers already. "Those are supposed to be our friends."

"I'm honest," he corrects. "And you're the one who's laughing."

"Am not."

"Well, it's not our fault our friends can't all be blessed with brains and bodies like ours," Dominic jokes in his best drag queen voice, as he calls it, raising the cases of beer into biceps curls.

"Yeah," I scoff. "Or your modesty."

"I'm done with modesty!" he yells into the night air, and it echoes against the brick-walled buildings of our high school.

"Who's there? DiCarlo? Miller!" a voice yells from the stands, perfectly imitating our old coach. "Get your asses up here!" Zac yells.

"This is so stupid," I groan.

"Now, *you* be nice." Dominic laughs, but stops abruptly when he catches a glimpse of Zac. "Oh my God," Dominic says under his breath. "Is he . . . ?"

"Still wearing his high school varsity jacket?" I finish. "Yes, he is."

"Never mind. Forget what I said, you don't have to be nice," he mumbles as we trudge up the steps of the bleachers.

There are about a dozen people here. A few were there at the concert, including Zac, who I managed to dodge until now. They're rowdy, drunk already. We'll be lucky if no one calls the cops on us for trespassing. Most I recognize from school. Zac seems to be the self-appointed ringleader. At one time I thought he was my best friend. But everything changed senior year. After Eden. But most things changed for me after Eden. He called her a slut once after we broke up—even after I confided in him about how much I loved her—and still, more than two years later, it's the first thing I think of when I see him.

"How does it feel to be back?" Zac says, laughing, spreading his arms out wide like he's gesturing to some kind of vast kingdom.

"Looks like *you* never left." I don't know if I'm messing with him or trying to start a fight, but he just smiles at me anyway. He doesn't get it, which is probably for the best.

I turn around and look out at the view. This place that felt so important, so life-and-death, seems small now. It's really just four brick buildings, an old scoreboard, a tennis court, a soccer field, empty parking lots, and a rusty flagpole in the center of it all.

"Victorious!" Dominic answers. I don't know if he's being serious or not now. He might really feel victorious—he wasn't exactly out back then, not with our teammates, anyway. Being gay *and* black in a mostly straight, mostly white school, I think he tried to make himself invisible, except for when he was on the court. "Being a big-shot college basketball star agrees with me."

"I bet," Zac murmurs, and I can hear the jealousy in his voice without even needing to look at him. "Miller, heads up." I turn back around just in time to catch the can of beer he's tossing to me.

I give him a nod and retreat up to the top level of the bleachers. I can see Dominic is making the rounds, working his way over to the one guy he's really here to see. I'll go introduce myself to him in a while—after all, Dominic was nice to Eden tonight even though he thinks she's bad for me. It's hard to explain her to him, how wrong he is about her, what she means to me, without telling him things it's not my place to tell.

Three of the guys hop the fence and start racing each other around the track, and two of the girls, who I think must've been cheerleaders, follow them onto the field. They start enacting old cheers I recognize from basketball season, only they're stumbling and laughing through them, falling over each other and screaming. As I look around at everyone in their little groups, I wonder if they're all pretending to be having fun or if they really are and there's something wrong with me that I can't be that person anymore.

I set the beer on the bench next to me and take my phone out. I want to text her, but it's like she said, there's too much to say in a text right now. I put my phone away instead.

That girl from the show is not being very discreet about watching me. I wish I could hang a sign around my neck that says STAY BACK 100 FEET. As soon as I have that thought, Zac zeroes in on me and starts climbing the steps. I pop open the beer, and it protests with a carbonated hiss. I take a long swig. I won't be able to get through a conversation with him sober.

"Buddy," he says, taking a seat next to me. "Been a minute."

"Yeah," I agree. Chug. Chug. Chug.

"So?" he says. "Tell me! What's been going on with you?"

I shrug, finish the rest of the beer. He pulls another can out of his jacket pocket like magic and hands it to me. "Thanks." I crack it open.

"What's with you, man?" he asks, side-eyeing me.

"Nothing's with me."

"If you say so." He takes a giant gulp. "Hey, see that girl?" he asks, pointing at her with the neck of his bottle. "She was asking about you before you got here."

"Hm."

"*Hm*? That's it, hm?" He snorts through a laugh, keeps drinking. "Big man on campus. Guess you must be swimming in it."

"Hey," I warn him, and take another sip. "Come on."

"Unless living with DiCarlo is rubbing off on you," he says, cracking himself up.

"Hey!" I tell him, more firmly this time. "Do you see me laughing?"

"Loosen up, bro," he shouts, reaching around me and squeezing my shoulder.

"God, were you always like this?" I say, more to myself as I shrug him off me.

"Were you always like *this*?" he comes back at me.

"I'm just not interested, okay?" I answer, so he'll drop it. And I take another sip, trying to pace myself.

"Okay, okay." He holds up his hands like I'm the one being an asshole right now. "Saw you talking to that girl at the concert. Was that . . . uh . . . ?" He looks off, snapping his fingers like he's trying to summon her name.

"Eden," I answer.

"Right," he says. "Question, though. Didn't she kinda screw you over last time? Like cheat on you or something?"

"No, she didn't."

"We're talking about Caelin McCrorey's little sister, right?"

"Yep." I watch him as I take another long pull and swallow. "I seem to remember you once called her a slut, didn't you?"

He chuckles like it's nothing. "Is *that* why you're pissed at me?"

"Who said I was pissed at you?"

"Man, that was a million years ago." He stares at me, and there's this weird smile edging onto his face, like he's half amused with himself, half scared of me. "What is this? Did she say something about me or . . . ?" He trails off. "'Cause it was just a joke."

She never mentioned a word to me about Zac, but now he's making me wonder if there's something more than that one slut cough in the hallway senior year.

"Like what?" I ask. "What would she say about you?"

Before he can answer, the three guys who had been racing around the track are bounding up the bleachers toward us, the former cheerleaders trailing behind them. Dominic is walking over to us now too, his arm around the shoulder of the guy he likes—not so secretly, it seems—and the rest of them are following.

"Dude, did someone just say something about Caelin McCrorey?" one of them asks as they're approaching. "Did you hear what happened to him?"

"Oh yeah," another answers. "Heard he got kicked outta school or something, right?"

"No, no. You're thinking of his friend," one of the cheerleaders answers. "Kevin, remember? Kevin Armstrong."

Hearing his name sends a chill up my spine. I try to catch Dominic's eye. *Eagle.*

"He didn't just get kicked out of school. I heard he's in prison or something."

"No, he's not in prison," someone else answers. "He did get arrested, though."

My heart is racing. *Eagle*, I shout in my mind.

"That Boy Scout?" Zac spits, laughing. "What the fuck for?"

I keep drinking. No one seems to know. My heart slows a little. Maybe they'll drop it.

"I know," the other cheerleader chimes in now, waiting until everyone looks at her before continuing, louder. "He raped someone."

There's an uproar of voices saying things like "what" and "are you serious" and "no way," but it's Zac's voice that breaks through: "Okay, now I want to know who's accusing him because that's bullshit!"

I turn to look at him, and I can't think of one word to say because all my thoughts are preoccupied with restraining myself from knocking him on his ass right now.

"No, it's true," the first cheerleader says. "I know the girl. We met her." She points to the other cheerleader. "Remember? Kevin brought her home over Thanksgiving last year. Jen or Gin, something like that? She was his girlfriend." So Eden was right; people really have been talking.

"Obviously not anymore," the other girl adds, snorting through her words before dissolving into laughter.

"Oh, his girlfriend?" Zac shouts, throwing one of his arms forward, all sloppy. "Well, there you go."

"What does that mean?" I finally say because I can't restrain myself this much.

"Come on, how's his girlfriend going to accuse him of rape?"

I clench the now-empty can between my hands. "You realize what a fucking asshole you sound like, right?"

"Whoa, Miller." Zac nudges me with his elbow. "Chill."

Dominic gives me a questioning look. He has my back, though

he has no idea why; that's what makes him a good friend. "No really, Zac," he taunts. "Tell us you're an asshole *without* telling us you're an asshole, am I right?"

People laugh at that, but Zac's still looking at me like I really had knocked him on his ass. *Good.*

"Well, it's not just her," the cheerleader says. "There's like at least one or two other girls. I don't know who they are, but it's a whole thing."

"*Forreal*," the other girl adds, slurring. "Like I heard there's'posed to be a trial and everything."

I spot a case of beer someone has brought up, and gesture for one. I open it immediately. Drink fast. This is too hard.

"Is it terrible," a small voice says, "that I wouldn't be surprised if it's true?"

Next to me, on the bench below mine, I see it's that girl who's spoken. Hannah, the one from the show, the one Zac was talking about. She looks up at me and smiles quickly before looking away.

"Oh my God," her friend who's sitting next to her says, gripping her arm. "What do you mean?"

"No! God, no. He never did anything to me," she responds, "but I was alone with him once after a game, and he totally creeped me out."

"How?" I ask. Dominic shoots me another look, making me aware that I'm being too intense. "I mean, why, wh-what did he do?"

"Oh, um," she stutters, blushing like she's surprised I'm talking to her. "It wasn't really anything he did, exactly," she continues. "Just a feeling, I don't know." She shrugs. "The way he was looking at me, maybe? Like, weird. Sort of . . ." She pauses and stares off like she's trying to remember more clearly.

And for a second—a split second, now that I'm really looking at her—I see something in her that reminds me of Eden somehow. I take a drink. It's not that she looks like her; she doesn't. It's something deeper, and I think it must be a shyness in her gestures that reminds me of her. It hits me with way too much clarity as I wait for her to finish talking. Kevin must've seen this quality too, whatever it is, in this girl. Just like he must've seen it in Eden. Like some part of her is unprotected, vulnerable. The thought that I might be seeing something he saw scares me.

"Predatory," she finishes with confidence, but then shakes her head and lets out this small laugh. "Whatever, I don't know. I just know it made me not want to ever be alone with him again. Like ever."

"Yeah, that's probably a good thing." I nod, biting back any more words. Someone's handing me another drink. I'm drinking way too much, too fast, but I take it anyway. Dominic is making some kind of hand gesture, like *slow down*, but if he had any idea how hard this is right now, he wouldn't blame me.

"Well, this all makes so much sense," Hannah's friend says. "I always thought Kevin Armstrong was super hot. And I'm only attracted to complete psychopaths. So yeah, that tracks."

Everyone laughs like it's all a big joke.

I stand too quickly, and the world sways. I have to grab the railing to stay balanced.

"Where you goin'?" Zac yells after me. "Hey, Miller!"

I don't even acknowledge him. Just concentrate on walking

down these steps without spilling my drink. I make it to the bottom, and somehow Dominic is suddenly there, standing in front of me. I turn around to look—wasn't he just up there with the rest of them? And as I'm turning back to face him, he's got his hand on my shoulder like he's steadying me.

"Hey, are you okay?"

"Yeah, I'm fine," I lie. "I'm gonna fly solo for a bit, that's all."

"What?" he asks, looking thoroughly confused.

"You know, the *eagle* metaphor thing?"

"You are shwasted right now and still using the word 'metaphor,'" he tells me, shaking his head. "How are you so drunk already?"

"I don't drink, 'member?"

"Listen, I'm gonna need to sober up a little before I can drive us. You really okay on your own for a while?"

"I'm fine. I'm just—I'm gonna talk a walk."

"You're gonna talk a walk?" he repeats.

"Take," I correct myself, enunciating carefully. "Yes! Go. Seriously. Be with your . . . *man*," I settle on after shuffling through "boy" and "friend" and "boyfriend" and "guy" and "guy friend" in my head.

"Oh, he's my man now? Okay." Dominic laughs hysterically. "I'm so giving you shit for this later."

"You're a good friend, you know that?"

"Okay, okay. You too. Go talk your walk, we'll leave soon, all right?"

I wander back toward the school, and I don't really know where I'm going until I'm standing there, this swath of grass between the tennis court and the student parking lot. I go to take another sip but realize the can is empty. I crunch it up and aim for the garbage bin at the entrance of the tennis court.

"He shoots," I say out loud. "He *scores*."

I hear clapping behind me; I turn around.

"Nice shot," she says. Hannah.

"Oh. Didn't see you there."

"Is it okay if I join you?" she asks, pulling a flask out of her purse. "Brought the good stuff."

"Sure," I tell her reluctantly, if only to keep Zac away from her.

We sit in the spot I sat with Eden the day she said she'd go out with me. There were dandelions growing all over then; we had this whole thing with dandelions and making wishes. And she was doing her tough-girl routine but let me in just a little bit anyway. I can close my eyes and see her sitting here in the sun so clearly.

I run my hands along the grass. It's freshly mown. Nothing growing here now.

"I liked what you said back there," she tells me as she holds the flask out.

I take it from her and bring it to my lips. Whiskey. *Small sips this time*, I tell myself. I shrug and hand it back to her. "I guess I'm just kinda over this whole scene."

She nods and takes a much longer sip, scrunching up her face as she swallows it.

"I have to tell you, I had the biggest crush on you when we were in school. I'm sure you didn't know I existed."

She passes the flask back to me, and I take a sip before trying to figure out how to respond.

"God, I just totally made that weird, didn't I?" She laughs and covers her face with her hands, then spreads two fingers to peek at me.

"Uh, no," I finally say. "No, I'm just not really in a place to—I mean, I'm flattered to hear that, but—"

"But you have a girlfriend, right? Of course you would, why wouldn't you?"

"I don't actually, but I'm not—" I stop midsentence because I don't know how to say what it is. It's true I don't have a girlfriend, but I don't feel quite available somehow, either. "I mean I guess it's sort of . . ."

"Complicated?" she finishes with a knowing laugh.

"Exactly."

She takes a big sip, hands it back to me, and as I'm drinking, she looks around and says, "Well, it's just us here now."

"You seem very sweet, I just—"

She leans in so fast I can't stop her. Her mouth is wet on mine, the taste of whiskey strong on her tongue, making me feel even drunker. I'm kissing her back even though I shouldn't. And it feels good even though I don't want it to. I haven't kissed anyone since that day four months ago when I kissed Eden . . . or she kissed me.

She's climbing onto my lap, her legs straddling me, her long skirt pulling up. She takes my hands in hers and runs them up her thighs. I can't help but think of Eden's bare legs earlier. Her skin is so warm. Soft. And now her hands are on my chest, pushing me to the ground. And I pull her down with me. I'm drifting away, my head so fuzzy. I wish I would've kissed her tonight. I wish I would have found the right words to tell her everything. She was right there. Right here in my arms. And I let her go. Again.

I feel myself being pulled back to my body as I open my eyes. I'm on my back in the grass now, and it's not her body pressed up against mine, not her hair my hands are tangled up in. She's holding herself up over me, and she's laughing, saying, "It's Hannah, actually."

"Wh-what?"

"You just called me Eden."

"Shit, I'm sorry," I say, trying to catch my breath. "My head is—I'm not really thinking clearly. I know your name, I promise."

"It's okay," she says, her hand rubbing against my jeans. "Kiss me like that again, and you can call me anything you want."

"No, I—I'm not really in a place to—I'm just—" I'm getting flustered, my head feeling so full as I struggle to sit up. "God," I mutter to myself, "fuck me."

"Yeah." She giggles. "That's kinda what I'm trying to do." She leans in to kiss me again, and I have to push her hands off me.

"No, really. I can't." I scramble away from her and stand up, buttoning my jeans and quickly threading my belt back through the buckle. She looks up at me, so strangely, so confused. "I'm sorry, it's really not you."

She doesn't say anything as she gets up and walks away. Doesn't even look back.

"It's not you," I call after her. "Really."

It's *not* her. She's not Eden.

I kick at the grass and hit the metal flask, nearly toppling over as I bend to pick it up. I sit back down, take another swig, and pull my phone out of my pocket.

EDEN

We're dozing to a movie playing on Steve's laptop when my phone vibrates on the nightstand. I raise my head from its spot on his chest to look at the time.

He tightens his arms around me as we settle back in. But then, in the next beat, suddenly he's sitting up, dumping me off him. "Seriously!" he shouts, looking down at my phone as the screen darkens. "Why's he texting you at one thirty in the morning?"

"I don't know," I say. "Do you really want me to check?"

"No," he says abruptly.

I reach across him and flip my phone over, facedown, pretending I don't care that he's just looked at my phone without my permission, that I don't care about whatever it is Josh has said. Steve is staring at me as if I should have some kind of explanation.

"Are we still on this?" I ask. "Because if we're going to have this fight again, I'd rather just go home."

Reluctantly, he lies down next to me. It vibrates a second time, and we both ignore it. The third time, Steve sits up again. "Oh my God, what the hell does he want?"

I reach for my phone, and this time I turn it off, but not before I catch a glimpse of the beginnings of each message lighting up the screen:

It was nice to . . .

I'm sorry if I . . .

Can I see you . . . ?

"I don't know. I don't care," I lie. "Forget about it," I tell him. Even though I'm already trying to fill in the ends of each sentence, even though all I want to do is stare at the words and overthink each and every one for hours on end.

"Sorry," Steve says, closing his laptop and setting it on the floor. "That kinda ruined the mood." The mood was already ruined, though, before we even got here. He lies back down next to me in a huff.

"Again, I feel like you're blaming me or something. It's not like I asked him to text me."

"I know," Steve says. "I'm not blaming you. I blame *him*, believe me."

I hesitate to say the rest, which is, again, we're friends and friends text each other and I don't like him thinking he has any say in the matter. But instead of that, I ask him, "Do you still want me here?"

"Of course," he answers, softening a bit as he looks at me.

"Well, can I borrow a T-shirt or something to sleep in? I hadn't planned on not going home tonight."

"Oh, yeah. Sorry, I should've offered," he says, remembering that he's supposed to be a nice guy. He jumps out of bed, and I follow him over to his dresser, where he opens a drawer overflowing with his signature nerdy graphic tees, all in various states of unfolded. "Take your pick."

I sift through until I find the one I've seen him wear so many times over the years of being friends, then not being friends, then being sort of friends again, and now this, whatever we're trying to be now. It's got a picture of a cat holding up a bone, with the caption I FOUND THIS HUMERUS. I drape it over the front of me and turn to look at him. "How about this one?"

He laughs and nods. "Perfect."

And I start to relax for the first time since I let go of Josh's hand earlier tonight. Face-to-face, I think we both realize at the same time neither of us knows quite what to do. We've seen each other without clothes a few times before, but it wasn't like this, just standing in front of each other.

"Um," he says, nervously pushing his hand back through his hair. "Want me to turn around or . . . ?"

"No," I say uncertainly as I pull my shirt off over my head and set it on top of the dresser. Except now I'm feeling a little self-conscious just standing here in my bra, so I start unbuttoning and unzipping my shorts to have something to do with my hands. Steve takes his jeans off and sets them next to my shirt, making us even. Now he's wearing only his boxers and the band T-shirt from earlier.

He reaches for the humerus shirt and raises it up over my head so I can easily slip my arms into it. Thankfully it's big enough that it falls past my butt.

"Thanks."

I finish taking my shorts off and reach under the shirt to take my bra off. We get into bed, and he looks down at me, grinning in this shy way that reminds me of the chubby, awkward freshman version of Steve I used to be friends with.

"What?"

"I just never would've thought that shirt could look so sexy."

I reach up to turn off the light, laughing. But he kisses me, hard, swallowing the sound. He moves his hands over the shirt more confidently, more freely than he has ever touched me in the three months we've officially been together. He's usually so timid when things heat up, but the way he's pulling my whole body closer to him, it sort of takes my breath away. Maybe it's because of his dad being gone, or Josh, still no doubt in the back of his mind.

I don't know. Whatever it is, I want to let myself go with it. I don't want to fight it, don't want to keep waiting for every last thing to feel right before I get to enjoy this. The kissing and the weight of him, the closeness. He pushes the shirt up my stomach and pulls his own off over his head so we're skin to skin. He pulls my leg up around his waist, rubbing himself against my hip, his thigh pressing between my legs.

"Do you like that?" he whispers.

I nod in the small space between us.

I don't care that I don't love him. I like him; I trust him. Pretty much, anyway. Even if the events of the evening have only shown me that he clearly doesn't trust me, I try to shove the rest of this night out of my mind. He trails his hand down my stomach, inside my underwear, and groans as his fingers slide against me.

"I have a condom," he says with his lips to mine. "If you want to try again."

We've tried to have sex three times, but something always goes wrong. The first time I was the one to freak out, the second time he was, and the third, we were both too nervous and it didn't last long enough to count it as having happened. I would say yes right now if I thought it would be easy. But these things are never simple with him, and I don't think I can take one more emotional hit today.

"Wait," I say, pulling his hand out of my underwear. "Can we just stay like this for now?" I ask him, drawing his body closer with my arms and legs. "This feels really good."

"I'll do whatever you want." He's kissing me as he repositions himself between my legs so that his whole body is against me now, only a couple of thin layers of underwear between us to dull the sensation of how hard he's pressing down on me, the friction of our bodies barely absorbed by the fabric. "Is this good?" he asks, breathless.

I gasp, "Yes."

We're both breathing heavier and moving faster. And as his hands roam under my shirt now, I can't get Josh out of my head. I can't stop thinking about *his* hands touching me, his arms, his breath, his voice, his body. I open my eyes in the dark to try to remind myself of where I am, but it's no use because it becomes Josh's room.

A moan escapes my mouth, and I get scared that somehow he's going to be able to tell it's not for him. He thrusts harder, though, and I start to wonder if maybe his head is somewhere else too. I can't help but think about how if we were really having sex and not unceremoniously grinding on each other, he'd really be hurting me. But we're not, I tell myself, we're not, so he's not. It's okay.

"God, I'm close," he's saying as I'm thinking all this.

I close my eyes again and try now, try so hard, to think of Josh and not Steve. I am a bad person, I know. But I don't want this to end. I don't know when I'll get to feel this way again, and I want to savor it as long as I can. He's pushing against me so hard, I stretch my arms up over my head, reaching for the wall behind us, just to have something solid to hold on to.

"I'm so close," he breathes against my neck.

But before I can even consider how close or far I am, he grabs my arms so abruptly, it shocks me back into reality.

"Steve." *That's too hard*, I want to say, but it's all happening so fast. He wraps his hands around my wrists and holds my arms down against the bed. "Steve?" I repeat, but he's not looking at me, not hearing me. I push and pull my arms. I try to move. I can't. I squeeze my legs around him, trying to make him slow down. I try to call his name again, but my voice is frayed, and I'm not getting any volume.

It feels like something in my heart stretches and snaps like a rubber band, some force rushing toward me like hands pulling me underwater. Dark, freezing-cold water that I can't see through.

I'm pulled through this murky darkness until I'm back there again. And it's not Steve anymore; it's not Josh. My wrists are pinned, twisted together, held so tight I'm afraid they're slowly breaking. Again. Another hand around my throat. Again. A voice telling me to shut up. *Again*. I'm drowning. I can't fight this. I struggle against him. Yell at him to stop—I think I do, at least. Not breathing. For too long, I'm not breathing. I'm drowning, I must be. And then, when I'm sure I'm going to just let go, sink, die, those hands holding me under release their grip, and I break the surface of the dark water, gasping, flailing.

On my feet, I turn the light back on. I'm breathing heavily, coughing, pacing, trying to stave off the memories that just invaded my mind, my body, without warning.

Steve watches me for several seconds, sitting there in bed, a pillow pulled across his lap. "Edy!" he shouts, his eyes wide, like this isn't the first time he's said my name. "Edy, where were you just now?"

"Where were *you*?" I shoot back at him.

"I was here," he says. "I—I'm here." And he's looking at me so innocently, I can't take it. I turn around and place my hands against his desk, trying to brace myself, and I let out a slow, shaky breath. I look up at myself in the mirror. Clear, harsh edges. No blur, no disappearing acts. I am fully here.

"Please come back to bed, Edy," Steve says gently.

I meet his eyes in the mirror and have to look away again. "I need a minute," I manage to tell him between breaths. And then I watch as his reflection gets out of bed and cautiously walks up behind me.

"You're scaring me," he says. "Tell me what I did. Please?"

"Nothing," I choke out. "It wasn't you."

"It had to be," he counters. "Everything was fine—good, you said it felt *good*—and then something happened."

I shake my head. He places his hands on my shoulders, slowly turning me around to face him. He takes my hands in his. "Jesus, you're trembling."

I snatch them back from him and shake them out. "I'm fine."

"Is it a panic attack or anxiety attack or whatever?" He freezes, looking genuinely worried. "What should I do?"

"Just—just stay right there," I tell him, holding my arms out so he doesn't come any closer. "For a second." I gasp. "Okay?"

He nods. He doesn't move. I step back and lean against the desk again. Close my eyes. Breathe in and out. In and out. In and out until my lungs work again.

When I open my eyes, Steve is sitting on the edge of his bed. He's put his shirt back on.

"Come back, we'll just cuddle, okay?" he says, as he holds the blanket up for me to climb in. I do. I back up against him, and he wraps himself around me. He's always good at this part. "I'm not him," he says softly, smoothing my hair back. "You know that, right?"

If I speak, I might cry, so I just nod. Because I know what he's talking about. He's not Kevin. Of course he's not. But he's not Josh, either.

JOSH

“He’s a really good guy,” I hear Dominic saying. “Seriously the best guy friend I’ve ever had. He’s just messed up over this girl, I think. Plus, he hardly ever drinks, so he’s just sloppy AF tonight.”

“No, I get it,” someone else responds. “Been there. Well, not over a girl, but—you know . . .”

I open my eyes. Streetlights flash through the car windows. I’m on my side, scrunched up across the back seat of Dominic’s car. I hear myself groan. Every sound echoes in my head.

“Hey, sleeping beauty,” Dominic’s secret admirer guy says, smiling as he turns around to look at me from the passenger seat.

“Sleeping beauty, my ass,” Dominic says. “Do not vomit in my back seat.”

I reach for my phone, the screen blurry as I try to focus. It’s three in the morning. “She didn’t text me back,” I mumble.

"Luke, will you take that from him? We don't need him drunk dialing his ex."

"Here, why don't you give that to me for now?" He's so polite and gentle, I hand it right over.

"Luke," I repeat his name. "I'm so rude, I d-did-in't-introduce myself."

"You introduced yourself, Josh," Luke replies.

"Like five times," Dominic adds.

"She didn't text," I hear myself say again.

"I know," Dominic responds. "It's okay."

The next thing I know, I'm standing, sort of, between Dominic and Luke. They're holding me up on each side, their arms under mine, and I'm stumbling up my front steps. Dominic is reaching into my pocket for my keys as if I can't get my own keys. And I want to tell them they really don't have to do all this, but I can't seem to make the words come out.

Then we're crashing through the door, and I reach out to grab the handle so it doesn't smash into the wall and wake up my mom, but somehow I trip and we all fall forward on top of each other.

I'm laughing even though I'm trying to be quiet. Dominic is *shhshh*-ing me.

Next they're spilling me onto the couch.

Then Dominic and Luke are standing across the living room with their backs to me, time skipping forward again, my mom and dad here now in their bathrobes and slippers. They're all talking too quietly for me to hear.

Now they're standing over me, and Mom has her hand over her mouth, shaking her head. Dad is looking at me like there's something seriously wrong with me, as if I'm horribly disfigured or something. I bring my hand to my face with difficulty, feeling around for my eyes and nose and mouth, all of which seem to be in the right place.

I let my eyes drift shut again.

EDEN

He wakes up as I'm reaching over him to pick up my phone, still turned off. "What are you doing?" he asks me, voice all rough and groggy as he squints against the daylight. "Aww, no. Why'd you take my shirt off?"

"I need to get home," I whisper.

"It's Saturday," he groans, reaching for me. "Why are you dressed already?"

"I have to go," I tell him again softly.

"No, please don't go. Stay awhile. Come on, when are we gonna be able to do this again?"

I sit down on the bed next to him and let him pull me close because I don't know when we'll do this again. *If* we'll do this again. My head is resting on his shoulder; his arm is around me. I close my eyes, and I feel the rise and fall of his chest. It would be easy to stay like this. I almost let myself float back to sleep, but then he inhales deeply and says, "Edy?"

"Mm-hmm?"

"Can we talk about last night?"

I'm not entirely sure which part of last night he wants to talk about—Josh, our fight, or our latest sad and humiliating attempt at intimacy—but I feel like the conclusion is going to be the same no matter what.

"Do we have to?" I ask him.

"Well, kind of," he says, sitting up, making me sit up along with him. He maneuvers around so that we're facing each other, and he rubs the sleep out of his eyes. "Right?"

"Probably," I admit.

He takes my hand and kisses it. "I'm sorry," he says.

"What for?"

"Everything."

"*Steve*, stop, you don't have to—"

"No, I knew I was pressuring you to come out last night. I just wanted you there. But that was selfish. And I know I was really out of line when I said that stupid shit about you and . . . *him*." I guess he can't bring himself to say Josh's name. Sometimes I can't, either, but I'm guessing it's for a very different reason in Steve's case.

"Thanks."

"And then here, in bed," he begins but pauses, touching his mouth, suppressing the urge to bite a fingernail. "I feel like I really messed up."

"No, you didn't."

"I gave you a panic attack, Edy."

"It really wasn't your fault," I try to tell him, but that's not entirely true.

"Please just tell me what I did so I don't do it again."

He's looking at me so intently, holding his breath, like maybe whatever he's thinking he did is worse than what actually happened. "It's not—it wasn't *that* bad," I begin, and he leans in closer. "You just, like, sort of grabbed my arms."

"Okay," he says, expecting more from me.

"Pretty hard," I add.

"Oh," he breathes, his eyebrows squishing together.

"I mean, you were holding me down. *Really* hard."

"Well, but I thought you wanted it like that." He looks down at the rumpled sheets, the spot where we were lying as if he's replaying it. "You were enjoying it, I thought?"

"I—I was," I assure him. "Until then, anyway. I couldn't move and I got really scared and I was trying to tell you to stop and I felt like you weren't listening to me."

"I did, though. I did stop. I stopped right away."

I don't remember that. I don't remember him stopping. But then, I don't really know what happened between that being-pulled-underwater feeling and jumping up, already mid-anxiety attack. "You did?" I ask.

"Of course," he insists, taking both of my hands now. "Of course I did. I swear I stopped the second you said stop. You—you believe me, don't you?"

"I believe you; I just can't remember," I admit, and I'm not sure which one of us is more upset by that realization. "It made me think of . . . what happened. I mean, *he* did that too. Kevin," I add, because DA Silverman told me I needed to practice saying his name with confidence and stop sounding so uncertain.

"Jesus, I didn't realize," Steve says, rubbing his forehead. "I'm so sorry."

"I know. It's—"

"But you know I would let you up. I mean, I didn't even think I was holding you down that hard in the first place. I figured you could get up if you . . ." But his words fade as I shake my head. I think he's only realizing right now how easily he could overpower me if he wanted to because he leans over my lap and kisses both my wrists in the place where his hands had been. When he sits back up, his eyes are shiny. "You know I wouldn't hurt you or try to force you—"

"I know, I know that." At least, my head knows that. My body hasn't gotten the message though. "But at the moment, that's not what I was thinking about."

He nods and clears his throat like he's about to say something else, but he hesitates before continuing.

"What?"

"I love you," he says quietly.

I look down at our hands, and I feel this massive pressure climbing up the back of my throat. Last night I didn't care about love, but this morning I have to care.

"You don't have to say it back," he adds. "But I do, I love you." Every time he says it, I feel like he's stabbing me in the heart. "I've loved you since Yearbook Club ninth grade, hell, probably even since middle school."

"No, Steve," I say, and I let go of one of his hands so I can rub the tears collecting at the corners of my eyes. "You don't."

"Don't tell me how I feel," he argues gently as he reaches up to touch my face.

“Okay, I won’t tell you how you feel, but can I tell you what I think?”

He nods.

“I think you love the person you knew back then, the person you believe I can become again one day. But that’s not the same as loving me the way I am now.”

“Edy, don’t say that. That’s not—”

“No, even that, Steve. *Edy*. I don’t want to be called ‘Edy,’ and everybody calls me that anyway. But I’m not her.” I can’t hold back now; I can’t do this halfway. “I’m not her and I—I don’t think I can do this anymore.”

“What are you saying?” he asks, biting his lip, like he’s afraid to let the words out. “Are you . . . ? You’re not breaking up with me?”

I nod, and he lets his head fall into his hands. I hate that this isn’t the first time I’ve made Steve cry. “I’m sorry.” I reach out but can’t quite make myself touch him. “I wanted this to work, I swear, I really did.”

He looks up at me with tears in his eyes. “It could if you tried,” he pleads.

“You think I’m not trying?” My voice breaks over the words, but I continue. “Every minute I’m trying. So hard. Too hard.” And now we’re both crying. “Do you hate me?” I ask him. “Please don’t hate me.”

He shakes his head, and now he leans into me, and for the first time ever, I’m the one to hold him. My arm falls asleep, but I don’t move.

“Steve?” I finally say after our breathing slows and there are no more gasps or sniffles.

"Yeah?" he answers, his voice ragged.

"You really are a ten, you know that, right?"

He laughs. "You're a liar."

"I am not."

He looks up at me and smiles.

"Can I tell you something else?"

He nods.

"I'm not coming back to school."

He opens his mouth but then closes it.

"I just can't handle it there," I explain. "Too much has happened."

"I know," he says, laying his head back on my shoulder. "Can we stay like this just a little longer?" he asks.

"Sure," I answer.

JOSH

I wake up in my bed. The light coming in from the window is so bright it feels like I'm staring directly into the sun. I close my eyes again, and I have this flash of my dad and Dominic walking me up the stairs. Through my bedroom door. Dumping me onto my bed.

Still in my clothes from yesterday, I check my pockets for my phone. Not there. I sit up, and my body is so heavy, my head pounding. I feel all around the bed, look under the sheets, on the floor. I stand up and am immediately knocked back down by gravity.

Slower this time, I stand again. I check my desk, move papers around, toss books on the floor. It's not here. I start walking toward my door. I'll retrace my steps. I must've dropped it.

My mom comes in first. "Josh, why are you throwing things around?"

"I'm not throwing anything; I'm looking for my phone," I tell her. "Have you seen it? I think it fell out of my pocket."

"Your phone can wait," my dad answers, suddenly there in my doorway. They come inside like they've been standing in the hall all morning, just waiting for me to wake up. Mom flips the covers back over my bed and sits down on top of it, patting the spot next to her.

"We need to talk, sweetheart," Mom says. "Sit down."

Dad nods in agreement and steps forward.

I sit. The last time they sat me down like this was when I was ten and our first cat died.

"What happened?" I ask.

"You tell us," Dad answers.

"What do you mean?"

"Josh," Mom says, suddenly irritated. "Last night. What the hell happened?"

"Nothing happened." My head cracks open with each syllable they force me to speak.

"Joshua," Mom says, pulling out the full name. "You couldn't make it through the door without—"

"That's what this is all about?" I try to laugh like I'm not about to die. "You guys are overreacting. I drank too much. Everyone there drank too much."

"Oh, well, if everyone was doing it"—Mom throws her hands up—"then never mind; it's fine."

"It was one night." I can't believe they're coming down on me like this. "It's not like I was driving."

"It's not like you were walking by the end of it, either," Dad accuses.

I stand up now. I'm not taking this sitting down. Certainly not from him.

"Can I not have one fuck-up?" I say, feeling my heart pumping faster.

They just stare at me.

"No, I'm actually asking," I tell them. "I did *nothing* wrong in high school, do I need to remind you? I never skipped school, didn't drink, never did drugs, never even smoked once. Hell, I never even got a detention!"

"You're not in high school anymore," Mom says.

"Fine. Exactly. I'm not a kid. I don't even live here anymore. I'm twenty years old, and this is the first time I've ever—"

"This was not the first time you've been this drunk, Joshua," Mom interrupts, standing back up now too. "Though I'm grateful you didn't come home beaten up this time."

"*Mom*," I begin—how could she bring that up? "That was different."

"Whoa, wait, what do you mean?" Dad says, giving us the *time-out* sign with his hands just like he used to do when he coached my peewee games and the ref would call a foul on me. "When did he get beaten up?"

"Winter break. His senior year, Matt," Mom says, practically pulling the exact date out of her brain. When I got in a fight with Eden's brother, or rather when he got in a fight with me; it actually wasn't much of a fight at all since I could barely muster the will to even defend myself.

"Of course you would remember the *one* time I actually dared to act my age, right?" I snap at her, and her eyes widen with my betrayal—we've always been on the same team.

"Stumbling home drunk with bloody knuckles and bruises

and a black eye is not acting like *any* age. It's acting foolish and dangerous. And no, you're wrong. This . . ." She waves her hands over me. "This is all too similar."

"Why am I just hearing about this?" Dad asks, talking over Mom.

"How is this similar?" I say, ignoring him.

"Why am I just now hearing about this?" Dad repeats, louder.

"You were there, Matthew!" Mom yells at my dad. "How could you forget this? That girl's brother attacked him."

"Okay, he did not *attack* me," I try to say, but she's focused on Dad now. *Of course he doesn't remember.* He was drinking back then, among other things.

"This is all over the same girl as last time," she tells him, then turns on me again. "Josh, every time you get involved with this girl—"

"Will you stop calling her 'this girl,' Mom?"

"So, this is the same girl from a few months ago, too?" Dad says, catching up too slowly for Mom's rapidly dwindling patience.

"This is not over Eden. It's not over anything. It's not even anything!"

She looks back and forth between us, shaking her head as she walks out of my room, muttering, "I can't with you two right now. I just can't."

As she exits, the air in the room feels slightly lighter. I exhale, roll my neck from side to side. "Have you seen my phone?" I ask him, resuming my search under my bed.

"No. Joshie," he says, all exasperated. "Forget about the goddamn phone and talk to me."

"Talk about what?" I sit back down on my bed, suddenly dizzy after bending over.

"Dominic said you ran into the girl—this ex-girlfriend—at some concert, and next thing it's this again, you're falling-down drunk. So, what happened?"

As I look up at him, meeting his eyes, I have the strongest urge to laugh. Because of course he wants to talk about her *now*. "Dad, you know her name. If you call her 'the girl' one more time, I swear to God—" But I stop myself; there's no point in arguing. "And besides, I already said this has nothing to do with her. It was a party. There was drinking. End of story."

"Eden," he corrects himself. "Okay? I remember her name is Eden. What's the deal exactly with this g—with Eden?" he asks. Then he steps closer, lowering his voice. "What is it? Just say it, Josh. You can tell me."

"Tell you what? I don't know what you want me to say."

"Is she pregnant?"

"What?" I stand up again. "What are we even talking about?"

"Did you get her pregnant?" he repeats quieter, casting a quick glance over his shoulder. He's looking at me so earnestly, so concerned and ready to step in and help that I do laugh now. "Hey, I'm serious here. Is that what's been tormenting you? Because we can figure it out."

"No, I didn't get her pregnant, Dad. But that was a good guess. Do you wanna try again?"

"I am trying, I promise."

"You really don't remember anything I told you, do you?"

He closes his eyes, as if I'm the one hurting him rather than the other way around. My dad has blacked out huge portions of my life, and most of them I couldn't care less about, but this was one of the big ones I needed him to remember. And it's clear it's just not there. He has no recollection of me pouring my heart out to him, telling him everything, begging for advice, reassurance. Of course, it wasn't until he came over to my side of the kitchen table and put his arm around me that I smelled the alcohol on him. It wasn't until I stopped crying that I recognized that vacant look in his eye.

"I wanted to talk to you about this back in December. I came to you then. Do you remember at all?" I ask him. "I'd understand if you don't, since it turned out you were in the middle of a bender at the time."

"I remember you were very upset. I do remember that. I've tried to talk to you about this since, and you've pushed me away every time. You didn't even come home over the holidays, Josh—"

"Yeah, I really didn't want to see you," I tell him, not caring if I hurt his feelings.

"And you know what? I understand that," he says, "but let's deal with this thing now."

"Does Mom even know, or does she think you've been sober this whole time?"

"She knows about my relapse, yes. But I'm back on track now and . . ." He reaches into his pocket and pulls out a token I've seen so many times before. "Got my ninety-day chip just last week."

"You know what, Dad? I don't care. Get high. Drink yourself to death. I honestly don't care. I can't care anymore." I start toward the door. "I need to find my phone. Do you mind?"

"Joshie, come on." He holds his hands up like he's not going to let me pass. "I'm listening now. You needed me and I wasn't there for you. I'm sorry if my not being there is why things have been going off the rails for you lately, but you can't mess up everything you have going for you because you're mad at me."

"Not everything is about you! Believe it or not, I have my own problems that have absolutely nothing to do with you."

"You're clearly numbing yourself. You've been reckless. You're throwing basketball away—throwing your future away."

"Basketball?" I scoff. "Basketball is not my future."

"And if you'd been kicked off the team for showing up drunk to that game at the beginning of the year, what would've happened then, huh? Your scholarship would've been pulled. Do you know how many hours I spent on the phone with your coaches, with the dean, with your adviser, to make sure you only got benched for the rest of the semester?"

"I wasn't drunk," I lie. I'd been in that black hole, as D called it, all of winter break. I barely left the apartment. I was sick over Eden, over my dad, over me—not being able to do anything about any of it. And I was sick of feeling sick. So, I had some drinks before the game. It worked. I felt better. I didn't think I was *drunk*, though. Didn't think anyone would notice. But Coach did. He noticed right away and had one of the assistants drive me home before anyone else noticed too.

Dad stands there staring at me with his jaw clenched, holding back his words.

"I was sick," I tell him. He thinks that's a lie too but I can't explain why it's not, so I continue, "And I never asked you to do that—I would've dealt with the consequences myself."

"You were *hungover*," he says, thinking he's correcting me. "Like you are right now."

"You of all people?" I shout at him. "How can you stand there and lecture me?"

"Because I know better than anyone!" he yells back. "Don't do this to yourself. God, you're so much like me," he mutters to himself. "Please don't be like me."

"I am nothing like you; stop saying that!" All the yelling is making my head throb, my heart pound, my stomach queasy. "Dad, move—I'm gonna throw up," I manage to say, dodging past him.

I make it to the bathroom, and as I empty my entire body, Dad keeps patting my back. "Get it out," he's saying, over and over. "Get it out. You're gonna be fine."

After I'm sure I'm finished, I sit on the floor with my back against the wall. The cold tiles feel good against my skin. I watch as my dad gets a washcloth from the cabinet and runs it under water from the sink. He wrings it out and then sits down next to me. He places the washcloth on the back of my neck.

"Stop, Dad." I push his hands away.

"I'm only trying to help."

I toss the washcloth up onto the counter because some part of me doesn't really *want* to feel better. I won't say that, though; that would only make him think there's even more wrong with me than he already does.

He sighs, and because I don't want any more lecturing, I open my mouth. The first thing that comes out is "Mom's wrong about Eden."

"All right?" he prompts. "I'm listening."

"None of this is because of her. Okay, maybe it's partially because of her, but not because of anything she did. She didn't do anything to me. I just . . ."

"You what?" he asks, nudging me in the arm. "Tell me what's going on then. Please."

"She's special. I really care about her."

"But?"

"Don't tell Mom about this, all right? I'm really not supposed to be talking about it."

He holds both hands up in front of his chest and shakes his head. "You know I can't promise until I know what it is."

"She was raped."

He clicks his tongue. "Jesus."

"It happened before we were together. And I didn't find out until after we broke up. A long time after we broke up. She just told me a few months ago and—"

"In December?" he asks.

I nod. "And I've just been so . . . I don't know. I was the first person she ever told about what happened, and I didn't know what to do or say." I stop myself from saying, *which is why I needed you.* "I felt helpless. Hell, I still feel helpless."

"I'm sorry," Dad says.

"I guess I just wish I would've known earlier about what happened. I feel like I should've known, anyway, without her having to tell me. Like maybe I could've done something to help her. I don't know, it's like a million thoughts running through my head all at once. Like what if I did anything when we were together to make things worse for her? If I wasn't paying attention or I pressured—"

"Do you mean sexually or . . . ?" For all his faults, he has always been easygoing about this kind of stuff, so I know his question is strictly for clarity—no judgment involved.

I nod. "Mostly, yeah. But other times too."

"Come on, Josh. You've always been a stand-up guy. I'm sure you were a gentleman."

"How can you be sure? I'm not. There were times I got really mad at her, lost my patience. But only because I didn't understand what was going on. Now that I do, I've questioned a lot of what happened between us. Sometimes I wish I could do our whole relationship over. If I could do it differently, I would."

"It's never too late to try again. Right?"

I shake my head. "I don't know, it's probably better that we stay just friends. It feels too . . . complicated," I land on, borrowing Hannah's word from last night. "That is, until I see her, and then it feels like it would be so freaking easy. But now she's with someone else, and anyway, there's this age difference—"

"Oh." He breathes the word, the subtlest interruption, and I can see the worry stitching across his forehead. "How much of a difference are we talking about here, Josh?"

"She's seventeen. So, it's not terrible, but it's—it's there. We were only two grades apart in school," I try to explain. "Anyway, she's about to graduate."

"All right," he says, seeming to relax a bit. "Go on, sorry."

"I want to . . . ," I begin. "I don't know, I just can't . . . I guess I thought . . ." But I'm not even sure what I'm trying to say, not sure what I want anymore, what I think. "I just thought I'd moved on," I finally admit.

He sighs and squeezes my shoulder, holding the space for those words to exist for a minute. "Well, it sounds like you're going to have to find a way to really move on, bud. A different way than this," he says, gesturing all around us—this, meaning hungover and half-dead on the bathroom floor.

"Yeah," I agree.

"Grab a shower. Drink some water. Take a nap." Dad pats my back again as he stands. "You're gonna be okay, I promise." And he leaves me in the bathroom, closing the door gently behind him. "I'll find your phone," he calls to me from the hall.

EDEN

I wait until I'm out of the shower, in clean clothes, sitting at my desk in my bedroom, calm and collected, before I finally look at his texts.

> It was nice to run into you tonight. I've missed talking to you.
>
> I'm sorry if I made things weird with your boyfriend. He seemed pretty pissed. I hope he understood . . . the way things are between us. Do you want me to tell him there's nothing going on? I will if you need me to. I just want you to be happy
>
> Can I see you again before I head back to school?

I've missed talking with you too

You didn't make things weird, they just . . . were

Tell me when/where. I'll be there.

I wait an hour. I even call. I wait another thirty minutes. As I'm walking up to his house, I'm going over all the times I've done this before. In the dark. In the cold. Their house never changes. His cat darts off the porch as I approach, prancing down the steps like she was expecting me. When I reach down to pet her, I see something in the crack between the steps and the shrubbery. And as I get closer, I can tell it's a phone. I pick it up and turn it over in my hands. Josh's phone. The screen is cracked; the power is off.

The door swings open before I have the chance to knock.

"Oh!" I yelp, jumping back, nearly dropping Josh's phone.

"I'm sorry," the man who is basically an older version of Josh says. I'm momentarily muted as I take in the similarities. Same stature, same build, same facial structure, same eyes. If not for his weathered features or his salt-and-pepper hair, slightly different nose, this *is* Josh. "Can I help you?"

"Oh, um, I found this," I tell him, holding the phone out. "It was lying in the walkway. I texted him, but I guess he didn't get it. I called, too. Obviously this is why he didn't answer." I'm rambling now, and I can't seem to stop myself. "But I thought maybe I should just come to see him instead. I wasn't sure how long he'll be staying in town and didn't want to miss him."

"Eden?" he asks, squinting at me as he takes the phone.

"Oh, right. Sorry, yes. I'm Eden." I fidget as I stand there, getting so nervous—I hadn't thought about his parents being here on a Saturday morning. Parents tend to hate me. Like they can smell trouble on me, fear that I'll rub off on their kids.

"Matt," he offers, pointing at himself, and I immediately think of the time Josh told me his middle name. *Joshua Matthew Miller*, he'd said, and I thought that sounded like the best name in the world. "The dad," he adds when I don't respond.

"Right, of course. Hi," I say stupidly. "Is, um, is Josh home?"

The door opens wider, and his mom steps forward. I saw her only once before, when she was picking Josh up from school one day, but I immediately see Josh in her too. The same nose, same pretty mouth. But there's a tightness in her features, a sharpness in her jaw as she meets my eyes.

"This isn't a good time," she tells me.

"Oh, sure. Okay, yeah." I fumble with my words. "Can you let him know I stopped by?" I ask, and instantly regret it as his mom levels me with the most intense glare I think I've ever received from anyone and turns away without another word, leaving his dad there.

"S-sorry," I stutter involuntarily, as I back away from the door. "I didn't mean to interrupt anything."

"No, wait," his dad says, and steps out onto the porch, pulling the door closed behind him. "There's no need to apologize, you just caught us on a rough morning here."

I nod. Of course I understand. I'm having a pretty rough morning myself. I don't say that, though. I look around, trying to get my bearings, and that's when I realize his car isn't here. "Is

Josh . . . okay?" I ask, my eyes setting anew on the shattered screen of his phone in his father's hand.

"He'll be fine," he answers, which worries me even more.

I feel my hand go to my heart as it starts racing with my darkening thoughts. "His car's not here. Nothing happened, right? There wasn't some kind of accident or—I mean, he's all right. Right? He's not hurt or anything?"

"No," he's quick to answer. "God, no. Nothing like that. He's just nursing a pretty wicked hangover this morning."

"*Josh* is?" My voice squeaks. None of that makes sense. "But I saw him last night. He wasn't drinking. He doesn't drink," I tell his father, who continues looking at me in a way that's eerily similar to how Josh looks at me when he seems to think I know more than I'm letting on.

"Well," he breathes. "He sure did last night."

"Oh." I exhale and let my hand fall to my side. "Okay. Will you tell him I came by?" I ask again, pretty sure his mom isn't going to let him know.

"I can see you care about him," he says. "Don't you?"

"Yeah, I care about him more than . . ." I feel a little embarrassed at my honesty, but it makes his dad take another step toward me and I think maybe he'll tell Josh I'm here after all. "Anyone," I finish.

But he doesn't let me in; he nods somberly and sits down on the top step of the porch. "You got a minute?" he asks.

I nod. He gestures for me to sit down. I do. He doesn't say anything at first, and I start to wonder if I'm supposed to be speaking. I really don't know the parental protocol here. He pats his shirt pocket and pulls out a soft pack of cigarettes, which looks rumpled and crushed like it's been around for a while. "Do you mind?" he asks me, tapping the pack against his palm, a lighter tumbling out.

"No," I tell him. "It's okay."

He plucks a cigarette from the pack and brings it to his mouth. He lights it, and as the smoke swirls around us, I feel my heart pounding, craving that relief, the immediacy of it.

He inhales deeply and says, while holding the smoke in his lungs, "Always trying to quit, but . . ." and then turns his face away from me to blow the stream of smoke out of his mouth. I'm suddenly so tempted to ask him for one, but then he immediately stubs it out against the concrete step after only that one long, deep drag. I'm not sure I'd have that kind of self-control.

"I remember when Josh was a kid, he loved comic books." He pauses, smiling as he looks out into the yard. "We'd always read them together."

I smile back, but I'm suddenly entirely unclear about where this conversation is heading.

"Every superhero has a fatal flaw," he continues. "The thing about Josh is . . . he's always been one of those people who cleans up well, if you know what I mean. Always so together on the outside, it's easy to forget it doesn't mean that's how he really is inside. I've always thought that was sort of his fatal flaw."

"I know," I tell him, and he looks at me like he's trying to figure out whether I really do know that about Josh or if I'm only agreeing for the sake of being agreeable.

"He's turned into such a good person—no thanks to me, I'm sure you know that, too," he slips in, but quickly continues. "I'm so proud of him, but I'm worried about him," he admits. "He just cares so much about everyone else. He wants everyone to be okay. But I think he can get so consumed with worrying about other people, he isn't caring enough about himself right now. Which scares me."

I hold my breath, then exhale a short, nervous laugh. "I can't tell if you're blaming me or asking me to help."

"Neither," he says, standing up, bringing the shorted cigarette with him. "I just thought you should know."

"Okay." I stand up too. "Thanks for letting me know."

"It was nice meeting you, Eden," he tells me.

"Yeah, same." I take only a couple of steps before I turn around. "Um, maybe don't tell him I was here, then. I'll just—I can catch up with him some other time, I guess. A better time," I add, thinking of his mom's words.

He gives me a classic crooked Josh smile as he holds up the phone. "I'll make sure he gets this."

PART TWO

July

JOSH

I'm sitting behind the front desk at the athletic center, scanning in a student ID every few minutes, making sure the picture in the database matches the person entering the building. The afternoon sun is streaming in through floor-to-ceiling windows, making me tired.

Fridays are always dead here, especially during summer sessions, so I finally have a chance to study. I'm wading my way through the chapter on research methods for my psych class, when I hear Coach's telltale key chain jingling down the hall. I straighten up, take a sip of coffee, try to look more alert than I am.

As he walks up to the desk, he says, "Bright and early Monday morning, yes?"

"Yes," I agree, "see you Monday."

"Tell your father hello for me," he adds.

"Will do, thanks, Coach. Have a good weekend."

I've almost earned my way back into my coach's good graces.

He got me this work-study position for the summer, I think, mostly to keep tabs on me. He's tried hard to make sure there's been no time for study, no time for anything, except working my ass off to prove myself. Which has meant basically being errand boy for the whole department. Someone needs lunch, I go get it. A visiting bigwig donor or VIP needs to be picked up at the airport, I'm their chauffeur. Gym equipment needs cleaning, I'm the janitor. Struggling athlete requires tutor—that's me too. He did at least let me take the weekend to go home; I told him it was a family thing, and I was thankful he didn't press me for details.

I guess I deserve the punishment, considering what I did.

But every morning when my alarm goes off at the crack of dawn for practice, I have this tug-of-war in my head. Between the part of me that knows I'm lucky to have this chance and wants to follow through on my commitment. Because I made a commitment to take the scholarship and play on this team. Plus, I know it makes my dad happy. Then there's the other part of me that just wants to sleep in every once in a while, wants to be a regular student, here to get an education instead of play a game I rarely enjoy.

Most of the guys on the team only take three classes during the semester because there just aren't enough hours in the day for any more than that, but I've forced myself to take four this last year, against my adviser's recommendation. This summer, I'm trying to get at least two more classes under my belt; otherwise, I'll end up in college for an extra year at this rate, and I do not want to be playing any longer than I have to.

It's not like I didn't know what I was getting into, all the stupid sacrifice and pressure. But to be so burned out after two years and still not be even halfway through makes me want to leave it all behind some days. Basketball, school even. But this morning before class, my psych professor asked me something I hadn't considered before and haven't stopped thinking about since; she wanted to know if I'd be declaring a minor this fall.

"A minor?" I repeated—I've barely declared a *major* as it is. Sports medicine was something Bella talked me into freshman year, and it seemed logical at the time. She was pre-med—still is, I'm sure—and she made a very convincing case.

"A minor in psychology," Dr. Gupta clarified when she saw I wasn't computing what she meant. "You have all the prerequisites already." I've taken two classes with Dr. Gupta, and another psych class last semester to fulfill a social science requirement. I had my AP Psychology credits from high school, so I didn't need to take any extra intro-level courses to start taking psych classes—it made sense. After all, I'm interested in the subject, but it wasn't part of some larger plan. Just sort of happened. So, I didn't know how to answer her.

"Think about it," she told me. "Let me know if you have questions."

But now that I'm sitting here, really thinking about it all, Bella's argument was mainly that *I* played a sport and *she* was studying medicine, so we would be able to take some classes together.

I take my phone out—she texted me at the beginning of the week. The first time I've heard from her since we broke up in December. She wrote:

> Are you on campus for the summer?
> Want to get a drink sometime, catch up?

I've been putting off responding because I'd feel bad if I said no, but if I said yes, I can foresee what would happen. She'd take me back even though I hurt her, and I'd let myself go along with it because we made sense on paper. And that rational part of me, the one that keeps my commitments even when I don't want to, does sometimes wonder if I threw away a good thing with her. It wonders what would've happened if I hadn't answered Eden's call that night. I'm 99 percent sure Bella and I would still be together and I wouldn't have found out about what happened to Eden and I'd be blissfully ignorant about my dad's relapse and I never would've screwed up basketball last winter, and these last seven months would've been smooth sailing, everything going as planned.

But even as I reread her text now, I'm reminded of the things off paper that didn't work.

She asked if I wanted to get a drink because she doesn't even know I don't like to drink. Because I'd never told her. And I never told her because then she'd ask why and I'd also have to tell her about my dad and how the handful of times I've been drinking in my life, I've drunk way too much and ended up massively regretting it and being terrified that I'm more like my dad in that way than I want to admit. Because even though we lived together and we got along and I genuinely liked her—loved her, I thought—there still were things I could never say to her. Not like Eden.

I leave Bella's text sitting there and switch over to Eden's text from this morning, the one that made me literally laugh out loud in the locker room.

At work rn, perfecting the art of latte foam design

She sent a picture of a wide-rimmed mug with the Bean logo from back home—she'd mentioned a couple of weeks ago she got a job there.

I know, I know. a lot of baristas go for the obvious heart or rosette, but my signature shape is . . . the blob.

It's very blobby (sp?). Starbucks has nothin on the Bean

thank you.

i'll make you my special vanilla blob latte next time you're here

I keep debating whether I should tell her I'll be home this weekend. We never did see each other again over spring break. She called, left me a voice mail, which I listened to way too many times over the last few months. She told me she wanted to see me. I gave her excuses—lost phone, broke phone, got sick, had to get a new phone, got busy, had to leave early—none of which were lies, exactly, even if I felt like they were.

She's been texting pretty regularly, but it's all light and airy surface stuff like our communication is suddenly quantity over quality. It's never been this way with her before. I feel like something has changed but I don't know what or why, and I'm too scared to ask her about it. Thankfully, she doesn't talk about *Steve*, at least. I don't think I could handle that yet . . . or ever.

I leave for home the next morning, stop for gas at the gas station I always stop at, twenty miles into the five-hour drive. I look up at the number on the pump. Two. The exact one I used the last time I was driving home, back in December.

It was snowing that afternoon when she called the first time and hung up. I was on my way to practice. She called and hung up four times in a row. I deleted her number from my phone years ago, but I could tell it was her from one breath.

I tried to put it out of my mind as best as I could, but then later that night, we were sitting at our kitchen table, books all spread out, studying for finals, when her next call interrupted us. I answered, but she hung up again, three times.

"What the hell?" Bella said, telling me on the fourth call, "Just ignore it."

But I couldn't. "Eden, is this you?" I answered.

And then she hung up on me again.

"*Eden*, as in your ex-girlfriend Eden?" Bella asked, setting her highlighter down in the binding of her textbook. "What does *she* want?"

I shook my head and stood from the table. I called her back. I was getting so mad while I waited for her to answer and I didn't even really know why—because Bella was getting upset or because I was starting to care whether I heard her voice or not.

She answered but still wouldn't say anything, and Bella was right there listening, so I told her not to call back. But then I was immediately relieved when she called a second later anyway.

"Is she stalking you or something?" Bella hissed, sounding meaner than I'd ever heard her before. "Do *not* answer that, Josh—she's messing with you."

But I did. And when she finally spoke, her voice nearly crushed me. She didn't sound right at all. She kept saying "I cared." I didn't know what she meant, but then she repeated it. "I cared about you. I always cared about you."

She'd never said that to me before, and hearing it now, this way, it scared me.

"Did you know?" she asked. "Did you know I cared?"

I didn't know what to say, so I told her the truth. "Sometimes."

She went off about all these random things she'd lied to me about and what a horrible person she was and how much she hated herself and how I should hate her too. She was being so cryptic and erratic and I was really hoping it was just that she'd been drinking or something, but when I asked her that, she laughed and said no, and I could tell she was starting to cry.

Something was wrong. I didn't know what, but I knew she wasn't messing around. I tried to keep her on the phone, but I could feel her getting farther and farther away with every word I said to her. I asked her what she needed, how I could help.

"You can't," she cried.

I started getting more than scared because she was winding down, or maybe winding up; either way, I was losing her, quickly. She was saying things like "I'm sorry" and "I shouldn't have called," and I tried to tell her it was okay but it was like she couldn't even hear me anymore.

"I just miss you so much sometimes, and I wanted you to know that I cared. I really did," she said so quietly I had to cover my other ear just so I could hear her. "And there wasn't anyone else. Ever. I hope you'll believe me."

"Wait, Eden," I yelled, because I knew—she was done. "Don't hang up," I said, even though it was too late.

Bella was watching me as I paced our tiny apartment, frantically trying to call Eden back, leaving message after message. We'd been together for over a year—I was planning on taking her home with me over winter break to meet my parents—but she'd never seen me like this.

"Calm down," she kept saying. "You're really overreacting right now."

But I couldn't calm down. And I wasn't overreacting.

"You don't still love her," she said at first, suppressing a laugh. She didn't say it like a question, though; she was telling me. *Of course, you're not still in love with a girl in high school who was never really your girlfriend in the first place*. I was trying to tell myself that same thing. I could go months without having her even cross my mind. I was over her. But if that were really true, then how was it that she could call out of the blue after years, and I just crumble at the sound of her voice?

"You're not," she repeated when I didn't answer. "Josh?"

"What, God?" I snapped at her, another thing she'd never seen me do before.

"Hey, don't yell at me," she said, standing from the table. She walked over and stood directly in the path of my pacing, studying me. "Why are you freaking out over this?"

"Bella, just give me some space. You don't understand. Something is seriously wrong, okay?"

"Well, help me understand, then." So practical, she waited, standing there in front of me, like I could *explain* Eden to her. Like this was one of our Advanced Calculus problems we could figure out if we just put our minds together. But I could never explain Eden to anyone, not even myself.

"Okay," Bella said, crossing her arms as I stood there, silent. "I can't believe I have to ask you this, but is there something going on with you and her?"

"Bella, come on" was the best defense I could muster. Because of course there was something going on with us, there always had been. We never ended. We barely began.

"It's not a trick question, Josh, just tell me the truth," she demanded.

The truth was too complicated, though, to be able to tell Bella, who, I was just realizing at that moment, didn't understand that *I* was complicated too.

But the truth about us was also simple. Eden was angry and I was sad, and we shouldn't have worked but we did. We worked like we weren't too damaged to work. Maybe only sometimes, when other things weren't getting in the way. Like all that sadness, all that anger. And other people and bad timing and petty teenager shit. Of course, there were also her lies. The secrets I always knew she was keeping from me.

But in spite of all that, I called her back anyway. I left my girlfriend in our new apartment in the middle of the night—in the middle of a fight—anyway. I remember thinking, even at the moment, I shouldn't be willing to throw everything away for her. I shouldn't be able to not listen when my girlfriend cries actual tears, pleading with me to stay. To feel her pulling my arm and to keep going anyway. To hear her, and believe her, when she gives me the first and last ultimatum of our relationship: "Don't you dare go to her, not if you want to come back here." And to not even be able to say I'm sorry and mean it. To close the door on her and get in my car anyway.

All because she called me. All because I was scared. Scared because it had suddenly occurred to me that maybe I was now the one who was angry and she'd turned sad—*too* sad, maybe.

I left her a voice mail while I stood here at the gas station, in this spot, freezing, in the middle of the night. I told her I was coming and then I prayed to all the gods in all the universes that by the time the tank was full, she'd have called me back and told me to turn around. I wanted her to be lying. I wanted her to call me back and tell me she was fine. She didn't need me. She didn't care. She never did.

I wanted to believe that her phone call was not her saying goodbye—in a permanent way. Because, of the many things I was not sure about when it came to her, I was sure about that. She was capable of it. I don't know why I knew that, but I just did. And even though I'd gone without her for so long, I didn't know if I could go on without her in the world.

"Please, Eden," I whispered, the words coming out in a white cloud of cold. "Just fucking call."

The gas lever pops, and I'm suddenly thrust back into the daylight, into the heat, the sun beating down on my neck and shoulders. I look down at my arms, goose bumps rising on my flesh, a shiver running down my spine.

I transfer the pump back into the cradle and watch as the numbers on the screen flash and reset to zero. I take a breath and try to shake off the cold I didn't realize was still lingering in my bones from that night.

I get in the car and pull out my phone to text Bella back:

> I don't think meeting up would be a good idea for me. But I hope you're doing well, Bella. I'm sorry.

EDEN

The applications were garbage, I knew that. I submitted identical materials to every school, complete with a stupid boilerplate cookie-cutter essay my guidance counselor practically wrote for me, checking all the boxes, she said, of what these schools are looking for. I remember thinking, fleetingly, *What about what I'm looking for*?

All except for the one application I didn't think would matter.

For that one, I wrote something that probably should've been locked in a journal somewhere away from the world. It was part apology to myself, part love letter to Josh, part victim impact statement to anyone who would listen . . . all in the form of my essay to the admissions office at Tucker Hill University. It was overly precious and overly honest and dripping with metaphor and too many shiny words, but I was proud of it. All about second chances and lost time and regrets and feeling hopeful about the future. And I believed, I wrote with such confidence, that my future was there.

I meant it when I wrote it. It was a shot in the dark, a wish that was unlikely to come true. And the improbability of it actually happening made me feel brave enough to try.

It was the very end of January, and I was flying high off the knowledge that Kevin had been arrested and people seemed to believe me and I still thought that counted for something. I thought he'd soon be locked up and out of my life—out of *all* our lives—for good. I felt free. Josh and I had been talking again, before I left school, before Steve, before things got so much harder. And so I cranked out that essay in the eleventh hour. I had no idea that months later, still nothing would've happened to move anything forward with the trial or that I'd be feeling less free, less hopeful, with every day that passed.

I had no idea how any of this legal stuff worked, so when DA Silverman and our court-appointed advocate, Lane, explained that it wasn't going to just be a trial that consisted of me, alone, against him, that it was the state against him and I was just one piece of something bigger, I felt so relieved. Almost powerful. Protected even. Because it was three against one—me and Amanda and Gennifer—finally the odds felt fair. Strength in numbers. I imagined the three of us walking into some fancy courtroom like a gang or something from a movie poster: the ex-girlfriend, the little sister, and the girl next door, all tough and strong, arms locked in solidarity.

It was a nice dream.

But that feeling didn't last. Because, as DA Silverman and Lane made abundantly clear when they explained the whole evidence collecting, hearing, and trial process: under no circumstances were we allowed to talk to each other about anything related to the case, Kevin, or what happened to any of us. Because we could be accused of . . . I'm not sure what, lying, I guess, creating some mastermind narrative. Didn't they realize Kevin was the real mastermind behind it all in the first place?

I barely remember the person I was when I wrote that essay. I thought about it twenty-four-seven, for weeks, until the cold, blissful realization washed over me: I could stop hoping. One look at my transcripts would ensure no one would ever read it.

Which is why I'm having trouble processing the email I'm staring at on my phone. It says I've been taken off the wait list and am being offered admission. I read the words ten times, but I still don't understand them. This has to be some kind of mix-up.

I frantically search for their previous email.

I'd barely read it the first time. My eyes scanned for the word "unfortunately," and then I immediately closed it—never even looked at it again. But it wasn't a rejection. They told me I was wait-listed. I go back to today's email. Yes, it clearly states: *We are pleased to offer you admission for the fall semester.*

"Oh my God," I whisper.

"What?" my brother, Caelin, says as he shuffles into the kitchen, where I'm standing frozen, with the microwave door still open, my burrito getting cold, still in my polo shirt and visor from the Bean, the scent of coffee clinging to my hair and my skin.

"I—I got in," I stammer, looking up at him. "To Tucker Hill University."

"Holy shit, Eeds." He smiles as I hand him my phone, and I realize how long it's been since I've seen him smile. "Seriously, this is amazing. I didn't even know you applied there. Tucker Hill is a really decent school."

"I know. Which is why I thought I'd never get in in a million years."

"Congratulations," he says, and he holds his arms out like he might lean in to hug me, but then he stops short.

"Well, but it's not like I can really go, can I? I mean, it's expensive and far away—"

"Eden, you have to go," he interrupts. "It's really not that far away; it's not even out of state. It's gotta be four or five hours, max."

"Okay, but it *is* expensive."

"Oh, fuck money," he says, dismissively waving his hand through the air. "There's financial aid and scholarships, grants . . . loans."

"It's so soon, though. I don't have enough time to get ready, and with everything else going on." The trial is supposed to start in the fall, which we haven't discussed, the two of us. What it'll be like for him to see his former best friend like that . . . his sister.

"Yeah, that's all the more reason you should get out of here—you can come back when you need to," he says, conveniently not saying *for the trial*. "And you have over a month. That's plenty of time."

"Mom and Dad won't think this is a good idea at all. Me, being on my own—they don't even trust me to borrow a car to get to work. And that's another thing . . . I don't have a car."

"Stop, stop, okay?" He brings his hands together like he's praying. "First, since when do you give a shit what they think . . . or what *I* think, for that matter?" He laughs, and so do I, because, of course, that's true. "And you can find a car. Hell, I'll give you my car!" he shouts. "Stop making excuses."

"You need your car."

"What do I need a car for? I'm taking the semester off," he reminds me. "You're doing this."

I'm trying to picture how any of it could work, how any of this is not crazy. I let out a laugh and cover my mouth, shaking my head as I look down at my phone again. I suddenly feel giddy and nauseated with the overwhelming sense of possibility blooming in my chest.

"Tucker Hill," Caelin says. "Isn't that where Josh Miller goes?"

I nod slowly.

"So, does this mean you and him are like a thing again or . . . ?" he asks awkwardly.

"He has a girlfriend," I hear myself automatically reply. It's the sentence that has been constantly running through my mind for months, even if that's not exactly what he asked. "I mean, we're just friends," I conclude.

I bring my lukewarm burrito into my bedroom and close the door, open my laptop. I want a cigarette so badly, because I'm feeling all these emotions bubbling up, fear and excitement and joy and dread, all fighting for top billing.

But I take a breath, slowly in, slowly out, and I open my email, double-checking, as if the message would've changed from my phone to my computer. It didn't. I follow the link to the English department grants and scholarships. English, I'd said my intended major was English. I try to picture myself there, as one of the people in these idyllic pictures online. Maybe I could be that girl there, sitting under a tree with a blanket and a book, reading. Or that kid smiling in the lecture hall. I could be in that group of people walking together, talking, laughing—friends. I close my eyes and try to dream it: big buildings and vast libraries, living in a real city.

And then there's the other part. I close my laptop. The Josh part. The whole Josh . . . *thing*, as Mara said the night of the concert.

I'm picking at the salad on my dinner plate that evening, trying to find the right time to bring it up. Caelin keeps looking over at me, waiting for me to say something. Mom is reading on her phone. Dad, who barely speaks to me these days, is hunched over his chicken, eating in silence, as usual.

"So," Caelin announces, "Eden got some really good news today."

Mom looks up from her phone and brings her napkin to the corner of her mouth. "Good news? We could use some good news around here."

"Uh, yeah. So, it turns out I got into Tucker Hill University for the fall."

"What?" Dad says, setting down his fork, looking back and forth between me and Caelin like we've been keeping some sort of secret.

"I just found out today," I add.

"And you . . . want . . . to go?" Mom asks, her words coming out slow and uncertain.

"I mean . . . ," I begin, but just the way she said it makes me feel like I shouldn't want to go, like I don't have a right to want it.

Caelin interrupts. "Of course she wants to go."

"Right, of course you do," Mom says, and I can feel a *but* coming next.

"This is a good thing," Caelin says in my defense, bolstering my resolve just a little bit.

"Yeah," I agree. "Why do I feel like I'm breaking bad news to you guys?"

"No, it's great news. Really," Mom says. "Just somewhat unexpected."

"Okay," I scoff. "Are you even happy for me at all?"

"Of course!" Mom says. "Yes, of course we are. Sorry, I'm just thinking of everything you have going on. You know, it finally seems like things are settling here for you, with your *appointments* and your job and . . . and you have a routine. I just worry that a big change isn't what you need right now."

"Or it's exactly what I need. I already called my therapist's office and I can keep meeting with her over the phone. I can definitely find another part-time job making overpriced coffee. And I can come back for the hearing, if it even happens—I mean, it could get postponed again. Why am I putting my whole life on hold?"

Dad sighs loudly, shaking his head.

"What?" Caelin asks our dad, and even I hear the challenge in his voice.

Dad narrows his eyes at Caelin. "Excuse me?"

"I said the word 'therapist,'" I mutter under my breath. "I mentioned the hearing—I know we're supposed to be acting like none of this is happening."

"Eden," Mom says. "No one is—"

But Dad interrupts her. "She's gonna do what she wants to do. Why even ask us?"

"Who, *me*?" I say loudly, Caelin's boldness catching, because I'm so sick of Dad not talking to me ever since this all came out, like *I* did something wrong. "So, you mean to say you actually want me here? Because you barely say two words to me."

"This is . . . ," Dad starts, pushing away from the table, looking at Mom. "She's too young, Vanessa. She's too young to go away. This is," he repeats, "this is not happening."

"You won't even look at me, seriously?" I shout.

"Eden," my mom says. "Calm down."

"Oh my God," Caelin mumbles.

"What do you want me to do here?" I ask, and I'm not even trying to control the volume of my voice now. "What, work at the Bean for the rest of my life, take a community college class every once in a while. I am capable of doing things, you know. This is something I want. I don't know why you're being this way."

Dad stands from the table now, he's walking toward the door, grabbing his car keys.

And I finally say the thing I've been holding back for the last seven months. "You think this is all my fault, don't you?"

He turns around, actually looks at me for the first time in months.

"Well, I didn't ask for any of this to be happening. What Kevin did is not my fault, and I'm sick of you blaming me every single day!" I shout.

"Your father does not blame you." Mom stands up now too. "Conner, say it," she demands.

Caelin stands up too, looking at my dad, then at me, as he says, "No, he blames me, Eden." He pushes his chair in calmly and then goes to his room.

Dad turns back around, opens the door, and leaves.

"For God's sake," my mom hisses. "Eden, I'll be right back. We'll figure it out—let me just . . ." And then she follows after my dad. I'm left alone, sitting at the table with four half-eaten plates of food.

"I'm going," I say to no one.

It takes me all night to work up the courage to text him. Ever since that conversation I had with his dad on their front porch, I've been trying so hard not to dump all my shit on him. Been trying so hard to be there in case *he* needed me for a change. I've tried to ask him so many times how he's doing, but he hasn't opened up to me at all. I've started to worry maybe our time has just come to an end. That we've missed too many chances and have finally run out of them.

I lie on my back, staring at the blur of my ceiling fan, letting it lull me into some kind of weird meditative state. I have to drag my eyes away. I roll to my side, sit up, and take a deep breath, pulling up our texts for the millionth time. If I wait any longer, it's going to be too late and I'll have to do this all over again tomorrow.

I know it's late . . . but can I call?

My phone immediately vibrates in my hand.

JOSH

It rings too many times before she answers, my head already swirling with all kinds of terrible scenarios, too much adrenaline racing through my body.

"Hey," she says quietly.

"Hi. What's wrong?"

She laughs, saying, "Okay, why is 'what's wrong' the first thing you say to me?"

I try to analyze her voice. "Sorry. It's just in all the years I've known you, you've only ever called me when something's wrong."

"Is that true?"

"Oh, I don't know," I mumble, not wanting her to feel bad, not wanting to think about that phone call again.

"Well, nothing's wrong, I just"—she inhales deeply and breathes out slowly—"wanted to talk to you. Is that okay?"

"Of course. I told you, call me anytime."

"I know you said that, but—okay, thank you." She pauses. "Um, is your girlfriend there?"

I never did get around to telling her that we'd broken up. There never seemed to be a time when it wouldn't come out like I don't have some ulterior motive of trying to get her to be with me.

"Will she get upset that I'm calling so late?"

"Well, *I* called *you*, so . . ." I switch the phone to my other ear, like that might help me think better. "Why, would your boyfriend be upset?" I ask her instead.

"Yeah, probably." She laughs that perfect laugh of hers—her real one. "If he were still my boyfriend."

"Oh," I breathe.

She laughs again, waiting for me to join her, but I can't.

"Wait, is that true?" I ask before my heart gets too carried away. "You're not together anymore?"

"Yeah," she answers. "I mean, yes, it's true. No, we're not together anymore."

"Oh," I repeat.

"Josh?"

"Sorry. Um, no, the only one who'd be upset we're talking right now is Harley." Now it's my turn to wait for her to laugh, but she doesn't. "You know, my cat . . . Harley Quinn? Never mind. I'm, uh, actually home right now."

"Home like at your parents'?" she asks.

"Yeah, just for the weekend."

"You weren't gonna tell me?"

"Oh, it's just a short trip."

"But . . . were you going to tell me?"

"Well, I wasn't sure I'd have the time to see you, so . . ." I drift off, hoping she'll say something, because how am I supposed to tell her the truth? *I'm not sure I trust myself to be around you.*

"Eden?"

"Yeah, no, I'm here," she says gently.

"What if . . . ?"

"What if what?"

"What if we talked in person instead?" I ask her. "Could I come over?"

I hold my breath through the silence on the other end of the line. She's never let me come over before. I don't know why I even asked. I should've just invited her here.

"It's okay if you don't—" I start, but she interrupts.

"Come over."

I changed my T-shirt and brushed my teeth, and less than ten minutes later, I'm pulling up outside her house. In all the time I've known her, I never once picked her up or dropped her off here, never went inside. Her house is really dark, but as I'm pocketing my car keys and walking up the driveway, the front porch light turns on.

She opens the door as I approach, stepping outside in bare feet. She smiles and steps down to meet me just as I'm stepping up, and we kind of awkwardly hug on the stairs, both of us falling into each other and wobbling.

"Hi," she murmurs as she pulls away and steps aside. "Sorry, I went in for that hug a little too ambitiously, I guess."

"I don't mind ambitious hugs if they're from you."

That was literally one of the stupidest things I've ever said in my life, but she's wearing shorts again—this time soft pajama-type shorts, and I can see there's a matching tank top, which she's wearing underneath an oversize hoodie and I'm having a hard time thinking of anything but that. I follow her inside, trying to conjure up some modicum of chill.

There are shoes lined up in the entryway, so I take the cue and remove mine.

"Thanks," she says quietly as she stands there shifting her weight from foot to foot, scratching her thigh, looking over her shoulder. She seems oddly, tangibly uncomfortable in her own house. Or maybe she can tell that I'm nervous, and it's making her nervous too. "My parents are upstairs," she adds, not quite whispering but letting me know we need to be relatively quiet.

"Oh, okay," I say, nodding.

"I'm this way." She leads me into the living room and down a hallway where I can hear muffled TV sounds coming from one of the rooms, a thin line of light under the door. "My brother," she explains. I momentarily flash back to the New Year's party my senior year. Rumors had been flying about Eden, and I was trying, unsuccessfully, since I was drunk—the first time in my life I ever drank—to explain that those rumors were just lies. Looking back, I'm sure I only made it worse. So then, when her brother confronted me later that night, I tried to tell him that she wasn't just some hookup to me, but before I could fully explain that I really loved her, he'd already knocked me to the ground. My first fight. My first black eye. My first hangover.

She closes the door behind us, and I try to take a quick look around without being too obvious. Everything's very minimal and sparse, more like a showroom than a real room. "So, this is it, my bedroom."

"It's different than I thought it would be, somehow."

She looks around like she's seeing it for the first time as well.

"I mean, it's nice," I backpedal.

"No," she says. "I know it's weird. There's not much of me in here anymore."

I'm not sure what that means, and I guess it shows on my face because she explains.

"My mom, like, went on this IKEA spree and just totally got rid of everything that had been here before. Repainted and made everything very . . . gray. I guess I haven't really spent much time putting my own touches back in. Except for my lamp," she says, moving toward her desk to turn on this small stained-glass lamp, which is the only source of color in the entire room. "I found this at a thrift store. I'm very proud of it. But I'm rambling. Sorry. I guess I'm nervous."

"It's okay, I might be a little nervous too." I pause. "Being here for the first time makes me feel like I'm in high school again."

She releases a short laugh. Then she reaches around me to turn off the light switch at the wall. The overhead light goes out, and her desk lamp casts a kind of yellow glow around the room. "There, that's better," she says. "Not so bright."

"Yeah," I agree, watching her as she stands in front of me in the dim light now, looking even more . . . *captivating*, is the word that keeps flashing through my mind.

"I've never had anyone in here. I mean, Mara, obviously. But I've never had a *boy*," she whispers through cupped hands, "in my room like this. Before." She inhales deeply and says, "Sorry, that was supposed to be cute or funny or something."

"No, it was," I tell her, but really, I'm thinking about *Steve*. Was he really never here, and what does that mean?

"Um. Do you wanna sit or, oh, do you want something to drink?"

"I'm fine," I tell her. "It's okay."

She says, "Okay," but she's still twirling her fingers around the drawstrings of her hoodie, which she clearly threw on over her pajamas right before I got here. And something about that sends my mind off in the wrong direction again. I have to look away.

"Should we start over?" I ask. "Proper hug?"

She nods.

"Yeah? Okay. Come here." I hold my hands out, and she takes them, moves toward me, and clasps her arms around my waist. I let my arms fold around her and rest my chin on top of her hair, which smells amazing as usual. She presses her face against my chest and holds on so tight. She keeps taking these slow, deliberately deep breaths like she's trying to calm down. Part of me wants to ask if she's okay, but it's pretty clear she isn't, so I try to breathe with her, try to calm myself down too. Gradually, her grip loosens, and we back away from each other.

"Sorry, I've just been—it's just been a lot lately, but I'm glad you're here. I always like talking to you in person better."

She hadn't mentioned anything in our texts *being a lot lately*, but I guess I haven't exactly been forthcoming about my stuff either. We sit on her bed, facing each other, the same way we'd sat on that picnic table.

"So, what did you want to talk about?" I'm asking, just as she's saying, "Why are you home?" As usual, we talk over each other.

"Sorry, you first," I tell her.

"Okay, so why are you home right now?" she repeats.

"It's my dad. He's six months sober this weekend. There's a ceremony, and then we're doing a family celebration sort of thing."

"Oh. Wow, six months. That's a big deal, right?"

I nod. "Yeah. I mean, I've seen him get his six-month chip quite a few times before, but . . ."

"But what?"

"I'll probably regret saying this, but something does feel a little different with him this time."

"Good," she says, with this slow blink, like she really means it.

"I don't know, I'm being cautiously optimistic, I guess."

"I'm really glad, Josh. You deserve that."

"*I* do?" I ask.

"Yeah, you deserve to have your dad healthy and . . . and there for you. I mean, I know how much this has hurt you over the years." She reaches out and takes my hand, inching closer to me, and I catch this sheen falling over her eyes. "I just"—she pauses to close her eyes for a moment—"I want it to be different for you this time too."

I reach out and take her other hand now, thinking I may finally understand something important about her that I'm not sure I've fully realized before. She spent so much of our relationship hiding her emotions because *this* is how she feels things—deeply, completely. That and this: she really has always cared.

"Eden," I begin, but I don't have anything else to say, so I settle on "thank you."

“I’m sorry about the phone call,” she says. “I was just surprised that you didn’t mention you’d be here. It’s not like you *have* to tell me every time you’re going to be in town.”

“No, I wanted to tell you.” I move a little closer to her now too. “But things have felt . . .” I try to find the right word. “Strained. Since last time. Or maybe it’s just me, I don’t know.”

“It’s not just you.”

There’s a silence that I feel it’s my turn to fill.

“I’ve gotta be honest, it was hard to see you with another guy. But more than that—I just felt like maybe I should try to leave you alone.”

“No,” she says, squeezing my hands in hers. “I would never want you to leave me alone.”

“Well, I thought, if you’ve moved on, I should try to do the same, and maybe that would make things easier or—”

“If *I’ve* moved on,” she repeats, her voice turning harder now as she lets go of my hands. “You’re the one who has a serious girlfriend.”

I shake my head as she speaks. “No, I don’t. That’s not—it’s been over for a while.”

“What?”

“It’s over,” I repeat.

“Since when?”

“Since I came to see you that night. In December. She wasn’t actually okay with it.”

“You lied to me?”

“Yes,” I admit. She nods slowly, and I watch as she pulls her bottom lip between her teeth and then looks at her hands in her lap, her hair hanging down over her face. I angle my head to try to see her expression, but she brings her hand up to her forehead like she's shielding her eyes from the sun. "Eden?" I reach out and raise her chin until I can see her face . . . *smiling.*

"Oh, don't look so broken up about it," I joke.

She looks up now and covers her mouth. "No, I'm sorry. I'm not smiling," she says, but she's losing her voice as she muffles a laugh.

"No, you're laughing!" Which only makes me start laughing too because it's so absurd. "What's so funny?"

"No, nothing—I'm sorry!" She bats her hand at my arm. "Stop it," she demands, but then she cracks up all over again.

"*You* stop." Her laugh is a drug. "You're the one laughing at me."

"I'm sorry, I don't know why I'm laughing. I'm sorry," she repeats. "I'm not laughing at you, I promise."

"No, don't worry. It's okay," I tease. "It's just my heart."

"Oh my God," she sighs, pulling herself together. "I'm the worst."

I nod, pretending to agree, stopping myself from saying, *No, you're the best.*

When we finally stop laughing, we've somehow drawn even closer to each other. "It's just that I've been obsessing about you and this, like, *dream girl*, and now . . ." She shakes her head for a moment and then looks at me so intensely, her cheeks flushed.

"What?" I ask her.

"I do care about your heart, you know." She reaches out and lets her hand hover over the center of my chest, her fingers barely touching my shirt. "A lot, actually."

I cover her hand with mine, pressing it flat against my chest. We're so close now, and I wonder if she can feel my heart pounding through my shirt. She inches toward me and touches my face with her other hand, the way she had the night of the concert, so softly. I turn my head and kiss her palm, and as her hand moves down to my neck, she pulls herself closer to me. She leans in and presses her lips to my cheek for a moment before pulling back to look at me. Her other hand tightens around the fabric of my shirt, and her eyes dip down to focus on my mouth. I watch as she takes this tiny sip of air—God, I don't know how I could've forgotten this detail. It used to get me every time, the way she'd always take that little breath right before she kissed me. I close my eyes, and I can feel the warmth of her mouth, our lips nearly touching.

I can barely catch my breath—because this is happening—but then, as I wait for her to close this impossibly small distance between us, her hand loosens its grip on my shirt and presses against my chest now. I open my eyes to see her backing away.

EDEN

I am two people right now. The first one wants to throw herself into this, into him. Her tunnel vision is focused only on how good it will feel, how right, how pure and honest. But the second girl? She doesn't see him at all, really. She has X-ray vision. For her, the room is so cluttered with all the things that have happened here, he's barely even there. She sees beyond the freshly painted walls and the new furniture and the clean linens and everything in perfect monochrome order, all the scars hiding underneath.

One of us pulls him closer, the other one pushes him away, and I hate them both because neither of them feels like *me*.

"I'm sorry," I breathe.

"No, I am. Did I just really misread this?"

I don't know what words to say to explain. I barely understand what's going through my head right now, but I take his hands and hold them tightly because that's all I can do. "You didn't misread anything. It's just . . . not here. I can't. Not here," I repeat, glancing around the room as if the walls are watching us. I feel like they can do that sometimes.

"That's okay," he says, so gently, though he must be even more confused than me.

"It happened here," I try to explain. "You . . . you know what I'm talking about, right?"

I see the wave of recognition pass over his eyes. He squeezes my hands and nods. "Yeah," he whispers. "Right. Of course."

"That's sort of what I wanted to talk to you about."

"Oh," he breathes, straightening his posture. "Okay."

"No, not *that*. Don't worry."

"I'm not worried, you know you can talk to me about it."

I close my eyes and shake my head. "No. I mean, thank you. But no. What I meant is I wanted to talk to you about the . . . the *here* part of everything."

"The here part?" he repeats as if he might understand what that means if he says it out loud. "All right."

"I know I'm not making any fucking sense and I'm all over the place."

"It's okay, I'm following," he says with a cautious smile. "Mostly."

"I'm not trying to ignore what just happened. Or almost happened. I don't want to forget about that. I'm *not* forgetting about it, believe me, but—" I pull his hands toward me and lean over to kiss the backs of each of them. "Can we just put a pin in that for a minute? Or whatever that saying is. Because I really did want to talk to you about something."

"Sure, we can do that. Yeah."

"Okay." I inhale and exhale, trying to get some of this tension out of me. In with the good, out with the bad, I tell myself, just like my therapist taught me. "You know I've been trying really hard to make things work here."

He nods.

"But it's just not," I finally admit out loud. "And the more I think about it, the more I'm pretty sure it's not going to. Like, I try to imagine myself here a year from now and I just don't even see anything." I pause to clear the thickness those words leave behind in my throat. "I can't be here anymore. In this house, in this town. Too much has happened. I don't fit anymore. I haven't in a long time."

"Mm-hmm," he murmurs, nodding encouragingly. "I can understand why you'd feel that way."

"So, I've been thinking about leaving."

"Leaving?" His eyebrows pull together, and he shakes his head slightly. "What do you mean? Where would you go?"

"Well, what would you think if I applied to your school? Would that be weird for you or—"

"To Tucker?" he interrupts. "Are you kidding? No, that would be . . ." He pauses, searching for a word. "Perfect."

"Yeah?" I exhale. "Really, you mean that?"

"Really, I mean it. Hundred percent—a thousand percent."

I try to stop myself from smiling like this, but it's hard not to when he's smiling at me like that. "Okay, I'm really glad you said that because I did."

"You did?"

"And I got in."

"Wait, you got in?" he says, too loudly for almost midnight.

"And I think I really, really want to go."

"You got in," he repeats. "Seriously, Eden?"

I nod.

"That's amazing!" He throws his arms around me, and I suddenly feel freer already. "I'm so happy," he whispers into my hair. "I'm so fucking happy for you."

"You are?" I ask, hating how small and stupid my voice sounds.

As we pull apart, he tucks my hair behind both ears and holds my face in his hands for a moment, still smiling as he looks me in the eye. "Don't ask me that; you know I am." He kisses my forehead quickly, a peck, sweet and chaste. He holds my gaze for a moment longer and then scoots away from me, this time with his back against the wall. I sit directly next to him now, my back to the wall, my arm against his arm, my leg against his leg.

He's suddenly so quiet.

"What are you thinking?" I ask him.

He shakes his head and says, "I don't know, a lot of things."

"Like what?"

"Like I'm really proud of you—is that weird to say?"

"No," I tell him. But I watch as he swallows hard and looks around my room, differently than he had before. "What else are you thinking?"

He turns his head to look at me, and he squints just a bit. "Honestly? I'm mostly trying *not* to think about you . . . in this room . . . *him*," he adds, his speech halting.

"Sorry," I say. Because maybe it wasn't fair to put those thoughts in his head.

"Why are you sorry? I didn't mean that like you shouldn't

have said anything about it; I'm glad you did. You have nothing to be sorry about."

"Looks like such a nice room, doesn't it?" I say, and I don't know if I'm trying to make light or if I'm genuinely asking. I wanted him to understand how much I need to leave, but it's hard to watch him actively seeing my life the way it really is, the way no one else seems to get.

"No, it doesn't," he says immediately. "Sorry, I just don't know how you do it."

"Do what?"

"Live in here . . . after everything."

"I don't. Not really. I mean, I can't sleep in here very well. It's a brand-new bed, but I still end up on the couch most nights. It's better than before. All through high school, I literally slept on my floor in a sleeping bag. I—I've never told anyone that."

He exhales a long stream of air and puts his arm around me. I let myself lean into his side. "The only time I slept in a real bed was at Mara's house or—"

"Or what?" he asks.

"Or when I was with you," I finish, stealing a quick glance up at him, and he's watching me with the most devastated look on his face. "Sorry."

"Don't be."

"I don't know why I'm saying all this right now. I'm really tired." I sigh. "I know I'm rambling and making this all weird and negative, aren't I?"

"No, you're not. Please don't say that, okay?"

Before I can answer, he's shifting away from me, and I think for a second that maybe I really have messed this up, but then he's lying down, his head on my pillow, and he's holding his arm open to the side. "Come here, I'll stay till you fall asleep."

"Really?"

"If that's okay, yeah."

I nod and crawl into the space next to him.

"Comfortable?" he asks.

I sit back up because my hoodie is making me too hot. I only put it on because I was in pajamas and not wearing a bra, but that seems so silly now, so I unzip it, and he helps me pull my arms out of the sleeves. I lie back down, resting my head in that perfect spot I've tried to find on so many other people but has never felt quite like this.

"Want me to turn the light off?" he asks, reaching toward my desk for the stained-glass lamp.

"*No*, don't." It comes out too fast, and he draws his hand back, almost startled. "I mean, do you mind if we leave it on?"

"That's fine," he says softly. "Is that a thing you do? Keeping the light on?"

"I'm not, like, scared of the dark," I try to explain, raising my head to look at him. "I just sort of am in here, that's all. Yet another thing I've never told anyone."

He doesn't speak, just nods. I lay my head back down, let my arm rest across his stomach while his fingers trail up and down my bare skin like a lullaby.

"Eden?" he says so quietly I can barely hear him. "Can I ask you something?"

"Okay."

His chest rises as he fills his lungs with air, and I can feel his heart beating faster beneath me. "When we were together, did I ever . . . ?" He pauses, and I wait. "I mean, I realize our relationship moved really fast and it started out very, um—"

"Sexual?" I offer, since this is clearly difficult for him.

"I was going to say physical, but yeah." He pauses again and swallows before continuing. "And you were younger than I thought you were."

"Because I lied to you."

He ignores that, continues as if I hadn't said anything. "Did I ever do anything that wasn't okay with you or that made you feel . . . ? I mean, did I ever not listen or pressure you to—"

I see where he's going with this, so I cut him off. "Josh, *no*."

"No, don't—" he says, and the way his voice is trembling, I have to look at him. "Don't just say what you think I want to hear. I really need to know the truth. It's killing me," he adds, his words punching me in the heart.

"I am telling you the truth."

"Sometimes I think back and I'm not sure anymore how well I treated you. It's just, I knew something was wrong. Even the first time we were together. I knew, but I didn't do any—"

"What were you supposed to do? You tried to ask me about it, and I basically told you to fuck off."

"But I—"

"Stop. You never *ever* did anything wrong; I promise." When I reach to touch his face, he takes my hand and holds it there against his cheek, looking into my eyes.

"You promise," he repeats. "Really?"

"I do." He lets go of my hand, and I lie back down against him. "Please, don't even think that for a second, Josh. If anything, it was the opposite."

"Okay," he whispers, stroking my hair with one hand and holding my arm with the other. "I'll let you sleep, I'm sorry."

"It's all right."

He doesn't think I hear it when he whispers, a few minutes later, "Thank you."

JOSH

I stare at her ceiling for I don't know how long. I should feel better, finally having my answer, but her words keep replaying in my head.

"The opposite," I hear myself say out loud. "What's the opposite?"

"Hmm?" she mumbles.

"You said 'if anything, it was the opposite,' but what does that mean?"

"Oh," she breathes, her voice already heavy with sleep. "I don't know. You always made me feel . . . safe. Too safe, maybe." She lets out the tiniest laugh. "Kind of ruined me for anyone else."

"I don't know how to take that," I whisper, but I cling to that small laugh.

"It's just—you know, no one else is like you."

Within seconds her breathing turns slower, deeper, as she drifts to sleep.

"No one else is like you, either," I say, even though I know she won't hear me.

The next thing I know, I'm opening my eyes, and I can tell I've been out for a while. Eden's still asleep, her leg draped over mine now. I move slowly, reaching into my back pocket for my phone. It's almost four o'clock. I shift her leg first, then, as carefully as I can, slip my arm out from behind her neck. I don't want to wake her, but I don't want to just leave, either. On her desk, near the lamp, there's a stack of sticky notes and a jar of markers and pens.

To be continued . . . Sleep well, J

I cover her with the knit blanket that's folded over the back of her chair and place the note on the pillow next to her.

I tiptoe through her house in the dark, barely even breathing. I don't know who would be worse to run into in the middle of the night: one of her parents, who have no idea who I am and might think I'm some kind of intruder, or her brother. I make it to the entryway, where I scoop my shoes up and carry them the rest of the way. It's not until I close the door behind me that I finally let myself exhale. I lean against the railing and try to balance myself while I slide my sneakers back on.

"Hey, Miller."

"Jesus fuck!" I nearly fall down the steps when I look up and see her brother sitting there in the dark.

"Sorry," he says. "I was trying to *not* scare you, actually."

"No, it's fine," I say, struggling to get my other shoe on quickly, just in case I need to make a break for it. "Um, I know what this probably looks like, but I'm not sneaking out or anything like that."

He laughs slowly. "Yeah, this is a little awkward, huh?" he mutters as he lights up a cigarette, illuminating his face, and that's when I realize he's got a whole collection of bottles next to him.

"You all right, man?" I ask him, because he looks rough as fuck. Nothing like the MVP, voted-most-likely-to-be-an-NBA-all-star-by-the-age-of-twenty guy I used to play with in high school; he barely even resembles that guy who beat me up at the New Year's party.

He shrugs. "You want one?" he asks, nearly dropping the bottle of beer he's trying to hand me. If I ever needed motivation to not drink again, this might just be it.

"No, I'm good. It's late; I should probably get home."

He nods and opens the bottle for himself instead.

"Good seeing you, though," I tell him, even though it's actually sort of horrible seeing him. Like this, anyway.

"Miller?" he says, as I take one step off the porch. "Did you know?"

I don't need to ask him what he's talking about. "No, I didn't know. I wish I had, honestly."

"Is she okay, do you think?"

I'm not sure what to say, but I try to answer anyway. "I think she's . . . doing her best. You should ask her yourself," I add.

He nods but doesn't say anything. I raise my hand to wave and take a step away from him. "Hey, for the record, Josh . . . ," he calls after me. "I'm sorry for punching you in the face that time."

"It's all right," I tell him. I take another step but stop and turn around again. "You know, I really do care about her. I always have. It was never what you thought."

Caelin nods again and stands, taking a couple of unsteady steps toward me, extending his hand. And as I take it, he reaches around me to pat my back, much like we'd have done after a game back in the day. "I'm glad she has you . . . as a friend, or whatever," he says.

"Yeah, well, I'm glad I have her too," I tell him, hoping he'll remember this conversation in the morning. "Take care, all right?"

"Yep. Later."

By the time I'm pulling away from the house, he's already inside.

EDEN

We stand in my driveway. All of us. Like the farewell scene in *The Wizard of Oz*. Except instead of ruby slippers, my magical transport is a borrowed beige Toyota. And, of course, I'm not going home; I'm leaving it.

It's amazing how fast time passes when you're trying to get your entire mess of a life in order. I had to quit my job at the Bean, register for classes, find a place to live, get a new job, and cram in as many appointments with my therapist as I could. I'm beyond exhausted.

But I did it. And now we're here. Mara's ugly crying, and, to everyone's surprise, so is my dad, and it's harder to hold it together than I thought it would be, even after taking an extra pill. But I do it.

"Eden, are you sure we can't follow behind you?" my mom asks again. "Just to get you settled in."

"No, it's okay. Really, I have plenty of help there. And I'll be home again next month for the . . ." I pause, meeting Caelin's eye before he looks down at his feet. "Hearing," I finish.

"Are you sure you didn't forget anything?" she asks, looking back toward the house.

"Probably, but I can always get it next time."

"Wish we at least knew this Joshua person you're going to be living with," my dad mutters.

"I'm not living *with* him, Dad," I correct, not wanting to be too harsh, as these are probably the most words he's said to me, or near me, since the dinner table fight. "We'll just be in the same building."

"I know him," Caelin says. "He's a decent guy."

That seems to put my dad at ease, which sparks a tiny flame in my chest. Because why isn't *me* knowing him, vouching for him, trusting him, good enough? My stomach clenches at that thought, extinguishing the fire before it makes its way to my brain and I say something I'll feel guilty for later. That's not the way I want this to end. Or begin.

We all look at each other, then at Caelin's car, filled to the brim with boxes and bags and my still-newish mattress wrapped in plastic and strapped to the top with bungee cords.

"Well," Mom says, pressing her fingers to the corners of her eyes. "I hate this."

"So do I," Mara sobs.

I go to each of them—Mom, Dad, and Caelin. I hug them and tell them I love them. Mara, my scarecrow, I save for last. "*I think I'll miss you most of all*," I whisper in her ear.

"Stop," she laughs, even as she whimpers, "I can't believe you're leaving."

“You better visit me,” I say through her hair in my face and her arms clasped around my neck, her whole body shaking with sobs as I hug her back.

“Let us know when you get there,” my mom calls to me as I’m pulling out of the driveway.

I’m almost at the highway when I realize I don’t know where I’m going. I pull down a side street and park. I see a text from Amanda from fifteen minutes earlier.

All it says is: ur really coming back right

I wonder if she was watching us in my driveway. I can feel the panic coming off those words. She means coming back for the hearing. When I asked the DA if I had to, she said they could make me. Though she used the word “compel.” I guess Mandy doesn’t know that. I can’t deal with her right now. I shake the chills out and copy the address from Josh’s text and paste it into my navigator.

Take a breath. Begin again.

Twenty minutes into the drive, I almost die when I swerve into the left lane while trying to check my directions. The truck driver I nearly collided with honks twice and gives me the finger. But after I make it past the city limits, I’m feeling pretty good. The road is clear, and I’m driving fast with the window rolled down, radio on, the playlist Mara made for me blasting all the songs I know by heart. I start thinking maybe this wasn’t such a crazy idea, maybe this could actually be a good thing. The sky is gray, but it seems just right. Like the perfect day to try to change.

I text Josh my ETA at the halfway point, when I stop for gas and a bathroom break. I keep the radio off for the second leg of the trip. I hadn’t actually gotten this far in my plan. I mean, I know classes start in one week and that Monday morning I have new student orientation and a campus tour with a group of incoming freshmen like me. And that my roommate's name is Parker Kim, a second-year undergrad on the women's swim team, who lives in Josh's building.

I slow down to the exact speed limit, try to prepare myself.

All our talks and texts have been strictly logistics. About the colossal shortage of student housing on campus and how all the apartment listings I sent him to check out for me were apparently in terrible neighborhoods and far from campus. About the vacancy in his friend's apartment—her former roommate just moved in with their girlfriend and she needed a new roommate fast, almost as much as I did. "It's perfect, right?" Josh had said. And I took it at face value, trying not to read too little or too much into him wanting me to be so close.

But for the past six weeks, throughout all the planning and preparing and back-and-forth, that almost-kiss has stayed pinned securely in place, not budging. The closest he's come to giving me any kind of sign about what he's thinking was when he sent me a link to a work-study job in the library, accompanied by some confusingly suggestive emojis.

You should apply for this. I remember you used to volunteer in the school library back when you were hiding from me . . . And your 🔥 book club thing 😉

I reread that text so many times, even had Mara analyze it. She was pretty sure he was flirting with me, but I'm still not convinced. I did, however, apply for the job, and after a five-minute phone interview, I got it. Twelve hours per week. I'd still have to find something else, but this would be a good start.

GPS says I'm only two minutes away now. I pull over several blocks from the building, swish some lukewarm bottled water around my mouth, and pop a breath mint. I am rummaging in my purse when my hand makes contact with one of my now three prescription bottles. One for depression, one for sleeping, and one for when I'm actively having a panic attack. I consider taking another one, just to take the edge off. But instead, I apply a little lip gloss, pulling my windblown nest of hair back into a slightly less messy bun. Just in case. Of what exactly, I don't know.

JOSH

I could barely sleep last night. I'm sitting with Parker on the roof of our building, drinking coffee, even though I've already had way too much caffeine today.

"Your leg bouncing is about to drive me crazy," Parker tells me. "Do I need to cut you off?" she asks, gesturing to the mug trembling in my hand. I set it down, and the coffee sloshes over the side onto the table. I check my phone. Again.

"She should be here any minute."

"Can I just ask," Parker says, peering over the rim of her coffee mug at me, "is this weird nervous thing you're doing anxiety or excitement?"

I'm not sure what to say because I really can't distinguish between those two emotions right now.

"Because I'm getting some red flag vibes off you," Parker continues, but I'm too busy staring at Eden's last message, and

Parker's voice drifts to the background of my thoughts.

"Josh!" she shouts, snapping her fingers in my face.

"Sorry, what?"

"She's, like, *cool*, right?" she finally asks. "I'm gonna be living with this person, and your weirdness is giving me doubts!"

"No, she's great, really. It's me. I'm just not . . ."

"Cool?"

"Funny." I force a smile. "No, it's just that we kinda left things unclear. About what we are. The lines between friendship and something more are just very blurred right now, and I don't know what to expect."

"Well, what do you want it to be?"

I shrug, wishing I could say with certainty that friendship would be enough. "I mean, I'll take whatever she gives me."

"Great, that sounds healthy. No drama there at all."

"Okay, obviously, I want more."

She just keeps staring at me, a smirk stretching across her face. "You" is all she says.

"Me, what?"

"*You* . . ." She stands up and points her finger at me. "Better not cause drama with *my* roommate. Because then that means there's drama with *me*." Now she points at herself. "And I don't do drama."

"I don't either."

"Uh-huh." She does not sound convinced.

My phone dings. "She's here."

I jog down the first flight of stairs, Parker calling behind me, "*Run, Josh-wah, run*!" Quoting the movie we watched in our

American History course, where we were randomly paired to work on a presentation together. It took me a full year before I understood that she didn't actually hate me. She likes to tease and poke and jab.

And as I knock on my door, stick my head in—"D, she's here!"—I wonder if I've made the best call in setting her up with Parker. Underneath, I know she's a nice person, but she can have such a gruff exterior sometimes.

"Yeah, I'm coming," Dominic yells as I close the door.

I stop and wait for Parker to catch up.

"What?" she says.

"It's just—you're gonna be nice to her, right?" I try to ask as gently as possible.

"I'm always nice, you dick."

"Okay, but she's got a lot going on and—"

"Most girls do," she says, cutting me off. "Josh, listen. I can read between the lines. I get it. I'll be nice to her." And for the first time maybe ever, there's no hint of sarcasm in her voice, no shadow of a grin on her face. "Just don't try to control so much."

"All right," Dominic says, appearing in the hallway between us, clapping his hands. "I'm ready. Let's do this."

"Okay," I say—to both of them.

I walk down the next flight of stairs, forcing a slower pace, because Parker's right, I can't try to control what happens next. Outside, I see Eden's brother's car parked on the street in front of our building; it's easy to spot, overflowing with a mattress strapped to the top of the car. But I don't see Eden. I bend down to look through the passenger-side window. Her phone's sitting there in the cupholder, the lamp from her bedroom sticking out of the top of a bag on the floor.

"Relax," Parker sings from behind me. "Besides, I think that's her over there, isn't it?"

I follow the direction Parker is looking, across the street, at a girl standing at the crosswalk. She has her hair pulled back and is wearing sunglasses, the strap of her bag pulled across her body, and she's carrying a tray of drinks from the café on the corner. At first I don't recognize her. I don't know why exactly. I guess I was expecting her to seem out of place here, expecting to have to help her get acclimated, protect her, even. But she already looks like she belongs, like she's always been here. The traffic light changes, and she starts walking toward us, waving when she spots me.

"Hi!" she says as she approaches us. "I come bearing frozen cappuccinos."

Parker steps forward and says, "Oh, this is the beginning of a beautiful friendship, I can tell already."

"You must be Parker," Eden says, raising her sunglasses with her free hand.

"And you must be Eden." Parker moves in with open arms but stops. "Are you a hugger?"

"Um, sure," Eden says, her eyes flashing to mine just for a moment. "Yeah."

"I've heard so much about you," Parker says, giving Eden a hug—something I've never seen Parker do with anyone before. "Welcome to the building, to Tuck Hill, you're gonna like it here, I promise."

"Thank you," Eden says. "I'm glad to be here."

"Hello again, dear," Dominic adds, not even hinting at any of his many misgivings he hasn't been shy about sharing with me, as he pulls Eden into a brief one-armed hug. "I'll gladly take one of those off your hands."

"Good to see you again," she tells him as she hands him one of the drinks she's carrying, giving one to Parker as well.

And then her eyes meet mine. She smiles so brightly, I literally cannot find any words to say except "Hey, you."

We step toward each other on the sidewalk, and as I put my arms around her, Parker takes the drink tray from Eden. And now I feel both her hands pressed against my back, pulling me in. I allow myself to savor it for a moment, but because I would stay like this all day if we could, I let go first.

EDEN

I follow Parker up the stairs into my new life. She's talking without any trouble the whole two flights, while I'm struggling to catch my breath. I guess it must be her swimming lungs. Or maybe I've been holding my breath so long, I don't know what it's like to breathe easily anymore.

"Laundry room is in the basement. Josh and D stay on the floor above us," she's saying as she leads me down a long narrow hallway. "Oh, and after this, remind one of us to show you our spot up on the roof."

"Okay," I manage to get out.

At the very end of the hall, she says, "Here we are, 2C. Home sweet home."

Part of me also wonders if my racing heart is me not being used to stairs or my anxiety meds wearing off or if it might just have something to do with Josh and the rush of finally being able to hug him, touch him, in the daylight, in public, without fear of who might see us and what they might think or if I'm doing anything wrong or pretending it's something it's not.

She pushes the door open and holds her arm out, gesturing for me to walk in first. It's a large, bright, open room. With windows on two walls. A well-worn formerly vibrant red couch sits in the middle. A small table with mismatched chairs in the corner. A tiny kitchen with old white appliances and a narrow bar that separates the space.

"I know it's not much," Parker says as I look around. "It's small, and we share a bathroom, but it's still way better than campus housing."

"No, this is . . ." It's neat and clean and nothing like home. As I take a step, the old hardwood floors creak under my feet. "I love it."

"Your room's this way," she says, smiling as she leads me to a wooden door on the opposite side of the apartment. "My old roommate left a few things. Just a dresser, bookcase, desk, and chair. We can get rid of them if you want, but I thought I'd leave it and see if you need any of them first."

My room.

The wooden floors continue, and as I cross the threshold, it feels like the room is drawing me in. It's smaller than my bedroom back home. But there's a large window with a tree outside it, and the old, chipped furniture is warm and inviting. I run my hand along the top of the desk and feel the grooves of pen marks crisscrossed along the surface.

"What do you think?" Josh's voice says behind me.

When I turn back around, Parker is gone and Josh is standing in the doorway with two of my bags at his feet, cradling my little stained-glass lamp in one arm like it's a baby.

Our fingers touch as I take it from him, the brass body of the lamp warm from his hands. I bring my lamp over to the desk—*my* desk—plug it in at the wall socket, and turn the little key-shaped knob to switch it on.

"Perfect," I say, turning back around to face him. He leans against the doorframe and smiles the way he always does. That perfectly imperfect smile of his. But this time it sparks something in me, like that key-shaped switch. Like I'm seeing him in full color for the very first time. My feet are frozen in place. But in my mind, I'm walking over to him. Because all I want to do is pull him inside the room, *my* room, close the door, take his hands in mine, and put them on me. I want to kiss him everywhere, feel his mouth on my skin. I want to—

"You okay?" he asks, picking up the bags and walking toward me like he's definitely not thinking any of the things I am right now.

I swallow, watching his arms working so easily, so smoothly, as he sets the bags down next to the closet door. "Yeah. I'm just . . ." I bring the backs of my hands to my cheeks. They're flaming. I've always been attracted to him, but this is different—this churning inside me is like a gnawing hunger but deeper. I usually have so many firewalls up when I start thinking about him, the sudden vividness of this fantasy catches me off guard. "Just hot. Warm," I correct.

I don't know what is happening to me. Is this just how I feel about him when I'm not filtering my emotions and censoring my every thought?

He walks past me, his arm just grazing mine, as he goes to the window. "Let me see if I can get this open. All these old windows stick really bad in the summer." He unlocks the metal latch at the top and gives the wooden frame a sharp jab before it squeals open, ushering in a fresh breeze, which hits my skin, cooling me down just enough to stop me from rushing over to him and acting out the things that won't stop playing in my head.

"Thanks," I tell him, reaching out as he passes me. My fingers catch the sleeve of his shirt, my hand grasping his forearm as he stops. I want to pull him in, want him to reach for me too, but he stands there and covers my hand with his for only a moment before letting go.

"No problem," he says, all nonchalant, and goes to the doorway as if I were really only thanking him for opening the window.

I make my way downstairs, feeling slightly dizzy as my senses attune to him, just steps behind me. All day long we're in such close contact, passing in the hallway, squeezing by each other on the stairs. Every single time I want to reach out to touch him. But he doesn't seem to be having the same problem at all, and I don't know what to make of that.

The day is only getting hotter and more humid when I find myself alone outside. I take one last sip of my now melted frozen cappuccino and decide I can at least try to undo the bungee cords holding the mattress and box spring in place.

Standing up on the inside of the car door, stretching on my tiptoes, I reach under the mattress, trying to feel the spot where the two hooks connect. I can't see it, but I can feel it right at the edge of my fingertips.

"Don't be a hero, Eden!" Parker calls out, suddenly behind me. "Let the guys get that one. It's not anti-feminist, I promise. Or if it is, whatever, I won't tell anyone."

"I got it," I say, even though I can feel my grip slipping.

"Here," Josh says as he comes up behind me. I feel his leg next to mine, his hand resting on my back for a moment as he reaches his other arm around me, his body pressed up against mine now. "You almost had it," he says with his hand moving along my arm to the place where my fingers almost reach the hook. He pulls the cords closer and says, his mouth painfully close to me, "Hold this side." He slips the hook into my hand and then reaches farther, pressing tighter against me, to unclasp the two.

My heart stutters at the feeling of his body on me like this. He has to be feeling it too.

As he steps down, I lose my balance. "Oh, ya good?" he says, normal as anything, as he places his hands on my waist to stabilize me. If I turn around, I'm afraid I won't be able to look him in the eye without kissing him.

And because I don't think I should do that here, in the middle of the street, I just mutter, "Yeah, all good." I keep my back to him as I slip under his arms. I go stand at a safe distance on the sidewalk with Parker while we watch the two of them maneuver my mattress off the car.

I run up the steps to hold the front door open for them, and as Josh passes, he says, "Thanks."

I let myself look up for only a split second, and I can tell he has all these questions in his eyes as if *I'm* the one being weird.

As the door swings closed behind them, Parker snorts a laugh.

"Well, then." She breathes out an exaggerated sigh, almost a whistle. "You could cut that with a knife."

“What?” I ask, even though, of course, I know.

She tilts her head and smiles.

I press my hands to my cheeks again, feeling the blood simmering under the surface of my skin. “Um. So, food?” I say, instead of acknowledging what is apparently obvious to everyone around us. “I’m gonna order us some food. What’s good around here?”

Thirty minutes later, we’re all on the roof with a large pizza and a two-liter of soda. Dominic brought up paper plates and plastic cups and hands them to each of us.

Parker says, “You’re destroying the planet with these—you know that, right?”

Dominic doesn’t skip a beat. “No, the energy companies and big-ass corporations are destroying the planet. I am being thoughtful and making our hard-earned dinner a little more civilized.”

Josh scoots over on the wicker love seat, making room for me to sit down next to him. “You’ll get used to their bickering,” he says, smiling as he meets my eyes. It feels like the first time he’s even looked at me all day.

“No, it’s nice,” I say. And it is. My house has felt so dead these past months, with no one talking to each other. No one joking around. No one laughing. “This whole place is nice,” I add, taking in this little patch of space on the roof, filled with mismatched outdoor furniture, a patio table and chairs, potted plants.

With the sun finally retreating behind the taller buildings in the distance, a comfortable quiet washes over us as we sit with our slices of pizza. Until Dominic sees me trying to blot my oily fingers on a clean spot on my grease-stained paper plate.

"Oh shit, forgot . . ." He pulls a wad of napkins he'd had bunched up in his pocket and hands me one. "Here you go."

"More paper products?" Parker shouts through her last bite.

"Well, you can just use your pants as a napkin if you prefer!"

Parker holds both hands up in the air and then brings them down against her thighs, smearing them all over her jeans. Dominic stands abruptly, commanding everyone's attention, holds up one finger like he's about to launch into some kind of serious monologue, but then his only response is "Ew."

I can't help but laugh, even though I'm not entirely sure how much they're joking with each other. Next to me Josh exhales a short snicker but restrains himself.

Parker stands up with a satisfied grin on her face. "All right, kids. I'm gonna try to get in a swim before it gets too late."

"And I have a hot date I need to get ready for," Dominic says. "And by hot date, I mean a video call in my room." My confusion must show on my face because he continues. "Me and Luke—you know him, I think, Lucas Ramirez from school?"

"Oh yeah," I say. "He was a year ahead of me."

"We're doing the long distance thing for now. Trying to convince him to come out here like you did, but—" He stops talking suddenly, and Josh sort of squirms next to me. "Well, I mean, not that it's the same thing. I'm not saying you came here just to be with—"

"Oh-*kay*," Josh interrupts. "Don't wanna be late, do you?"

Parker puts both of her hands on Dominic's back, steering him toward the door. "We're leaving, but you two enjoy this totally unromantic sunset. Later, roomie."

"Wow," Josh breathes as they clamor for the door, their laughter echoing after it closes. "I'm sorry about them. They're being weird and immature."

"They're fine." What I really want to say is he's the one who's being weird and immature. "I like them."

I set my paper plate on top of the empty pizza box and lean back into the cushions, feeling all the tension in my muscles coming to the surface. But the view is beautiful as the light hits the buildings that make up the small city of the university and then a landscape of rolling green hills just beyond. So much nicer than the flat monotony of back home.

The breeze flows over us and rattles the leaves of the nearby trees, cooling my hot skin and sweat of the day. This would be the perfect moment for him to kiss me, talk to me, do literally anything to me.

JOSH

I've been waiting to be alone with her all day, trying so hard to play it cool and not force anything or make it awkward, but now we're finally here and I'm not sure what to do.

"Well," Eden says. "She wasn't wrong about the sunset."

I turn to look at her, how she's watching the sky, the way it's casting this golden creamsicle light over her, but the only thing I can think of as a response is "Yeah."

She sighs and leans back, bringing her legs up onto the seat and crossing them beneath her. Turning her head from side to side, she sits up straight, then curves her back and starts kneading her shoulders with her hands. "God, I'm really out of shape," she says with a small laugh.

There's nothing I can think to say about her shape that will not incriminate me in some way, so I just sit here, trying not to look at her.

"I guess I'm not used to all the lifting and carrying," she continues, rolling her shoulders forward and back.

"Oh, right," I manage.

"Josh?"

When I look up, she's stopped moving around and is now staring at me. "Are you okay?"

"Me?" I ask. "Yes, why?"

"I don't know. You've been really quiet all day." She pauses. "Did I do something? Are you not happy I'm here?"

"*No*." So my playing it cool has completely backfired. "Oh my God, no. I'm happy you're here; I'm just trying to give you space."

"Why, do you want me to give *you* space?"

"No," I almost shout. "It's not that at all. You just got here, and I don't want you to feel like there's any big rush to figure out what we're doing."

"Oh." She nods, seeming to think about this for a few seconds. "Yeah, I didn't get that at all."

"Sorry," I mumble. "I probably should've just come out and said that, huh?"

"Aren't you supposed to be the good communicator in this relationship?" she says with a short laugh, but then quickly adds, "I mean, not *relationship*-relationship—you know what I mean." She reaches around to the back of her neck again, squeezing the muscles while turning her head.

"Guess I'm slipping." I feel slightly more relaxed after getting that out in the open . . . and seeing her fumble through the word relationship. "Do you need a hand?"

"Yes, please." She pivots on the seat so her back is facing me. "I thought you'd never ask. It's like, right here"—she runs her hand from her neck to her shoulder—"where it hurts."

Her skin is warm as my hands dip under the collar of her T-shirt, and I have to exercise such restraint to not lean down and kiss that spot. I feel her whole body exhale and start to sway and melt under my hands. She makes these small moans every time I press down. I'm glad I'm sitting behind her so she can't see how much her noises are affecting me. If I didn't know her better, part of me would wonder if she was doing it on purpose to turn me on, but she doesn't think like that. She doesn't even know what she's doing to me. She never did.

"All right," I say, stopping abruptly because I want this too much right now.

"Oh, don't stop," she groans, glancing over her shoulder at me. "That felt so good."

"Yeah, it was feeling a little too good to me too," I mumble.

"What?" she asks, and I don't know if she didn't hear me or if she just doesn't know what I mean.

I clear my throat, trying to decide if I should tell her or not. "N-nothing."

"No, what? Tell me." She twists around so that she's facing me now.

"Eden, you—" I start, but I can't help laughing. "You were . . ."

"What?" she repeats.

"You were making . . . sex noises."

Her mouth opens and she gasps, and I watch as her face flushes right before my eyes. But I can tell she's trying not to laugh too. "Oh my God, Josh!"

“What, you were!”

“I was not!” she shrieks, swatting at me before covering her face with her hands.

“You were too—I would know.”

Her laughter fades as she keeps gazing back and forth between me and the last remnants of color left over from the sunset.

“Sorry,” I tell her, trying to keep the lighthearted mood going a little longer. “I could only take so much.”

She sits back again and looks out at the darkening sky, shaking her head and letting out a little burst of laughter every so often. “Sex noises,” she scoffs. And then she turns toward me again. “Um, okay. So, speaking of . . . that,” she begins. “Is it time to take the pin out, you think?”

“It’s honestly your call.” I’m trying to keep the ball in her court, but it’s so hard to know when I’m giving her too much space or not enough. “For me, it’ll hold. I mean, if you want to wait or need more time, we can talk about it when we’re not totally exhausted.”

“Right.” She sighs and then immediately yawns. “It has been a big day.”

“Yeah,” I agree. “I guess we should probably go in, huh? I’m sure you have a lot of unpacking and stuff.”

She nods as she stands, then holds her hand out to help me up. I take it, and we sort of loosely hold hands as we walk across the roof deck.

We reach my floor first.

“So, this is me,” I tell her. “Want me to walk you down to yours?”

"No, it's all right."

We stand in front of my door, and she moves in to hug me first, reaching up to wrap her arms around my neck. "I'm really glad you're here," I tell her one more time.

"So am I," she whispers, her mouth close to my ear. "I've missed you." She gives the side of my neck the smallest, faintest kiss before pulling away, leaving me with these shock waves radiating from my heart.

"Okay," I say for absolutely no reason, probably blushing and grinning like an idiot. "Well, you know where to find me if you need me."

She catches my hand as she moves away, giving it a tiny pulse before she lets me drift out of her grasp. "You too," she adds, and there's something in her tone, in her smile—is she flirting with me? *God, don't tempt me.*

"Good night," I call after her. She turns around when she reaches the end of the hall at the staircase and waves.

Inside, I can hear Dominic talking with Luke behind his bedroom door. I can still feel the press of her lips against my neck. I look at the time on my phone. It's only eight thirty. What the fuck am I doing here? Why didn't I just tell her that I can't stop thinking about her, that the only thing I want to know in the world is what she's thinking about us? *For me, it'll hold*—is that what I actually said? I mean, it will. It *has*. For months, years.

I realize I'm pacing. I force my feet to stop. I go to the door, but my hand refuses to turn the knob. I should wait. I can wait. No, I can't. I open the door and jog down the hallway, down the stairs, all the way to her door. I raise my hand to knock, but I don't follow through. I start to head back the way I came but stop again. Go back. And now I'm essentially pacing again, but in her hallway this time.

She's right there, I tell myself.

I go back to her door. I'm doing this.

I raise my hand and knock, too loud and fast.

There's some shuffling on the other side of the door, and when she opens it, she looks surprised to see me standing there. Her hair is down now, sort of messy, and it just makes her look even more beautiful to me somehow.

"Hi," she says.

I take a breath, bypass a greeting, and blurt out, "Eden, would you please go on a date with me tomorrow night?"

"A date?" she asks.

"Uh-huh. A date. With me. Tomorrow. Please."

She looks down at her feet and smiles, and it takes everything to keep my hands in my pockets and not reach out to move her hair out of her face.

"Okay," she agrees, finally lifting her head to look at me again.

"Okay?" I repeat.

"Okay," she says again, and lets out this small laugh.

"Okay." I start to back away and nearly trip over my own feet like I'm a twelve-year-old and this is the first time I've ever asked a girl out.

"Good night," she says. "Again."

"Good night again."

She closes the door, and I'm halfway down the hall, feeling completely reenergized after this utterly exhausting day of trying to watch my every move and word and thought. But I could run a marathon right now. I pick up my pace, preparing to take the stairs two at a time, burn off some of this excitement, when I hear a door click and snap behind me.

"Josh, wait!"

I turn to see her skipping after me. When she reaches me, she stops quickly and takes a few fast, shallow breaths and stands so close, pausing for a moment before she reaches for my hands. "I just . . . um," she starts but doesn't finish. Instead, she lets her hands trail up the length of my arms, to my shoulders to my neck to my face, where I can feel her fingers trembling slightly against my cheek, her thumb grazing my bottom lip.

She opens her mouth and it looks like she's going to say something else, but then she takes that tiny breath I love so much and tilts her head up to me. Her eyes search mine for my answer. I don't think I could speak if I tried, but I nod because whatever the question, whatever she wants, my answer is always going to be yes.

Her lips are so soft as they part mine, her mouth warm, and as my tongue tastes hers, she kisses me harder. We breathe each other in, heavier and deeper and she's making those sounds from the roof again, and I can't even believe how good it feels to be kissing her. To *only* be kissing her.

My hands want her face and hair and arms and hips all at the same time. She holds on to my waist and pushes against me as I pull her closer, until we're backing up into the wall, where my elbow lands with a thud. "Oh," Eden breathes into my mouth as she places her hand between my elbow and the wall. And I have no idea why such a simple gesture should make my heart start pounding uncontrollably like this, but it does, and I want her to bring me back to her room so badly it hurts.

Someone opens their door, and we pull apart just in time to see the older man who lives in 2E poke his head out and mumble, "Get a goddamn room" before shutting the door again.

We look back at each other, and as much as I want to keep kissing her here, like this, for at least another few hours, we both bust out laughing.

"Sorry!" Eden calls in the direction of the closed door. "Not sorry," she whispers to me.

I shake my head. "Definitely not."

She brings both hands up to my shoulders and pulls me down just enough for her to kiss me one more time, softly, slowly. Resting her head against my chest, she sighs, and I can feel the warmth of her breath through my shirt. She looks up at me, placing her hand over my heart. "To be continued?" she asks.

I nod, but I can't speak, can't move. Even as she backs away and takes her hand from me, I replace it with mine, exactly where hers was, not wanting the feeling of her touching me to be gone. She drifts down the hall, turning around once to smile. She covers her mouth as she lets out the briefest giggle and jogs back to her door. I stand there for at least a full minute, just in case she comes back. But as I make my way up the stairs, slowly, one at a time, all I can think is: this is how it always should've been, how it should've started between us.

EDEN

I spent all day sending Mara pics of every outfit combination I have in my current wardrobe, which is not that much. She kept saying I should wear the one dress I brought with me, but a dress felt like too much pressure for our very first real date. There's enough pressure after waiting for this for almost three years, I don't need to add any more.

So, I opt for the jean shorts I wore the night of the concert. They're newish and I know I caught him checking out my legs in them that night. A simple T-shirt with tiny yellow flowers. Pretty but not sexy. Sandals. I shave my legs and armpits. Because, just in case. I try to follow this video Mara sent me on cute styles for shoulder-length hair. I manage something with a twist and bobby pins that looks decent enough—from the front anyway. Lip gloss, mascara, bracelet, necklace, earrings.

He picks me up at eight o'clock on the dot, just like he said he would, and he looks and smells so good, I almost don't want to go anywhere with him except back inside. But then he leans down and kisses me on the cheek, which makes me laugh for some reason. And when we get outside onto the sidewalk, he takes my hand, except it's so tender and unexpected and honest that it makes me almost want to cry.

We hold hands as we take our time walking, smiling, and glancing over at each other for the entire three blocks it takes to get to the restaurant.

Nonna's Little Italy is the name of the place. It's small and dark and cozy, and I could smell the herbs and baking cheese and garlic and oil from the street. If comfort food could be an entire environment, this would be it. The woman who seats us does so with not many words, but she smiles warmly at us both when she hands us our menus. A second, younger man, comes by to leave a basket of freshly baked bread wrapped in the same kind of cloth napkin our silverware is tucked inside.

After we place our orders, Josh says, "So?" neatly pulling back the towel from the bread, like he's trying not to rip wrapping paper on a gift. "How's the date going for you so far? And don't let the fact that I've been trying to plan this basically as long as we've known each other influence your answer in any way at all."

"Well, for starters, you showed up on time. Looking very handsome, I might add." I pause because, did I just say *handsome* out loud? I feel like I should be embarrassed, showing my hand so easily, but then . . . we've waited too long for games. That's something old Eden would do. So, I force myself to add, "The kiss on the cheek was also a nice touch."

"Oh, I'm glad," he says, blushing. "I wasn't sure that went over like I'd hoped."

"No, it did," I assure him. "And this place. You might as well have read my mind. Nonna's Little Italy might be my new favorite restaurant, and I haven't even tried the bread yet."

He pushes the basket toward me, and I tear off a piece, still almost too hot to touch. But the butter melts into it perfectly. He waits for me to take a bite.

"And now that you've tried the bread?" he asks.

I take my time chewing and swallowing and open my mouth like I'm going to answer him but then take another bite, which makes him laugh, which makes me all warm and inexplicably soft inside. "Best date I've ever been on," I answer.

"Wow. That's better than I thought," he says.

"Well, full disclosure. This is also kind of the *only* date I've ever been on."

"Steve didn't take you on dates?"

I had sort of forgotten Josh knew about Steve. In my mind, I was thinking more about the plethora of random guys I'd hooked up with after Josh—the ones I met at parties or other sordid drunk and high encounters. Faceless, mostly. Nameless. People I never saw again, let alone went out on dates with. "Not really," I finally answer. "But not for lack of trying on his part," I add, in Steve's defense.

Josh looks down at his plate, and when he looks back up at me, he's sort of grimacing. "Okay, that's gotta be like first date rule number one, right? Don't mention the other person's ex. Jesus, maybe this is my first date too," he tries to joke, taking a sip of water.

"No, it's okay." But now that it's out there, I feel obligated to say something. "Steve was a pretty good person. We just should've only been friends, that's all."

Josh is nodding, and right as he's about to say something, our food comes. We start eating in silence, and I worry I've somehow messed this up, but then Josh finally speaks. "So, does that mean you're still friends with him?"

"You mean like you and I are still friends?" I ask.

"Sort of," he admits.

"No. We're friends. But we're not friends like you and I are *friends*. If you know what I mean?"

He smiles, both bright and bold, yet a little shy, all at the same time. "I think I know what you mean, yeah."

"Good." I twirl a bite of my pasta around my fork and stuff it in my mouth so I stop talking.

"And just so you know," he says, "I'm not *friends* with anyone else right now either."

"Noted." And even I have to laugh at how nerdy and awkward we're being. "Thank you for the information," I add.

"You're very welcome."

Full of pasta and sauce and bread and cheese, we leave Nonna's, but when we get outside, Josh starts walking in the opposite direction from which we came.

"Not this way?" I ask.

"The date's not over yet," he says.

"There's more?"

"Yeah, there's sort of a whole theme."

"I get a *themed* date?" I ask, genuinely impressed, flattered even. "What is it, the theme?"

"It's more of a loose theme or . . . or a theme within a theme," he says, motioning with his hands as he tries to explain.

We walk about half a block, past some apartment buildings that look a lot like ours, with storefronts at the ground level that are closed already. Old trees line the streets here, their roots pushing up the cement of the sidewalk into tiny mountains that make the ground uneven. Josh reaches for my hand again and I let him. But he keeps holding on even after we pass the broken parts of the sidewalk.

"We've never done this," he points out, interlacing his fingers with mine. "You always used to pull away when I'd try to hold your hand."

I nod. "I like it now. It's nice." But it's more than nice. And I more than like it. I just don't know exactly how to say that.

He smiles at the ground, and I squeeze his hand once. He squeezes back. Like some kind of private Morse code between the two of us. We turn on a dark corner and the wind suddenly picks up, blowing our clothes and hair. I have the distinct thought that I wouldn't want to be walking here alone at night without him.

"We're close," he says as if he can tell what I'm thinking.

We stop in front of a little shop I think is a coffeehouse at first, because the neon sign in the window says GREATER THAN > GROUNDS. As we walk in, a bell dings. There's no one in sight, and when we step up to the counter, I see there are at least twenty different flavors of gelato lined up in the freezer case. The hand-lettered sign at the register says: COME FOR THE COFFEE, STAY FOR THE GELATO.

"Mm, gelato for dessert?" I ask.

"I took a chance," he says, half squinting, half side-eyeing me like he's holding his breath. "You do like gelato, then?"

"Well, yeah. I like ice cream, so . . ."

A girl pops up from behind the counter, proclaiming, as she straightens her glasses, "Gelato is not ice cream. Ice cream is not gelato. Gelato is a thousand times better than ice cream. It's just a fact."

"I agree," Josh says, but he barely glances at her, this girl who kind of reminds me of myself in a weird way. Maybe it's just the glasses and the similar hair and height, but I find myself imagining her as an alternate-universe version of myself.

She puts on a fresh pair of plastic gloves and says, "My name is Chelsea. I'll be your barista today." And then she sighs, like saying her name is the worst part of her job. "Let me know if you want to sample any flavors."

"Thanks," Josh tells her as we peruse the selections.

I can't help glancing over at her. She's looking at Josh—of course, I understand why—and when she sees me noticing, she pushes her glasses up, just like I always used to do when I was nervous.

"Um, can I try the pistachio mint?" I ask her.

She shovels a tiny plastic spoonful and hands it to me across the counter. Out of the corner of my eye, I can see that Josh is watching me put it in my mouth. "What?"

"Nothing. It's just, pistachio mint? What are you, a senior citizen?"

"It's good! Here, try," I tell him, hovering the spoon in front of his face.

“Gross, keep your old-person pistachio mint.” The barista, Chelsea, sighs again, thoroughly unamused. Part of me wonders if she’s looking at me and looking at Josh and wondering how—*why*—he’s here with me and not giving her a second glance when we’re so similar.

“Can I try the chocolate peanut butter?” Josh says, either not picking up on the barista’s annoyance or just not caring. She gives Josh his sample, and we both watch him as he presses the spoon onto his tongue and closes his eyes.

“Chocolate peanut butter, really? That’s what does it for you?”

“What’s wrong with chocolate peanut butter? It’s a classic flavor combination.”

“I know I’m in the minority, but there are just some things that don’t go together.”

The barista says, completely monotone, “Oh my God, take it back.”

Josh looks at the barista, then at me, and for a second I wonder if he sees it too. But then he says, “Okay, I’m sorry, but this isn’t gonna work out after all.” He turns like he’s going for the door, and I try to laugh because I know he’s joking, but then, out of nowhere, I collide into this wall of panic that rushes into me at the thought of him saying that for real someday.

I reach for him, but he floats through my fingers because they’re going all tingly. Time seems to expand in the second he takes to stop and turn back around and pull me into his arms.

“Just kidding,” he whispers into my hair. He looks down at me and kisses my lips, quickly. Time resets. And *I’m here,* I tell myself, *I’m okay.* I can keep myself here.

I see: Josh. *I feel*: Josh. *I hear*: Josh. *I smell*: Josh. *I taste*: Josh.

He brings his hand to my neck and tilts my face toward him. "You know I'm just kidding, right?" he says quietly, sweeping his thumb across my cheek.

"Yeah," I breathe, finding my voice again. Not disappearing. Not tonight. Not with him.

The barista clears her throat and says loudly, "So, one pistachio mint and one chocolate peanut butter?"

I look at her again, and maybe I don't see as much of a resemblance anymore. She is just a girl named Chelsea who has her own life and will probably never think about us again after we walk out of here. "Yes, please," I answer, stepping away from Josh and feeling my feet and hands and legs and arms regaining their strength as I walk up to the register.

"I can get it, Eden," Josh says.

"No, I insist," I tell him. "You got dinner; I'm getting dessert."

"Okay," he agrees. "Thank you."

Chelsea slides our cups of gelato across the counter and says, "Have a good night," adding, under her breath, "I'm sure you will."

We take our little paper cups of gelato and tiny flat spoons to go, eating as Josh leads us down the street. "So, I sorta got the feeling that girl didn't like us very much," he says with a laugh.

"Well, in her defense we were being a tad . . . *cute*."

"You mean *you* were." He nudges me in the arm, but I sidestep the sweet comment because even though I'm trying here, I'm still me, and I still can't seem to acknowledge even the most innocent compliment.

"So, I'd like to guess at the theme of the evening."

"Okay," he says, scraping the sides of his dish and licking his mini spoon.

"Something Italian, obviously," I say, tapping my chin with my finger and pretending to give this my serious and undivided attention. "Delicious Italian foods?"

"Clo-ose," he says, drawing the word out. "Remember, though, it's more of a theme within a theme. We do still have one more stop."

"Are you taking me to Italy next?"

"Yeah." He smiles as he tosses his cup into a garbage can. "I wish."

"I have one more bite of my pistachio mint. You sure you don't wanna try? It's really good, I promise. I wouldn't steer you wrong."

He studies the contents of my cup and then says, "Okay, I'll try."

I gather a spoonful and then can't decide if I should hand it to him or feed it to him. He laughs at my awkwardness and ducks his head to meet the spoon, holding my hand in his as he brings it to his mouth. He watches me while he tastes it. And there's something almost unbearably intimate about this moment, standing on the sidewalk on an empty street, the wind picking up all around us, my hand still in his while we pause, taste, savor.

Slowly, he begins to nod. "Hmm."

"Hmm . . . good?"

"Different," he says, licking his lips. "It's different than I thought it would be, but I kinda like it. Actually, I really like it."

"See?"

He takes my empty cup and spoon and tosses them into the

garbage can a few steps away, and when he comes back, he stands in front of me and touches my cheek again, the way he had in the shop. He presses his lips to mine so softly, not rushed like before, and as I kiss him back, I can taste all the flavors.

"I wanted to make up for that weird little spur-of-the-moment kiss back there and couldn't wait until the end of the night." He holds his hand out for me to take again and adds, "Sorry."

"Don't be. I liked them both." I squeeze his hand again, and he squeezes back as we keep walking in the direction of campus.

We enter a parklike setting right off the street. I read the sign out loud. "Tucker Hill Memorial Garden. Is this part of the school?"

"It is, yeah. I used to live over here my first year," he says, pointing farther down the street. "And this is how I would get on campus every day."

"It's really pretty here," I tell him. We continue down this little pathway through the garden. There are different types of plants and flowers, with benches parked under trees every so often, small lights that shine along the way, plaques engraved with people's names adorning everything in sight.

"Confession," Josh says, giving my hand a squeeze. "I actually used to think about you all the time when I came through here."

"You did?" I ask, feeling my heart racing at the thought of him here, thinking of me.

He nods.

"Why?"

He shrugs. "It's always quiet here and beautiful—every season has different things in bloom. It's also a little sad, but peaceful. I guess I kind of thought this might be your sort of thing."

I let his words sink in as I catch a long sweeping branch of a young willow tree and let it fall through my hand as we walk. When I turn my head to look back at him, he's already watching me. I let go of his hand and loop my arm with his instead, wanting him closer.

"What are you thinking?" he asks. "Am I talking too much?"

"No, I love when you talk to me." He pulls me in closer, and our feet kind of stumble into each other. "It just catches me off guard every time you do that."

"Do what?"

"Just . . . get me. So right, so often."

"Well, I can't take all the credit," he says, seeming to sidestep my compliment this time. "There's one more part up here that deserves most of it."

I can't imagine what he means by that, but as we continue down the foliage-lined pathway, I see there's a light ahead, a clearing that opens up into a larger space. As we get closer, I can hear water running, splashing.

"Wow," I say, letting go of Josh's arm to get a better look. It's a fountain in the shape of an apple, made of stone and metal and sitting on a giant circle of granite, no barrier to prevent anyone from walking right up to it. And so I do. But when I get too close, water spouts begin spraying all around it, like a challenge to try to walk through and remain dry. The exterior of the apple is shiny red like a fire engine, and the water sprays out of the top where the stem curves up and over the side of the apple, a metal leaf dangling in the wind, held there by a wire or chain of some sort.

But as I walk around to get the full view, I see the other side of the apple is carved out, meant to look like there have been giant bites taken out of the fruit, leaving the hourglass shape of the core behind, and the seeds, made of a dark metal, all overflowing with water. Inside the round part of the apple, there's a bench with two sculpted seats in the shape of leaves, just like the metal leaf from the stem, shielded from the waterfalls. It reminds me of the pumpkin carriage from *Cinderella*, except grittier, less elegant . . . more dangerous and even sensual, somehow.

Josh stands in place, waiting for me to come back around—I guess he's seen it enough times. "This is really . . . ," I begin as I make my way back to him. "I've never seen anything like this. It's strangely . . . beautiful."

He's smiling as he watches me, and then he points to something on the ground in front of him. I come to stand next to him and look down. There's a plaque there that reads:

FONTANA DELL'EDEN / FOUNTAIN OF EDEN.

"Oh my God," I say.

"See, I can't take all the credit," he repeats.

"The apple thing makes more sense now," I say, looking at the fountain again.

"I'm glad you like it."

"I'm surprised *you* like it—it's so edgy and weird."

"I like edgy and weird," he says as he moves the strand of hair that's fallen out of my half-assed attempt at an updo. "My favorite person in the world is a little edgy and weird, herself."

"Josh," I begin, but I don't really know what to say.

He stares into the water, lights shining up from underneath, casting reflections of movement all around us.

"Every day, when I would pass by, seeing your name there, I would sort of daydream about you being here. Or me bringing you here."

"You know I thought about you too, right?"

He nods, taking both of my hands.

But I need him to really know. "It's not that I just *thought* about you, though. I . . ." *Ached* is the word I'm having trouble getting out.

"I know," he says softly, but I wonder if he really does. "You know, I always thought if we got a second chance, I wanted to do it right this time," he continues, drawing his eyebrows together. "Do you know what I mean?"

This time I nod.

"Because I want this with you," he says, eyes fastened to mine. "I really do."

"I do too," I tell him. "More than anything."

He smiles now, and I can see his whole body relax, his grip on my hands loosening. "So, then . . . we're doing this for real this time?"

JOSH

My words hang there in the space between us, my heart racing while I wait. I keep imagining that I'm missing her answer in the sound of the falling water. But then she starts nodding.

"Yes," she finally answers.

We stand there holding hands, smiling at each other. I lean down and try to kiss her, but she backs up a couple of steps. I'm confused. She doesn't let go of my hands and doesn't stop smiling either. *Is she . . . playing with me?* She's changed—it's not the first time I've thought it over the last few months, but it's the first time I know for sure it's true.

"No?" I ask her.

She shakes her head.

"No kiss, not even after my big speech?" I joke with her, trying my best to play along.

"You'll get your kiss, don't worry," she says, pulling me by the arm as she moves closer to the fountain. "Come with me."

She walks me around to the opposite side of the fountain, our footsteps setting off the series of what must be motion-activated streams of water shooting out from the platform and arching over the walkway.

"See that little bench inside?" She points to the metal bench of vines and leaves on the other side of the cascading water. "Let's go," she says, holding my hand tighter.

"Go?"

"Yeah, we can make it."

I look around. There's no one here and probably no one nearby on a Sunday night when the semester isn't even in session yet. "I don't think we're supposed to—" But before I even finish my sentence, she drops my hand and is racing forward under the tunnel of water. "Wait, what are you doing?" I shout after her.

She outran it, though. She turns and makes this adorable *whoop* sound from underneath the apple, still dry. "Come on!" she calls, motioning me forward with her hands.

I laugh to myself because I'm going to have to do this now.

"Ready?" she yells. "Go!"

I start but stop.

"Josh, come on! You have to just do it. Run. Now!"

So, I do. I run, either too fast or too slow, and end up getting hit full-on by every single stream of water. By the time I reach her, I am soaked all the way through my clothes.

She's covering her mouth, laughing. "Oops," she mumbles through her hand. "Or maybe you should've waited."

"Oh, that's funny?" I wrap her in my arms, and she lets out

this gasp-shriek as my cold wet clothes press against her, my hair dripping down onto her face as she looks up at me.

"Okay, okay," she shouts. Then she pushes my hair back and slides her hands down my neck, letting them rest on my shoulders. And like always, she takes that small breath of air, slowly letting it out as she kisses me, deeper, more fully.

My hands follow down the curve of her back to her waist, fitting perfectly over her hips. She lets me pull her even closer, raising herself onto her toes to reach my mouth. I tighten my arms around her and lift her just enough for our mouths to find each other. Our kiss deepens, and as I feel the full weight of her body against me now, I just want more of her.

"Hold on to me," I whisper, and she folds her arms around the back of my neck. I reach down and place my hands under her thighs and hoist them up around my waist. She inhales sharply and lets out this soft breathy cry.

"Okay," she says, her lips moving against mine. I can feel the muscles in her arms and legs contract all around me. "I'm not laughing anymore."

"Me neither," I tell her between kisses, my breathing growing faster, with hers. I feel her lungs expand against my chest as she opens her mouth to take a deep breath. I kiss her neck, damp with the spray of water bouncing off the walls.

"*God*," she exhales.

I look up at her, and her eyes are so bright, even in the dark, and I don't think I have ever wanted anything or anyone, even her, more than I do right now.

She looks at me like she's going to say something else but

kisses me instead. I take a few steps to move us to the wall, so I can get a better grip on her, but as her back presses against the dome shape of the apple, she lets out a short scream. Her whole body tenses and jerks, and I realize I've just walked her right into a stream of water, as it now cascades over her.

I pull back and set her down on the ground, and she stands there frozen for a moment, mouth open. "I'm so sorry," I tell her.

"Cold," she says, drenched head to toe. "That was *really* cold." She gasps as she looks at me. "Did you do that on purpose?"

"I swear, I would not have purposely interrupted what was just happening." But now I'm the one covering my mouth to laugh.

"Oh, I see," she says, taking my hands. "You were just seducing me so you could have your revenge."

"No—" I start to say, but then she pulls me forward into her arms, so that we're both directly under the water. "Oh!" I shudder. "Holy shit, that is fucking freezing."

"I know, it is!" She laughs and kisses me once more. "Can you take me home now?"

"Yes," I tell her, and I hold out my arm.

"Will you stay with me tonight?"

We're trying to be quiet as we enter our building, but by the time we get to her door, leaving puddles in our wake, our shoes squeaking and squelching, we're both laughing hysterically.

"Oh my God," Eden groans, as she wipes under her eye and pulls her hand away with a black smear left on it. "What do I even look like right now?"

"Beautiful," I answer.

But she just sort of rolls her eyes dismissively and starts taking her hair down. “Will you give me a few minutes?” she asks. “I’m just going to take care of . . . this situation here,” she says, floating her hand in a circle in front of her face.

“You look beautiful,” I try again.

She doesn’t acknowledge what I’ve said, but she does kiss me.

“Okay, I’m gonna run upstairs and take care of this”—I look down at my drenched clothing—“situation too.”

She laughs silently but then says, more seriously, “You’re coming back though, right?”

“Of course.”

“If I’m not out of the bathroom, just come in and wait in my room, okay?” she whispers. “I’ll leave this unlocked.”

Dominic is standing in the kitchen eating cereal when I walk in. “What the hell?” he says, turning to look out the window. “Is it raining?”

“Nope,” I tell him, rushing past without explaining.

I brush my teeth and take the world’s quickest shower to wash the chlorine smell off my skin. I hang my wet clothes on the back of my door and get into clean ones. T-shirt, boxer briefs, because they’re comfortable and I also read somewhere that women find them the sexiest, a statistic I didn’t think I cared about or even remembered before, well, this very moment. I go back and forth about jeans versus shorts—Dominic’s voice in my head telling me cargoes should be outlawed—but if we’re just in her room, sleeping, it can be casual. I decide to go with one of my newer pairs of athletic shorts. I hesitate at my nightstand, not sure if I should bring them.

Is it presumptuous or just being prepared? I open the drawer and decide to take one, just in case.

In the kitchen, Dominic is watching me rush around.

"Do I look all right?"

"All right for . . . *what*?" he asks, this horrified yet baffled expression twisting his face.

"Sleeping over," I admit.

"Do you really want to have this conversation?"

"No, actually." I grab a bottle of water from our fridge. "Thank you. Gotta go."

"Have fun, stud," he calls after me. "Remember, practice in the morning—don't overexert yourself!"

I'm back at her door within ten minutes. I knock quietly before I open it and tiptoe through their kitchen, past the straight line of light from under the bathroom door.

I let myself into her room. I would sit, but she has a bunch of clothes spread out on her bed and chair. So I stand in the center of her tiny room instead. It's dark except for the dim light coming from the small lamp on her desk, and it reminds me of when I was in her room back home. How oppressive it felt in there.

But this room feels like Eden already. I admire her things spread out all haphazardly. She has her laptop open on her desk with a music app on pause and a copy of this year's course catalog and some other books and papers teetering dangerously close to the edge. But that's when something else on her desk catches my eye. Three prescription bottles, tucked in behind a tube of lotion and some hair products.

It's none of my business, God, how I know that.

But, my brain insists.

Because all my stupid brain can think of is my dad and his problems, all the times he would hide pills and bottles—all the times we'd have to hide them *from* him. She's not my dad, though. She told me all that stuff was in the past, and I believe her.

The sound of the shower turning off carries through the quiet of the apartment.

"All right," I say out loud, taking a deep breath and forcing myself to look at something else. Her bookcase. Perfect. I go over, but I can't seem to focus enough to read a single title. I walk back over to her desk and glance at the closed door once more.

I don't need to know *what* they are; I just need to know that they're hers. Carefully, I reach for the first one, memorizing their exact positions. Her name's on the label. And the second one. And the third. All prescribed to her. By a doctor in our hometown. Nothing wrong with any of this. It's absolutely none of my business.

But, again.

Now I do kind of need to know, at least, what they're *not*. And I still hear the fan going in the bathroom.

God, I hate myself.

I go back to her desk. The labels don't say what they're for, but I also don't recognize the names, which is a good thing. The only drug names I'm familiar with—because of my dad, of course—are the dangerous pain-related controlled substances. And at least these aren't that. The first one says to take once a day, the second is one tablet at night, and the third says as needed. All have refills. I set them back down in their spots.

There is no reason for me to fixate on this. It's not even

surprising that she would be on some kind of medication after everything she's been through. Fuck, *I* should probably be medicated too.

Just then, the fan shuts off, and I hear the bathroom door creak open. Quickly, I park myself in front of her bookcase, bending down to slide one of the books out, as if I'd been standing here reading the jacket this whole time.

"Hey," she whispers. "You're here."

And as I turn around to see her face, the glorious fruit and flower scents following along behind her, I can almost forget about the things that are none of my business. "Of course I'm here," I tell her, setting the book down as she starts walking toward me.

But then she stops short, looking at her desk, and my heart starts racing like she might be able to tell I've handled the bottles. "I'm sorry it's so messy in here." She turns around and gathers up all the clothes from her bed and tosses them on top of the desk, covering all the stuff I am now pretty certain she didn't want me to see.

"No, I—I don't mind. I mean, it's really not messy," I lie.

She comes to me now and wraps her arms around my waist. "It is messy, but that's only because I was super nervous getting ready for an important date with this guy I really like."

And now I genuinely fucking hate myself. But coming clean wouldn't make me feel any less guilty and would only make her think I don't trust her or she can't trust me. There's no reason to ruin what has been an amazing night because I'm paranoid that everyone I love is going to turn into an addict.

I clear my throat, breathe her in, and say, "Oh?" As she looks up at me, I lean down to kiss her. "Think you'll see him again?"

She smiles and lets out a small laugh as she presses her cheek against my chest, her wet hair leaving a damp spot on my shirt.

"Tonight was the most fun I've had in a really long time," I tell her, a different truth, instead. And it *was* fun, but it was also equally sexy and romantic and meaningful, but I'm not sure how to say all that.

"Hmm, me too," she sings. "But—"

"But what?" I ask, starting to get worried. Is she already having second thoughts?

"You have to tell me the theme."

"Oh." I exhale too forcefully, but she doesn't seem to notice.

"I mean, Italian restaurant. Italian dessert. Italian fountain. That's the theme within the theme part, right?"

"Right."

"So, what's the bigger theme? I still don't think I got it."

"You. Being here. Me. Being so beyond happy about you being here. I guess that's the real theme I was going for."

"Oh." She pauses. "Well, then, I guess I did get it, after all."

"Good." I touch her cheeks where they're blushing. "You know, I feel like I'm getting to see this whole other side of you here," I tell her, moving my hands through her wet hair.

"Really?" She brings her hands up around my neck and looks at me with this easy smile. "You didn't know I could be fun before?"

"I did, but I'm realizing you're also kind of . . . wild."

"Me?" she gasps. "What about *you*?"

"What about me? I assure you no one has ever once accused me of being wild. Responsible, dependable, sensible?" I count them on my fingers as I list the words. "Yes. Wild? Never."

"Do I need to replay the footage from that whole steamy fountain kissing scene?" she asks, and her fingers are so light as they dance up and down my arms that I feel momentarily dizzy. "Because that seems to be playing on a loop in my head right now. The part before you walked me into a freezing waterfall, I mean." She pauses to let her grin disappear before she continues, more serious. "The part right before that was . . . *intense*."

I lean to kiss her neck just so she doesn't see my face turning red, but I pull myself together and look at her again, so she knows. "I never would've done that with anyone else."

"Me neither."

My hands go to her bare arms. She's wearing only a thin tank top and shorts, and as I lean down to kiss the other side of her neck, I can't help but notice that she's not wearing a bra. She touches my face and brings my mouth to hers while her fingers trail up my stomach, under my shirt.

"Can we take this off?" she asks me as her hands start to push my shirt up. Something in me melts a little at the way she said "we."

So we do. We pull my shirt off over my head together and let it fall to the floor, but before I can start kissing her again, I feel her mouth planting these soft, warm kisses across my chest and stomach, sending chills through my whole body.

"Oh God," I breathe. "That feels so good."

She takes my hands from where I lost my train of thought and left them perched lazily in her hair and presses them against her over the front of her shirt. I raise her shirt just enough to touch her skin, and then her hands are there too, moving my hands up under the fabric, over the gentle curve of her stomach.

"This is okay?" I ask, even though she's the one who placed my hands there. "Can we . . . ?" I begin, suddenly unable to finish the sentence. "Can we take this off too?"

"Mm-hmm," she murmurs, her voice muffled as she pulls the shirt off over her head. She brings her arms in front of her chest and moves in close to me before I can really look at her. The feeling of her bare skin, her body pressed against mine, has my heart going so fast. Even though I've seen every naked inch of her so many times before, this feels brand-new. Because it's not only her attitude that's changed in all this time apart, but it's her body too—every part of her fuller, stronger, softer, from the arch of her back to the shape of her shoulders, her thighs and hips and waist—I need this minute to prepare myself. I take a deep breath as her fingers work under the band of my shorts, hands roaming gently over my carefully selected underwear, gradually edging the athletic shorts down over my hips.

"Can I?" she asks as she pulls away to let space in between us.

I finally look down at her, and she is so much more magnificent than I remember, all I can manage to do is nod. She slides my shorts down my legs and onto the floor, then quickly slides hers off too, and I hold her hands as she steps out of them. And we stand in front of each other, in only underwear, for the first time in years.

"You are so beautiful," I tell her, squeezing her hands in mine like we'd been doing all night. "I know you're gonna keep ignoring me when I say that, but I wish you wouldn't because I really mean it."

"Sorry." She shakes her head but smiles in that rare shy way she does sometimes, only for a moment. "I'm nervous," she whispers.

"It's okay, I am too," I assure her. I've had sex with five people in my life—two casual, three relationships, including her—and I feel as nervous as if this were my first time.

"I didn't think I would be so nervous," she says.

"We don't have to do anything tonight."

She pauses, studying my face.

It's almost like she's trying to determine if I really mean that or not—she should know I do, but in case she doesn't, I add, "Have I ever told you what an amazing kisser you are?"

She grins. "No, you've never mentioned that."

"Well, you are the best kisser in the world—hey, you're laughing, but I'm completely serious," I tell her. "And I would *seriously* be more than happy to just lie down with you here and keep kissing you. We really don't have to do anything else."

"I know. Thank you for that." She inhales deeply and exhales before continuing. "But I want to. I mean, if you do."

"Oh, I do." I look down, feeling like I should somehow apologize for not having more control over myself. "Obviously, I do. There's no rush, though."

She nods, placing my hands on her hips like she knows how much I love the way they feel. And as she reaches out, running her hands along my face and down my chest and stomach, she's not even trying to hide the fact that she's looking at my body. Staring. Gazing. I have the urge to make some kind of stupid joke, like *hey lady, my eyes are up here*, because standing in front of her like this, under her hands, her eyes on me, it's intense—that was the word she used earlier—almost too intense to bear.

"You are so gorgeous," she whispers.

"W-what?" I stutter. There's literally nothing she could've said that would've shocked me more. She's never said anything remotely like that to me before. I almost think she's joking. But then she lets her hands float down my back and rest on my hips. And it doesn't feel like a joke at all.

"Do you even know?" she asks, and her eyes meet mine again like she's expecting an answer.

EDEN

There was a time when I was afraid to look at him too closely. Afraid of how beautiful his body was, afraid of the things he could do, the ways he could hurt me with it.

But not now, not anymore. Right now I'm not afraid of anything. I can't stop watching his face as I touch him. His eyes are closed like they were earlier, with the bite of gelato melting on his tongue.

"Eden . . . ," he says, breathless, as he pulls my hand away and places it on his chest instead.

"Sorry, was that not—"

"Oh my God, no." He smooths my hair back and touches my lips. "That was . . ." He shakes his head almost imperceptibly, and I can feel his heart racing under my hand. "I just need a second. It's been a while since I've done this. And . . . I just need to slow down for a second."

“Oh,” I say awkwardly, “okay.” I back away from him and try to cover myself with my arms as I sit down on the edge of the bed. But then he’s right there with me a moment later, like it’s a choreographed dance, suddenly kneeling on the floor in front of me so we’re at eye level. He kisses my knees and lets out a long sigh, laying his head on my lap. It feels so strange and sweet and vulnerable, I reach out and run my hands down his back, through his hair, still damp.

He raises his head slowly and kisses my thighs, running his hands up and down my legs, moving forward as I part them, wanting to let him come closer. I lie back on the bed and pull him down on top of me. I can feel my pulse everywhere, all at once. He places his arm behind my back—if he tells me to *hold on to* him again, I might go into cardiac arrest—but he doesn’t; he somehow manages to gracefully scoot us up on the bed so that my head is resting on the pillow.

“Thanks,” I whisper.

We start this sort of slow kiss, rocking our bodies together, and it feels so good to be this close to him. I’m holding my breath as his hand travels down my body until he’s touching me over my underwear. “Is this okay?” he whispers, kissing my neck right under my ear.

I manage to gather enough air in my lungs to say, “Yes.”

And then his hand, so warm against my stomach, dips down beneath my underwear, and I switch from barely breathing to breathing too fast. My heart races while he takes his time. Moving down my body slowly kissing, kissing everywhere, and when he rakes his teeth along my hip bone, I don’t even know what involuntary sound it is that I make. He gets to my underwear, and I don't know what more I can possibly take. I have to close my eyes.

"Can I?" he asks, his fingers curling under the elastic band. I nod, and he must be looking at my face because he breathes, "Okay," and starts sliding my underwear down. I open my eyes again, and he's there kneeling between my legs, kissing my ankles, then my calves and knees. When he gets to my inner thighs, his mouth trailing closer and closer, I start to lose track of myself. He lowers himself to his stomach and wraps his arms around my legs, hands pressing down on my hips. Every part of me wants this, but the better it feels, the more I'm slipping away.

We've done this all before, though, I remind myself. It's safe with him, safe to let it feel good. It's safe to stay in this place.

I reach down to find some part of him to hold on to—his hair, the back of his neck, his arms, his wrists—and when his hands meet mine, it's like an anchor, our fingers interlacing, pulling me back. He's pushing me right up to the edge, but I can't let myself go. Because I'm looking up at my ceiling, and it looks too much like too many other unfamiliar ceilings I've been under, and even though it's him, *us*, it's different now than it was back then.

I've had so much practice keeping Kevin out of my head in these moments, and I mostly succeed. It's the others, though, this time. The nameless, faceless ones, dragging me away from here. I close my eyes again, trying to focus on how good this feels, his mouth, his tongue, the warmth, the rush of it all, but—

I let go of his hands. "Josh . . . ?"

"Yeah?" He crawls back up to me. "What is it, are you okay?"

I nod and try my best to smile. "I'm okay, I just—"

"That was too much, too fast, wasn't it?" he says. "I'm sorry."

"No, it wasn't. It felt so good, really; I was just starting to get in my head a little. It's, um, been a while since I've done this too."

"Oh," he breathes, looking at me like he hadn't considered this. "Okay. Well, just tell me what you need."

"Can you just stay here with me, close to me, I mean?"

"Yeah, of course." He lies down next to me, kisses my shoulder, and says, "I'm staying right here. Do you want to stop? We can. I promise I won't mind."

I shake my head and take his hand, sliding it down my body again, guiding him to where I want him. "I don't want to stop," I tell him. I want to be here for this—all of it. I want to feel everything. I don't want to let these fucking ghosts in my head win.

I'd forgotten the way he pays attention, as if nothing exists but us. I pull him close, so I can feel his weight against me. There's no fear or impatience or self-consciousness in his touch. He holds steady, watching my face, keeping me with him. I feel my breath coming faster, trembling as he tips me over the edge in a way I've never known before, feeling it somehow beyond my body, even. And then he's kissing my lips, my neck, my chest.

"You are amazing," he's whispering, breathing heavily now like he'd been holding his breath that whole time. "God, I want you so bad—sorry, can I say that?"

"Yes," I answer, trying to catch my breath while stopping myself from smiling at his words. I open my eyes, not even realizing I'd closed them. "But you have something, right?"

He looks over at our clothes on the floor. "I do. You want me to get it now?"

I nod.

"I'll be right back," he whispers. I watch as he walks over and fishes the condom out of the pocket of his shorts. The way he's looking at me as he climbs back into bed—like I'm the best thing he's ever seen—I could just die. "Just tell me if we need to stop at all, okay?"

"I will."

He's going slow, being careful. The way he's watching me so closely, his eyes dark and deep and warm, has me sort of hypnotized. I have a montage running in the background of my mind of all the times he's looked at me like this—making me feel weak and strong, all at the same time. He moves gently, his breath even and paced now, and I can tell he's trying to restrain himself.

"I love you so much," he says quietly, his mouth against mine. "You know that, right?"

I nod because I do know. But I can't speak because I feel the walls of my throat suddenly caving in, heavy with too many competing emotions, and words sitting there waiting, trying to figure out how to get out of me. I clutch his shoulders as we move faster, together, breathing each other in.

It's kind. Delicate. This giving and taking.

I've never been so present. Never this connected to anyone, not even him. I'm holding on to him so tight and I have to bury my face in his neck because, I realize, I'm crying. Crying because I've never felt this way before. About him, about myself. I don't even know what *it* is, but I feel it in my body, my heart, my mind, everywhere—it's everything.

And then I know, all at once: This feeling is freedom.

Even as he finishes, he's still being so gentle with me. We pant against each other for a few moments before he tries to raise himself up off my body. But I hold on, keep him close. "No, stay," I tell him.

"Look at me, Eden," he whispers, brushing my hair aside. I turn my face away because I don't know how to explain. "You're crying."

"No, I'm not," I try to say, but I hear my own voice, all wet and raspy.

"Yes, you are." His hands are on my face now, his eyes searching mine. "Talk to me. Did I . . . ?" He pauses. "Did I hurt you?"

"*No*," I gasp, and the tears are coming faster now. "No, I'm crying because I've just never felt like this. Ever. I've never felt so . . ." *So happy, cared for, respected, even.* But then I say what all those things really mean: "So loved."

"Oh," he exhales, relieved, seeming to understand. "You are. I mean, I do. I love you," he says again. "And I—I've never felt this way before either."

I let him wipe the tears from my cheeks, and as he looks down at me, even his eyes turn shiny. He smiles and blinks fast. "Jesus, you're gonna make me cry now."

"Sorry." I sniffle, almost laughing at myself.

He releases a breath of a laugh too. "It's okay."

We readjust our positions, and when he gets up to throw the condom away, he asks if I want him to leave the lamp on—I don't, I won't need it if he's here. He climbs into bed and covers us with the sheet, laying his head on my chest while we hold each other.

"Josh?" I hear myself say into the darkness.

"Hmm?" he says, his voice all loose and sleepy.

"I love you too."

He raises his head and looks down at me, squinting slightly like he's confused or didn't quite hear me, but then he kisses my lips softly and says, "I know how hard that was for you to say."

I shake my head. "No, it wasn't."

PART THREE

September

JOSH

I left her asleep in my bed this morning. She didn't even stir when my alarm went off at five. I was so tempted to stay with her. But I'm not quite off the coach's shit list yet, so I can't afford to be late to a single practice or workout if I have any hope of playing this season.

The first month of the semester has flown by. Between my practice schedule and Eden working, plus our course loads, it seems like we have less and less time for each other every day.

I make it through morning training from six to eight, then the team meeting before my first class at nine. I text her good morning on the way. But she's usually running too late; she won't text back until after her first class ends at ten thirty. I only have an hour break between morning classes, and then it's back to prep for practice again.

I hate that there's no time to just relax together. I don't know how we'd see each other at all if we weren't in the same building. She got a second job at the café across the street from our apartment, but the manager's already being a dick about her availability. I don't know what he expects. This is a college town; everyone's schedules are crazy. I've gone in there to study when she works on the weekends. I tell her it's so I can spend a little more time around her. That's mostly true, but I also don't trust the guy. It seems like he has it out for her for no reason, criticizing everything she does, wanting her to come in early, stay late.

I was there once when she dropped a mug on the floor and it broke.

She laughed for about two seconds out of embarrassment—it was charming and cute and everyone thought so, giving her these sympathetic nods and smiles. And then, as she was literally kneeling on the floor to clean it up, the manager came over all red-faced and tossed a rag down next to her, muttering, "It's not funny. Pay attention to what you're doing. If you can't be more careful, you can't work here."

The way he said it, though, he was so angry, way angrier than he should've been over a cheap ceramic mug. And the way she looked up at him. I saw something flash in her eyes. She was scared, for just a second, I could tell. I stood up and walked over, not even knowing what I was going to do or say, but I had the most intense urge to grab the guy by his stupid apron and push him up against the wall, drag him outside. Not a familiar feeling for me; I didn't like how quickly it came on.

"Look, I distracted her," I told him. "I'll pay for the mug."

He didn't even speak to me; he just glared at us both and walked away.

I squatted next to her and said quietly, "You absolutely do not need to put up with that shit."

"Please," she scoffed. "I've dealt with bigger douchebags than him. But you should probably go. You didn't make me drop the mug, but your face *is* very distracting. Plus, all these girls keep checking you out. I'm getting jealous."

I looked around. No one was checking me out. But someone was checking *her* out. A guy in the kitchen was watching her through the window where the servers pick up the food, his eyes lingering for just a little too long. I stared him down until he walked away.

I really want her to quit the second job. Not only because I hate her boss and her creepy male coworkers, but we're not even one full month into the semester and she's already running herself ragged. The only nice part of being so busy is that it makes the time we do have feel more special.

Her classes are all on the opposite side of campus. Most days we can at least walk home together, though. Sometimes we can sneak a lunch in. Today I stop by the student union for sandwiches and then have to jog to the library if I want to make it in time to see her at all before I have to head back to the athletic center to get changed for afternoon practice.

I smuggle the paper bag of food in my backpack and head up to the fourth floor of the Arts and Sciences Library. I find her toward the end of one of the aisles, near our spot in the back corner, where we can usually get a few minutes of privacy. I stand there and watch her for a minute. She has a cart of returned books she's supposed to be shelving, but she's standing on top of one of those little plastic stepstools, flipping through the pages of a book, before she reaches up to place it in its designated spot on the shelf. Then she takes down the book next to it and starts skimming the pages instead. I glance at the titles as I walk toward her. Biographies, looks like. She's so absorbed, she doesn't even notice I'm standing right next to her.

"Excuse me, miss?" I whisper.

"God!" she yelps, and the book she was holding clatters to the floor.

"Shh," I tell her, bending down to pick it up. "This is a library."

As she takes the book from me, she smiles and says, "When are you going to stop sneaking up on me?"

"I wasn't trying to—you're just very focused."

She looks both ways before reaching out to pull me closer and leans down to kiss me. "So this is what it feels like to be tall," she muses, still standing on the stool and a full two inches taller than me. "It's a whole different world up here."

"Want me to start carrying around a stool for you everywhere we go?" I ask.

"Why do I think you're not entirely joking?"

"Hey, if you really wanted that, you know I would do it." I hold her hands as she steps down and pull her in for a hug. "Hungry?" I ask.

She nods and checks again to be sure no one will see us, as we go to the end of the aisle and make our way to our corner table, which is hidden from view. As I unpack our sandwiches, she leans her head on my shoulder and groans, "I wish we could go home and lie in bed all day."

"So do I," I sigh. "You were out cold this morning. How late did you stay up last night?"

"I don't know," she says, rubbing her eyes. "I had a lot of reading to catch up on."

I touch her face; she has these dark circles under her eyes. "Baby, you look so tired."

"It's okay, I can sleep in tomorrow; I don't have to be at the café until the afternoon. Still on for date night tonight, right?" she asks.

"Definitely," I tell her. "Practice ends at six, but if I hurry I can probably be home by like six forty-five-ish."

"You don't have to rush," she says, covering her mouth as she takes a bite of her sandwich. "Our reservation isn't until eight."

"Reservation? Fancy." I wait a beat, try to judge her mood a little better. "Are you proposing?"

She coughs and widens her eyes at me. "It's not *that* fancy."

I laugh. But if she were, I'd totally say yes.

"You're insane, you know that?" she says with a grin.

"Me? You're the one proposing after one month," I joke.

"Let's at least get it straight; it's more like three years."

"So, you *are* proposing?"

She shakes her head, trying not to laugh. "Oh my God, you're ridiculous."

I nudge her shoulder with mine. "You love it."

She nods. "Mm-hmm. You're right, I do."

We're kissing when someone clears their throat.

"Oh," Eden says. "Hey."

"Uh, sorry." A boy who looks too young to be in college is

standing there—I can see he has the same work-study ID badge Eden has. "We need some help downstairs at the circulation desk."

"Sure, yeah. Sorry. I was just taking a quick break."

He shrugs and shuffles back down the aisle.

She stands and takes one more bite before wrapping up the second half of her sandwich, trying to stuff it in the pocket of her hoodie. "Obvious?" she asks.

"No," I lie. "Just make sure you finish that at some point."

"I will." She squeezes my hand before walking away, turning around to whisper-shout, "I'm picking you up at seven forty-five—don't forget."

I finish my lunch and check my phone. I forgot my dad texted when I was in line at the sandwich shop.

> Your mom and I are looking forward to seeing you for your bday next week. The big 21! Tuesday still good? Can't wait to meet Eden.—

Except I haven't exactly told Eden that my parents will be here or that they want to take us out for dinner, get to know her. I haven't wanted to stress her out or put any extra pressure on her. But I'm going to have to. Tonight. I'll tell her tonight.

EDEN

I sit in the back of the lecture hall so I can slip out a few minutes early without drawing too much attention. I've come early to each of my classes this week to explain why, so soon in the semester, I'd have to be out next week. I got the time off cleared with the library and sort of cleared with Captain Douchebag at the café. I traded shifts with someone, but he said he still needed to approve it.

At this point, let him fire me. There are at least five more coffee places in a ten-minute radius of campus. I'm sure at least one of them is hiring.

I walk to my next class, fast, on a mission. This is the last formal explanation I'd need to give. *I'm a witness in a court case in my hometown; I have to appear at a hearing next week, so I'll need to miss class.* That was the statement it took me and my therapist the better part of my last fifty-minute phone session to figure out. And that was what I told every one of my professors. Each time, it went over pretty well. No real follow-up questions or concerns. No emotional outpourings on my part.

I have my lines memorized.

I make my way down the steps to the lecture hall floor, where my professor's standing at the podium trying to connect her laptop to the projector, muttering, "Goddamn thing!" And there's something so human about her, all frustrated, that reminds me of my mom.

"Um, hi—sorry," I say as I approach.

She looks up at me and brings her glasses down from the top of her head, puts them on before speaking. "Hello, what can I do for you?"

"My name's Eden McCrorey. I'm in your World History section this afternoon."

She nods and glances back down at her laptop, not quite paying attention. "Okay . . . and?" she mumbles, distracted. Again reminding me of my mom.

I take a deep breath. "It's just that I'm going to have to miss class next week."

She removes her glasses now and stares at me, as if to say, *Oh, really?*

I open my mouth to continue, but I realize I've already messed up the order of my lines.

"I mean," I try to start over, "I have to appear as a witness in a trial in my hometown. Or, not a trial." I stumble and fall over the words. "Yet, anyway. It's actually just a hearing." But then I have my therapist's voice in my head, saying, *Don't minimize, don't apologize*. "Well, not that it's *just* a hearing," I add.

She takes a step toward me and turns her head slightly, like she's having trouble understanding me. I'm not explaining this right. This wasn't what I was supposed to say.

"It—it's just a preliminary hearing," I stutter. "To see if there's going to even be a trial."

I take a breath and pinch the bridge of my nose. Hard. Trying to drive back the tears I'm feeling working their way through my skull. "Um . . . sorry, I just—"

My lungs are suddenly out of air, and I'm having a hard time refilling them.

"Oh," she coos. "It's Eden, right?"

I nod, unable to answer her for some reason. And then she's taking a step toward me, her arms outstretched. I don't understand. She's hugging me before I even realize I've started crying.

"Oh, sorry," I sniffle through her poofy hair in my face.

"It's okay," she says, and sort of rocks me back and forth. I feel my cheek collapse into her shoulder, I let my weight fall against her. "It's okay," she repeats.

Out of nowhere, I'm sobbing like a child in this total stranger's arms—she's smaller than me, and I can actually feel my body shaking hers as I clutch the sharp bones of her shoulders. But I can't stop myself. "Oh my God, I'm really sorry," I blather, pulling away from her. I pull my sleeves down over my hands and wipe my eyes. But it's ugly crying, all snotty and gross.

She turns around and goes to her briefcase, rummaging around for a moment before pulling out a tiny rectangular package of tissues. "Here," she says, pulling one out and handing it to me.

"I'm really sorry," I repeat. "This is just the fifth time I've had to explain this. First time I've cried though, lucky you." I try to laugh.

"It's quite all right, Eden." She gives me a frowning smile, a head tilt, and one final pat on the back. "It's no problem. Why don't you come to my office hours after you return, and we'll figure out some way to make up the time?"

"That would be great," I gasp, my breathing erratic. "Thank you." *Thank you*, I silently tell her, *for not asking why I'm crying or if I'm okay.*

She hands me the whole package of tissues now. "If you need to miss today's lecture, I can have Lauren, my teaching assistant, send you the presentation."

"No, it's fine. I'm fine, really," I say by default.

"Self-care is more important than sitting here listening to me bang on for two hours about the politics of ancient Rome. Really," she says. "Please."

Say yes, I plead with myself. *Just say yes.*

"Actually"—gasp, gasp, gasp—"I think that might be helpful if you're sure you don't mind. It's been a really long week." My therapist would be so proud of me for accepting this small offer of grace.

But now it's three o'clock in the afternoon and I have nothing I'm supposed to be doing. It's a strange, unsettling feeling, after months of rushing and endless things needing to be done, to have time. I get a coffee and decide to stop at the store on my way home, thinking maybe I need to stock up on some travel packs of tissues if I'm going to be spontaneously ugly crying in public.

I pass the customer service desk at the front of the store and eye the racks of cigarettes tucked safely behind the counter. I could buy a pack. Just have one, throw the rest away, and feel so much more capable of handling everything right now. I get in line, behind the older woman holding her stack of scratch-off lotto tickets. But I won't have just one, I know this. And Josh would smell the smoke on my hair, taste it on my tongue. Then he'd worry. I watch as the lady in front of me hands over her winning tickets and the twentysomething cashier scans them, reciting how much each ticket should be worth.

I step out of line. Tell myself I don't need the cigarettes. I tell myself maybe it's only hormones—I started on the pill just a couple of weeks ago. I've never been on birth control before, and Mara warned me it could mess with my emotions. I don't exactly need any more interference on that front, but with the amount of sex Josh and I have been having, I couldn't risk anything happening. I tell myself it's this and not that I'm slowly unraveling as the hearing gets closer.

I'm walking up and down the aisles, not even sure what I'm doing. I smell a package of strawberries and set it back down. I pick up a pear and squeeze it gently. I sample a cube of cheddar speared with a toothpick.

I select a bag of organic coffee that is way too expensive and carry it like a baby as I continue down the aisle. And then I see cake and brownie and muffin mixes. I exchange the bag of coffee for a chocolate cake mix.

I'm surprising Josh with a fun dinner at this hibachi place he told me his parents took him to for his birthday last year. I'm trying to do something special to preemptively make up for missing his birthday next week. Of course, I haven't told him I'll be gone, because I haven't told him about the hearing yet. I've been telling myself for weeks, *Tomorrow. I'll tell him tomorrow.* But then tomorrow never comes.

I take my phone out. It barely rings before my mom picks up.

"Hello?" she answers, sounding alarmed. I can't remember the last time I called her instead of texting. "Eden, you there?"

"Hi. Yeah. Are you busy?"

"No, not at all," she says, though I can hear phones ringing in the background at her work. "What's going on?"

"Nothing, I just had the afternoon off and I'm in the grocery store."

"Okay . . ."

"I'm trying to get stuff to make a cake. For Josh's birthday," I add. "And I thought maybe you'd have some ideas. I want to do sort of like a peanut butter chocolate flavor."

"That sounds nice," she says. "So, things are going well with him? With Josh," she inserts, making a point to say his name.

"Yeah," I tell her. "It's good. Things are good."

"Good."

There's a painfully awkward pause.

"Um, so I have this chocolate cake mix, but I don't see any kind of peanut butter type frosting. I don't know, I just remember you always made different flavored frostings for our birthday cakes when we were kids."

She laughs. "Watermelon vanilla. That was your ninth birthday," she says.

"Right. I remember. That was a good one."

"Let me see." I can hear her typing on her work computer. And as I wait, listening to her breathing into the phone, sort of humming to herself as she scrolls, I wish she were with me right now. "Oh, here we go. I think I found something. Yes, this is an easy frosting recipe.

All you need is peanut butter, whipped topping, chocolate syrup, and mini peanut butter cups—all of which you should really have stocked in your kitchen anyway, as a college student."

It takes me a second to realize she actually made a joke. "Oh." I laugh. "I thought you were serious for a minute there."

"I am serious! You should have lots of junk food around for all your late-night studying."

"Okay, I'll get right on that."

"I'll email you the recipe," she says, and I can hear the smile in her voice. "Or, I could try to text it."

"Email's fine. I can get it on my phone either way."

"Sending now." I hear her typing again.

"Thanks, I'll let you know how it turns out."

"Well, let me know if you need help."

"Okay."

"See you next week. And, Eden?" she adds. "You've got this."

I'm not sure if she's talking about the cake or the hearing, and I don't know that I agree with either, but I tell her, "Thanks, Mom."

A minute after I hang up, I get a notification from my bank that my mom has sent me thirty dollars with the note: *For the birthday cake fund!*

Since I've been away, she's been surprising me with these small gestures that tell me she really does care that I'm doing all right here.

I decided to buy everything—mixing bowls, a baking pan, a whisk, a spatula, measuring cups—because I correctly assumed we didn't have any of those things at the apartment.

It feels good to not have to be thinking about anything but whisking the eggs and water and oil into the powdery chocolate mix. To be doing something for someone else.

Parker gets home just as I'm putting the cake in the oven.

"Whoa, what's happening in here?" she asks, stopping at the kitchen island to run her finger along the inside of the bowl. "I honestly didn't even know if that thing worked."

"What, the oven?"

She nods and licks the cake batter off her finger, murmuring, "Yum."

"I'm making a birthday cake for Josh."

"Aww, roomie." She gives me these big doe eyes. "That's really freaking sweet."

"You're still coming tonight, right?" I ask her for the twentieth time.

She hesitates. "Actually, I was thinking about staying in because this week has kicked my ass, but okay. You convinced me with this damn cake. What time should I be there?"

"Eight. Sharp. No, seven forty-five. You and Dominic are bringing the balloons with you so he doesn't suspect anything."

"So, what you're saying is I really never had a choice in the matter, did I?"

I smile, shake my head. "Nope."

"Fine, you master manipulator you," she says, and drags her bag behind her as she heads to her bedroom. "Grabbing a nap. Wake me at seven fifteen."

"Okay," I call after her.

I've never had a friend like Parker. But then, I haven't really had many different kinds of friends at all. I like her, though. She's not very touchy-feely with emotions or overly polite or warm, but somehow it feels good. She doesn't seem to mind that Josh is here all the time or that I spend half my time there. She's comfortable with who she is, and for some reason that makes me feel comfortable too. Like, neither of us has to pretend to be anything other than who we are. Although we have created an alter ego for takeout by combining our names "Kim McCrorey" and "Eden Parker." We laughed way too hard about it the other night when a delivery guy buzzed up to our apartment and said that he had an order for a Kimberly.

I go to pull up the recipe for the frosting and see that I have a text from my mom:

> Hi Eden, Mom here. Remember that you need to let the cake cool for at least two hours before frosting it. Let it sit out at room temperature for 30 mins and then you can put it in the fridge for the rest of the time. Love, Mom

If this wasn't so new for us, maybe I'd poke at her, say something like, *you don't have to use formal salutations in your texts.* But I just write back: OK, I will. Thx

I follow the directions, step by step, measuring out and mixing in the peanut butter, whipped topping, chocolate syrup, and mini peanut butter cups. I set it in the fridge to chill and sit down on the faded red couch while I wait for the cake to finish baking.

Twenty-three minutes still left on the oven timer.

Twenty-three minutes to just sit and do nothing.

My brain jumps on the opportunity to terrorize me with doubts and questions I don't have answers to. I pull up the emails from Lane that I've been avoiding looking at over the past month. She'd offered to hop on the phone with me multiple times to talk through the hearing process. And it's only right now, at five thirty on the last Friday before everything begins Monday morning, when she's sure to be out of the office, that I finally feel the urgent need to talk to her. Today's email from Lane:

> Happy Friday, Eden:
>
> Just a reminder that we're touring the courthouse/courtroom at 8AM Monday. Try to spend some time this weekend reviewing the police report and the statement you gave Det. Dodgson so it's all fresh in your mind. I know DA Silverman sent over a hard copy, but attached you'll find a pdf for your convenience.
>
> Make sure you dress in something comfy and natural (modest, for lack of a better word). Think business casual.
>
> Let me know if you have any questions.
>
> See you soon,
>
> Lane

I wonder if she sent Mandy and Gennifer the same thing. There have been so many times I've wondered if the lawyers would really know if we talked, wondered if we could get around the rules. Because on some very deep level, I wanted to know what he did to them, and I wanted them to know what he did to me. Not the details, but more the *how* of it. I'm not sure why—I guess because I'm still not sure even, all these years later, how it happened to me.

But I resist.

Instead, I search the term business casual and see a lot of blazers over brightly colored tops. I'm thinking anything bright is not the way to go. And I do not own a single blazer.

I finally text Amanda back now. I think about apologizing for taking so long. Trying to come up with an excuse for why it's taken me a month to get back to her, but she probably doesn't care about that; she just wants my answer, so I give it to her.

Yes. I'll be coming back.

I immediately see the three dots beside her name, dancing like excited atoms. I wait for a response. It doesn't come.

The oven timer goes off. I toss my phone on the couch and run over, opening the oven door and reaching in, forgetting the brand-new set of oven mitts I'd lain out on the counter.

"Shit!" I hiss. "Fuck fuck fuck fuck fuck," I whisper as I turn the faucet on and run my hand under the cold water. I look back at the cake sitting there, the oven door wide open like a mouth, and then I watch as two red lines bloom across the palm of my left hand, a bite mark from some kind of rabid animal.

JOSH

She knocks on my door at exactly seven forty-five. I open it, ready, but not prepared for how she looks. "Oh wow."

She laughs. "Oh wow to you too."

"Sorry, but you look . . ." She glances down at herself. She's wearing a dress—the only time I'd ever seen her in a dress before was the first time she ever came to my house. It was supposed to be our first date, except she didn't want to go anywhere. "You look really . . ."

"Really?"

"Really amazing."

"*You* look really amazing," she says, and pulls me close to her for a kiss. "You ready?"

She leads the way down the stairs and to her car. "We're driving?"

"It's not too far, but . . ." She lifts her heel in this adorable way that makes her look like she's about to dance. "Not in these shoes."

"Are you sure this isn't fancy?"

"Oh my God, I'm not proposing, Josh!" She laughs as she unlocks the doors.

I get in and buckle up. "I feel underdressed."

"You're not, I'm just overdressed."

"Hmm, well . . . to me, you're always overdressed."

"What do you mean?" She side-eyes me as she pulls away from the curb. "I never dress up."

"No," I tell her, reaching over to touch her bare knee. "I mean, overdressed as in you're always wearing too much."

She gasps, pretending to be scandalized. "Well, I never!" She lets her hand float to her heart, and I notice it's wrapped in a bandage. "Get your mind out of the gutter, Miller." She laughs. "Or at least have the decency to wait until I've proposed."

"Okay, mind officially out of the gutter." I take her hand and try to see around the bandage. "What the hell happened to your hand?"

"Oh, nothing," she says, shaking her head. "Just had a little kitchen accident."

"Did you cut yourself?"

"No, it's like a tiny burn. It's fine."

"Are you sure? That doesn't look tiny."

"Yes, I'm sure. I'm tough, you know. I can take a little burn."

"I know you're tough." I bring her hand to my lips and kiss the outside of the bandage, kind of shocked at how upset I feel to know she got hurt in any way. "But still."

She takes her hand back and touches my face as she glances over at me. "You worry too much."

"Get used to it," I tell her. "That's my whole shtick."

She smiles but doesn't say anything. And I'm watching her so closely, I don't even realize the car has stopped until she turns to look at me and says, "We're here."

"Here?" I look out my window. "Wait, we're going here? The Flaming Bowl. I love this place."

"I know," she says with a tiny giggle. "That's why I brought you."

We walk in a few minutes before eight. Eden gives the host her name, and we're directed to the bar area to wait until our table's ready. I reach for Eden's hand, but she tenses up and gently pulls away. "Shit, sorry. I forgot."

"It's okay," she says softly, and moves to the other side of me, offering her right hand instead. "I'm not going to break."

I see Eden look behind me and grin, but before I can ask why, I hear two distinct voices, one in each ear, say in a whisper, "Surprise!"

I jump and spin around. Dominic and Parker are yelping and shouting, "Oh my God, your face!"

"Did you see it?" Parker exclaims, pulling Eden in for a hug as she hands off a bunch of balloons, strings tied together, floating over our heads.

"What . . . what is this?" I ask.

"It's your surprise birthday party!" Eden shouts, throwing her arms around me.

"My birthday isn't until next week."

"I know, that's the surprise," she says, laughing. "Are you really surprised?"

"Yes!" I am definitely surprised.

"Thank God you're finally here. Someone already stopped me to ask where the bathroom was," Parker says, taking a sip from her tiny ceramic cup of sake.

"Why would someone ask you where the bathroom was?" Eden asks.

"Well, because I'm Asian I must work here."

"Oh my God, what did you say?"

Dominic starts laughing, and so do I.

"What am I missing?" Eden asks.

"This happens a lot, you'll see. So my go-to response is to tell them in Korean *I don't fucking work here, asshole.* They walk away real fast."

"That's brilliant!" Eden claps and laughs with her whole body.

I look up at Dominic, smiling as he's watching me watching Eden. "What?" I ask him, moving closer to stand next to him.

He shakes his head and passes me a Coke with lime, which he's already ordered for me from the bar. "It's just good to see you happy, that's all." He raises his glass. "Happy birthday, man."

"Thanks."

All through dinner, we talk and laugh and Eden makes sure she keeps telling everyone it's my birthday. And the chef keeps calling me "the birthday boy" even while he's performing all the theatrics of the meal, balancing and chopping and tossing ingredients and setting the whole grill on fire. I would normally feel weird about the special attention—I never used to let my parents tell restaurants it was my birthday when I was younger for fear they'd have the whole staff come out and sing "Happy Birthday." And that's exactly what happens. Parker takes a video. I would be embarrassed, with the whole restaurant clapping for me, but I can tell it's making Eden so happy. And then she kisses me right there in front of everyone—really kisses me—and they all erupt in raucous cheers.

I lean in close and say, "I love you."

She rests her head on my shoulder for just a moment and says quickly, quietly, "You too."

After the performance art that is hibachi, we're left to finish eating. Eden says, "Save room for dessert, everybody."

Parker sets her chopsticks down and says, "Oh yeah. I got a little sneak peek, and we're definitely gonna want to save room."

We all pile into Eden's car, with our to-go containers and the balloons filling the back seat.

"Thank you," I tell them again. "This was a really fun birthday surprise."

Dominic says, "It was all your girlfriend."

My girlfriend, I repeat in my head, I love the way that sounds.

"And . . . ," Eden adds. "There's still one more thing."

"More?" I ask.

"Yes, you're not the only one who can plan multipart dates."

As we arrive home, Eden instructs Dominic and Parker to escort me to the roof. "I'll be up in a minute," she says.

While we wait up on the roof, Parker clears her throat and announces, "So, we've been conferring tonight, and we just want you to know that we think you really found a good one."

"I know I had my share of doubts earlier," Dominic admits, "but you clearly make each other deliriously happy, so there's no arguing with that."

"Not that you need our blessing or anything," Parker adds. "Just thought we'd give you a little unsolicited feedback."

Before I can say anything, Eden is backing through the door of the roof, and as she turns around and lets the door fall closed behind her, I see she's carrying a cake with candles lit all over it. They start singing to me for the second time tonight, and as she sets the cake down on the wicker table, I see that there are tiny peanut butter cups mixed into the frosting.

"Oh my God, you didn't," I say. "Peanut butter cups?"

"Make a wish," she answers, squeezing in next to me on the love seat, draping her arm around my shoulder.

I look over at her and think, *I have nothing left to wish for*. But I don't say that. I lean forward and blow out the candles anyway. She kisses me on the cheek, then stands up to get a bag from the corner and pulls out plates and utensils—not paper—that she must've brought up here earlier.

"You really planned this all out, didn't you?" I ask her.

She shrugs, but she can't hide her smile as she plucks the candles out of the cake and sets them on a napkin. "Okay, since it's your birthday, you have to make the first cut, and then whoever's birthday comes next has to take the knife out."

"I've never heard of that," Dominic says.

Parker shakes her head. "Me neither."

"Really?" Eden asks. "We always did that in my family."

"I like that tradition," I tell her. I try to position the knife to make a decent-size slice.

"Bigger," Parker shouts.

"Okay, how's this?"

"Perfect," Eden says. "So, who's birthday is next?"

Dominic raises his hand and says, "July."

"April," Parker adds.

"Guess it's me, then. November," Eden explains, placing her hand over mine on the handle of the knife.

She passes around the plates of cake and distributes the forks, and I can't help thinking that this is the best birthday I've ever had. She watches me as I take a bite. "Do you like it?" she asks.

"It's delicious." I take another bite, and now she does too. "But I thought you were anti peanut butter and chocolate?"

"You might have converted me."

"Josh," Parker says, "you know Eden made this cake, right?"

"Wait, *you* made this?"

"Well, not from scratch, but yeah."

"Oh my God, it tastes like it's from a real bakery."

She takes another bite. "Okay, it is pretty good. For chocolate peanut butter."

When we get inside my room, Eden sets her purse on my dresser and slides her shoes off, peels her sweater down her arms and hangs it on the back of my chair. I love that she seems comfortable here. If it weren't so soon, I'd ask her to move in with me.

"Thank you for tonight." I wrap my arms around her waist from behind. "You're so thoughtful, you know that?" I kiss her hair, her neck. "So sweet."

"Really?" She spins around to face me. "Thoughtful *and* sweet? No one's said that to me in a very long time."

"Well, you are."

"No, you are," she says, touching the side of my face with her non-bandaged hand.

"You're physically incapable of taking a compliment, aren't you?"

She looks up and smiles in this way that makes me feel almost lightheaded as she brings her arms up around my shoulders. My hands find her hips automatically, and we sort of clumsily sway from side to side a little as we pull each other closer.

"What, are we dancing or something?" she asks.

"Why not?" I ask back, rocking her more intentionally.

"There's no music," she points out.

"Well, there's music playing in my head," I joke, committing to this cheesy giddiness welling up inside my chest.

She throws her head back in laughter. "Oh my God, did you really just say that?" She giggles, her whole face lighting up as she moves in to kiss me. "You giant nerd."

I take her hand from the spot where it's resting on my neck, raise it in the air, and awkwardly twirl her in a slow circle. As I pull her back in, she pushes up against me, standing on her toes to kiss me again, not laughing this time.

"Look at me," she says, holding my chin. "I love everything about you."

I like to think I'm so level all the time, but she can come out of nowhere sometimes, like right now, and say something so wonderful and dizzying it makes me come undone completely. She pulls my shirt off over my head, her mouth on my skin, and I move my hands all over her dress, testing from the top and bottom, trying to figure out which way it comes off. "How do you—I don't see . . . ?"

"Zipper." She laughs and turns around so I can unzip her

dress. "But wait, there's a little hook at the top that you have to undo first."

"I see it." Carefully, I unlatch the delicate little eye hook and slowly unzip the dress. I trace the curve of her back as the two sides separate. She reaches up to pull her hair out of its clip, and as she runs her fingers through it to shake it out, I can smell her shampoo or whatever it is that never fails to make me want her even more than I always already do.

She moves on top of me as we climb into bed together, her hair falling over my bare skin as she kisses my chest, my arms, my stomach. I don't know how she can both relax me and turn me on at the same time—something I never knew I was missing out on before her. I can feel her breath as she plants tiny kisses up the center of my body, feel her mouth smiling when she reaches my lips. Then she leans on her elbow, shifting to the side of me, her hands so warm on my waist as she looks down. "You know I really love you, right?"

"I know," I tell her, letting my finger trace the shape of her lips. "I really love you too."

She lays her head against my chest and inhales deeply, arranging herself in my arms. "Can we just lie here for a minute?" she whispers.

"We can just lie here all night."

She raises her head. "Yeah?" she asks.

"I'm actually really tired," I admit. "I mean, don't get me wrong, I could definitely rally."

She releases a short burst of air against my neck, a silent laugh, as she lays her head back down. "I could too," she says, as she stretches out alongside my body, draping her leg over mine. "But this feels nice," she whispers.

“It does,” I agree, my arm finding a perfect resting spot along the small of her back.

This would be the time to tell her about my parents coming to visit. I set my other hand on top of hers on my chest, feeling the gauzy bandage underneath. “You burned your hand making my cake, didn’t you?”

“Amateur mistake,” she says. “Forgot the oven mitts.”

I kiss the palm of her hand. “Did you put something on it, like aloe or something?”

She nods. “Yes, don’t worry.”

I wake up to a strange rattling sound I can’t place. I open my eyes and roll over in bed. It takes me a second to remember we’re in my room and not hers. She’s not in bed. I squint as I look across the room.

It’s too dark to see much more than Eden’s silhouette from the moonlight coming in from the window. I’m about to tell her how beautiful she looks, standing there with her back to me.

But then I realize what the noise was.

Pills. I hear the plastic scrape of the lid being twisted back onto the bottle. And I see her arm reach down to stick it back in her purse. She brings her cupped hand to her mouth and picks up an old water bottle on my dresser, tips it to her lips.

When she turns around, I close my eyes. The bed creaks as she climbs in next to me again. Her body feels cold now as she backs up against me and pulls my arm around her stomach. I feel her inhale deeply and then sigh.

“Hey. You okay?” I ask her.

“Mm-hmm,” she hums.

I kiss the back of her neck and pull her closer. "I know it's not my business, but . . . ," I start, and she twists around to face me. "What are you taking?" I whisper.

"Oh," she breathes. "It's nothing."

"Well, I've seen you do that a few times now, when you think I'm sleeping." I push her hair back behind her ear, try to be gentle. "I know it's none of my business," I repeat. "But are you okay?"

"It's just to help me sleep."

"You're having trouble sleeping again?"

"Not again," she corrects me. "Still."

How did I not know that? "Oh. I'm sorry," I whisper. "What can I do?"

She curls up to me and says, "This."

I tighten my arms around her and decide not to mention the other pills I saw in her room.

"It's not 'none of your business,' Josh," she says. "I was going to tell you; I just didn't want you to worry."

"Thanks for telling me now. It actually makes me worry a little less just knowing."

"Really?" she asks, her voice sounding small in the silence of the night.

I nod.

"There's something else I need to tell you."

"All right?" I answer, trying to prepare myself to act surprised about the other pills.

"One of the reasons I wanted to have your birthday early," she begins, "is because I have to be away next week."

And now she's surprised me for a second time tonight. "Wait, where? Why?"

"There's a hearing. I'll have to be back home for a couple of days at least. The DA said I should plan for the whole week, just in case."

"*What*?" I say too loudly. "But they can't just expect you to drop everything at the last minute."

"Yeah," she whispers, looking down as she runs her fingers along my collarbone, neck, jaw. "I've known about it for a few months."

I don't know what to say. I don't know why she wouldn't have told me. That's not the important thing right now, though, so I try to push that out of my head. "I'm coming with you, obviously."

"No." She stops touching my face and finally meets my eyes. "It's really not a huge deal."

"It *is* a huge deal." I sit up now. "Can I just ask, why didn't you tell me before now?"

She sits up too and pulls the sheet close to her body. "Don't be mad—"

"No, I'm not mad," I interrupt. "I'm not mad at you at all, I'm just . . ." I stop myself from saying "worried" and settle on "confused."

"Things have been so wonderful," she says, rubbing her head like it hurts.

"Yeah," I agree. "They have. They are."

"Well, I didn't want to ruin it by talking about all this fucked-up shit."

"Okay, but we can't just ignore it, either."

"You think I don't know that?" she snaps at me.

I shake my head. "No, of course not. That's not what I meant."

She sighs. "I know, sorry."

"It's okay."

"Jesus Christ. See?" she says, her voice shaking. "This is why. This is exactly why I didn't want to let this get in." She waves her hand through the air, this tiny space between us. "It ruins everything."

"Hey, listen to me," I tell her, reaching for her hand. "Everything's fine, okay?"

She starts to shake her head.

"With us, I mean. Everything's fine with us. Nothing can ruin this." What I don't say is that *it* is already in. It's always been there. "Let me come with you, though."

"No."

"Eden—"

"I won't be able to do it if you're there, Josh."

I can't imagine what my face is doing right now, but I try my best to wipe it clean of any reaction.

"No, what I mean is, I don't want you to hear the details. I honestly don't want anyone to hear any of this." She pauses and looks at me, waiting, debating. "He's going to be there. You really want to be in the same room with him?" she asks, but doesn't wait for an answer. "I don't."

"So, you're just gonna do it alone?"

"Yes."

"What about your mom? I'm sure she'd want to—"

She shakes her head. "She's testifying too, so she can't be there for mine; I can't be there for hers. And I wouldn't want her to be there anyway. The only way I'm going to be able to do this is by myself." She stares at me. "What? Why are you looking at me like that?"

"No—nothing. I'm just thinking. Just trying to understand." Why would she rather do this alone when I'm offering to be there with her? I have so many questions, I barely know where to start. "But I thought your mom didn't know anything about what happened. She didn't, right?" I ask, because that would be incredibly fucked up if she did. But what I say is, "What is she going to testify about if she didn't know?"

"Josh," she moans, "puh-lease, please, I don't want to—"

"I just want to help, Eden." I touch her face, kiss her forehead before she can back away. "I just want to know what's going on."

She rolls onto her back and looks up at the ceiling. "My mom didn't know. But she saw something. Something that she thought was something else."

"What does that mean?" I ask. "What did she see?"

"The next morning, she saw blood on my nightgown and legs, the sheets."

Blood. The word echoes in my head. My heart starts racing—no, it races, then stops abruptly, stuttering.

Eden clears her throat and continues, quieter. "She assumed I just got my period. I guess. I mean, why would she think anything else?" she adds, more to herself. "And that morning, I kind of tried to tell her—my brother too—but I didn't actually tell them. I—I wasn't clear. I wanted them to guess. I didn't want to have to say it. I didn't know how to say it. So, I don't know. I think they want to know about that morning from my mom and Caelin's perspectives."

These are the details. Nightgown. Legs. Sheets. Blood. This is why she doesn't want me there.

"See?" she asks. "You don't feel any better knowing that, do you?"

"That's not—that doesn't matter, I . . ." I try to find the right thing to say, but I can't.

"I'm getting tired," she says, turning to press her back against me, pulling my arm around her again, ending the conversation. She brings my hand to her mouth and kisses my fingertips softly. "Thank you for offering, though, really."

I try my best to relax, but my whole body is tense now. I hold her while she falls asleep and I try not to think about her blood or nightgown or legs or sheets. Try not to think about her waiting for someone to see, to guess, what had happened. And finally, I try not to imagine what I'd do if I ever found myself in a room with him again.

EDEN

It takes all my willpower to drag myself out of Josh's bed the next morning. I pull my dress back on and gather my purse and sweater and shoes. He's lying on his stomach with his arms around his pillow. I sit on the edge of his bed, allowing myself this rare moment of quiet to admire him. I run my hand along his back and lean over to kiss his shoulder, but he's so tired he doesn't wake up.

Downstairs, Parker is in the kitchen, stretching, with her earbuds still in—she's already been out for a run this morning—drinking one of her healthy green smoothies, looking all glowy and vibrant, compared to me. Dull and exhausted in yesterday's makeup and messy hair, the zipper of my dress inching down my back with every move I make.

She pulls her earbuds out and laughs when she sees me. "Hey, roomie," she says. "I see you're embracing that stride of pride this morning."

"The what?" I mumble, setting my purse down on the counter and letting my shoes clatter to the floor.

"You know, the trek of triumph, the sultry saunter, the booty-call boun—"

"Are you just making these up right now?" I ask with a laugh.

"You need to get your nose out of the so-called important *lit-tra-ture*," she says, in what I think is supposed to be a British accent. "Pick up a magazine every once in a while, woman."

"For your information," I tell her as I pour myself some water from the fridge. "We had a very nice snuggle sesh last night."

"Snuggles, sure," she says, lunging forward into a stretch. "You want a smoothie?"

"Ugh, gross. No. I'll get some coffee at work."

"Ah, yes. Coffee and no food, the breakfast of champions."

I open the cabinet and pull out a granola bar. "Happy?"

She brings one arm across her chest and then the other, saying, "I guess."

"Do you need to get in there?" I ask, gesturing to the bathroom. "I have to get ready."

"All yours," she says as she starts to jog off toward her bedroom. "I'm about to hit the pool anyway."

"Hey, Parker, um, can I . . . ?" I start, not really knowing how to finish.

Turning around, hands poised near her head, about to put her earbuds back in, she looks at me. "What?"

"It's not a big deal or anything, but I wanted to tell you I'm going to be gone for a few days next week. I just have to go home for something."

"Oh." She lets her hands drop and takes a step toward me. "Is everything okay?"

"Yeah, yeah. It's just—" I could tell her. Right now I could tell her the truth, but something stops me, like always. "Everything's fine, I'm just letting you know."

"You sure?"

"Yes." I nod and smile and start pulling back the wrapper of my granola bar. She watches me for a few seconds, until I take a bite and chew and swallow. "Really, that's all."

"Okay," she says slowly, then finally turns to go into her room.

I eat the rest of my granola bar and get into the shower. By the time I get out, Parker's gone and I've worked myself up into a panic just thinking about what's going to happen this week. My heart is racing and I'm breathing heavy. I walk into the kitchen in a towel, dripping water everywhere, dumping the contents of my entire purse out onto the counter so I can find my pills. I take two. I don't have time for a fucking anxiety attack right now.

I clock in at 12:02, and Captain Douchebag is standing there at the lockers, waiting to tell me that this is the third time I've been late and that I should consider this my verbal warning.

"Sorry," I mumble.

"Don't be sorry," he snaps at me. "Just get here on time. It's not that hard."

He walks away, and as I'm putting my things in my locker, pulling out my apron to tie around my waist, I realize one of the cooks, Perry, has just caught me rolling my eyes at our manager. But he just nods and laughs silently, thankfully understanding. I sort of shrug and smile in return.

Halfway through my shift, at four o'clock, there's a girl in line, a little older than me. She's staring at me. When it's her turn, she steps up to the counter and smiles in this strange way. Like I should know her, but I don't.

"Hi," she says hesitantly, eyes flashing down to read my name tag. "Eden."

I smile back. "What can I get started for you?"

"Oh, um . . ." She looks all around, confused, as if she suddenly found herself inside a coffeehouse by chance and wasn't prepared to be asked this question. "Can I just order a . . . ? Oh, I don't know, what's your favorite drink?"

"My favorite?" I repeat. "Huh, nobody's ever asked me that. I guess you can't go wrong with the pumpkin pie latte. Sometimes I add a little vanilla to it, which I love, but—"

"That sounds great," she says, her eyes fixed on me so intently I have to look away.

"Great," I repeat. "For here or to go?"

"Here," she says, but then quickly adds, "No, actually, to go. I think. Yes, to go."

"All right, can I get a name?" I ask, marker in hand, tip already pressed against the cup.

"It's Gen," she says quietly. "With a G."

My heart struggles to race, weighted down under the double dose of meds still working through my body. I look at her more closely now, the way she's been looking at me. I'd searched for her online months ago. In my mind she's been existing as just a static image on the screen. I recognize her now, but it's different seeing her in person. "You're Gennifer?" I breathe. "Gen," I correct.

She nods, smiles again—I realize she has a very pretty smile, the kind that can cover up all sorts of terrible things. "You wouldn't be able to take a quick break or anything, would you?"

Perry covers the counter for me while I sit down across from her at a table in the corner.

"Sorry," she begins. "I was just passing through on my way back for the hearing and I knew you worked here. Your brother mentioned it—I promise I haven't been cyber-stalking you or anything." She pauses and sort of laughs. "I can definitely see the family resemblance."

"Oh" is all I manage to say. I don't know why I seem to have forgotten that my brother knows her—they were friends, he'd told me that. They still are, it seems.

"I guess I just didn't want the first time we met to be in a courthouse. I don't know, is that weird?" she asks, taking a sip of her latte. "This is really good, by the way."

"No, it's not weird," I tell her.

"I know we're not supposed to talk, but . . ." She looks through the window, her smile fading. "Do you ever wonder why? Why he would do this—" She starts but stops. "Like, that's the part I'm stuck on. I even tried to ask him. The next day. I went home that night and told my roommate what happened, and she took me to the hospital. Got the rape kit done and it was so horrible, but I didn't want to report it right then because I thought for sure there had to be a *reason*. Do you know what I mean?"

"I . . . Yeah, I think so," I tell her, because even though I know we shouldn't be doing this, talking, I desperately want to hear what she has to say.

She sits up a little straighter. "I wanted to believe that he somehow must not have realized or it was some kind of, like, mental break or . . . but it just turned out that I—" She stops abruptly, taking another sip of her latte. "I just didn't know him. At all."

It's strange, this realization slithering through my brain, as I listen to her. I don't think I've ever *wondered* why. Because deep down, in that place beyond logical thinking, I thought I knew. He did what he did because *I* had done something to make it happen. I could never quite put my finger on what it was, whether it was just one thing or a combination of things. My head could disagree all day, tell me it wasn't my fault, but my heart knew, always, it was me.

Until now, maybe.

"I really thought I did—I thought I knew him," she repeats. "I genuinely trusted him."

"Me too," I hear myself say.

She looks at me and tries to smile again, but it doesn't fool me this time. "Sorry I'm dumping this on you."

"It's okay," I tell her. "I mean, I get it."

"Yeah," she says softly. "I thought you might."

I can only nod because there are too many things I want to say, but none of them are things I'm allowed to tell her.

"I know you have to get back to work; I hope I haven't ruined your whole day or made you feel—"

"No, you didn't. I'm glad we got to meet. Like this, instead."

"I guess I just wanted to tell you face-to-face that I'm really . . ." She pauses, tracing a circle around her cup as she finds whatever word it is she's looking for. "Thankful. To not have to be doing this all by myself."

"I am too," I tell her. "If it weren't for you and Amanda, I couldn't have . . ." I shake my head—I can't even finish the sentence.

"I have a feeling you could have," she tells me, as she reaches across the table, sliding her latte receipt toward me, her number already written on it. "For when this is all over, if you want?"

As I watch her leave and get in her car and drive away, I realize there is a version of this where Gen never says anything. She lets it go and just keeps wondering why. Where Amanda stays scared and angry and hurt and continues to blame me for everything. It's the version where I lose myself forever and never find my way back. And for the first time, I think I understand—in my head *and* my heart—why we're really doing this.

For us.

We're doing this for us. Somehow that makes this all so much more real, more frightening.

JOSH

I'm sitting in bed reading, when I hear Dominic call from the other room, "Your girlfriend's here!" I look at my phone; it's not even five o'clock.

She walks into my room and closes the door behind her, still wearing her apron.

"What, did Captain Douchebag let you leave early?" I ask.

She shakes her head and drops her bag on the floor like it was too heavy to hold on to for another second. There's this faraway look in her eyes as she slips out of her shoes and walks toward me. I set my textbooks down on the nightstand to make space for her, because she's crawling into my lap without a word, curling up against me.

"Hey, you okay?" I can smell the coffee in her hair as I place my arms around her—she didn't even stop by her apartment before coming up here. My mind immediately goes to her asshole manager, to that cook who's always leering at her. "Eden, did something happen?"

"No," she whispers. "I just missed you."

"Are you sure?"

"Yeah," she mumbles against my neck.

"You would tell me if one of those guys from the café messed with you, right?"

She finally looks up at me, searches my face, clearly has no idea what I'm talking about. "What do you mean, what guys?"

"No, never mind," I tell her, shaking my head. "Nothing."

We spend the rest of the weekend in bed, half the time dozing, the other half exploring each other in the daylight for a change. More sleeping, making love, feeding each other leftover cake. Heaven.

Sunday afternoon turns into Sunday night and I know I have to let her go, but I keep wanting just a few more minutes with her. She lets me redress her burn, and I watch her pack her bag. At the car, I try one more time to convince her to let me come.

"I heard you, okay?" I say. "I don't need to be there in the courtroom if that isn't going to help, but at least let me be there before and after."

"You *are* here with me before." She takes my hands. "And you'll be here waiting for me after, right?"

I nod. "I'll be here."

"Thank you, that's what I need from you," she says, and I try to believe her.

We kiss goodbye, and my heart aches to think of not seeing her for possibly a whole week. It's kind of scary how attached I am after only a month of being together again.

"You're allowed to change your mind, okay?" I tell her as I bend down and lean into the car window. "If you decide you want me there, I'm there."

She smiles and says, "Okay," even though I have a feeling she won't change her mind.

I kiss her once more, squeeze her hand, tell her "I love you" one last time.

And then I stand there on the sidewalk, that same helpless feeling I had before burrowing deeper into my stomach, while I watch as the car shrinks smaller and smaller in the distance.

EDEN

Mom drives me and Caelin to the courthouse in the morning for the walk-through. Lane meets us on the other side of the security checkpoint and escorts us to the courtroom we'll be in. There's less wood than I expected from all the TV courtrooms, less everything—the space is utilitarian, with no warmth or character or ornamentation of any kind. I can hear all three of us breathing, no one wanting to talk, so the room swallows our breath.

DA Silverman struts in a few minutes later, in her high heels and impeccable suit, which is decidedly not business casual. Behind her are Amanda and her mom, and Gen, looking younger today, somehow, than she had at the café. There's an older man with her who I assume must be her father.

The parents greet one another like they're at a funeral, small syllables, all hushed and subtle. Gen steps close to me, and for a second I get scared that she's going to hug me or something and possibly give away the fact that we'd met the other day. But that's not what she does; she pulls my brother in for a brief hug.

And he sounds like someone else as he says, "Hey, Gen, Mandy, Mrs. A." But as Amanda and her mom nod and smile politely back at Caelin, I realize it's that he actually sounds like himself—his old self, the one I haven't seen in months. It's strange to see him here, not just my brother but someone who is *something* to all these people too.

The three of us—me, Amanda, and Gen—exchange our awkward hellos and look at one another like maybe we're looking into some kind of distorted fun house mirror at ourselves. We take turns smiling at each other, then frowning and looking away.

"So," DA Silverman says, her voice cutting through all this emotion taking up all the air. "We just want to walk everyone through what's going to happen this week, just to make sure we're all on the same page, and if anyone has any questions, then we can address them now. We all know testimonies start tomorrow. And as you know, we all must remain separate. We have a private room down the hall where we'll have you wait until it's your turn."

Gennifer's father, whose name I already forgot, says, "So, there's no jury at this point, correct?"

"That's right," Lane responds, her voice way too chipper. "A hearing is really not all that different from a trial. Think of this as a pre-trial, without a jury. That part comes later."

"But he'll be here, in the courtroom, while the girls are on the stand?" he asks.

I see Mrs. Armstrong's jaw clench. I wonder if Gennifer's dad realizes that she's Kevin's mom too. I wonder what she thinks now, every time she hears her son's name. It can't be good.

"Yes," DA Silverman says, and leads us up to the witness box, tells us to look out. "So, Kevin will be sitting there with his attorney." She points at one of the tables in front of us. "I'll be over here on this side."

"And I'll be sitting out here," Lane says, pointing to an area of seating. "On your side, with the detectives who worked your cases and whoever else you'll have here for you. So, if you need somewhere to look at any time, just look at me."

I can't stop staring at the table where Kevin will be sitting.

"You all right?" my mom says quietly.

"That's really close" is all I say. What happened to all those big fancy sprawling TV courtrooms? This is tiny. Claustrofucking-phobic. Stuck in the 1980s. I want to raise my hand. I have a question: *Why is that table so fucking close to the witness stand?* I want to scream. *Who fucking designed this place?*

"So, we'll start the process tomorrow," DA Silverman says with a self-assured nod. "Just remember to remain calm and be honest. If you don't know something you're asked, it's okay to say you don't know. Keep your phones close. If there are any changes to the schedule or order, I'll let you know via text."

Mom takes me and Caelin for breakfast at IHOP afterward, the same one, off the highway, where Josh brought me that day last December, when he came for me. This was where I told him about Kevin, about me, about all of it.

We pick at our food in mostly silence.

I'm distracted by the fall decorations everywhere—pumpkins and ghosts and cornucopias—thinking about the way time passes. It felt like it took so long to get to this point, but now it's here and I barely feel ready at all. Wasn't it just summer? Just spring? Just winter before that, when I was here last, in that booth right over there by the window, trusting Josh with my heart, soul, mind, everything.

In the car, Mom looks at both of us and says, "You know that your father has never been good at talking about his feelings, but he doesn't blame any of what's happening on either of you. You need to know that, both of you. He's just so angry still," she tries to explain.

"Yeah, at *who*?" Caelin asks. "That's the real question."

"Not you," Mom says. And then she twists around to look at me in the back seat. "And not you, either."

I nod, sort of understanding—that kind of anger, that kind of silence—too well.

I call Mara once we get back home. I was planning on joking with her about business casual. *Like, what even is that?* I could hear myself saying. Asking her if she has a blazer I could borrow, but when I hear her voice on the line, something changes.

"Hey," I say. "You busy in a few hours?"

Instead, I ask her to meet me at our playground. The one where we used to play when we were kids and then where we used to hang out drinking and smoking and getting high with randos, all post-Josh and pre-Cameron.

Our giant wooden castle—our private magical realm—still standing after all this time.

When I pull into the parking lot, she's there waiting for me, sitting on a tire swing that's shaped like a horse, swaying back and forth, sidesaddle. My headlights shine a spotlight on her. When I get out of the car, she runs and slams into me, full-body hug.

"Oh my God, I've missed you," she whines. "I'm so happy to see you, Edy."

"I missed you too," I tell her, and I mean it, but things feel different somehow. It's only been a month since I've seen her, but so much has changed for me.

We climb up to the highest tower and sit down, crossed-legged, opposite each other. She keeps making this awkward nervous half laugh I don't know what to make of. "So, Josh being good to you?" she asks. "Treating you like a queen, I hope."

"He's being very good to me," I tell her, but I can't seem to force a smile right now the way she is. "He really wanted to come with me. Be here for the hearing. But I said no."

She finally nods, straight faced, and says, "Why not?"

I shrug. "I don't know."

Mara looks down at her hands. "Edy, can I ask you something?"

"Sure."

"Why didn't you ever tell me?"

I open my mouth to answer but change my mind. "You know, I almost just said 'I don't know' again? Because for so long I really didn't know. I guess saying 'I don't know' is easier to say than to try to list all the reasons."

"I want to know all the reasons," she says. "Because I would've believed you."

"That's probably the biggest one. You would have believed me, and if you knew, then I couldn't pretend anymore and I would've had to do something about it. And I couldn't. Or at least, I didn't think I could."

She nods but chews on the inside of her cheek like she's trying to not say something.

"And you were all I had. I didn't want anything to change."

"It wouldn't have," she argues.

"It has, though. You feel it, don't you? Things are just different now."

She looks down again. "You never gave me the chance to be a good friend to you. As much as I love you, I'm mad too, and I know that makes me a total bitch. I'm mad because I would've been there for you if I'd known."

"I know."

"But I understand, too," she adds. "Who's to say I wouldn't have done the same thing?"

I shrug, nod, say, "I guess."

We sit there for a moment, looking out on this small patch that once held so many things from our childhood, our high school indiscretions. Somewhere in the distance a car horn honks, a muffled reprieve from the bittersweet reverie of this place.

"Can I ask you for a huge favor, Mara?"

"Anything."

"Will you come to the hearing?"

"Of course," she says, no hesitation.

"Really?"

"Yes. What do I have to do?"

"Just sit there," I tell her. "Let me look at you while I'm testifying. Can you do that?"

She nods.

"I'll have to go over everything that happened. The details. Like, probably everything that ever happened between me and—" I cough, clear my throat. "Me and him. Me and Kevin," I finally say. "But especially what happened that night, I guess. It's just that, he's going to be there, and I don't want to accidentally look at him and then freeze or break down or fly into a rage or something."

"Would it help if you told me now?" she asks. "Like as practice?"

"Maybe."

I tell her about the Monopoly game earlier that night, how he flirted with me, even though I didn't really understand that was what he was doing at the time. I tell her about how I woke up to him in my bedroom at 2:48 in the morning—I looked at my clock because it didn't make sense, why he'd be in my room. How I thought at first, he must be playing some kind of joke. How he climbed on top of me and covered my mouth, pinned my arms down. How he was crushing me, hurting me, how he told me to shut up. He put his hand around my throat. He wasn't laughing. He was serious. It wasn't a joke.

Mara's squeezing my hands so hard.

"Then what happened?"

Mara stares at me and nods, her eyes wide, unblinking, from across the room now.

"He pulled my underwear down my legs and yanked my nightgown up so hard it ripped," I say. "And then he shoved it into my mouth."

"Why did he do that?" DA Silverman asks.

Out of the corner of my eye, I see his lawyer's white-haired head pop up, his hand rising in the air, but I keep my eyes on Mara. "Speculation," he says.

"What happened then, with the nightgown in your mouth?" she asks instead.

"I was trying to scream, but I couldn't."

"And what do you remember next?"

"He was kicking at my legs, trying to separate them. I got one of my arms free and I hit him, but he just held me down harder, tightened his hand around my throat. He kept telling me to stop, to hold still. I didn't, though, and he was getting more and more angry." I clear my throat.

"Was he yelling?"

"He was whispering, but directly in my ear. His face was right next to mine, and he said, 'fucking do it,' and I remember that because I didn't know what he wanted me to do."

"Can you tell us again how old you were then, on December twenty-ninth?"

"I had just turned fourteen in November."

"And Kevin was a few weeks away from turning twenty years old?"

I look her in the eye. Was that true? Was he that old then? I don't know. But I don't have a chance to answer because his lawyer does that hand-raise thing again, this time laughing. "Your Honor, relevance?"

"Had you ever had sex before?" she asks instead.

"No. I had never even kissed anyone."

"Again." Hand. "Relevance?"

She spins on her heel and looks directly at White Hair, practically spits the words "I'm trying to establish why, when the *twenty*-year-old man told the *thirteen*-year-old girl to 'fucking do it,' she didn't know what that meant."

Now he stands. Takes off his tiny wire-framed glasses and shakes his head, even lets his mouth hang open for a moment as if he has no words to express how deeply he objects. "Your Honor . . ." is all he says.

"Withdrawn," she says, and turns back to me. "After he said 'fucking do it,' what happened?"

I lock eyes with Mara. "He forced my legs apart. I—I was getting weaker. I couldn't breathe."

"Because of the nightgown in your mouth?"

"Yes, and because he was squeezing my throat tighter and tighter."

"What do you remember happening next?"

"He . . . um . . ." I close my eyes. I picture the wooden playground. Just me and Mara. The softness of the night all around us. Mara's hand holding mine.

"Do you need a break?"

I open my eyes. "No."

"What happened next?" she repeats.

"He raped me," I finally say, the word sounding too small and simple to convey its own meaning.

"Okay, and did he hurt you?"

"Yes."

"Did he know he was hurting you?"

"Your Honor." He raises his hand and stands up now. "Again, speculation."

"I'll rephrase. Could you indicate to him in some way that he was hurting you?"

"I was crying. I mean, I couldn't speak or yell because he was still choking me, and I couldn't move because he was holding mc down, but I was crying, and I didn't know until later, but I was bleeding. He knew he was hurting me—he wanted to hurt me."

White Hair raises his hand again, almost bored now, not even bothering to look up from his folder. "Move to strike everything after the first sentence, 'I was crying.' She'd already answered the question."

I see Mara's face turning red.

I want to look at the man so badly, want to make him look at me as he deletes my words from the record. But I keep my eyes on Mara, let her be angry for us both. I know for sure I've made the right decision now. I couldn't have had Josh here listening to this. And I couldn't do it alone, either.

"Do you know how long he was raping you?"

"Five minutes."

"How do you know?"

"I looked at the clock when I could move again. I remember thinking it felt like hours. I thought the clock had to be wrong."

"And what happened next?" she asks. I think hard, trying to put the events in the right order, but my brain keeps skipping ahead to the end. "What's the next thing you remember?" she rephrases, somehow reading my mind.

"He let go of my throat and he ripped the nightgown out of

my mouth and I started coughing and he kept telling me to shut up. He was moving my hair out of my eyes—it was stuck to my face because my face was wet from crying. He wanted me to look at him."

Hand raise.

"He *said*, 'Look at me,'" I correct myself. I was catching on now—emotions are not allowed here, feelings aren't facts. "He told me to listen, and he held my face so that I had to look into his eyes."

"He told you to listen—what did he say?"

"He said, 'No one will ever believe you.'"

"Then what? Did he leave?"

"No. He sat up but was still kneeling between my legs, staring at me—at my body. I tried to cover myself, but he moved my hands away. He made me promise that I wasn't going to tell anyone."

"And did you promise?"

"Yes."

"Why?"

"He said that if I told anyone, he would kill me. He said, 'I swear to God, I'll fucking kill you,' and given what had just happened, I believed him."

"So did he leave then?"

"No." I hear my voice shaking, I feel my throat caving in, just like it had that night.

"What happened next?"

I can't even look at Mara—I'd left this part out at the wooden playground. I cough, try to clear my throat. "He, um . . . he kissed me. And then he got up, put his underwear back on, and told me to go back to sleep."

"And then he left?"

"Yes."

"Thank you. Nothing further."

I let myself exhale. I let myself think maybe I was doing okay. But then his lawyer stands up, buttons his jacket, and smiles at me, just like Kevin had smiled at me that night, in between shoving his tongue in my mouth and putting his boxers on—I had forgotten to say that. *He kissed me, smiled at me, and then he got up.* Too late.

"Good afternoon, Eden," he begins, pretending to be a human being. "I'll keep this brief; I just have a few questions.

"How long have you known Kevin?"

"Since I was like seven or eight. That was when my brother became friends with him."

"And didn't you have a crush on him?"

"What?"

"A crush." He shrugs. "You know, a playful infatuation."

"Maybe when I was younger, but that doesn't mean—"

"Just yes or no."

The thing about a crush is that you have them because, on some level, it's unattainable, and if you're being honest with yourself, you wouldn't really want it anyway even if you could have it. But all there's room to say here is "Yes."

"And that night, you said you wanted to play a game with Kevin. Monopoly, right?"

I didn't say I wanted to play a game with him—it was his idea. When had I said that? Did I say that today? I can't remember. But wait, why is this even important?

"Eden, can you answer the question?"

"We played Monopoly."

"The board game?"

Of course the fucking board game. I look at the DA, are these serious questions? I thought we'd be sticking to what I said in the police report.

"Eden?"

"Yes, the board game Monopoly."

"And that night when you were playing, didn't you tell Kevin that you wanted a boyfriend?"

"I didn't say that."

"But you did ask if Kevin had a girlfriend, right?"

I shake my head. Where is this coming from?

"I don't—" I close my eyes, try to remember. "No. No, we were talking about my brother having a girlfriend. He was on the phone with her and that's why it was just me and Kevin. He was the one who got the game out," I add, remembering more clearly now. "*Monopoly*."

"Right, and then you asked if Kevin had a girlfriend."

"Maybe I—"

"Yes or no."

"Y-yes."

"You said earlier that you were fourteen at the time?"

"Yes."

"And did you know how old Kevin was at the time?"

"He was almost twenty," I say, repeating what the DA had said.

"So, he was nineteen, right?"

"Right."

"But did you know at the time how old he was? At the time?"

Except now I'm doubting myself. Did I think he was eighteen, nineteen, twenty? "I mean, I really don't know if I knew exactly."

DA Silverman stands up and sighs. "Is this going anywhere?"

"Did he know how old you were at the time?"

She sits down and then shoots right back up. "Speculation, Your Honor."

"Did you have a conversation about how old you were?"

"Well, he knew I was in ninth grade."

"Yes or no—did you have a conversation about age?"

"No."

And so it continues for what feels like hours. Pointless questions mixed in with important ones, always with *right* or *didn't you* tacked on to the end. Dissecting all of my sentences into smaller and smaller fragments until they barely make sense anymore.

"One last question, Eden. Did you ever say no?"

"Say no?"

"Did you ever verbally say no at any point that night?"

"I couldn't speak. He covered my mouth immediately, and then he—"

"Did you say no?"

"I fought him, I hit him, I kicked him, I—"

"But did you ever say the word no?"

I look at Mara, then Lane, then the DA.

"I—I already said I couldn't speak."

"Your Honor, please instruct the witness to answer the question."

"Please answer the question," the judge says.

"No, but—"

"Thank you," he says, and smiles again, like I'd just handed him a fucking cappuccino or something. "I have nothing further."

And as he turns around and walks back to the table, I make the mistake of watching him—this old, frail, white-haired fossilized monster—and as he sits down, my eyes drift too far until I realize I'm looking at him. Kevin. And he's looking at me. He has me pinned like a dead insect mounted on a foam block, with only his eyes, like he had that night.

I hear this sound in my ears like the ocean. I close my eyes. I'm going. Leaving my body. Disappearing. Gone. The next thing I know I'm in the bathroom, Lane there, telling me how great I did. "Great" is the word she used. It echoes in my head. *Great great great*. And she's smiling at me in the mirror.

I look at my hands—I'm washing them at the sink. I've torn my bandage up into ribbons, the tape peeling off, the two red welts on my palm, only just starting to scab, now picked over and bleeding in patches. I don't remember doing that. I don't remember leaving the courtroom.

"How does that fucking lawyer sleep at night?" Mara says.

"I want to go," I say out loud to no one in particular.

Lane touches my shoulder, and I flinch. "Sorry, honey. You did really well, I mean it."

"Whatever, I don't care. It's over. I just wanna go."

JOSH

Eden called me last night at midnight to tell me happy birthday. She said she thought through what I'd said to her about doing it alone and she'd asked Mara to go with her. I stayed on the phone with her until she fell asleep. She didn't say so, but I could tell she was really nervous. I wished she would've just let me come.

I've been distracted all day waiting for word from her. I spaced out during our team meeting this morning, and Coach reamed me out in front of everyone. Even Dominic pulled me aside in the locker room to ask what was going on with me.

"Nothing," I told him. "I'm just tired." Which was true; even after Eden finally fell asleep around two o'clock and I hung up the phone, I couldn't sleep at all.

I texted her before afternoon practice to check in.

When I get out at six, I still haven't heard from her. I call and leave a voice mail.

"Hey, just me. Thinking of you. Hope everything's going okay. Well, call me when you can. I love you. Miss you."

On my walk home, I'm barely paying attention to anything—not other people or traffic or street signs—I'm staring at my phone the whole time.

"Josh!" my mom's voice calls out to me, laughing. "What are you doing?"

I look up. I've walked right past my building, past my parents, waiting on the front stoop, each holding coffee cups from Eden's work.

"Head in the clouds much?" Dad says as he steps closer and hugs me.

Mom stands now and passes her coffee to Dad. She places her hands on my shoulders and holds me at arm's length, smiling as she studies me for a moment. "Happy birthday, sweetheart."

"Happy birthday, Josh," Dad echoes.

I honestly don't know if I've ever been happier to see them in my life.

"You look tired," Mom says as we walk up to the apartment. "Are you getting enough sleep?"

I shrug. "I don't know."

"You don't know?" she repeats, her voice an octave higher than usual. And as I glance back, I see her looking at my dad, all wide-eyed.

"Mom," I groan. "I'm fine."

I unlock the door to my apartment and let them in.

"So, where's Dominic?" Dad asks.

"He went to get dinner with some of the other guys on the team."

Mom says, in her best casual voice, "And what about Eden,

where's she?" Then looks all around like she's searching for evidence of her having been here.

I sit down on the couch in the living room, and they follow.

"Listen, she's not gonna be able to make it tonight."

"What?" Mom shouts as she sits down on the couch next to me, then adjusts her volume. "She's not going to make it for your birthday?"

"We celebrated on Friday. She had to go out of town."

"Out of town?" she repeats, like that's the most absurd thing she ever heard. "In the middle of the semester?" She shakes her head. "*Joshua*."

"No, don't say my name like that."

"Like what?"

"Like I'm naive or getting taken advantage of or being lied to or something. I'm not. It's not like that."

"Well, tell me." She crosses her arms and looks at my dad like he should be getting upset along with her. "What's it like, then?"

I glance up at my dad, sitting on the ottoman next to the couch. He gives me a half smile, a nod, sort of squints, drawing his eyebrows together, tilts his head in Mom's direction.

"What's this?" Mom asks, not missing anything. "What's going on with you two?"

Dad sighs. "Just tell her, Joshie."

"Dear God, tell me what?" she says, clutching the collar of her shirt. "She's not pregnant, please tell me she's not preg—"

"No!"

"Thank you thank you thank you," she whispers into her clasped hands.

"Why is that the first thing you guys jump to? Do you really think I'm that irresponsible?"

"No," Mom says. "But shit happens, Josh. You can be careful ninety-nine percent of the time and all it takes is one—"

"Oh my God, please," I say, raising my voice. "All the safe sex talks are scarred into my memory for life, I assure you. Can we drop this now?"

"Not until you tell me what's going on," Mom insists. "I don't like this. I have to be honest. I don't like this girl for you, Josh, I just—"

"Fine," I relent. "Just please stop saying that."

So I tell them everything. And by the time I finish, they're sitting on either side of me on the couch, Mom's arm around me, Dad's hand resting on my knee. When I look up at Mom, she has tears running down her face.

"Sorry," she says, wiping her cheeks with the backs of her hands. "That's a lot, Josh."

"I know," I agree, "it's been a lot for her."

"Well, for you too," Mom says.

"No, come on." I shake my head. "I'm not comparing anything I might be feeling to what she's going through."

Dad speaks up. "No one's saying you should compare anything, but just acknowledge, all right, this is not an easy thing to be dealing with in any relationship."

I nod. I know he's right. But I don't know how to explain that when we're together it doesn't feel hard. When we're together it feels like we can handle it—could handle anything.

We order food and stay in. D and Parker join us. Parker

shows my parents the video from the hibachi restaurant of everyone singing "Happy Birthday." Eden kissing me at the end, with total abandon. Everyone cheering.

"Let me see that." Mom takes the phone and watches the video two more times, smiling by the end of it. "You look happy, Josh," she says quietly.

They leave to go to their motel at eleven. Outside, at the car, Dad says, "Come on, group hug." And they both wrap me in a giant hug. A different day I might've said something stupid like *aren't I getting a little old for this*, but not today. Today I just let them and feel grateful.

"You need more rest." Mom jabs her finger into my chest. "Hear me?"

"Yes."

"We love you," Dad says.

"Love you guys too."

I watch as they drive away, my dad's arm darting out from the passenger-side window to wave at me all the way down the road. I walk down to the end of the block and back again, just to burn off some of this anxiety I've had building up in me all day. I pull out my phone again, just in case I've somehow missed her.

Still nothing.

Upstairs, I try to fall asleep, but I toss and turn.

EDEN

It's almost midnight when I wake up on the couch in the living room, in the dark. Josh just texted me a minute ago.

> I hope you're sleeping well right now. Talk tomorrow? I love you

I call him back. He answers right away.

"Hey," he says, and I want to start weeping at the sound of his voice. "There you are."

"Hi," I whisper, throat scratchy and worn from all the talking earlier. "I'm sorry. I lay down after I got home, and no one woke me up."

"It's okay. How . . . ?" He pauses. "How are you? How did it go?"

"It was a fucking shit show." I force a bitter laugh only to not start crying again.

“Eden, baby . . . ,” he says so softly, I let his voice wrap around me. “I can be there in the morning if you—”

“No, don’t worry about it. It’s over.”

“What do you mean?”

“No, *it’s* not over, but my part’s done. My mom and Caelin go tomorrow. I was thinking of staying one more day and coming back Thurs—” I start coughing and reach for the room-temperature glass of water sitting on the side table next to me.

“You okay?” he’s asking as I pull the phone away from my face.

“Yeah, sorry,” I croak, and swallow most of the glass in one gulp my throat is so dry. “Thursday,” I finish. “Early Thursday.”

“Hey, are you getting sick?” he asks.

“No, I don’t think so. My throat just hurts like hell from talking so much. I was talking for hours today. It felt like they asked me a thousand questions.”

He makes a sound I can’t quite decipher.

“I won’t keep you, okay? I’m glad to hear your voice though, even if it’s scratchy.”

“Wait, Josh.” I try to laugh, but I just end up coughing again. “Don’t hang up. I’m not trying to get off the phone. Tell me about your day. How was your birthday?”

“Oh,” he says. “It was fine. I mean, last weekend was really the main event. With you. Best birthday ever.”

“Mmm.”

“You sound exhausted.”

“I wish I was there with you right now,” I whisper.

“So do I, you have no idea.”

“Josh?”

"Yeah?"

"I know it's dumb, but could you stay on the phone with me again tonight?"

"It's not dumb." I hear some shuffling and the creaking of his mattress. I close my eyes and can picture him getting settled in bed. "I just put you on speaker."

"I love you," I tell him.

"I love you too."

"Thank you."

"For what, loving you?" he asks, a small laugh in his voice.

I smile—it hurts my face. "Yes."

JOSH

I wake in the morning to my five o'clock alarm, as usual. Still dark out, I see a text already sitting there from my mom.

Is this her?

With a link to an article in the local paper. The headline reads THREE WOMEN TESTIFY AGAINST BASKETBALL MVP IN *PEOPLE V. ARMSTRONG*. I quickly scan for her name. Not there, thankfully. They haven't listed any of their names. There's a highlighted pull quote, enlarged in bold: "Harrowing . . . if true."

It's that ellipsis that gets me. *Harrowing*—dot dot dot—*if true*. Like someone pushing me from behind. *Dot dot dot*. Harder, harder, harder.

Now I'm off.

There are other articles, and I find each and every one. One put out by a college paper, titled HE SAID, SHE SAID, BLAH BLAH BLAH. Another calls the "lack of physical evidence shocking." Here I make the mistake of scrolling down to the comments.

Some commentators are restrained enough to write just a word or two, like "LIARS!" or "poor guy" while others write longer comments. "Five minutes, really? Sending a college kid to prison for something that lasted five minutes! Smh, what is this country coming to?" And then there are the tirades that span multiple paragraphs, some longer than the damn article itself, full of hate and typos.

I feel sick to my stomach.

I only hope she hasn't seen any of this bullshit.

There's a knock on my door. "Hey, you awake?" Dominic. "Leaving for the gym. You coming?"

I click the power off on my phone. "Yeah," I call back.

I work out harder than I have in a while. I can't tell if it's anger, sadness, or what that's fueling me. All I know is that something has crawled inside me, and it's making me want to fight it. Coach walks by and gives me a nod of approval.

Part of me wants to stand up and tell him I couldn't give two shits about this fucking team right now. That they're so stupid to think that any of this matters at all. But then I think of my dad, freshly sober, spending hours on the phone trying to save my ass from getting kicked off the team. And I just work harder. Because I don't know what else to do.

She can't get back soon enough.

EDEN

Thursday morning, freshly showered, I sit at my kitchen table. In my dining room with my brother, my mother, my father, sipping orange juice from a glass I've used a million times before. Bacon, pancakes, coffee.

Mom asks if I want sugar and cream. I do, but I shake my head no.

Dad is asking who wants eggs. I don't. But when he comes into the dining room holding the skillet in one hand, scooping up a portion of scrambled eggs, smiling at me, I hold my plate out and take them anyway.

Then we're all sitting here. Chewing. Forks scraping against plates, awkward silence descending over us. I poke at my syrup-soaked pancake. Neither Mom nor Caelin said a word about how it went for them in court yesterday, but I could see their telltale puffy and bloodshot eyes this morning.

“What a fuckin’ week, huh?” I say, just to break the tension.

Caelin laughs, spitting out the sip of juice he’d just taken. “Perfect timing,” he mumbles into a napkin.

Mom scoffs and says, “Edy, good God.”

“So, when you headed back to school?” Dad asks, pretending the tension isn’t happening at all. “Do we at least get you for the weekend?”

I take a sip of my plain coffee, let it burn the roof of my mouth. “I think I’m gonna head out pretty soon, actually. Maybe I can make my last class today, and then I won’t have to miss tomorrow.”

He nods but doesn’t say anything.

“I just don’t want to have so much to make up.”

“And I’m sure you want to get back to Josh, too,” Mom adds. “Your brother showed me his picture online—”

“Mom,” Caelin interrupts. “I didn’t *show* her,” he says to me. “She needed help searching for him on the team website—”

“Oh, fine,” Mom interrupts him back, tossing her napkin in his direction. “I was snooping.”

“*Stalking*,” Caelin mutters through a fake cough.

Dad actually laughs.

“Anyway, he’s a very cute boy,” Mom says. “I don’t blame you for wanting to rush back to him.”

“Well,” I begin. “I really do have work to make up.”

She grins at me from across the table.

“So, Eden,” Dad says. “When do we get to meet this very cute boy?”

“Maybe after you all quit calling him a very cute boy.”

“Hey.” Caelin holds his hand up. “For the record, all I’ve ever called him is a *decent guy*; I never called him a very cute anything."

And just like that, we've had our first semi-normal family interaction in years. I send a silent thank-you across the state to Josh, who's probably walking to his first class right now, for being so damn decent and handsome, he let my family salvage our last morning together.

After breakfast I help clean up, start the dishwasher, try not to act like I'm in a hurry to leave. I pack up a bag of fall clothes, my soft scarf and matching gloves, a heavy coat, and some of my long sleeves and sweaters from the back of my closet. I have to pull out my old clarinet case to get to my boots, and as my fingers fit around the handle, I have this vivid flashback of freshman year, carrying this thing with me everywhere I went. I set it on my bed next to my other bag and open it up.

Like some kind of time capsule from another life, I find the sheet music I was working on when I decided to quit, the booklet still folded open to the exact page. I take each item out and hold them in my hands for a moment: the plastic case for my reeds; polishing cloth, soft against my fingers; the tiny screwdriver everyone always needed to borrow from me because no one else ever had one; the tube of nearly empty cork grease that Mara once mistook for lip balm; the mouthpiece, barrel, bell, upper joint, lower joint . . . all the pieces of the clarinet disassembled and put away neatly. Exactly as I'd left them, not knowing that would be the last time I played.

I'm not sure why, but I take it with me, along with my fuzzy socks and warm clothes.

I say my goodbyes. Caelin hugs me for the first time in months. Dad tells me he just transferred two hundred dollars into my account, for which I am wholeheartedly thankful. Mom walks me out to the car, tells me, "Take care of yourself. Be safe. And let me know when you hear anything from the DA, okay?"

"I will."

The drive home, back to Josh and my new life, which has nothing to do with this old one, feels so long. Too long. My eyes just want to close. I only make it an hour and a half before I have to pull off at a rest stop. I push my seat all the way back and pull one of my big sweaters from the bag in the passenger seat, wrap myself up in it.

Just as I'm feeling myself fading to sleep, I'm back in the courtroom, eyes locked on Kevin's. Then I'm back in my old bedroom, that night, with him looking down on me.

My eyes snap open.

The tree I'm parked beneath is letting the fluttering light filter through the windshield onto my face. It feels so gentle, I allow myself to close my eyes again. The judge is telling me I'm dismissed. "Dismissed." That was the word. How appropriate, I thought, even then.

How had I forgotten this part?

But I can't move. Not until Kevin's dickhead lawyer whispers something to him, making him break eye contact with me. I see Lane and Mara standing up, waiting. DA Silverman nodding, watching me as I step down from the box.

I stare straight down at my feet, but I still feel his eyes on me the whole time.

When I wake up, I'm in the shade now, cold and somehow more exhausted than I was to begin with. I pull my seat upright again and put the sweater on all the way, trying to gather some warmth around me. I dump my travel mug of cold plain coffee from my house and go inside the rest stop for something with sugar and caffeine and calories.

It gets me through the rest of the drive. I make it home in the middle of the afternoon while everyone's still gone for the day. I trudge up the two flights of stairs with my arms full, unlock the door, make it to my room, and sit down directly on the floor.

Breathe. I need to breathe.

I lie flat on my back, close my eyes, and concentrate on the hard floor under me, find the points where the floor supports my body, like my therapist told me.

I place my hand on my stomach and feel it expand and contract with each breath. In and out, over and over. I'm nearly asleep when I hear my phone vibrating from my bag, and I realize I never texted to let anyone know that I made it home.

I sit up too quickly and pull my purse down on the floor, digging through it until my hand finds my phone. But the text waiting there isn't from Josh or my mom; it's from DA Silverman.

I have news . . .

No.

I won't open it. I can't. Whatever it is, I don't want to know yet. Either our case is dead or it's moving forward. And I can't know either of those things right now. I stand, leaving the phone there on the floor. It lights up again, and I kick it away from me this time. It skids across the floor and under the dresser, out of sight.

I lug my bags onto my bed, start unpacking. Keep my hands busy—that's another tip my therapist gave me. I can still hear the vibration of my phone, rattling now, shoved up against the baseboard.

I open my laptop, cue up my moody sad-girl playlist. Florence + the Machine croons out in a darkly lyrical dance. But I can still feel the phone vibrating—inside my chest now, somehow. I turn the volume up.

I put away all my clothes, literally fold every article of clothing, even my bras and underwear. I match up every last sock with its mate and divide half a drawer for all of Josh's clothes I've found lying around. I hang up my sweaters in the closet and line my boots up with my other shoes. Carefully, I slide my clarinet case up on the top shelf of the closet. Next, I organize my desk. Move my hair and makeup stuff over to my dresser. I line up my meds in a row, rounding them out with the packet of birth control pills and the bottle of Tylenol I've been popping like candy all week for my never-ending headaches.

I had an in-person with my therapist on Wednesday. She asked how I'd been feeling with the new meds, and I had to admit that I forget to take them a lot, so I couldn't be sure if they were really helping much. When she asked me why, I didn't tell her it's because I keep them hidden half the time; I just shrugged. The thing is, I know Josh is literally the last person on the planet who would make me feel weird about any of it—he understood about the sleeping pills, as I knew he would. It's me.

So I decide—force myself—to just leave them there, out in the open.

My playlist comes to an abrupt end, plunging me into silence.

I look around. Everything's in order here. Bed made. Books lined up in neat rows. My life ready for me to dive back in. But I don't dive. I drag myself over to my bed. I don't even have the energy to lift the covers. I lay my head on the pillow, curl up inside my sweater, and face the wall, just waiting to feel normal again.

JOSH

After practice, Coach calls us all together for a meeting in the locker room. There's a tightness, a tension in the air. Everyone's tired and hungry and ready to go. I just want to get to my phone to see if she's texted me back yet.

"All right, guys," Coach begins. "Quick announcement. This is coming down directly from the dean. We'll be talking to all the teams, so don't feel special. Okay, I'm sure some of you have heard about the sexual assault case involving a student athlete over at Eastland U."

My heart starts racing.

"Obviously, there's no tolerance for this kind of thing at Tucker Hill," he continues, looking down at his clipboard, reading. "Zero tolerance for any form of harassment or so-called 'locker room talk' on this team or any team on this campus. Got it?"

I look around. There are heads nodding.

Someone raises a hand. "Uh, Coach, has someone complained, or . . . ?"

"No. Thank God. The dean wanted us to preemptively talk with you all, as a reminder that this shit won't fly here."

Okay, so this is just a general PSA. I start to relax.

Coach squints at his clipboard again. "THU will be issuing a formal statement regarding its commitment to . . ." He trails off, skipping ahead. "So, basically, the moral of the story is eyes are on teams like ours right now, and we can't afford any bad press, gentlemen."

Bad press, so that's really all that matters here.

"Such bullshit," I hear someone mutter under their breath. When I look up, Jon, one of the bench players, has a stupid shit-eating grin on his face. He leans in to the guy next to him, whispers something, and I see both of them Jell-O-shaking with silent laughter. Something inside me picks up like a swelling wave, and I can feel my fists tightening at my sides.

Coach dismisses us, and I look around—I completely missed the end of the meeting.

I try to shake off this feeling.

I'm finishing getting dressed at my locker, checking my phone—still nothing from her—when I hear Jon's dumbass guffaw over the bank of lockers.

"You know she wanted it, and then when he didn't want a relationship, she decided to screw his career." That wave returns now, and I can feel my face getting red. "That is exactly why you don't dip your dick in crazy."

I know I shouldn't, but that wave is pushing me down, and

someone else, this other version of myself is rising up instead. I walk around the corner and see Jon toweling off his hair as he regales two freshmen benchers with his opinions.

"I dunno, man," one of them is bold enough to pipe up, "I read there were three girls he did it to. . . ."

"Yeah, well, maybe he's attracted to psychos," Jon says, and shrugs. "Bitches probably want a payout! You know how the pussy is. . . ."

I can't even hear the rest of his sentence because the wave is pushing at me as I step behind him, too close, it pushes past my chest, into my throat, out of my mouth. "Hey, do you ever just shut the fuck up?"

Jon turns, stupid mean grin still on his face, and behind him, the freshmen's eyes go wide—I must be looking like something scary to them.

"Sorry, my bad, did I upset your delicate sensibilities?" he says, patting my shoulder in mock comfort, the spot he touches radiating heat, practically vibrating. I know I should leave, but the other Josh has a point to make.

"No, *I'm* sorry, do you have some kind of problem with not sexually harassing women, or what?"

"Fuck off," he mutters dismissively. "You know what my problem is?"

"No, what's that?" I challenge. "Please, tell me."

"You." Somehow this makes the wave retreat. Me, I can deal with that.

"Me?" I cross my arms. "Okay."

"Yeah, with you half-assing every practice and wasting a

starting spot on the team, and now you're trying to make *me* look bad?" He looks at the crowd, which has suddenly gathered around us, and I can't tell if they're on his side or not.

"You make yourself look bad all on your own."

"And you shouldn't even be here!" he shouts. "Not after what you pulled last season. Everyone thinks so."

Dominic walks up then, interrupts. "Hey, speak for yourself, Jon—why don't you just take off, all right?"

"Why? It's true," he argues.

"No, it's not," Dominic says.

"Whatever." I grab my bag and close my locker. "I don't have time for this."

"Sure, but you have time to push your woke agenda about a bunch of bitches crying rape? Please, you're so—"

And that wave is back—a tidal wave now—no fighting it. It is the buzzing in my head, a tingling in my limbs, this sick rush of adrenaline pulsing through me.

It's oddly quiet for a moment.

And then sound erupts all around us, yelling, shouting.

It takes me a second to process why Dominic is standing between us. Why someone's holding my arms. Why Jon is on the floor. Why Coach is storming in here, screaming, "Break it up, you assholes!"

He drags us both into his office.

"What do you wanna do?" he's asking Jon. "You can lodge a complaint if you want—it's within your rights."

Jon looks at me, sort of smirks, like this is all just an amusement to him. "Nah," he finally says. "It was just a shove. It's really not a big deal."

"Fine." Coach stands, points to the door. "You go," he tells him.

I start to stand as well, but Coach presses down on my shoulder. "You," he orders, through clenched teeth, "siddown."

He closes the door behind Jon and throws his clipboard against the wall, making me jump.

"What the hell is wrong with you?" he yells. "I swear, it's one step forward, twenty steps back with you. Every damn time. Tell me something, do you even want to be on this team?"

I clench my jaw shut so I don't say it: *No*.

"Huh?" he yells. "Well, do you?"

"Yes," I lie.

"Then screw your damn head on right, get your priorities straight!" he shouts, the veins in his neck throbbing. "You're on thin ice—paper thin. One more incident, you're suspended. I don't care how talented you are. I don't give a shit what's going on in your personal life. When you're here, you don't *have* a personal life!" he yells. "You understand me?"

"Yeah, I understand."

It's dark in Eden's room, but I can see her lying on her bed. I'm relieved at first. She's here, she's safe. But the way she's curled up in the fetal position, lying so still, gives me that full-body rush of adrenaline chill again. I feel unsteady as I walk toward her.

EDEN

I wake up to the click of my lamp being turned on. It's dark outside my window. I hear the door latch shut, then his light footsteps behind me. The quiet swish of sneakers being removed. He doesn't need to say a word for me to know it's him. The sigh in his breath might as well be a fingerprint.

The bed sinks as he climbs in softly. He moves my hair and touches my waist as he eases in beside me, bending his knees into mine, fitting himself around me like a missing puzzle piece. He slowly moves his arm so that it's resting on top of mine.

"Hey," I breathe, pulling his arm around me tighter.

"Sorry," he whispers, kissing the back of my neck. "I was trying not to wake you."

"No, it's okay," I say, my voice still worn and raspy. "What time is it?"

"It's, like, almost eight."

"Mm." I stretch out a little and clear my throat. "I've been asleep all afternoon."

With his face in my hair, he breathes in and says, "God, I missed you." He grips my sweater in handfuls, pulling me so close. There's something about it, the way he's holding me like he's scared I'm going to float away, that makes me nervous.

"Josh?" I turn around to face him. "What's wrong?"

"Nothing." He touches my face and smiles, but it doesn't quite reach his eyes. "Nothing's wrong," he repeats, this sadness in his voice. "I just really missed you."

I kiss him. "I missed you too."

He wraps both arms around me, pressing me to his body, kissing my hair, my forehead, my cheeks.

"Wait, let me look at you." I pull away from him enough to see him more clearly and take his face in my hands. "Aw, your beard is back."

"Stubble," he corrects, and finally he gives me a small but real smile.

"Okay, fine, stubble," I repeat. "I like it."

"College era me, right?" he asks, the slightest laugh in his voice.

"More like sexy-era you," I tease, though I'm really not joking at all.

He buries his face in my neck and laughs.

"I love when you get all shy."

"Shy?" he repeats slowly, letting his head rest on my chest, like he's trying to remember what the word means, whether it's a good or bad thing.

"It's very cute."

"Okay," he says quietly.

"Hey, are you really all right?" I ask him.

"Yeah." He raises his head to look at me then. "I'm more concerned about how you are."

"You just seem kinda sad."

"No, I'm fine. I just didn't sleep much while you were gone and, I don't know, I was worried when I didn't hear from you earlier."

"Oh. Sorry, my phone—" I glance over toward my dresser. "It's under there. I forgot to pick it up. Sorry."

"No, don't be sorry." He takes my rebandaged hand in his and kisses it—examines my haphazard placement of Band-Aids for a moment but doesn't comment on it. "I'm glad you were resting."

"I'm glad you came," I tell him, running my other hand over his face.

"So, how are you feeling?" he asks.

"Okay." I prop myself up so I can kiss him. He nods like he wants more from me. "Better now that you're here."

He kisses me softly, quickly, like he's consciously not wanting it to get too steamy.

"You don't want to kiss me," I say. "What, do I have bad breath or something?"

He scoffs. "No, come on."

He rolls onto his back, and I try to tell myself he's not moving away from me; he's making room for me, inviting me in. So I kiss him. I kiss him deeper and deeper. He holds on to me, his hands on my hips, but he's not giving me much.

I push his shirt up and kiss his stomach—that spot that always makes him squirm. He at least lets out a little sigh, a deep breath in, a small groan. I move on top of him and sit up, one knee on either side of his hips, and pull my sweater off. The T-shirt I wore underneath starts to come off with it, but he reaches out and pulls it down, his fingers barely grazing my skin as he covers my stomach back up.

He gazes at me and opens his mouth like he wants to say something.

"What?"

"Nothing." He places his hands on my thighs, watches as I take my T-shirt off.

He sits up now, with me in his lap, and kisses me once, lets his forehead rest against the center of my chest. I reach around behind me to unfasten my bra, but his hand catches mine and brings it back around the front, holding it in his.

"Eden." He breathes my name out slowly. "Hold on, don't you wanna talk?"

"What do you mean?"

"Well, just to catch up, you know?" he says so gently. "You've been gone."

"Oh," I say. "My God, am I being like a horny teenage boy right now or something?"

He cracks a smile and shakes his head. "I mean . . . I wouldn't say it like that."

"I'm sorry, okay," I tell him, scooting so I'm sitting a bit farther back on his thighs instead of right up against him. "Yeah, please. Talk to me."

"No, I meant I want *you* to talk to me."

"What about?"

He turns his head, sort of tips his hands open toward the ceiling. "Everything. What happened while you were gone, with the hearing and all? How it was being home. I mean, do you know what happens next? You haven't really told me anything."

I climb off him now.

"Eden, don't—"

"Don't what?"

"Don't shut me out," he says, reaching for me.

"I feel like you're the one shutting me out right now," I tell him.

He squints at me. "How am *I* shutting you out?"

"You, like, clearly aren't interested in having sex with me," I mumble as I pull my sweater back on over my head and shove my arms through the sleeves. "What, am I too sad and pathetic?"

"No, who said anything like that?"

"Too damaged? Too messed up?" I continue, gaining steam. "What, tainted?"

"Hey!" he says, his voice stern. "You know that's not what I think." He pauses, his chest moving in and out as he breathes heavier. "Don't put words into my mouth—that's not what we—we don't do that."

"Well, I feel like you're rejecting me or something."

I climb over him to get out of the bed. I walk to my dresser, have the urge to take one of my pills. Then I have the greater urge to open up the top drawer and sweep them all inside, close it up tight.

"I'm not rejecting you; I'm just not going to have sex with you when I have no idea where your head's at right now. I'm worried about you, okay?"

I look over at him, sitting there, so in control of his emotions, so perfectly rational all the time, always doing the right thing. I sit down in my desk chair, try to slow my racing thoughts, try to calm myself, try to feel the chair under me, feel my feet on the floor.

"I know, I'm sorry."

"Don't be sorry," he says, moving to the edge of the bed, reaching for my hands. "I just feel like I'm in the dark here."

"I don't want to talk about the hearing."

"Okay." He reaches for the arms of the chair now and pulls me toward him so we're facing each other. "That's fine, just tell me how you're feeling, then?"

"I feel . . . ," I begin, closing my eyes, letting him take my hands again. "I feel like . . ." I search my brain for anything, a concrete thought, a fleeting image. "A pumpkin," I tell him. *That's stupid.*

"A pumpkin?" he asks. He draws his eyebrows together like he's not sure if I'm being serious or joking. I don't really know at this point either.

"No, not a pumpkin, but like a jack-o'-lantern. You know?"

"Okay," he says, nodding.

"Like someone drew a face on me and carved it into my skin. Scooped out my insides. Just hollowed out, everything scraped clean. And then lit a fire in me and left me out in the cold. And I just . . ." I stop because I'm hearing myself and I feel my mouth twitching, like I could either start bawling or laughing, and I don't know which. Because I don't know if I'm being ridiculous or if this is actually the perfect sloppy metaphor for the way I feel right now.

"And you what?" he asks, giving my good hand a tiny squeeze.

"And I just, I don't know, want to feel human again," I finish. "As soon as possible."

His eyes get really deep as he watches me. And then his beautiful mouth just sort of collapses at the corners. He stands and pulls me up out of the chair too. Holds me close, pressing my face against his chest, kissing my hair.

JOSH

As we stand in the middle of her room, I can sense it—that hollowed-out feeling—coming out of her and crawling into me.

"I'm so sorry," I whisper because I don't know what else to say.

"You didn't do anything," she mumbles into my shirt, hugging me back like somehow she knows I might need her arms around me right now just as much as she needs mine.

"I'm still sorry."

"Don't feel sorry for me, Josh." She looks up at me, her eyes so full and open. "Please."

"No, it's not that I feel sorry *for* you. I just feel sorry that you're having to go through all this. It's not fair. And I wish I could do something to—to help or to make it easier."

"You do help, though." She sets her head against me again. "You do make it easier."

"What do you want to do tonight?" I ask her. "Are you hungry at all, or do you want to go back to bed . . . watch a movie? It's whatever you want."

"Could we lie back down?"

As we get undressed, she starts taking her pants off and looks up at me with this small, mischievous grin. "I promise I'm not trying to have sex with you again; I'm just getting into pajamas."

"Stop," I groan, folding my jeans over the back of her chair. "You know why I said that."

"I'm just messing with you." She takes her sweater off again and hangs it on the doorknob of her closet, walks over to her dresser in a mismatched bra and underwear, looking so beautiful I almost wish she would try to have sex with me because I need to feel human again now too. She pulls out one of my T-shirts I hadn't even realized I'd left here. "Can I wear this?" she asks.

"Sure," I answer, trying not to sound too enthusiastic about seeing her in my clothes. But as I watch her take her bra off and slide on my old beat-up gray T-shirt with a hole in the collar, my feet won't let me not go to her. "By the way, I pretty much want to have sex with you constantly."

"Oh, *constantly*?" she repeats, laughing as she gently pushes me away.

"I'm not kidding. I think about it way more than I should." I follow her to the bed. "Truly, you'd be offended if you knew."

She's smiling as she pulls back the covers and climbs in first, but then she looks up at me with her eyes narrowed, like she's confused about why I'm saying this.

"So, I would never reject you," I tell her as I climb in beside her.

"Oh," she murmurs.

I kiss her the way she was kissing me earlier—deep, serious. "Never," I repeat. "Okay?"

"Okay," she whispers.

As we lie here, she curls up around me, her head on my chest, her arm and leg draped across me. I start to feel more like myself than I have all week. We breathe in and out together, and I can feel her drifting to sleep when her phone vibrates from somewhere in the room, muffled. I look around and notice that she's cleaned, rearranged things.

The phone keeps going off. She sighs loudly.

"Do you need to check that?" I ask her.

"I don't want to," she whines.

"It might be important."

"I know it's important, that's why I don't want to get it." She rolls off me and says quietly, "It's under the dresser."

I don't ask why it's under there; I just get out of bed and tell her, "I'll get it." But as I walk up to her dresser, my eyes go directly to the pills lined up on top of it. I glance back at her. She sees me seeing them.

"My full pharmacy," she explains. "Insomnia, depression, anxiety."

I nod. "Okay," I say because I don't know if there's anything else I should say. I'm happy she's not hiding them anymore, but I can't say that without letting her know that I knew about them already. I kneel down and press my face to the floor, see the phone all the way against the wall, glowing. I reach for it and pull it out, trying not to look at the screen.

I walk back over to her and hand her the phone, but she's just staring at me. "Does that bother you?"

"What?"

"Those," she says, gesturing to the dresser, the pills.

"No, they don't bother me. Why would they bother me?"

"Because of your dad."

"You need them, Eden. It's totally different."

"Yeah," she whispers sadly, holding her phone facedown against her chest. "I do."

She curls up to me again and breathes deeply, finally raises the phone.

I glance down. There's a whole screen full of notifications she's missed. Texts from me, her brother, Mara, someone named Lane, two missed calls from her mom. And a text from "DA Silverman." This is the one she opens.

"Sorry." I kiss her head, close my eyes. "I'm not looking, okay?" I tell her.

"You can." She tilts the screen toward me. "It's happening."

> I have news and wanted to make sure you're the first to know: we're going to trial. Congratulations, you girls did it! I'll be in touch when I know more, but plan for sometime in December, possibly January. Talk soon.

"Eden, this is really good," I start, but she clicks the phone off, reaches over me and tosses it onto her desk. She shakes her head and pulls herself against me tighter, tucking her head down so I can't see her face.

"Eden?" I try to get her to look at me. "Baby?"

She's clutching my shirt, breathing heavy, sniffling. And then I feel her body start shaking. She's crying. "I can't," she gasps, finally looking up at me, tears streaming down her face. "I can't do it again."

I kiss her forehead, try to wipe her tears away. "Yes, you can."

"No," she breathes. "I can't. I really can't."

"It's okay," I tell her, even though I don't know that for sure. I don't know if it's okay or if she's okay or if it will be okay. But I say it anyway.

She keeps repeating it: *I can't.* She says it over and over until it doesn't even sound like words anymore, just breathing. And then, after what feels like forever, she finally stills, falls silent. I think she's asleep, but then she says, her voice clear, calm now. "His lawyer asked me if I ever said no."

I raise my head. "What do you mean?"

"Like he assumed I was given a choice. Like I could choose to say yes or no. And I couldn't explain that there was nothing to say yes or no to—there wasn't a chance to say it—but he just kept interrupting me."

"Fuck," I say.

"But just because I couldn't say no doesn't mean I said yes, either."

"I know that."

She kisses me, then touches my face, just looks at me.

"I love you," I tell her, and I start to worry I'm saying it so much she's going to stop believing that I mean it.

She smiles and closes her eyes for a moment. "I don't know what I would do without you, Josh."

"Yeah," I agree. "Back atcha."

"It's sort of scary," she whispers, like it's a secret, "how much I need you."

"Don't be scared," I tell her, even though it scares me, too, how much I need her. "You won't ever have to be without me. I mean, unless you wanted that."

She looks me in the eye now, holding my face steady in her hands. "I would never want that."

I wake up to her moaning in her sleep. She's thrashing. Having a nightmare. "Eden?" I whisper.

"No," she moans, kicking my leg under the blanket. "No."

"Hey, hey, hey, Eden?" I try. "Eden, wake up."

I touch her face, but she turns away from me. "Stop," she says, her hand flopping lifelessly against my stomach. "Please," she whimpers, crying with her whole body.

I touch her arm now, try to rub it gently. "Eden," I repeat, louder this time.

She starts coughing, gasping, and then her hand goes to her throat, all the veins and tendons in her neck visible like she really can't breathe. I've got to get her to wake up somehow. "Eden!" I shake her shoulder.

Her eyes fly open, and she bolts up, swinging at me. She scratches my neck with one hand, my chest with the other. I grab her arms. "Eden, stop."

She screams, "Let go of me, let go of me!"

I do, but she hits me over and over. She's breathing so heavily, gasping for air. I back up against the wall, but then she's backing up too, about to fall right out of bed, so I lunge forward to grab her again. She's kicking me with both her feet. This time she cries just one word: "Mom."

"Eden, wake up!" I shout, but she doesn't hear me.

She yells, "Stop." I don't know what to do—she's going to hurt herself. But I let go of her arms, and I can do nothing but watch her fall. The sound is terrible—she hits the desk and her lamp crashes down, part of the glass shade breaking, but it's still on, lighting her at this severe angle that makes her look haunted. She looks up at me like I pushed her or something, like it hurts her to look at me.

"Eden?" I scramble to get down on the floor with her, but she flinches away when I reach for her. She looks around the room: at the lamp, me, her skinned knees bleeding, the palms of her hands scraped. "Eden," I repeat. I kneel next to her and she holds her arms out, but I can't tell if she's reaching for me or trying to keep me away. "Hey, it's just me. It's just me. You're okay."

"What?" her voice squeaks. "What happened?"

"You were having a nightmare. You—you fell out of bed," I stutter, trying to give her the gentlest version of the truth.

Parker's pounding on the door now, which makes her jump. "Eden?" Parker calls. "Eden, are you okay?"

Eden looks at me like she's not sure how to answer, but I don't think I should answer for her because I don't know either.

"Eden!" She knocks some more. "I'm coming in."

She opens the door, and her eyes go to the broken lamp, then to Eden, huddling against the wall, arms around her knees, then to me, crouching next to her. "What's happening in here?" she says to me, then to Eden, "Are you okay?"

"Yeah, I—I'm okay," Eden tells her.

Parker narrows her eyes at me. "Did you fucking hit her?"

"NO!" we both shout at the same time.

"Oh my God, Parker, no," Eden says, seeming to snap out of it, the focus coming back into her eyes. "It's okay, really. I was having a bad dream. I fell."

"You were screaming," Parker says.

Eden shakes her head. "I don't—I don't know. I don't remember that."

"I'm gonna go get something for these cuts, okay?" I tell her. "I'll be right back."

Parker follows me into the bathroom. "What the fuck, Josh?" she mutters under her breath.

"It's like she said, she had a really bad nightmare. I was trying to wake her up, and I freaked her out even more. That's all." I open the medicine cabinet, where I'd found the bandages for her hand last week. I get Band-Aids and a tube of ointment. "I swear to you I would never hit her."

"Did she hit you, though?" she asks.

"No!"

"Josh, look at yourself," she says.

I close the cabinet and look in the mirror. I'm bleeding. Scratches on my neck, my chest. The red welts of early bruises on my arms and chest and stomach. I look down at my legs. Marks on my thighs and shins. "I'm fine. She didn't even know what was happening." I turn away from her to wet a washcloth in the sink. My hands are shaking.

"Josh," Parker says. "Are you okay?"

"I don't want to leave her by herself," I tell her instead of answering, because the answer is *No, I'm not fucking okay*. "It's gonna be fine."

"Okay," she says, not convinced.

Back in Eden's room, she hasn't moved; she's just staring at the floor. I reach for her lamp and set it back on her desk because it hurts to look at her like this too. I set the Band-Aids and ointment and washcloth on her desk and reach my hands down to help her up, but she doesn't even look at me.

"Eden?" I sit next to her on the floor. "Can you hear me?"

"What happened?" she asks again, finally looking at me.

"You were just dreaming, okay?"

"No, I wasn't—this was different."

"Let's get you up. Hold on to me, all right? Arms around my neck."

She lets me help her up off the floor and set her on the bed. "I'm just gonna clean these real quick," I tell her, reaching for the washcloth and pressing it against her knee.

"Oh my God, Josh." She touches my neck, presses her hand against my chest. "I scratched you. I'm so sorry."

"It's okay," I tell her as I apply a row of Band-Aids to one knee. "That was fucking stupid of me to try to wake you up like that. It's my fault, I'm sorry."

"I thought you were him—I didn't know."

"No, I know." I bring the washcloth to her other knee, and she draws in a sharp breath. "Does that hurt?" I ask her.

She takes the washcloth from me, folds it over to the clean

side, and brings it to my neck, dabbing at it gently, her hands shaking so badly. "I'm so sorry."

"I'm fine," I tell her as I finish putting Band-Aids on her other knee. "I promise."

I get up and put my shirt on. She's already freaked out about the scratches; she doesn't need to see the bruises, too. "Do you want to keep the light on still?"

She shakes her head and gets back into bed.

I turn the lamp off, avoiding the broken glass.

Lying back down next to her, I feel uneasy. Afraid. Not of her, exactly, but of the things haunting her. She lays her head down in the spot she always lays her head down in and drapes her arm across me the way she always does. But everything feels different.

"I love you," she says. "Josh?"

"Yeah?"

"I love you," she repeats.

"I love you too."

"Are you mad?"

"Of course not," I tell her. I'm a lot of things right now, but mad—at her, anyway—isn't one of them. "Eden, does that happen a lot? Having nightmares like that, I mean."

"Sometimes," she answers. "It hasn't been this bad in a long time, though. I know I scared you. I'm sorry."

"Will you stop apologizing?" But then I worry I might sound too harsh. "Really, you don't have anything to be sorry about."

"Okay, I'll stop," she whispers. She touches my chest in the spot where she scratched me and kisses my shirt—it stings as the fabric rubs against my open skin.

"Eden, can I ask you something else?"

"Mm-hmm," she mumbles.

"Are you getting help for all this? More than the meds. Like counseling or something?"

"Yes."

"Really?"

"Yeah, I have a therapist back home. We talk once a week."

"Is it helping?"

"Mostly, I think."

"Good, I'm glad."

She gets so quiet for so long, I think she's fallen asleep. But then she raises her head to look at me and says, "What about you?"

"What? Sorry, what about me?"

"Have you ever seen anyone—I mean, for the stuff with your dad? Or just in general?"

"Oh." I think back to the Alateen meetings my mom brought me to when I was in middle school. "When I was younger, I went to a few group meetings but . . ."

"But what?" she asks me.

I shrug. "They just weren't for me, I guess." But as we lie here, I remember more clearly. That's not what happened. The meetings conflicted with basketball and I stopped going.

"Hey, you should really try to sleep, okay?" I tell her. "I'll be here the whole time."

EDEN

His alarm goes off at five, like every other morning. Except he doesn't wake up to it. And he's not holding me like he was when we fell asleep. He's facing away. I reach across him for his phone and snooze the alarm.

I whisper his name and touch his shoulder, run my hand along the side of his face. Nothing. "Josh?" I repeat, slightly louder.

He flinches awake. "Oh, what, what's wrong?"

"Nothing, nothing. Your alarm went off."

He takes a deep breath in and rolls onto his back, at least a little closer to me. "How is it morning already?" he groans.

"I know." I prop myself up next to him and look down at his face. My eyes travel to the cuts on his neck—they look even worse. I lean in and kiss the red lines as softly as I can.

He reaches up and touches my face, my hair. "It's okay," he whispers, reading my mind.

I lie against him, and he kind of tenses up before he puts his arm around me.

"I technically still have the day off," I tell him. "So I'm gonna try to get a call with my therapist today."

"Okay, that sounds good."

"Would you—no, never mind."

"No, what?" he asks. The alarm goes off again. "Dammit," he says, reaching to turn it off. "Would I what?"

"Would you . . . ?" I was going to ask if he'd be on the call, to tell her what happened, to tell *me* what happened too, but I feel like it's not fair to ask him to relive it. "Would you just hold me for a few more minutes before you go?" I ask instead.

"Yeah, come here," he says—of course he does. He rolls onto his side and wraps me up in his arms.

"Tighter," I say.

He pulls me closer, kisses my hair, and whispers, "I love you."

And for nine blissful minutes, things feel okay.

But then the alarm blares again.

He sighs. "I gotta get up, baby."

I watch him as he gets out of bed and turns my lamp on. He reaches into his bag for clothes, and even as he takes his shirt off, I notice he's keeping his back to me. "Josh?"

"Yeah?" he answers, still turned away.

I get out of bed and step around to the front of him. He quickly picks up a pair of joggers and sort of holds them in front of his body like he's trying to cover himself.

"What are you doing?" I ask, reaching for the pants.

"Eden, don't—" he says, but then lets go of them.

And then I see what he's hiding.

"Oh my God," I mumble, my hand over my mouth. "Did I—" I swallow hard. I feel the tears already swelling up under my eyes as they take in the dark purple bruises all over his arms, chest, stomach, even his legs. "Did I do this to you?"

"Come here come here come here," he says, pulling me in and holding me tight. "Shh, it's not your fault, okay? I'm fine."

"No," I say, shaking my head back and forth. Because this looks too familiar, the bruises up and down his body, just like my own bruises the next morning. I reach for my chair and have to sit down because my legs feel weak.

"Please look at me." He kneels on the floor in front of me. "You had no idea what was happening, okay? You weren't here; you were there."

I slide down to the floor too, touch the bruises. "What did I do?"

"You were just trying to get away from me—from him, I mean," he explains, but I still can't believe it.

"How could I have done all this?" I say out loud. But the other part of the sentence that I don't say out loud is: How could I have done all this to him, my love, the one person I feel safe with, when I couldn't do anything to defend myself against Kevin that night? And then I realize the difference, as he watches me with those soft, dark eyes. Josh wasn't fighting me off. He was just taking it.

"I grabbed you. I was trying to help, but I didn't know what to do, Eden. So, I grabbed you because I . . ." He let his hands float down my arms, to these reddish-purple rings around the forearm on my right side and my wrist on the left. "Eden, I swear I didn't mean to hurt you. You were falling, and I was afraid you were gonna hurt yourself, and I know I made it worse." He looks at me, his eyes filling with tears now. "I'm so sorry," he belts out quickly as he hunches forward and covers his face with his hands.

"No, I'm sorry, Josh. I'm so sorry. I'm sorry," I tell him over and over. I pull him toward me, and I know I will never forgive myself for this. We collapse onto the floor in each other's arms, both of us crying now. "I'm trying, I swear," I tell him.

"I know," he says. "I am too."

JOSH

It was just a week ago we were in my room dancing to no music, celebrating, and now I'm here on the floor, afraid that I'm losing her all over again.

We stay like this, tangled up in each other, for so long the sun comes up.

"Josh?" she finally says, repositioning herself so she's sitting with her back against the side of the bed.

I sit up straighter too, and she starts touching my face so gently, the only thing I want to do is crawl back into bed with her and sleep this all off.

"I want you to know," she begins. "I'm going to tell Parker about the trial and everything. I can't stand her thinking even for one second that you would do something to hurt me. I'll explain it all to her, okay?"

"You don't have to do that," I tell her. "Not on my account. Really."

"No, I've wanted to tell her for a while, anyway. I just couldn't find the right time—but this is the right time, I know."

"Only if it's what you want to do."

"It is."

I take a few breaths, practice the words a couple times in my head first. "You might get upset," I start, "but you should know I told my parents about the assault—the trial and everything. I know I'm not supposed to be talking about it, but—"

"No, it's okay," she says so quietly I can't tell if there's any uneasiness behind the words. "It's okay."

"Is it, though?" I ask. "Is it okay?"

She nods. "I mean, I trust your judgment—God, I trust your judgment more than mine. I know you're not going to be telling people you don't trust, who don't *need* to know, right?"

"Right. No, of course," I assure her. "It was just getting hard to keep it a secret."

"I get it. It's been a secret for too long. It's just . . ."

I wait, but she doesn't finish.

"Hey, I know you're probably worrying about getting to practice," she says. "Go, really, you should go."

"Okay," I tell her even though practice is the farthest thing from my mind right now, but I'll go if that's what she wants. "Are you sure you're gonna be all right here, alone?"

"Of course, yeah," she says. She even smiles. "I promise. I think I'll probably just go back to sleep for a bit."

I'm shaky as I get to my feet. Almost weak, brittle feeling, as I take her hand and help her up off the floor. Dizzy as I get dressed and lean down to kiss her. Scared as I say "I love you." Unsteady as I leave her room and close the door behind me.

I make it to morning practice almost forty-five minutes late. Jon shakes his head when I walk into the gym. "Seriously?" he says out loud, looking around.

I don't even have the strength to get mad at him or try to defend myself, so I say nothing.

Dominic calls me over to the bench press. "Yo, Miller. Spot me." When I get over there, he says, under his breath, "Are you crazy showing up late after yesterday?" I barely have the energy to put two words together, though, to explain.

"I know" is all I can manage.

"I told Coach you had a last-minute problem with an assignment."

"Thanks," I tell him.

I grip the bar with both hands—thankful I'm not so shaky anymore, my blood pumping back through my body again—and help him with the lift-off.

"Got it," he says.

We take turns spotting each other, and I feel grateful that somehow he knows I shouldn't be alone right now. I keep catching him watching me too closely, but thankfully, he waits until after practice to ask me, when we're alone in the locker room.

"Parker called me in the middle of the night, you know. She was really scared. By the time I got down there, I guess it was over, whatever happened, but . . ." He gestures to the scratches on my neck; I pull my collar up. "Be real with me, what's going on with you? First you start a fight with Jon. Now whatever this is with Eden?"

"I didn't start that—"

"No," he interrupts, holding up his hands. "He was being a total prick, I know, but you laid hands on him first. That's not you."

"I know," I sigh. "It's all just a long, complicated thing, I don't know . . ."

"I got time."

So, we skip our first classes and get breakfast instead. I tell him everything that's been going on. With me, with Eden. The trial. Last night. Everything.

"Damn, that's some heavy shit." He shakes his head. "I had no idea."

"Yeah, well, I didn't exactly want you to, but I just feel like I'm in over my head. Like, I've honestly never been so scared in my life. I don't know what to do. If this happens again, what do I do?"

"This is only a question, I'm not trying to be a dick," he says, prefacing something I'm sure I'm not going to like. "But is she worth all this to you?"

"Of course," I answer right away—there's no question about it.

"No, I mean really, because this is a lot. A lot for anyone, even you."

"Dominic. Stop. She's worth it." But I feel myself getting all emotional again—angry, sad, it's becoming harder to even know the difference anymore. "You know, this is all happening because literally everyone in her life has treated her like she's not worth it for so long."

"I get it," he says. "I do. I really do." He pauses. "If you're in this for the long haul, maybe you need to talk to someone too. Because you know I got your back, but I have no clue what to tell you in this situation."

"I don't know. Maybe."

"You know I love you man, but as your friend, can I be honest?"

"Yeah, okay."

"You're starting to spiral again," he says. "Like before."

PART FOUR

November

EDEN

It's been over a month since the nightmare, and things are finally getting back to normal. I'd taken an anxiety pill before Parker and I left the apartment. It's extra slow to kick in tonight, though, as I sit in the stands by myself, chaos erupting around me.

Someone taps me on the shoulder and gestures to the seat next to me. "It's taken, sorry!" I shout, but it's so loud in here, I can barely even hear myself. I set my coat down and try to create a mental bubble while I wait for Parker to get back from the bathroom. But it doesn't work; I can still feel the sweat on my palms. I can smell too many people in too small a place. I can see the wooden court shining like a lake that might swallow us all up.

The game won't even start for a half hour and the energy in here is already insane. Everything is . . . too much. I guess the first home game of the season is a big deal. It's so different from what I remember the last time I attended one of my brother's high school games, when I was still in middle school and could tuck myself away into a corner and read, somehow managing to block everything else out.

When we were lying in bed this morning, Josh told me I didn't have to come tonight—he knew I'd have trouble with a crowd this size. But when I said I wanted to, he laughed, reminding me that when we were in high school, I once told him that I'd never be the girl cheering him on at his games.

"Never," he emphasized, teasing me.

"Oh my God," I groaned into the pillow. "Why did you even like me back then?"

"Hey, I thought it was funny," he told me.

"It was *mean*."

"No, really, I found your honesty . . ." He paused, looking at the ceiling for the word. "Refreshing."

"Lucky for me," I said.

He smiled at me so sweetly I wanted to stay in bed, but I had to get ready for my shift at the café. When I got out of the shower and came back into my room wrapped in a towel that only just covered me, I thought he'd fallen asleep again, so I tried to be quiet as I started gathering my clothes.

But then he sighed quietly through the word "*God*."

I turned around to see him watching me.

"What?" I asked, but just the sound of his voice, that way, had already stirred up all these butterflies floating around in my stomach.

"How has it been so long since I've seen you like this?" he asked, sitting up.

"We've been busy," I told him, but that's only part of the truth.

The other part was the harder part to admit—that something happened that night neither of us has quite recovered from yet.

I walked over to the bed to kiss him, but he lingered there, taking my hands, pulling me closer. "You smell so good," he mumbled against my neck. As I drew back, the side of his face was all wet from my hair. I laughed and wiped his cheek with the corner of my towel.

He touched my stomach and brought his hands to my hips, then up to the spot in the center of my chest where I tucked the edge of the towel in to hold it in place. Then he gazed up at me, a look in his eye I haven't seen in a while. "Do you have a few minutes?"

"A few," I answered.

He crept over, making space for me. "Come back to bed for a little bit?"

As I lay next him, he kissed me and then studied my face for a few moments, running his finger along the scar above my eyebrow, smiling as he leaned down to kiss it. Then he kissed my mouth again, my neck, moving down, taking his time even though we didn't really have the time.

The towel peeled away from my body easily. I forgot about the clock.

Because his touch . . . his mouth on my skin, his hands. I couldn't remember the last time it felt easy like this. To just give in and let go and get lost. I reached down to touch him too, wanted him to feel as good as he was making me feel. But he took my hand and brought my arm up over my head, held it there, gently, for only a second.

"I feel greedy," I explained.

"Greedy?" he mumbled as he laughed with his mouth against my stomach. "Oh, if you had any idea how much I'm enjoying this, you would think I'm the greedy one. Besides, no pregaming for me."

"Oh, is that a rule?"

He nods. "Kinda."

"And I know you'd never break a rule."

"Well, there's no rule about after a game, though."

I got in trouble for being fifteen minutes late to work, but nothing could ruin my high. Not my asshole manager, not the rude businessmen or the distracted soccer moms, not even spilling an espresso all over a customer's shirt. Because I could just close my eyes, feel my heart racing again, and remember how unimportant everything else is.

I hold out my phone now and take a few selfies with the crowd in the background: one with a thumbs-up, another with a wink, another with a huge cheesy smile, and one of me blowing him a kiss. He hearts them all immediately and writes:

> I've been thinking about this morning all day long

"What are you smiling about?" Parker asks as she squeezes in next to me.

"Just a little pregame encouragement. What do you say before a game? Not break a leg?"

"God no, please don't say that! How about a simple 'good luck,'" she suggests, watching as I text him. "I'm glad you guys are doing better," she says, and gives my shoulder a little shake—she's been so supportive ever since I filled her in on everything, kind of like the sister I never had. I'm about to tell her that, when the cheerleaders come out and everyone around us gets on their feet, starts clapping and yelling.

They're all so pretty in their sparkly makeup and hair all done up and their perfect bodies. I find myself wondering if any of Josh's teammates saw the selfies I'd just sent him. Would they say, *Huh, well, she doesn't look like much*? Not compared to these girls. Jocks can be ruthless. But then, all guys can be ruthless.

When the teams come out, everyone stands up again and cheers. I spot Josh. His jersey is number 12, just like it was in high school. *How did I not know that?*

I can't take my eyes off him the whole time. It's like I'm experiencing this entirely different version of him. He looks so graceful, moving quickly and jumping and passing the ball like it's nothing. I'm sort of in awe, how he can just show himself like this, put himself out there, in front of all these people.

He looks up at me when they're in the middle of a huddle and smiles. I feel flattered, then giddy. But there's something else following right behind. It's a sinking feeling that settles into my stomach in the place where those butterflies were fluttering earlier, like someone just threw a bunch of gravel on top of them, smothering out their fire, destroying their wings. And with that image, I name the feeling: unworthy. I'm strangely, suddenly, acutely unworthy.

I close my eyes, trying to summon that light, airy, throbbing, aching release I'd felt just this morning. But it's gone now. I try to tell myself it's probably just the anxiety meds kicking in.

Afterward, Parker and I hang out by the locker room, waiting for Josh and Dominic. And as they come out, there are girls—and guys—waiting here too, ready to gush all over them. I stand back and wait for him to come to me. He kisses me right there in front of everyone, jostling that heavy stone of unworthiness around in my stomach. Part of me wants to stop him, say, *Josh, wait, what will they think of you—being with me? I'm nothing. And you're . . .*

I look down for a moment, and when I look back up, he's got this amused sort of grin on his face. "What?" I ask.

"Shy girl night?" he asks quietly, knowing me so well. "We don't have to go out with them. It's okay."

"No, let's go. I'll be fine."

"Yeah?"

"Yeah, besides, we should celebrate."

He shakes his head and laughs. "We lost."

"Oh, right." I knew that, but I guess my brain sort of misplaced the importance of the whole winning-losing concept in its attempt to make me stay present through the whole thing. "Well, so what? All the more reason to celebrate."

"Hey, I agree with your girlfriend, Miller," says a guy I know must've been playing just now, but I didn't really register anyone but Josh. He introduces himself and is friendly enough, but I forget his name immediately.

We walk to the restaurant, arm in arm, lagging behind the rest of the group. It's the kind of perfectly chilled yet not too cold early-November night that makes me love that my birthday is coming in just a few days.

"You're quiet," he says.

"Sorry."

"No, you don't have to be sorry. I just noticed, that's all."

"Oh. I was just thinking about the weather. It's really nice out."

He looks up at the sky, the clouds moving above us, faster than we're walking.

"I mean, I was also thinking about the game," I add. "I've never sat through an entire basketball game before, like actually paying close attention."

"Even with your brother playing all those years?"

I shake my head. "I never cared very much. But, Josh," I say, more seriously. "You were so good."

He laughs. "Again, we lost."

"Well, forgive me. I was just watching you the whole time—I wasn't really keeping track of anything else." *The way you move your body*—I feel my cheeks burning.

"Me?" he says with a laugh.

"Yes, you." I pull him closer to me, and our feet shuffle along in slow motion as we gaze at each other. "I don't know, I never thought I was one of those girls."

"One of what girls?"

"You know what I'm talking about. One of the five hundred girls here tonight who are probably going to go home and fantasize about you."

He smiles and narrows his eyes at me, head cocked just slightly like he doesn't quite believe that this is a thing. God, he's so cute when he doesn't know how cute he is.

"I'm just saying if you got sick of me, you could have an upgrade in under a minute."

He stops smiling now and rolls his eyes, resumes walking at a non-dreamy pace.

"No, I'm just saying . . . you have options."

"Do you have to do that?" he asks. "I'm not interested in options."

"Okay, but I'm just saying there were like a dozen very pretty girls in my immediate vicinity who would—"

"Oh my God," he groans. "Stop."

"I'm just being honest—I thought you said earlier you liked that about me."

"Well, now you're being mean," he whispers, leaning close to me. "To yourself."

JOSH

We go out with some of the team after the game to a restaurant nearby. Parker joins, I think to make Eden more comfortable. Lucas drove up for the weekend to be with Dominic. I told them I'd clear out of the apartment—stay with Eden and give them some space.

I wasn't sure I even wanted to go out tonight; part of me was hoping she'd say no, but now that we're here, it's actually nice. I forget sometimes how I love seeing her out like this; I can admire her differently than when it's just us. I notice new things or remember old ones. Like how she doesn't seem to have any interest in small talk—something I forget until I see her in social situations like these—to the point of almost coming off as a little rude. But then she pays such close attention when she's in a conversation with someone, talking about something real. She commits to it and doesn't let herself get distracted. That was, after all, how she got me hooked on her to begin with. She forced me to be real because she had no use for the other version of me, the one who could make polite chitchat with anyone, all day long, without ever once saying anything that mattered.

She's deep in conversation with Luke now—from what I can overhear, it sounds like they were in band together in high school. I'd forgotten Eden told me once that she'd played some kind of instrument. I start to ignore my own conversation to join in theirs instead.

I shout over the noisy restaurant, "What did you use to play again?"

Luke points at Eden and says, "Clarinet, right?"

"Yes!" she shouts, delighted. "Good memory. And you were . . . flute, I think?"

"How'd you even remember that?" Luke asks her. "Didn't you leave band after freshman year?"

I see it in her face—she turns pale, and her eyes sort of get this faraway stare for only a moment. I've come to recognize this look. It means she must've left after what happened, because of what happened. It passes quickly, and she nods and smiles but reaches for my hand under the table.

Thankfully Dominic joins in just then.

"Wait a second," he says. "I thought flute and clarinet were the same thing?"

Eden and Luke exchange a look, as if that's the craziest thing they've ever heard, and start laughing hysterically.

Luke shakes his head, leans over, and kisses Dominic's cheek. Then says, "No, honey. They're not the same thing."

I bring her hand up onto the tabletop now and squeeze once

before letting go. As she opens her hand, I can see that the pink scars from her burn are almost invisible now.

We're the first to leave. On the walk home, I look over to see her smiling. Not at me, just smiling.

"It seemed like you had a good time tonight."

"I actually did," she says. "I like Luke. Do you know I literally never once spoke to him in school; isn't it weird how things can change?"

"Yeah," I agree. "Um, so listen, I wanted to float something by you," I begin.

"Okay, this sounds serious," she says, slowing her pace as she glances up at me.

"Serious? I don't know." I shrug. "Not really. My parents wanted me to invite you for Thanksgiving."

"Oh, wow," she says. "Meeting the parents. That is serious."

"Is it?" I ask—I thought it was too, but I didn't want to make a big deal of it. "It seems like it's the right time, doesn't it?"

She looks down and smiles.

"So, is that a yes?"

"Yes," she answers, nodding. But then she lets out this small laugh.

"What?"

"You do know that you once told me that you'd never let me meet your parents, don't you?"

"*I* said that?"

"Yeah. It was during that same conversation when I was being *so honest* and told you I didn't want to be your cheerleader or your girlfriend or anything like that."

I think back and do sort of remember saying that now. But I was particularly furious at my parents then; they were trying to hide my dad's latest relapse from me. I felt like I couldn't trust them, and I was so done with their shit by the time I met Eden, I didn't want them involved in anything that could potentially become important to me.

"Like you said, things change."

Back in her room, the towel is still lying twisted on the bed from earlier. We don't even talk about it; we just start taking our clothes off. We don't need to talk about it. It feels so right, like all the distance and sadness and fear of the past month was never even real.

She doesn't stop kissing me the whole time. We're so close, all harmony and rhythm and connection like it was all the time before that one horrible, terrifying night. Breathless, she says my name at one point. I think she's just saying it at first, but then a few seconds later she says it again. "Josh, I . . . ," she starts, and she holds my face, looks so deep into my eyes but doesn't say anything else.

"Yeah?" I ask her, pausing to listen.

But she shakes her head and smiles, whispers, "I love you."

I say it back. Over and over, I say it back.

I fall asleep so easily, with my head resting on her stomach, my hand on her hip, her arms wrapped around me. I can't remember a time when I ever felt more at peace, more okay with my life than I do right now, my body rising and falling with her breath.

I wake up in the early hours of the morning and stretch, rolling out of her arms. She's lying next to me, staring straight up at the ceiling. "Hey," I whisper. But she doesn't move or respond. I prop myself up and look at her more closely. Her eyes are wide open, unblinking. I have this intense flush of adrenaline punch through my whole body. Because there's no life behind her eyes. She looks . . . *dead.* I grasp her arm now and say her name, louder. She blinks a few times, then turns to look at me. She's back to life.

"Huh?" she mutters.

"Are you okay?"

"Yeah," she breathes, and touches my face gently. "I was just thinking."

"What about?"

"Nothing, nothing. It'll be okay."

"What will?" I ask. "What's wrong?"

She licks her lips before she speaks, like they'd dried out while she was lying lifeless for who knows how long. "It's just—I missed some days, I think, with my birth control."

A cold wave of panic passes over me. "Wait, you think or you know?"

"I ran out the other day and I didn't have a chance to pick up the refill."

Now I'm sitting up, looking down at her. I don't know what face I'm making, but she frowns slightly at me.

"Well, for how long?"

"I don't know, just a few days, maybe."

"Shit." A few days is all it takes—I definitely did my homework on all of this months ago, when we decided to stop using condoms. I mean, it felt logical at the time. If the pill's more effective, anyway, why do both? But that only makes sense as long as she's taking it every day, which she swore she would.

"A week, maybe, at most."

"Shit!" I repeat. "Are you serious?"

She pushes up on her elbows so she's half sitting, too calm. "Yeah, well, it didn't feel like a priority since we haven't been all that . . . active lately."

"Oh my God," I sigh into my hands. "What, and you just realized this now?"

She opens her mouth but doesn't say anything.

"You realized this just now, right?"

"I mean, it's fine," she says, not answering the question. "I can get the morning-after pill. It's easy."

"Okay," I say. At least we have a plan. But there's this feeling in my chest like a screw tightening. "Wait, did you let me . . . when you knew?"

"I—"

"You did." I realize as I watch her face. "That's what you were gonna say to me. When you said 'I love you.' Jesus Christ, Eden! What were you thinking?"

"Don't yell at me," she says, her voice extra quiet. "Please."

"Why didn't you stop me?" I yell anyway.

She reaches for me. "I'm sorry, I—"

I can't help but back away from her. "Can you not touch me right now?"

She turns very still as she watches me climb out of bed; I start getting dressed, grabbing random clothes as I find them scattered on the floor.

"Josh, what are you doing?"

"I need some air," I tell her. She moves to get up out of bed too. "Don't follow me."

But she's with me on the roof a few minutes later. She comes and stands next to me at the railing where I'm looking out over campus, trying to process what has just happened. The wind blows, and she steps closer to me. When I look at her, I see that she's wearing my gray T-shirt again, the one with the hole in the collar, and a pair of my boxers. She's shivering as she places her hand on my arm.

"I'm sorry," she says again. "It's just that it felt like things were going back to normal. I thought it would be okay. Or, I don't know, I guess maybe I wasn't thinking. But it'll be fine, Josh. I've taken plan B before, and everything was fine."

I turn to face her now. "With me?"

"N-no," she stutters, and looks down. "You're not really mad, are you?"

"Yes, Eden. I really am mad."

"It was an accident," she argues.

"No, it wasn't!"

She pauses. I can see her thinking through something. . . . God, why couldn't she have thought it through this carefully last night? Hot anger rises to the surface now, almost matching my fear. "Well, okay, then it was a mistake. But can I point out that if anyone should be freaking out right now, shouldn't it really be me?"

"You know what?" I begin, trying to channel some of my dad's calmness, borrowing one of his lines. "Can you please just give me a little space?"

"Are you serious right now?" she shouts.

"Yeah, I'm serious."

Her hair blows across her face, so I can't tell what kind of look she's giving me. But she turns and walks toward the door. "You're coming back, though, right?" she calls to me.

I didn't answer her and I didn't come back. I went to my own bed instead. I tried to go to sleep but couldn't. So now it's 6:45 a.m., and I'm waiting outside the pharmacy before it even opens. What's amazing to me is how much angrier I'm getting as each minute goes by. I'm not calming down at all; I'm just getting more amped up.

We've always been so careful. I'm not the guy who's careless or has accidents or makes mistakes. I trusted her with this—*that* was my mistake. Walking up to the register, I feel so ashamed, I grab a bottle of water just to have something else in my hands.

I go directly to her apartment and knock on the door. Parker answers with an eye mask pushed up on her forehead, face all scrunched, one eye closed. All she says is "I hate you."

Eden is sitting up in her bed when I walk in, arms wrapped around her knees. She stands and rushes over to me as I close the door. When I turn around, she's there with her arms open, but I can't.

"Here." I push the plastic bag into her hands instead.

"What's this?" She peeks inside and brings the bag back over to her bed. "I would've taken care of this myself, you know."

"No, I don't actually know that. I don't know anything." I'm pacing back and forth in her tiny room. "Please just take the damn pill. I'm not fucking around."

"Josh, I don't understand why you're so mad. It's going to be fine."

"How do you not understand why I'm so mad?" I snap.

She scoffs as she takes the box and the bottle of water out of the bag. "So, what, you're just going to stand there and watch me take it?"

"Please just do it."

Her hands are shaking as she peels open the box and takes the pill out of the packaging. I reach over to open the water bottle for her. She sets the pill on her tongue and mumbles as she takes the water from me, "Well, you thought of everything." She looks me in the eye while she swallows. Then she wipes the water from her mouth with the back of her hand.

"Thank you," I say, and sit down on the edge of her bed, waiting for the relief to come. But it doesn't.

"I almost didn't even tell you," she says. "But I wanted to be honest."

"A little late for that." My words are mean. I can taste the meanness in my mouth, but I can't hold them back.

"Why are you being like this?"

"Why didn't you stop me? Did you think I *wouldn't* stop?"

"No, I just—"

"Then what?"

"It . . . I don't know, it felt good."

"It felt good?" I repeat. "Oh, that's mature."

"Not felt good, like physically good—I mean it did—but I'm saying it felt good to be together again. To be in that place." She pauses and tries to reach for my hand, but I pull away. "See? Things have been so off with us. I didn't want to ruin it by stopping you because then I'd have to tell you I haven't been keeping up with the pill and then you'd read into it all like you're doing right now and think I'm even more screwed up than I am—and now here we are." She throws her hands up and adds, "Here we are, anyway."

I let my head fall forward into my hands, her explanation still echoing in my mind. I try to understand, but—

"I can't," I hear myself say out loud.

"You can't what?"

"I can't . . . trust you," I admit. "I can't—I can't do this." I'm still leaning forward, seeing the floor through my fingers, my hands hot against my skin, I can't look at her face.

"What are you saying?"

The words tumble out, landing heavy like boulders. "I don't know, maybe we need to take a break or something."

"Take a break." She laughs. "Over this?" I look up, and she has this half grin on her face, full of disbelief, irritation. I guess I'm annoying her, which annoys the hell out of me, sparking something even deeper—she's not taking this seriously. She's not taking *me* seriously.

"Yes, over this!" I shout, and I'm on my feet again.

Now that I'm yelling, I see her getting that far-off look in her eyes, like last night in the restaurant, but now it just makes me angrier.

"No," she says. "If we're doing this, then at least tell me the truth. Give me your real reason."

"You're questioning *my* truth when you're the one who lied?"

"I never lied. I just . . ." She crosses her arms now and says, "Admit it, you've been wanting out ever since that night."

"What night?"

She scoffs and rolls her eyes, but her hands are still shaking, betraying her coolness. "Don't play dumb," she says, her voice sharp. "You know what night."

"This has nothing to do with that night," I tell her. "Eden, how am I supposed to trust you after this?"

"Because it's me."

"Yeah, exactly," I blurt out. "This is you."

The way she looks at me—like if I'd just slapped her, it would've hurt less—makes me want to die. I try to take it back. "Okay, don't—don't look at me like that. You know that's not what I meant."

"Yes, it was," she says quietly, looking down at the pill box and the plastic bag and the water bottle sitting on her bed. She starts putting everything inside the bag. I reach for her, but she ducks away. "No. You want to go, just go."

"Look, I don't want to go," I tell her. *Take it back, take it all back right now.* I step toward her again, and when she looks up, I can see that her eyes are filling with tears.

"Just go, Josh," she says, her voice sounding strangled as she wipes her eyes roughly with the heels of her hands. "There's the door. I'm not stopping you."

"Eden, don't—"

"Go!" she shouts, already losing her voice to the tears. She throws the water bottle, but it misses me. "Get out, God!" she yells. "Just fucking go."

Parker appears in the doorway and looks at me, fully awake now. "Josh," she says calmly, firmly, "you need to leave."

I do. But I can't force myself to go far. I sit down in the hallway outside her door with my back to the wall. I'll wait for her for however long it takes, I tell myself. In the meantime, I'm just trying to remember how to breathe. *A break*. I can't remember ever saying anything so fucking stupid in my entire life.

EDEN

Parker makes me a green smoothie later that morning. But I can't catch my breath long enough to even take a sip. She brings me a bowl of ice cream that night, but then I start crying all over again, thinking of fucking gelato.

Every time I manage to stop, all I see, all I hear, is him standing in my room, so angry, saying *This is you.* Over and over. *This is you.* I am this. I couldn't have said it better myself, but he's always been better with words than me.

I am this . . . disaster, I am this thing that is incapable of not fucking everything up, I am this curse on the people I love. I never thought anyone could hurt me worse than I hurt myself. But knowing that he thinks the same terrible things about me that I do—it's too much to even process.

I wear his ripped gray T-shirt and lie in bed, sobbing, weeping, hyperventilating, for forty-eight hours straight. And even though all I want is him, I decline his calls, ignore his texts, tell Parker not to let him in. Because I am this, and someone needs to protect him from this, even if it has to be me.

I miss classes on Monday because I can't physically get out of bed. That night she comes into my room with soup. I ask her to bring me my pills instead. I take all three.

And finally, I sleep, dreamless.

On Tuesday, my birthday, I go to class and work in the library and somehow manage to not talk to a single person all day long. I skip my afternoon therapy session and don't even answer when the office calls to check in. Instead of calling them back, I pick up a shift at the café. Since I no longer have birthday dinner plans.

I mess up orders and drop a plate and I'm rude to the customers. Halfway through my shift, I say I'm taking a five-minute break, but I'm gone for twenty. Because I start having a panic attack in the bathroom when I wash my hands and catch a glimpse of the plasticky pink scars on my palm and suddenly remember all over again that this has all really happened—he really loved me, he really left me. And then I'm crying on the dirty floor. I avoid eye contact with anyone as I come out and try to act like I'm okay. I exit through the back door and walk down to the convenience store the next block over and buy a pack of cigarettes—legally, for the first time, since I'm now officially eighteen.

The cashier checks my ID and tells me "happy birthday." And in her next breath, as she slides the cigarettes across the counter: "You know those things'll kill you."

"Thanks, I know," I mumble back, and flash her a big smile. I think for a tiny moment it wouldn't be the worst thing.

"Need a lighter?" she asks, and I nod.

I consider just walking off and not going back to the café, but assuming I don't actually die from this invisible knife lodged in the center of my heart, I'll still need this job. When I get back, Captain Douchebag tells me he's writing me up. Fine. I take at least three more breaks to smoke in the side alley by the dumpsters, where there's a decommissioned table with uneven legs and a fading, scraped-up paint job. It's been almost a year since I've smoked, I'm already feeling so light-headed and weak when the back door to the café slams shut.

"Oh, hey, Eden." It's Perry, and it occurs to me now that I still don't know whether that's his first or last name. He takes a vape pen out of his shirt pocket. "Slow tonight."

I nod.

"Didn't know you smoked," he says.

"Yeah, I quit, but . . . not very well, I guess."

He looks up at me, like he's only just now seeing me—he's never taken a second glance at me before. "So, listen, would you mind if I smoked something a little stronger than this?" he asks.

I shake my head and wave my hand.

"There it is!" He points at me and grins. "I knew you were a cool kid." And then he takes a different vape out now—this one I can smell right away—that earthy sweet sticky scent. I laugh out loud because the universe has got to be testing me, offering up all my vices in such an organized, obvious way.

"Hmm?" he mumbles as he holds the smoke in his lungs. "What's funny?" he croaks before exhaling.

"Nothing," I lie. "Just imagining what Captain Douchebag would say if he came out here right now."

“Oh, that asshole left an hour ago,” Perry says.

I light up another cigarette. “Then I won’t rush getting back in.”

“So, Captain Douchebag, is that what you kids are calling him these days?”

I shrug.

He nods again, takes another hit.

“Hey, you want some of this?” I look over at him, and he takes a step closer. He’s easily ten years older than me. I must be giving off some kind of fucked-up sad-girl distress signal hormone that calls them to me like a beacon, a sonar frequency vibration, or something. *Hey, here I am, alone, vulnerable, ready to be messed with! Come at me!*

“Well, it is my birthday today,” I tell him, in spite of myself.

“Happy birthday!” I watch as his face lights up. “Hold on a minute.” He pops back inside for a few seconds and comes out with an open bottle of champagne and two flutes. He sets the glasses down on the wobbly table and fills them both. He passes one to me and holds his up, saying, “Cheers.” I hesitate, and he adds, “I won’t tell if you won’t.”

The universe wants to test me? Fine. Bring it on. I’ll fail—that’s what I’m best at.

“Cheers,” I say, and we clink our glasses together. Josh would be so disappointed in me—more disappointed in me than he already is. Cigarettes, weed, alcohol, rando. Check, check, check, and check. *This is you.* It keeps playing in my head. This is me. It’s inevitable.

“So,” he says, passing the vape next. “Boyfriend taking you

out later—the tall guy, right?" he asks, bringing his hand up above his head.

"Right," I say, and take a couple of hits. "The tall guy."

But the way he's looking at me, grinning. He knows, somehow, it's open season.

I lose track of the time while we sit there, lose track of what we were talking about. Don't even notice when he goes inside. I clean the same table a hundred times, it seems. I sweep the floors, it feels like, forever. From the front window, I can see my building. I imagine my apartment with X-ray vision, like I could even see into my bedroom, my unmade bed waiting there for me, calling to me.

After we close for the night, I'm shaky. Champagne on an empty stomach, cigarettes on a broken heart, weed on a shattered mind. Not a good combination, but I feel mostly lucid again by the time we're shutting off the lights and turning over the OPEN-CLOSED sign on the door. Perry places his hand on my lower back and asks if I need help getting home. I hate that I know it would be so much easier to go along with it than to try to be strong and stand up for myself.

But as I look at him, this stranger, the expectant smile on his face as he moves closer to me, it suddenly doesn't feel easy, like it used to. "No," I say quietly. "Thanks."

He keeps walking next to me anyway, though.

"What are you doing?" I ask him, stopping on the sidewalk, feeling my heart start pounding in that way that makes me afraid of what will happen next.

"I told you—I'm just making sure you get home okay."

"I literally just said I didn't need help."

"Yeah, but I—"

"Listen, thank you for the glass and a half of old, flat, left-over champagne that you stole from the kitchen. And thank you for exactly eight hits off your vape and . . . oh, let's see, thank you for telling me happy birthday," I say, gaining steam. "Really, thank you. So very much, okay? But I don't owe you anything."

"Whoa, simmer down. You've got the wrong idea," he tries to argue—he tries to laugh.

"No," I say. "No," I shout. "No!" I'm yelling in the street, louder and louder. "*No*," I scream at the top of my lungs.

Finally, he holds his hands up and starts backing away.

I cross the street and run up the steps to my building, close the front door behind me, and try to catch my breath. My legs feel boneless and weak as I make my way up the two flights of stairs. And as if I wasn't already about to collapse, there's a glass vase over-flowing with yellow flowers in it, sitting next to the door. A card attached, my name in his handwriting.

JOSH

I've tried to talk to her a hundred times. She won't come to the door. She's blocking my calls. I even left flowers for her birthday, and they're still sitting there a week later, all wilted and shriveled.

Every morning, when Dominic and I come down to leave for morning practice, he says the same thing as we approach the door. "Keep walking, just keep walking."

I go to practice, go to class, come home. Every day, the same.

We had an away game this week, and I thought maybe when I got back she'd be willing to talk to me. I told my parents she'd said yes to Thanksgiving, because I thought for sure by then we would've figured it out.

Tonight's practice goes as usual. Fifteen minutes warming up, stretching. Twenty minutes shooting, skill work, jump shots, rebounds. Coach walks around, watching us, keeps shouting, "Game speed, gentlemen!" Our assistant coach studies my shooting, takes some notes on his tablet.

One hour on defense drills. A half hour of offense, going over plays and sets. The assistant coach is watching me closely again, I can feel it, probably trying to catch me screwing up. The live section ends with a half-court scrimmage that seems to go so much more smoothly than usual. Everyone's playing well, calling the plays, cooperating. It doesn't feel like such a struggle just to make it through like it usually does. Coach is even in good spirits for a change, which helps.

"That was decent today, guys—good communication," he says, clapping his hands a few times. "You actually looked like a team out there for a change!" And then, to my disbelief, he adds, in front of everyone, "Nice work, Miller."

As practice winds down, we all do some more shooting. With only a few minutes left on the clock, everyone's loosening up, talking, chilling. "Too much laughing means you must not be tired yet!" Coach warns, and blows the whistle, adds ten more minutes. But I don't even notice it's over until a couple of the other guys stop at my basket on their way to the locker room.

"Damn, Miller," one of them says to me as they walk by.

"You're a machine, man!" the other says.

I catch the ball and stop. "Huh?" I ask, breathing heavily as I wipe the sweat from my face. I look around, suddenly feeling off-balance without the rhythm of the ball to match my pulse. They were the last ones out here. Coach is standing to the side of me, watching.

"Like night and day," he says, walking toward me, shaking his head. "Good to see you're back."

"What do you mean?" I ask.

"Oh, don't fish for praise, Miller. That's obnoxious."

"No, I wasn't, I—"

He interrupts me by holding his hand up, silencing me. "Whatever you're doing, just keep it up." He gives me a firm pat on the back and walks off the court, satisfied.

What *am* I doing?

I'm hating myself every minute of every day for hurting the last person in the world I ever wanted to hurt. I'm also sleeping too much and letting my classes slide. I'm lying to my parents about Eden. And pretty much my entire life is in the process of going down the toilet. But, dammit, I can play basketball. The one place I know what I'm supposed to do and I can do it well and make the people around me happy.

We win our next two games. I've honestly never played better. I'm magically redeemed in everyone's eyes now—at least everyone on the team. Even Jon has stopped giving the stink eye every time he looks at me. All I needed to do was be perfect. Easy.

But somehow it used to feel better.

That's what I'm thinking about when I'm walking out to meet Dominic at his car after this away game—in which we crushed the home team, embarrassingly so.

"Hey, Miller?" I hear Coach call out to me in the cold.

I stop and turn around. He's huddled outside the entrance with the assistants, talking with the coaches on the other team.

"Yeah, Coach?" I answer.

He takes a step toward me, bowing out of his conversation for a moment, to pay extra-special attention to me. Then he smiles, a rare genuine smile, and under his breath says something meant only for my ears: "Glad to see you finally got your priorities straight, son."

He's expecting a response, I know. But I can't seem to gather enough fucks to give him one, at least not one he'd approve of, so I just stand there, seeing my breath surrounding me in a fog.

"Go on," he says. "Get some rest. You've earned it. Enjoy Thanksgiving with your family."

"Thanks," I manage.

EDEN

I'm freezing on the roof at midnight. Just one more cigarette. Then, I promised myself, I'd go to bed. I've pulled one of the lawn chairs up to the edge of the roof, where I lean against the railing, letting my arm dangle over the edge.

As I inhale the mixture of cold air and smoke, tiny pinpricks stud the insides of my lungs. On the exhale, the cloud just keeps going, switching at some point from smoke to breath. I keep pushing out until my lungs feel tight, squeezed. The corners of my vision darken, until my body starts to burn and no more breath can come out. For a second I think about waiting just a little longer, letting myself pass out, find some kind of peace. But my body takes over and sucks in air, stubborn thing that it is.

Just as I'm putting out the cigarette, I hear a car door shut. Then another. Voices travel through the cold up from the street. The day before Thanksgiving, there's not much going on. I lean over to get a better view. They had to park across the street and around the corner.

I watch him from up here. I know his walk, know his voice by heart, even when I can't make out his words, I know it. It's been two and a half weeks. As I watch him now, all I want to do is race down the stairs to meet him, jump into his arms, and tell him to take me to his parents' house tomorrow. *Let's pretend,* I'd say. *Let's take a break from this ridiculous break.* I want it so badly. But even as I have that fleeting thought, a kind of paralysis takes over the lower half of my body, forcing me to sit, to remain still. *Wait,* my body commands me. *Stay.* It always wins.

It's completely silent outside by the time it allows me to move again. When I look down, the pack of cigarettes is crushed in my hand.

As I promised myself I would, I go to bed.

When I come out of my room in the morning, Parker has a suitcase and carry-on by the door, ready to go home with her. She's standing at the blender in her winter coat, filling two travel mugs with her classic green protein breakfast smoothie concoction, which she tries to foist on me every morning before she leaves for swim practice.

"You're drinking this," she orders. "You need the antioxidants with all the disgusting smoking you've been doing."

"Actually," I begin, but she stops me.

"No arguments, roomie!"

"What I was gonna say is, I quit. Again."

"When?" she asks, side-eyeing me.

"Last night."

"Well, it's about damn time," she says, rolling her eyes at me as she snaps the lid on both travel mugs, setting mine in the fridge.

"Okay, now that you're not actively murdering yourself, I'll remind you that my offer to come jogging with me still stands."

"Maybe I'll try when we get back. *Maybe*," I add, feeling in no position to be making promises to anyone, least of all myself.

"All right, come here," she says, and swishes toward me in her giant coat. Gives me a long hug. "Drive carefully, and take care of yourself, all right?" Then she scrunches her face up like she smells something bad and adds, "God, who the fuck am I turning into, my mother?"

My laugh muscles are out of practice from neglect, but they give a weak little huff. "Have a safe flight," I tell her. "See you in a few days."

She heads for the door but turns around and sort of half smiles, half frowns. "Honey, do me a favor and just think about changing out of that shirt, okay?"

"Oh." I look down at myself—the gray T-shirt is sticking out from under the collar of my hoodie—I had no idea it was that obvious I'd been wearing his shirt under my clothes every day. "Okay."

"Love you," she sings as she maneuvers through the door with her bags and mug, managing to nimbly close it behind her.

I take a breath but barely have a chance to let it out again when I hear his voice in the hall. I go to the door and look out through the peephole. In the tiny wide-frame convex circle, I can see their distorted figures: Josh standing on one side and Parker on the other.

Their voices are quiet, muffled.

Parker says, "Josh, I don't know what to tell you."

"At least tell me if she's okay?"

Parker puts her hand on her hip and brings her other hand to her mouth—I think, making the "shh" gesture, because she points at the door next. If she says anything, I can't hear it.

Josh brings his hand to his head. I hear him say something, followed by ". . . to tell her I'm sorry."

Parker shakes her head. Something mumbled. Then, "Don't. Just don't."

Josh throws his hands up and shakes his head. "But . . ." something indecipherable.

Parker reaches out and touches his arm for a second. "Let her come to you."

He says something short and nods.

I watch as Parker walks away. Josh watches her go. After a few moments he turns back toward the door, takes a step forward. I hold my breath as I watch him place a hand on either side of the door-frame and look down at the ground. My heart starts racing at how close we'd be if the door weren't between us. I can hear him sigh. Then he backs away and rubs his hands over his face—his stubble back now, nearly turning into a real beard this time. He looks at the door once more, and part of me is afraid that he might be able to tell somehow that I'm watching him. If he knocks right now, I'm not sure I'd be able to not let him in. I feel my fingers reaching for the knob—to keep me in or him out, I don't know which.

But then he walks away.

And I finally exhale.

I bring the green smoothie into the bathroom with me and sip on it as I get ready to take a shower. The cold rushes against my skin as I peel the T-shirt off my body. I feel more naked than naked even, like I've just removed a layer of skin and am now exposed to any number of dangerous contaminants from the world around me. But I let the shirt fall from my hands into the laundry hamper. I pile my other clothes on top of it and smoosh it down as hard as I can.

When I get out of the shower, I have a text from DA Silverman waiting for me:

> Happy Thanksgiving, Eden. I wanted to share this right away. We have a date. Clear your calendar for the second week of January. As always, let me know if you have any questions. Thanks, CeCe

CeCe. How strange it is to see her name there. I guess going to trial puts us on a first-name basis. I've seen her full name on paperwork as Cecelia Silverman, but I'd never imagined in real life she would go by CeCe. Such a normal nickname, a cute name even. Is she cute in her real life? I find myself wondering. Like, not a stoic powerhouse in heels and suits with her hair pulled back tight and shiny. Does she do cute things like make jokes and eat popcorn in movie theaters and sing off-key in the car? I write back immediately, still dripping wet, leaving puddles on the bathroom floor—I didn't realize I'd been needing this news so urgently until it came.

> Okay, thank you for the update. Happy Thanksgiving to you too, CeCe.

JOSH

I pull up to the curb in front of our mailbox. I turn the car off and wipe my hands on my jeans. Even closed up inside my car, I can hear the screech of the front door opening. I get out. Take my bags out of the trunk. Walk up the driveway.

I watch my feet the whole time; I can't look at them, standing there on the front porch. Dad comes down the steps to take one of the bags from me, and finally I meet his eyes—they're full of all kinds of concern and questions.

I try to smile but can't.

Mom stands on the top step, holding her hands up as she turns her head, the beginning of a word, "Wh . . ." hanging in the air. *What's wrong?* or *Where is she?* I'm sure, will be coming next, but she stops herself.

I silently thank them for at least letting me into the house before they say anything.

Harley comes racing up to me, rubs her head against my legs, purring loudly. They let me bend down to pick her up, having her in my arms as a buffer. And Mom finally asks, "Well, don't keep us in suspense. What's going on?"

And then they stand there, waiting for an explanation.

"We broke up," I admit, finally, after all these weeks of trying to deny it.

"Oh, sweetheart," Mom says. "Come here." She hugs me, and Harley leaps out of my arms. Dad pats me on the back.

When I look at him, he smiles sadly. "I'm sorry, bud."

I nod. *Not as sorry as I am*, I would say, if I could.

"Okay," Mom begins. "Come in, take your coat off. Do you want to talk about it?"

I shake my head. "Not really."

"You didn't break up over coming here, right?" she asks, probably thinking it must've just happened since this is the first they're hearing about it.

I laugh as I drop down onto the couch. "Yeah, I wish."

"Over the trial?" Mom asks, coming to sit next to me as she sets her hand on my knee.

"Mom?" I place my hand on top of hers. "Thank you, really. But I don't want to talk about it right now."

She looks up at my dad, then back at me. "Okay, honey." A timer goes off in the kitchen, and she stands.

"Need help?" Dad asks her.

"No, it's all under control. We're basically just waiting on the turkey at this point." And then she gives a not-very-subtle shooing gesture toward my dad, as if to say, *Do something about him.*

Dad sighs and sits down in his armchair across from me. "Wanna watch a game?" he asks, turning his head toward me in this gentle way.

"Sure," I tell him. "Anything but basketball."

He laughs. "Deal." He turns on a football game, and we both watch, not saying much, but it's sort of exactly what I needed. I stretch out on the couch, and Harley comes back to curl up on top of my chest.

"Someone missed you," my dad says, gesturing to the cat. I scritch under her chin, and the purring starts up like a tiny motor. "Joshie, you know I'm here, right? If you wanna talk."

"Yeah," I tell him. "Thanks."

I drift off, not quite asleep, but remembering this one time Eden slept over here when we were still in high school. We never even went upstairs. We ate pizza and watched TV and then fell asleep down here, on the couch, after talking late into the morning hours. We'd known each other only a few weeks and already I knew I was starting to fall in love with her that night. I told her secrets, about me, about my family, my dad's addiction. Things I'd never told anyone. Because I trusted her. I trusted that she would understand, and she did. She always did.

I open my eyes and look over at my dad.

He's been watching me.

"I really messed up," I tell him.

He shakes his head briefly, then says, "Don't we all?"

I nod in response, but what I really want to say is: no, we all *don't*, I don't—at least, I'm not supposed to mess up—not *this* bad, anyway.

Before we can get any farther, my aunt and two younger cousins, ten-year-old twins, Sasha and Shane, are barreling in, lots of noise and energy coming with them. A welcome distraction from my thoughts about how I'd imagined this day would go.

"Josh?" my aunt says as I stand to give her a hug. "Where's the girlfriend?"

Dad shakes his head to try to signal to her, drawing his finger across his throat, but it's too late.

"Oh," she says, putting her hand over her mouth. "Sorry."

"She's not coming," I tell her.

"*Ohh*," she repeats, drawing the word out this time, with a frown and a sympathetic head tilt. "I'm sorry, sweetie."

I shrug, try my best to pretend I'm not devastated.

"Josh, Josh!" Shane is hopping up and down next to me, shoving a basketball in my face. That familiar rubbery chemical new ball scent flooding my brain with memories. "Josh, look. Look at my new basketball. I just got it for my birthday."

"Nice," I tell him.

Sasha walks by and mutters, "You mean *our* birthday."

Shane rolls his eyes and sighs at her, and I laugh. I don't often think I've missed out on anything by being an only child, but when I see them together, it makes me wonder.

"And what did you get, Sasha?" I ask her.

"Mom bought me a clarinet," she announces, proud of herself.

"Wait, you play the clarinet?" I ask. Of course she does.

"Duh-uh," she says, full of attitude. "Only for two whole years now. Which you would know if you ever came to any of my school concerts."

"Sasha," my aunt interrupts. "Geez, give the guy a break. You know his games always fall on your concert dates."

"Sorry, Sash," I tell her. "What if I try to make the next one?"

She shrugs and skips off into the kitchen. She probably doesn't give a damn, but I feel terrible. I didn't even realize this was yet another thing I've been missing out on because of basketball. It's not like we have a big extended family; they can't just let me not show up for shit and then not even tell me.

I turn to my aunt. "Hey, I actually do want to try to come to her next concert. Will you let me know when it is?"

"Sure," she answers, seeming surprised. "If you really want to—but, honey, it's fine, we all know you're busy. Don't let the kid give you a guilt trip over it."

"Josh? Josh, Josh," Shane starts in again. "Wanna play before dinner?" He dribbles the ball twice, and his mom gives him the look—widening her eyes and pursing her lips—it's the same look my mom has given me so many times throughout my life.

"Not in the house, you little beast." She points to the door. Then she turns to me. "Do you mind indulging him for a bit, honey? It's literally all he's been talking about all week," she says under her breath. "My cousin Josh this, my cousin Josh that."

"Of course," I tell her quietly, happy to have an excuse to get out in the fresh air, where Eden's absence isn't taking up so much space. "Let's go, little man," I tell Shane. "Sasha, you wanna play too?" I call in the direction of the kitchen.

"I hate basketball!" she yells back.

I have to laugh at her candor; she makes it sound like such an easy thing to say.

"Thank you," my aunt whispers.

I follow Shane out to our driveway, where he runs and jumps for a shot into the basketball hoop my dad attached to our garage back when I was even younger than him.

"Good shot," I tell him. "You got some air on that jump, didn't you?"

He glows as he passes me the ball. We take turns shooting and passing and dribbling. I give him a few pointers here and there, which he seems delighted to receive.

"Square your shoulders," I say, and then I show him what I mean.

"Like this, Josh?" he keeps asking.

"Bend your knees a little more—that's it," I tell him. "Feet a little wider apart. Elbows in. Now when you shoot, you gotta follow through with your fingers."

And it's not until my dad comes out with some water bottles and I look up at him, smiling at us, that I realize I've been smiling too. I pass the ball to Shane, and he passes it to my dad.

"All right," Dad says, dribbling his way to the driveway. "Go easy on me, guys. I'm getting old." But then he turns and steps fast, driving past us both to deliver the most perfect layup, holding Shane in awe. And maybe me too, a little.

"Old?" I repeat. "Yeah, right. You see that?" I ask Shane.

"Uncle Matt, I didn't know you could jump that high," he says.

I nod in agreement.

Dad keeps playing with us, bringing a new energy in now, like he always used to when I was younger. Before long I realize my lungs are aching from breathing the cold air and laughing, shouting, joking with the two of them. It hasn't been like this between us in so long, I almost forgot it *could* be like this. The whole reason I ever got involved with basketball was because of this feeling. The fun, the connection we had. I don't know when that stopped.

I hold up my hand to signal I'm going to go grab a drink of water. Mom comes out then and stands beside me, puts her arm on my shoulder. "How you holding up, sweetheart?"

I nod. "Okay."

She looks up at me and smiles. "Dinner's ready, you guys," she calls out.

And as my dad walks by me, he holds his hand up. I give him a high five, and he pulls me in for a quick hug and kisses my forehead, in this way that makes me feel like I really am ten years old again. Shane passes me and then tosses the ball in the air over his shoulder. I catch it, and as I stand there in the walkway watching them go inside, I wish I could freeze this moment.

As we sit down to dinner, my heart feels lighter than it has in weeks, months really. Ever since that night. Eden was partially right about that night. Not that I wanted out. I didn't—I still don't. But ever since then, it's felt like someone's had a hand inside my chest, squeezing my heart, tighter and tighter, anytime I would try to feel anything good. And now I wonder if this is how she must feel all the time. If it is, I think maybe I can kind of understand now. Why feeling good, forgetting about the bad, would be enough to risk so much, just to hold on to it for a little longer.

EDEN

"Have you lost weight?" my mom asks while I'm helping her in the kitchen, putting all the side dishes into separate serving bowls and trying to rummage around the drawers for matching silverware.

I look down at my body quickly. I have no idea if I've lost weight, gained weight, still have all my appendages. I've been avoiding looking into mirrors as much as possible. Because every time I do, I'm just looking into my own eyes, invariably thinking, *This is you, this is you, this is you*, and wishing I could disappear on command for once.

"Uh, I don't think so," I tell her so she won't worry.

She asks about Josh, if he's having dinner with his family tonight.

"Mm-hmm," I tell her, not wanting to lie but also not able to tell the truth. My grandparents will be here soon, and if I burst into tears now, I won't have time to de-puff my eyes and look normal again before they arrive. At least, that's the reason I give myself for not telling her we broke up.

"Well, did you at least remember to ask him if he could join us a little later, for dessert?" she tries.

"Probably not," I tell her. "I think they're doing a whole big thing over there, so . . ." Still, not a lie, exactly.

"Oh, too bad," she sighs. "Well, ask him if he has time over the weekend to stop by."

I close myself in the bathroom and hold on to the sink. Try *not* to look in the mirror as I open the medicine cabinet for my pills. I'd already taken one earlier, but I guess it was no match for Josh talk. I take another now. And then I inhale and count to five, exhale to five, inhale, exhale, over and over. I don't come out until I hear my grandparents arrive. At least they don't know anything about what's going on with the trial, so that part should make things easier.

"Hi, Gma," I say, taking turns giving them each a hug. "Hey, Gpa."

My grandma holds my arm out and scans me, up and down, like she's cataloging everything wrong with me in her mind. "Good Lord, Eden Anne," she says, middle-naming me. "You look terrible."

"Oh" is all I can say. I try to laugh, but I don't do a very good job of pretending I'm not hurt by her bluntness.

Gpa just shrugs and shakes his head. "Well, you look lovely as ever to me, for what it's worth."

"Thanks," I say, forcing a smile.

"Yes, lovely," Gma agrees, batting her hand through the air. "But, honey, you're clearly not well."

I clear my throat. "I guess I've just been so busy, not really getting enough sleep."

"Vanessa!" Gma yells. "Look at Eden."

"Please, let's not." I turn to Caelin, who's been lingering behind me. "Caelin," I prompt, mumbling to him, "a little help?"

"Hey, Grandma." He hugs her, and then our grandpa reaches out to shake his hand instead of accepting a hug. I check Caelin's face, but he doesn't seem surprised—I wonder when that changed. Like, what age was Caelin when Gpa decided it was no longer acceptable to hug him? I hadn't noticed.

"Oh my God," Gma gasps, pulling on Caelin's arm so that he's in front of her again. "And look at you." She places her hand against his cheek. "What's going on around here? You look awful, too."

We share a look and start laughing.

"No, it's not funny," she says to us. "Where are your parents, hiding from me, I assume?"

"We're right here, Ma," Dad says, coming into the room holding two wineglasses—one red for Gpa, one white for Gma. Mom behind him, fake smile plastered on her face.

We all sit at the table, and mine and Caelin's appearances are the first order of conversation. "What are you feeding them, Vanessa?" she asks. "They need balanced diets. My God, they're just . . ." She pauses and casts her hand across the table in our direction. "*Languishing*," she finishes.

I can't quite locate the precise definition of the word "languishing" in my vocabulary at the moment, but I make a mental note to look it up, because something tells me it's an appropriate word to describe our current state.

Mom says under her breath, "I knew it was going to be my fault somehow."

"I didn't say that," Gma insists. "Conner, what are *you* feeding them?" she directs, pointedly, at my dad now, always the equal-opportunist insulter.

"Will you let it go?" Dad finally says. "They're college students, for God's sake; they're just worn out."

So I guess the trial isn't the only secret we're keeping from them. The part about Caelin not going back for his last semester must've never entered one of Dad's weekly Sunday-evening phone calls with Gma over the past year.

I look at Caelin, and he sighs. "Actually," he begins, but Dad tosses him a stern look that shuts him right down. Caelin shakes his head and pours himself a generous glass of wine, takes a big sip, then fills it up again. No one seems to notice. He sets it between us and tips his head toward me, gives me a small nod. I gladly take a giant sip, which, also, no one seems to notice.

Gpa asks about Dad's work, and that takes the focus off us for now. Mom busies herself with bringing dishes to the kitchen and refilling them with food. I pick at my mashed potatoes just so I'm not drinking on an empty stomach, but nothing really appeals to me with all these lies filling in the gaps between us.

"Oh," Gma says, holding her index finger up as if she just remembered something. "Caelin, we were reading in the paper about Kevin Armstrong. Tell me this isn't that little boy who was always hanging around here?" she says, shaking her head, already in disbelief. "Your roommate?"

Caelin wipes his mouth on his napkin before answering. "It is, actually," he answers. "The same one."

"Oh my," Gma breathes. "He's in a world of trouble from what I gather."

Caelin nods and takes a sip of wine. "Yeah, I hope so."

And then, out of nowhere, Dad slams his hand down on the table. Everyone flinches, the silverware jumps off the plates. "Dammit," he yells. "Can we just have a decent family dinner for once and not dredge up all this garbage?"

I take in a sharp breath of air and hold it, unable to let it go.

"Conner!" my mom shouts.

"What's all this about?" Gma asks, looking around the table. "What did I say?"

Then everyone's suddenly yelling at each other. I don't even know what they're saying anymore or who's on what side of which problem. Gma is still looking around, waiting for someone to tell her what's going on. I stand from the table and walk around to give her a kiss on the cheek. I do the same to Gpa. And then I continue through the kitchen, grab my coat from the hook by the back door, slide on my shoes, and go outside. The cold damp night air rushes into my lungs, and it's such a relief to breathe again that I laugh.

I sit down on the wooden seat of our ancient swing set and let my feet dangle beneath me, let my body rock back and forth in the wind. I lean all the way back and look at the stars, studying the white clouds of my breath, counting again, slowly this time. From one to five, in and out, over and over.

I hear the back door open and close. I sit upright and see my brother walking toward me, carrying the remainder of a bottle of wine.

"Well, they left," he says as he sits down in the seat next to me, offering me the bottle.

I shake my head. "Thanks, I think I've had enough."

"You okay?"

I shrug. "Ish."

"Okay-ish?"

"Yeah," I answer. "You?"

"Well, other than apparently looking like shit, I'm okay-ish too."

I start laughing, and so does he.

"Dude," he says, taking a sip from the bottle. "We really put the 'fun' in dysfunctional, don't we?"

"Pretty much," I agree. "Also, did you just call me 'dude'?"

"I've had a lot to drink," he says with a laugh, shaking his head.

"Hey, should you maybe slow down a little with that?" I ask, nodding toward the bottle between his hands. It's like we swapped places at some point. Now he's the screwup, and I'm supposed to be the good one, but I don't think he realizes I'm not done being the screwup yet. Our parents must be so proud.

"Yeah, I know," he says, brushing me off. "I will."

"When?"

"When that motherfucker's behind bars," he answers, and takes another mouthful.

"Well, but what if that doesn't happen?" I ask. "Then what?"

"Don't even say that," he tells me. "Don't even put that out there." He swings his arm toward the sky, *out there*, at the universe, and the wine spills all over both of us. "Sorry," he says. "Sorry."

"It's all right," I tell him, shaking the wine off the sleeve of my coat.

He sets the bottle down on the ground against the leg of the swing set and pulls a pack of cigarettes from his jacket pocket. Lights one up and offers it to me.

"Tempting," I admit. "But no thanks."

"Good," he says. "That's really good." He inhales, and the red tip of the cigarette burns bright in the darkness. He leans backward and exhales the smoke away from me. Then he holds the cigarette out in front of him and stares at it for a moment before depositing it into the wine bottle, where it sizzles and hisses. He looks at me for approval, and I hold my hand out for a little fist bump, which he returns.

"Hey, I bet you're sorry Josh couldn't make it for our lovely family gathering tonight?" he says, grinning. "Does he know we're crazy?"

"Oh, yeah." I can't help but laugh. "He definitely knows *I'm* crazy, anyway. Um, we broke up, actually," I say out loud for the first time.

"Oh no," he says, his voice softening with genuine concern. "Why?"

"Guess my craziness got to be a little much for the poor guy," I try to joke, but it's not funny, not even to me.

"You need me to go kick his ass again?" he asks. "I will."

"No, it's my fault." I look down and drag my foot through the patch of dirt under the swing. "I did something pretty messed up that really hurt him, and . . ." I shrug and sniffle, trying to hold back the tears. "I just don't know how we move on, really."

"I'm sorry," he says, but thankfully, he doesn't press for details about what I did that was so messed up.

"Yeah, me too."

Now if only I could figure out how to tell Josh that I'm sorry.

The next day, I'm with Mara in her car, eating drive-through tacos. She tells me about Thanksgiving with her dad and his fiancée and how they had the meal catered.

"It was really yummy," she admits. "But I didn't tell them that. It's still cheating to cater, even if it tastes better than the nasty turkey my mom always made. That dryness spells family." She tears open a packet of hot sauce and squeezes it into the cheese dip we're about to share, then asks me the question I've been dreading: "So, how are things going with you?"

I tell her what happened with Josh, but she interrupts me before I can tell her the worst part. "Oh my God, Edy, are you telling me you're pregnant, is that why you—"

"What? No! God, no. I got the morning-after pill—well, actually, Josh got it for me—wait, is that why I what?" I ask. "What were you gonna say?"

"Oh. Nothing. You just look a little . . ." She pauses, squinting as she stares at me. "A little rough. That's all."

"Yeah, that seems to be the consensus."

"Sorry, keep going," she says, dipping a tortilla chip into the queso and offering it to me. "How did this lead to you breaking up?"

"I knew I'd missed too many days, like I knew it was risky. But I let him . . . you know, come, anyway."

"Oh," she murmurs. "Um. *Why*?"

I shake my head. "I don't know anymore; I just did. And he's really pissed. I've never seen him so angry. And then I got angry that he was angry, and the next thing I know, he's telling me what a fuckup I am, and then we're taking a break and I'm throwing a water bottle at him." I pause, trying to recall whether I left anything out. "Yeah, that's pretty much what happened."

"You threw a water bottle at him?"

"It missed."

She nods, seeming to think about this detail for longer than feels necessary. "But wait, he really called you a fuckup? That doesn't sound like him."

"Well, okay, he didn't use the word 'fuckup,' but that's what he meant. And he was right," I continue. "I am a fuckup."

"Edy, don't say that."

"No, I am. What I did? That was fucked up—you think so too."

"Okay, but one fuckup doesn't make *you* a fuckup," she argues.

"I just keep thinking, if I hadn't told him and just dealt with it on my own . . ." I venture back into the loop my thoughts have kept getting stuck on these past few weeks. "But I guess that's not the point," I say, more to myself.

"Yeah," Mara agrees. "Can I say something to try to make you feel better that I also happen to believe is true?"

"Okay."

"I think you did the right thing telling him. I think that's actually you fucking up less, because you were honest. And I think you guys can work it out." She takes my hand. "Actually, I know you can."

I squeeze her hand in thanks, but it just reminds me of how that was our thing—me and Josh—the hand-squeeze private Morse code thing.

"Oh," I add. "And, of course, there's that whole little trial thing happening in January. So, I basically have a month to pull myself together and get ready to go through that whole fucking mess all over again."

She squeezes my hands even harder now. "You can do it."

I breathe in deeply through my nose and try to absorb some of the tears back into my body before they can make it out of me. "All right, I can't start crying again—I've been crying for three weeks straight. I can't physically cry again right now or I'm afraid I'm going to cause permanent damage to my body."

Mara's eyes light up. "Okay, that gives me an idea." She wraps up all our food and sticks it back in the carryout bag by my feet, then starts the car—all with this wild smirk across her face.

"Okay, why am I scared right now?" I ask her as she shifts the car into drive.

"Buckle up," she orders.

She takes us down the familiar roads of our tiny town until, twenty minutes later, we're pulling into the parking lot of a mostly abandoned strip mall that looks vaguely familiar. And then I see the sign: SKIN DEEP.

"No," I tell her.

"Hear me out," she begins. "I was just thinking that we need to do something that'll remind you of what a badass you are, and seriously, nothing makes me feel like more of a badass than getting a new piercing."

Mara has been collecting them. First her nose—I was there for that one—then her eyebrow, then her lip, then her tongue, then her navel, and who knows where else these days.

"Haven't you wanted to get your cartilage pierced since, like, forever?" she asks, reaching out to touch my ear. "It's very tasteful and cute."

I shrug. "Yeah, I guess."

"Well? Why not do it now?"

"I'm not sure the middle of an emotional crisis is really the best time to commit to permanent body alteration."

"Oh, please," she says, unbuckling her seat belt. "Emotional crises are literally the *only* time to do this kind of thing! And a piercing is hardly permanent. A tattoo—now, that's a lifetime commitment. No, you're getting your cartilage pierced, and if you hate it, you can take it out. Come on. Cameron's working today. He'll get us in right away."

"He still works here?"

"Yeah. After graduation he moved from piercer to apprentice tattoo artist."

I follow her inside and recognize the small waiting room from last time—somehow it seems less shady now, though, cleaner. The music playing through the speakers seems gentler, everything softer now than it was before. Cameron comes out from the back and actually looks happy to see me here with Mara.

"Hey, Eden. Wow, it's been a while," he says, all smiles.

"Edy's getting a piercing," she tells him.

"Actually," I say as I look around at all the artwork on the walls, "I was thinking I might get a tattoo." Because maybe I do need something permanent, something drastic. Something to bring me back to reality when I get in my head.

"What?" Mara shrieks. "Yes!"

Cameron sets me down with a bunch of books and says, "Here, look through these portfolios for ideas. I'm gonna finish up with this guy in the back and then we'll do it."

I look through the books, turning page after page, waiting for something to jump out at me, while Mara talks with the older tatted-up guy behind the front desk like they're old friends—and they might be. I've missed a lot.

And then I turn the page, and in the middle of all these different elaborate, pretty, floral designs, I see it. "Found it," I call out to Mara.

She skips over to me and looks. "A dandelion? That's sweet. Understated. Very *you*."

The guy from behind the counter comes over to look too, seeming excited for me. "Nice," he says. "Where are you getting it?"

I look down at my arms and push my sleeve up. "Maybe here?" I say, drawing a circle with my finger around the inside of my wrist.

"Yeah," he says with a smile, "that's gonna look good."

Mara hops and squeals. "Now you're making me want to get one too. But I'll wait. This is your day."

"No, it's not. It's . . ." I start to say, but then I freeze when I see who's coming out from the back room, Cameron following along behind him up to the counter. I can see he has the sleeve of his T-shirt rolled up, a fresh tattoo on his shoulder, covered with plastic wrap, but I can still make it out. A number. His number from basketball. Forever branded on his body.

It's Jock Guy. Again, haunting me like some kind of unresolved recurring nightmare.

I watch him as he pays Cameron; he doesn't even notice me sitting here. He may have chased me down before, but now it's my turn. Suddenly I'm on my feet, following him out, the chimes on the door dinging twice in quick succession.

"Hey," I call after him. "Hey!"

He turns around. "Yeah?"

"Do you remember me?" I ask him.

He starts to shake his head, but then I see something register on his face, "Oh. Yeah, you're Caelin's . . ." But he pauses. "I mean, your Josh's . . ." He starts again but stops.

"*I'm Caelin's, I'm Josh's,*" I mimic, savoring the sharpness in my tone. "Eden, my name's Eden."

"Right, yeah," he says, glancing around, maybe looking for Caelin, for Josh—to see if they're here to defend me. "So, what's up?"

"Just so you know, I remember what you did that day. When you and your buddy wanted to scare me after school that time. And I know you spread lies about me too."

"I don't know what you're talking about," he says, but he can't look me in the eye.

"Yes, you do."

"What do you want?" he asks. "An apology?"

I shake my head and continue. "I never told Josh you did that. But I just want you to know that it was really fucked up—pathetic, actually."

"Fine," he mutters. "That it?"

I shrug. "Yeah, that's it."

He nods and starts to turn away.

"You know, I don't even know your name," I call after him.

He turns back around and opens his mouth. "It's Za—"

"No, I don't *want* to know it," I tell him.

"Whatever," he mumbles, then turns back around, picks up his pace as he walks to his car.

When I go back inside, everyone's watching me from the window.

Cameron keeps asking if I'm okay, pausing as he dips the tip of the needle of the tattoo pen in the black ink. And I keep telling him I'm fine.

"It hurts, but not in the way I thought it would."

"Tough girl, huh?" he says admiringly.

I laugh, but he tells me to hold still.

"By the way, I never thanked you," he says.

"For what?"

"Finally cutting Steve loose," he answers, and looks up at me like he's trying to make sure I know he's genuinely thanking me. "I know I gave you a lot of shit about how you treated him in the beginning, but I didn't like how he started treating you, either. I'm just glad you ended it when you did, how you did. Before it got too . . ." He doesn't finish, but I think I know what he means: too volatile, painful, destructive. "For both of you, I mean."

I just nod in return.

My time with Steve feels like it was so long ago. I don't even feel like I'm the same person anymore. Back then I felt like I had no choice but to accept whatever kind of affection was offered to me even if it wasn't what I wanted or needed. But maybe we can only accept the love we think we deserve.

"I know I don't say it or show it very often," he adds, not looking up from my arm as he gently wipes the ink and blood off my skin. "But I do think of you as a friend, too, you know."

"Thank you," I tell him. "For saying that. And for being good to Mara all these years—she deserves to be loved that way."

He smiles but doesn't say anything.

"What do you think?" he asks after he finishes.

I look at my wrist, at my own personal dandelion, little seeds floating off toward the palm of my hand. Wishes, hopes. Mine.

JOSH

It's my last night home, and we're sitting around watching TV in the living room after eating leftover Thanksgiving dinner for the second night in a row. Mom stands abruptly, looks at her watch, and says, "I'm gonna run to the grocery for a bit. Any requests?"

"We have a house full of food," Dad points out, gesturing toward the kitchen.

"Well, sue me! I want something else," she claps back.

He holds his hands up. "Okay, okay," he says softly. "I was just saying."

I have a sudden flashback to when I'm twelve, hearing my mom give my dad this same excuse—except she'd say "we." *We* were going to the store or out for ice cream. Or *we* were going in search of something special I needed for a last-minute school assignment—me and her. Only we never went to the store or for ice cream or off to find that one missing item. She was taking me to a meeting. I remember she always had a bunch of go-to excuses at the ready, to pull out of her back pocket whenever she needed one. And as I look up at her now, I wonder if it's still that way, because Dad's right, after all, we have a ton of food in this house.

"Mom, can I come with you?" I ask, already getting off the couch.

She scrunches her eyebrows together and says, "To the store, really?"

"Yeah," I tell her.

She shakes her head and says, "Don't be silly. I'll be home soon. Text me if you think of anything you want. Or anything you want to bring back to school with you."

"No, Mom, I want to come," I try to say more firmly as I make my way over to the door and tug my sneakers on.

She looks at me, almost getting annoyed, but then I nod, widen my eyes, try to secretly tell her I know we're not actually going to the store.

"Oh," she says, pushing her arms through her coat. "All right."

She walks over to kiss my dad and says, "Be home soon."

He looks up at her, then at me. "Well, now I wanna come too," he jokes.

My mom swats his arm and shakes her head. "Goodbye," she calls over her shoulder.

Outside, she pulls on her gloves and looks over at me but doesn't say anything yet.

Once we're in the car, I ask, "You're going to a meeting, right?"

"Yes," she answers. "You really want to come?"

"Yeah, I've sorta been thinking about it lately. Thinking

maybe I should give it another try. As long as you don't mind me tagging along with you?"

She shakes her head. "Not at all."

We pull into the parking lot of a church and go inside, past all the stained glass and pews, down into the basement, to a room with a sign on the door that says AL-ANON MEETING TONIGHT 8PM.

The room is small and looks like it could be the basement of any home nearby, not much here to signal we're even in a church. There's a table set up with refreshments, white powdered doughnuts, and coffee. Pamphlets about Al-Anon and Alateen and AA and NA laid out for the taking. More and more people arrive, young and old, and my mom talks with everyone, lets me hang out in the back by the doughnuts. As everyone begins to find a seat around the circle, my mom gestures for me to come. I take the empty spot next to her.

"Well," I hear my mom say next to me, but when I turn to look at her, I realize she's not talking to me, she's talking to everyone. "It's a few minutes after eight, so why don't we go ahead and get started."

I look around the circle, trying to figure out who the facilitator is, the old man with the cane and the gray beard, the middle-aged woman in the fancy shoes who looks like she just came from a business meeting. Or maybe it's the—

"Welcome, everyone," my mom begins. "I'm Rosie, and my husband is an addict." My *mom* is running this meeting. I just watch her, admire her, while she tells our story—her story—kind of in awe of how she can just put herself out here like this. "I know how hard the holidays can be for all of us, not just our loved ones. I certainly do a lot more worrying around this time of year," she continues, and finally, she opens the floor. "Who would like to share?"

I just listen.

To the bearded man whose wife is an alcoholic. To the lady with the fancy shoes whose teenage daughter is relapsing right now. The girl who's probably not much older than me, talking about her fiancé. The man whose brother is getting out of rehab this week. When there's a lull in the conversation, my mom asks if anyone else would like to share and looks over at me.

"I'm Josh. My dad is . . . is an alcoholic, an addict," I say, finding it so hard to get those words out. "This is my first time doing this since I was a kid. I'm just observing today—listening, I mean—if that's okay."

"That's fine," Mom says, and heads nod up and down in agreement around the circle. "Often, it helps to just know there are other people out there who can relate."

Another person introduces themselves—a middle-aged man who could be anyone you pass on the street. "I'm struggling," he says, clasping his hands together in front of him. "I try so hard to let go of that compulsion to want to control everything she does." I'm not sure if his *she* is a wife or a child or what, but it doesn't matter because I watch him lean forward over his lap and start crying. "But it's so hard to trust her—hell, who am I kidding? It's hard to trust anyone," he finishes. Around the circle, heads nod in understanding and I realize I'm nodding along with them. The younger girl with the fiancé gets up and grabs the box of tissues that's sitting on the refreshment table and brings it over to the man.

The meeting ends with the Serenity Prayer, and the woman next to me grabs my hand, holds on tightly. My mom reaches for my other hand, and even though it's small in mine, it feels so strong, solid.

"I'm proud of you," she says, looking over at me while we're driving home.

"I didn't do anything. You were great, though, Mom," I tell her. "How long have you been doing that—leading the meetings, I mean?"

"A while." She shrugs, then smiles and reaches over to mess up my hair. "So, what did you think? Will you be going again—I'm sure you can find a meeting near campus pretty easily."

I nod. "Yeah, I think I might."

"That would be good for you, with everything that's been going on," she says. "I'm always here—you know that—but a mother isn't always what you need."

I'm not exactly sure what she means by that, not sure if she's talking about Dad or Eden or school or what, but I take this moment to ask her the question I've been too afraid to say out loud: "He seems different this time, right?"

She waits to look at me until we pull up to the red light. "He was really shaken when you didn't come home over winter break last year. It hurt him."

"I'm sorry," I begin. "I didn't mean to—"

"No, stop," she interrupts. "That's the point, you took a stand—you've never done that before."

"Oh," I mutter.

"And it didn't just hurt him, it scared him. He realized he could lose you. That's what's different this time. As far as I can tell, anyway."

"You've stood up to him lots of times," I point out.

"Well, it's different. He knows I'm not going anywhere. We're in this thing together. For better or worse, right? That's what I vowed, and I'll be damned, it looks like I'm sticking to it. But you?" She pokes my arm. "You made no such promise. I think he finally gets that."

"Do you regret it?" I ask her, though I'm not sure I'm ready for the answer. "Sticking to your promise, I mean."

"No," she responds. "Especially not lately."

When we get home, equipped with a few bags of random groceries for good measure, Dad is outside in the driveway, illuminated by the motion lights on the side of the garage. He's slowly dribbling one of my old basketballs I hadn't seen since middle school, and when he sees us pull up on the side of the street, he tosses his cigarette on the ground, steps on it quickly.

"Does he really think I don't know he's smoking?" Mom says, shaking her head as she unbuckles her seat belt and starts getting out of the car.

I reach into the back seat for the bags, but Mom comes up behind me and touches my arm.

"I'll get these," she tells me. "Why don't you go hang out with your father awhile, huh?"

"Yeah," I agree, "okay."

Dad starts walking down the driveway toward us, with the ball perched between his arm and his hip. "I was about to file a missing persons report on you two," he jokes.

"Mother-son bonding knows no time constraints," Mom says, always quick on her feet, in a different way than Dad is.

"Need help with those?" he asks.

"I've got it," Mom says, hurrying up the driveway, stopping for just a second as Dad gives her a kiss on the cheek. "Don't stay out here too late, boys," she calls over her shoulder. "And, Joshua, don't go too easy on him."

I stay behind. Not sure what to say, I hold my hands up. He passes me the ball. I pass it back. He goes for a shot, but I block him. I take the shot instead.

He claps his hands and waits for the pass.

He tries to get past me, but I block him again.

And again. And again.

"Wow, all right," Dad says, laughing. "You're really not gonna go easy on your old man, are you?"

"Nope."

"Good," he says, and I think we both know we're not talking about basketball anymore.

I pivot and jab, drive forward, stay a step ahead of him, make the basket. Over and over. I'm tiring him out, I can tell, but I don't stop. Not until he's standing there in the middle of our driveway, hands on hips, breathing heavy, smiling only a little when he says, "All right, all right." He raises his hands in the shape of a T and shakes his head. "Time-out, okay? Time-out."

"You done?" I call over to him.

"You got me." He breathes out forcefully, bends over with his hands on his knees for a second before standing upright again. "You got me, Joshie."

We go sit on the front steps, where Mom managed to stealthily leave two water bottles for us. He cracks open the first bottle and hands it to me, takes the second one for himself. We sit there side by side, drinking in long sips, both of us still catching our breath.

"Josh, do you know how proud I am of you?" he says, out of nowhere.

"Because of basketball."

"Well, no," he says. "I'm proud of you regardless of basketball."

"You are?"

"How can you even ask me that?" he says, letting out this short puff of air. "Of course. Of course I am. It's just a game."

I nod, letting his words sink in, trying to figure out why that doesn't feel true to me. It's a game, sure. A game I've grown to hate. A game that's taken so much from me, yet I can't seem to let go of it, even though I know it's just a game.

"It's not, though. It's not just a game to me," I hear myself telling him. "It's all I had."

"What do you mean?" He's shaking his head, squinting, not understanding. "Don't say that. You have so much going for you."

"No, I mean I clung to it. When you weren't there. When you weren't available."

"When I was using, you mean?" he says.

"Yeah."

"Josh, I—" he starts, but I'm not finished.

"I have held on to this game for so long, even when it's unhealthy, even when I hate how it makes me feel, even when I hate myself for being a part of this team right now." I have to stop and catch my breath, give my brain a chance to catch up with my words. "This fucking game has hijacked my life—and I hate it. God, I don't even know what I'm doing anymore!"

"Josh," he begins again, "no one is forcing you to stick with this if that's not—"

"No, *you* are!"

"Me? I have never—"

"Yes, Dad. I have been forced to keep this up because I don't trust that you're going to be there for me. But this?" I pick up the ball that's sitting between my feet. "This thing that's just a game—it might only be a game, but it's always there. It's been the constant, when that's what you should've been for me."

He's covering his mouth while he watches me, really listening to me.

"I—I'm a mess. I'm actively destroying my life over this," I continue, and I can feel hot tears on my face already, but I don't care. "Do you know *I* broke up with Eden? It was me. I broke up with her, even though I love her so much, because I thought I couldn't trust her. But it's you—you're the one I don't trust."

He shakes his head, and I see the tears in his eyes, hear the sheer sadness in his voice when he says, "I never—" But he stops and lets out this heart-shattering sob. "I never knew you felt this way." He gasps. "About any of it, I swear, I didn't know. I thought . . ." He pauses. "You had your mother, and she is so great, so *good*," he says, his voice trembling on that last word, as he jabs his fingers into the center of his chest, "so much better than me. I just thought—"

"Mom's great. Yes, she's a good person. She's an amazing mother, but I need you, too—I can't believe I have to tell *you* that."

He takes the ball from my hands and drops it, letting it roll down the steps into the grass, and he pulls me in with both arms, just holding on, both of us holding on.

“Thank you,” he says when we part. “Thank you for trusting me enough, right now, to tell me all of this. I can take it, I promise you. I’m here, all right? I’m not going anywhere this time.”

“Okay,” I tell him.

“Okay?” he repeats.

We stand, and as we start toward the door, I feel like I have a weight—a physical weight—lifted off me, the heaviness I’ve been carrying around inside me for so long, gone.

“Dad, wait,” I say. “I’m proud of you too, you know that, right?”

When I get back to school Sunday night, I send Coach an email letting him know I’m going to miss practice the next day. I tell him I have a personal matter to take care of, even though I know he said having a personal life isn’t allowed.

I’m waiting outside my adviser’s office first thing in the morning—I get there even before the department’s office assistants show up. Because I finally have my priorities straight.

EDEN

On Monday after class, I walk into the café and buy two bags of the nice dark-roast coffee with my employee discount. Then I go into the back to find Captain Douchebag at his desk.

"I have to quit," I tell him.

He looks at me, stone-faced, like I'm supposed to care that I'm making him mad. "I assume you're not giving two weeks' notice, either; you're just leaving."

"Yes," I tell him.

"Well." He breathes in, plucks the pen from behind his ear and tosses it onto his desk, and says, "I don't know what we'll do without you. You were such an asset."

I have the thought immediately and hold back for a moment, but then decide, why not? He really doesn't matter. There's nothing he can do to me. So I smile sweetly, then tell him, "And you were such an asshole."

I stand there for just a second so I can watch as his mouth drops open. Then I set my cleaned and folded apron on his desk and walk away.

"Don't expect a reference!" he yells after me.

I avoid eye contact with Perry on my way out, because he doesn't matter either.

I keep my next appointment with my therapist, and she even laughs when I relay my quitting story before going on to point out, more seriously, why this is a sign that I'm making progress.

I go to every class for the last two weeks of the semester and do not put Josh's shirt back on again even after I wash it. I'm sure this is somehow progress too, even though it doesn't feel like it. I let Parker drag me out for a jog a few times, and she tries not to laugh too hard when I can't make it more than thirty seconds without needing a break.

But I get better every time, especially when I realized that the breathing is not so different from when I used to play clarinet. Using the diaphragm, deep breaths all the way to the bottom of my lungs—it comes back to me so easily, somehow.

We have one week between the last day of classes and the first day of finals. The only obligation either of us has, other than swim practice for Parker and working in the library for me, is to study for our exams.

Parker is the only reason I know what to do with myself at all and don't get swallowed up by the overwhelming task of trying to figure out how to study. Everything was daunting and had me on the verge of multiple panic attacks until she initiated me into her

Study-a-Thon ritual. She brings me smoothies in the mornings and we order in food for Kim McCrorey each night. I make us a pot of dark roast to share in the afternoons, while we camp out in the living room with our books and notes and laptops. We stay up until midnight every night and wake up at seven to go jogging.

It feels good to use my brain for something other than worrying and hating myself. And it feels good to treat my body well for a change. For so long it seemed like the only time my body felt good was when Josh was making it feel that way. But this is different. *I'm* doing this. Working my muscles, getting stronger, feeding my body, actually taking care of myself for once.

I jog out on my own the Sunday before finals start because I'm so pumped with this new energy, Parker told me to go away and leave her alone so she could take a nap. So I run around the block at first, then back again, and it's not until I double back past the gelato place that I begin to feel how cold it's getting with the sun going down, my fingers and toes starting to go numb. I need something to warm me up before I head home. There's a handwritten WE'RE HIRING sign near the register this time. Chelsea pops up from her seat behind the counter, where she's got a book open in front of her.

"My name is Chelsea," she says, her voice flat and bored like last time. "I'll be your barista today."

"Oh, hi," I say, happy to see her for no reason. "I came in here once before when you were working. You probably don't remember me."

She just stares.

"You studying?" I ask her, gesturing to her open book.

"Yeah, well, it's been pretty dead all day. Guess no one wants gelato when it's doing"—her eyes shift to the drizzle hitting the window—"*that* outside."

I laugh, she doesn't.

"So?" she says.

"Oh, yeah. Can I get a hot chocolate to go?" I ask.

She starts making my drink and pushes her glasses up. While I stand there, I look around behind the counter, wondering if maybe this would be a safe place to work, if I could imagine myself slinging gelato and coffee here. But then I catch a glimpse of something familiar sitting next to Chelsea's seat. She comes back over and snaps a lid on the cup, slides it across the counter toward me, and says, "Here you are. One hot chocolate. To go."

"Hey, can I ask, what instrument do you play?" I gesture to her case—one that looks a lot more beat-up than mine, covered with stickers and scratches and scuff marks, having seen more of the world than mine has.

She glances down at her case too, and when she looks back up at me, she's actually smiling. "The sax," she answers. "Well, and piano, and guitar. You play?"

"Oh, I don't—I *used* to play clarinet in high school, but not anymore."

"Too bad, we actually need a clarinetist."

"Like for an orchestra or something?" I ask, puzzled by the strange flutter in my voice.

"Well, it's not quite that formal. I mean, I *am* in the university orchestra—I'm a music major, so . . . first year," she adds with a shrug. "But there's this other group that's open to all students. It's the Tuck Hill Campus Band."

"Oh," I say, feeling my body inching closer, curious.

"You haven't heard of it?"

"No, I haven't."

"Well, it's kind of an ensemble. But anyone can audition. We don't really do official concerts; we just perform at different campus events. I guess it's more about having fun." She looks around quickly, like she's caught off guard by her own talkativeness. "It's nice. We practice together once a week. Low pressure—*no* pressure, really—compared to everything else, I mean."

I feel my head nodding, because I know exactly what she means, this fellow first-year student, by pressure. It's different from high school. Everything's different here. It's only at this moment I realize that pressure, that difference, isn't something I've been able to talk about with anyone—not Josh or Parker or Dominic—because they're all already past the newness of it. But I'm not; I'm *in* it. Right now I'm directly in the middle of it.

"You interested, or . . . ?"

She lets the question dangle there.

"Me?" I double-check. "Seriously?"

"I'm always serious," she replies, monotone, but then flashes a brief smile. She's kind of strange, this girl, but I kind of like it.

"Oh God, I don't know, I'm really rusty. I haven't even taken my clarinet out of its case in—" I stop myself, because I was going to say *years*, but that's not true. I'd almost forgotten about my clarinet sitting there, waiting, on the top shelf of my closet. "I did play for like six years, though, before I stopped," I add, wondering who I'm trying to convince of my worthiness, myself or Chelsea.

"Six years isn't nothing," she says. "Rusty's okay. It's not like it's the symphony or anything."

"Um, all right."

"I can text you before the next practice if you wanna check it out. It won't be until after exam week, though. Will you be around over winter break?"

"Yes," I hear myself saying, making the decision right there on the spot, that I don't want to go home for winter break. "I'll be here."

She hands me her phone to put my number in.

"Okay," she says, looking at my contact info and adding, "Eden."

I walk home, sipping on my hot chocolate, realizing I completely forgot about asking for a job application. But I'm feeling pretty good about myself anyway, as the snow starts to fall, glistening as it collects on the ground and sticks to my hair and clothes.

An informal ensemble band, not for grades or credits. I smile to myself as I cross the street, remembering the feeling of being in a loud music room, the part right at the end of every rehearsal, when everyone would just sort of let loose and wail their instruments at the same time, to no particular tune or song or rhythm—just an all-at-once cacophony of sound—for fun.

When I come in the door, he's standing there at the bank of mailboxes. He's committed to the beard now. And he's wearing his green plaid flannel shirt that he once let me wear when I stayed over, and all I can think about is how soft and warm it was.

"Hi-hey," he says, seeming startled to be standing here face-to-face with me for the first time in a month.

"Hi," I manage to say back.

He searches my eyes, and I'm pretty sure I'm searching his right back, for some clue of what we're supposed to do. But I'm unable to look away, unable to speak, unable to move.

"Um," he utters. "You . . . look . . ."

"Cold?" I offer.

He smiles, and it's so beautiful I can't help but smile back. He licks his lips and swallows as he steps closer to me. He reaches for my hand, and I let him. "I miss you," he says quietly.

I nod and squeeze his hand once before forcing myself to let go and take a step away from him. "I miss you too," I tell him, because that's the truth. "But I'm not ready."

"Okay," he says. And he simply stands there holding his mail close to his chest while I walk up the stairs.

JOSH

There was so much I wanted to say; I'd been saving up all the things I needed to tell her. So much has happened in this month we've been apart. I wanted to tell her how I quit the team. How I've been going back and forth between my adviser and Dr. Gupta for weeks now, making a plan to switch my major to psychology. I think she'd really be happy for me about that one. I'd tell her how I managed to work with the financial aid office to cobble together a bunch of smaller scholarships and grants—and even a loan—to replace the stupid basketball scholarship that's been holding me hostage all this time.

I wanted to tell her how I've been going to these meetings, talking, listening, and doing all this thinking. And how strange it is to have so much time, suddenly, without basketball stealing it away from me. How all I wanted to do with it was to spend it with her, even just as friends—I wish I'd thought to at least tell her that. *I miss you*, I should've said, *not just as my girlfriend, but as my friend too—my best friend.* Because I'm pretty sure that's what she is.

But she's not ready.

That's okay.

I was half expecting her to just keep walking without acknowledging me at all. The fact that she spoke to me to tell me she's not ready is more than I was even hoping for.

When I get back to the apartment, Dominic is sitting at the table hunched over one of his textbooks, and when he glances up at me, he does a double take. "What the hell happened to you?"

"What do you mean?"

"You went downstairs as one person and came back as someone else. Like the opposite of going out and getting punched in the face."

"She talked to me," I answer.

"What'd she say?"

"That she didn't want to talk to me."

He squints and holds his hand in the air, teetering between a thumbs-up and a thumbs-down. "So . . . score?" he says uncertainly.

"Yes, because at least she talked to me," I repeat.

"Straight people really are different, aren't they?" he says to himself. "Oh, speaking of—do you mind if Luke comes up this weekend after finals?"

"No, sounds good," I tell him. "So, is it getting serious?" I ask.

He closes his textbook and looks up at me, trying not to smile. But then he nods slowly and says, "It's very serious. He's moving here. He just found out he can transfer next semester."

"That's amazing. I'm happy for you, man."

"Thank you, that really means a lot." He pauses and says, "And all joking aside, I'm happy she talked to you."

Exam week goes by in a caffeinated blur, as it always does. But that Saturday there's a gathering on the roof to celebrate the end of the semester. With all the students living in this building, it's sort of a given that someone's going to be throwing a party.

I head up before Dominic and Luke—wanted to give them some time alone. Part of me is wondering if she'll show up or not. These kinds of things were always hit or miss with her. I'm talking with a girl who was in my Intro to Forensic Psychology class last semester—she doesn't live here, but one of her roommates' friends does, apparently—when I spot Luke and Eden talking by the edge of the roof. Dominic and Parker are here now too. The girl from my class wanders off to find her roommate, and I go stand by the electric Crock-Pot of hot cider, because that seems like the best place to be either available if she wants to talk to me or to be easily avoidable if she doesn't want to talk to me.

"Hey." I turn around to see Parker standing there. She gives me an unprompted hug, which I find oddly comforting coming from her. "It's been a while since we got to hang out," she says.

"Yeah," I agree. "How have you been?"

"Okay. It's been a weird semester, but I think I'm growing fond of this new roommate-slash-friend role you thrust upon me by bringing her into my life."

"Good," I tell her. "I think, anyway." She stares at me for longer than feels comfortable. "What?" I finally ask.

"I was just waiting to see how long it would take you before you started pumping me for info about her."

"I wasn't—"

"No, I know," she interrupts, smiling. "That's progress." She looks behind me and sort of hitches her chin in the direction of something. When I look over my shoulder, I see that it's Eden standing there. And when I turn back around, Parker's gone.

"You guarding the cider?" she asks with a laugh.

"Um, I guess," I answer. "Want some?"

She nods, and I scoop a ladleful into one of the mismatched mugs sitting out on the table. "Thank you," she tells me as she cradles the mug between her hands and brings it to her face to smell.

"I can leave if you want," I offer.

"No, don't," she says. "We can't keep avoiding each other forever."

She drifts a few steps away and then looks over at me like I should be following, so I do.

I'm quick to tell her, "I was never avoiding you."

"Right." She nods. "Okay, then *I* can't keep avoiding you."

She leads us over to the wicker love seat with the flattened cushions, where we've sat so many other times together. Except this time it's not with her on my lap or me leaning on her shoulder. We just sit side by side like two normal people and look at each other.

"I like the beard," she tells me, adding, "It's not stubble this time, by the way."

I laugh—God, it feels good to laugh in her presence.

"So what else is new with you?" she asks. "Besides the beard, not stubble."

"I quit the team," I tell her.

"Oh my God, Josh. Okay, that's big." She smiles at me like she really does know just how big this is for me. "I knew you could do it."

"What, be a quitter?" I joke.

She pushes my arm a little, and it's the best feeling in the world. Then she looks off into the distance for a moment and smiles again, softer now, and says, "I seem to remember a wise young man once told me that just because you're good at something doesn't mean it makes you happy."

I look down at my mug—that was one of the secrets I told her that night at my house, lying on my couch, while we talked all night. "I can't believe you remember that."

"Why not? I remember everything you say to me."

My heart, flying high, suddenly drops to the ground with a splat.

"I am so sorry about what I said to you, Eden."

"Oh," she breathes. "No, I didn't mean—fuck, sorry—I wasn't talking about that. Really, I was just saying . . . I know basketball has been a huge drain on you for a long time. I wasn't trying to—we don't have to get into all that now."

"Okay. We can, though, if you want. Whenever you want, we can."

She looks at me in that way she does, that super-serious way that makes my heart pound in my throat. "I mean, I guess we can. If you want?" she asks uncertainly as she looks around us.

"Yeah, I would like to," I tell her. "A lot."

She inhales deeply and looks me in the eye. "Well, I finally realized why you were so mad at me," she begins.

"We don't have to do this here," I tell her. "You could come downstairs."

She laughs, my favorite of her laughs: the quick, semi-loud spontaneous one that she always means. "Let's just stay right here, okay? I somehow don't think going to your place is the best idea."

"Wait, you know that's not what I meant, right?"

"I know, but come on, Josh. It's *us*, after all."

Now I laugh, but in my head I'm replaying that word—*us*—over and over. Us. There's still an us to her. "Okay. Point taken. You were saying . . . ?"

She inhales deeply and starts again. "I just want you to know that I get it now. Why you were so mad. I know that sometimes I don't respect myself very much, and somehow, that night, it turned into me not respecting you, too, and I never meant for that to happen. I never wanted to hurt you—I never want to hurt you ever again." She pauses and reaches out to run her hand along my face. "I really am so sorry."

I take her hand in mine now. "Thank you for understanding. You always understand. It's your superpower," I tell her, and she looks down at our hands, that shy smile. "I think I understand, too, a little better anyway, about why it all happened the way it did. And I never meant to hurt you with what I said to you that night."

"This is you," she says, looking up at me.

"What?"

"That's what you said. *This is you*. This—the whole messed-up situation—*is* me."

God, it sounds even worse when she says it like that. "That's what I said, but you have to know that's not true. I mean, I didn't even believe it when I was saying it, and I don't believe it now, either. I swear to you, I never thought that. I would never think that about you. Not ever. I need you to know this."

She looks down at our hands again, and I can see her starting to breathe heavily, sniffing through her nose. Then she sets her mug on the ground, and I start to get afraid that she's going to leave, but then she takes my mug too and sets it down next to hers. She puts her arms around me, and I can feel her body shuddering, her head tucked under my chin. And I just hold her like that, everyone else around us disappearing.

"Thank you," she finally says as she pulls away from me. Her hair gets stuck on my beard-not-stubble, and I tuck it back behind her ear. "I guess I didn't even know how badly I needed to hear that."

She brings her hands up to her face to wipe her eyes, and I see something there on her arm, poking out from under her jacket. She brings her hand up again to run her fingers through her hair, and I know for sure I see something.

"What is this?" I ask her as I take her hand again and turn it over.

"Oh." She pulls her sleeve up. "Yeah, I got a tattoo," she says with a sniffle and a laugh.

"A dandelion?" My heart starts racing. Because. Dandelions. That was *our* thing. "It's beautiful."

"Thank you."

"Does it mean something?" I dare myself to ask.

She breathes in through her nose, gazes out, beyond all the people that are gathered here on the roof, and says, "Well, I guess it's about being free. And strong."

"I like that—it's perfect."

"And you too," she adds, quieter.

"What do you mean?"

"It's sort of about you, too," she says, making my pulse quicken again. "Just a reminder to"—she breathes in deeply again and exhales before continuing—"to try to be the kind of person you think I am."

"What kind of person is that?"

"I don't know, someone who's resilient instead of destructive. Hopeful instead of . . . you know, feeling doomed or powerless or whatever. Brave," she adds.

"That's not the kind of person I *think* you are. That's the way you really are, Eden."

"I'm trying to be."

I bring her wrist to my mouth and kiss that spot where the dandelion is. She touches my face again. And I can't resist the urge; I turn my head to kiss her palm now, that spot where she burned herself. Her fingers go to my lips.

"I really want to kiss you," she says, "but I'm not going to, okay?"

"Oh, okay," I answer.

"I want us to keep talking." She takes hold of both my hands. "I want us to be friends again."

I nod. "I want that too."

"But just friends for now. Because I'm still not ready to—"

"No, I understand. Really, I do."

"So, you'd be all right with that?" she asks. "You can do that?"

"Yeah," I agree. "I can definitely do that."

EDEN

Parker leaves the following Monday to go home to her family for the holidays. The first thing I do is go to the closet and pull down my clarinet case. I've been using this as an incentive to get through exams.

Chelsea texted that the band would be meeting at the end of this week and that it would be a smaller contingent—that was the word she texted, "contingent"—since a lot of the members have already left for winter break. I like that even though Chelsea and I have only had two very awkward conversations, she somehow gets that a smaller group to audition in front of is what I need.

As I take the pieces of my clarinet out of the case and begin putting them all together again, it feels like maybe some other pieces of my life are beginning to fall into place too. Like, maybe I can get back some of who I used to be—the good parts I thought were lost forever.

I promised Parker I'd keep up with jogging so we could continue after she gets back. And I keep my promise; I go for a jog almost every morning. Then practice my audition piece every afternoon, getting a little less rusty each time.

And on Thursday, after nearly a week of polite, friendly texts with Josh, I pull my hair into a messy bun, put on my sports bra, leggings and sweatpants, hoodie and a puffy vest, and thick socks and sneakers. I walk up the stairs, take a breath, and knock on Josh's door.

"Do you want to go jogging with me?" I ask him, forgetting to even say hello first.

He stares at me in the doorway for a moment, studying my face and looking down at my clothes. "I honestly can't tell if you're serious or joking."

"No, I'm really asking you," I tell him. "Jogging is something I do now."

"Since when?" he asks, this sort of half grin on his face.

I don't want to say *since you dumped me*, so I opt for: "I've been hanging around you jocks for so long, it was bound to rub off on me."

"Well, I'm not a jock anymore, remember?" He laughs and adds, "But I'll still go jogging with you."

We fill each other in on the gaps of time we've missed. I tell him about the books I've read for my classes, and I try not to stare at him too much while we run side by side. I think he goes slow for me, but I mostly hold my own as we work our way up and down the streets of our neighborhood. While we run, he tells me about all this stuff he's been doing—going to meetings and confronting his dad and changing his major to something he actually cares about. I can't believe how much has changed with him in such a short time. He's like this shiny new version of himself. I tell him about my clarinet breathing technique, about the audition tomorrow, and he stops running then.

"Seriously, Eden, that's awesome," he says, this huge beautiful smile on his face. "I'm so glad you're getting back into that. It always seemed like something you really missed."

"Yeah," I agree, stopping now too, my breath coming in heavy white puffs of air. "I have missed it."

JOSH

I go to knock on Eden's door the next morning, and as I get closer, I hear music. Not music playing from a speaker but actual music. When she answers the door, she's in pajamas and her favorite hoodie, holding her clarinet.

"Hi," she says with a smile, seeming genuinely happy to see me standing here.

"Morning," I say. "Was that you playing?"

"Depends," she says, narrowing her eyes at me. "Were you coming down here to complain about the noise?"

"No, it sounded really good."

"In that case, come in. Want some coffee?"

"No, I can't stay. I've gotta take care of some financial aid stuff before I leave. But speaking of which. Dominic left for home already—he's helping Luke move out of his dorm."

"Yeah, I heard. Luke's moving here. That's really great."

"Yeah, it is," I agree. "So, I just wanted to see if you want to ride home with me for the break. I know you have your audition later today, but when were you planning on leaving?"

"Oh," she says. "Thanks, but I'm actually staying here."

"By yourself for the holidays, why?"

"Ugh, it's a long story," she sighs. "When I was home for Thanksgiving, it was just—there's some toxic stuff working itself out there right now and I really need my head clear going into this trial."

"Makes sense," I tell her, especially considering how wrecked she was after the last hearing, how it nearly wrecked *us* for good. "You've got to take care of yourself."

"Yeah," she says sadly. "And besides, this time of year is always triggering anyway."

"You mean because of family stuff?"

"Oh," she breathes. "Sometimes I forget you can't actually read my mind. Um, no, it's—the holidays, that's when it happened. When Kevin—the assault," she says, and I somehow get the feeling she's trying to spare me from hearing the word "rape."

"You never told me that."

She sort of shrugs one shoulder.

"Um, just putting this out there. You could stay at my parents' house, with us, if you want. Strictly friends, I promise."

She smiles for a moment. "Thanks, but I think it's best if I just stay here."

I feel like I should offer to stay with her, but the fact is, I need to be home with my family this year. And for her reasons, she needs to be here. She doesn't need me to fix this or make it better or protect her. For once I feel like it'll be all right. Me. Her. This fledgling *us*.

"Okay," I tell her. "Well, in that case, I think I'm probably heading out after this financial aid appointment, so . . ."

She sets her clarinet down on the kitchen counter. Then walks over to me, hugs me tight, breathes in and out, her head, like always, fitting under my chin.

"If you need anything," I begin to say as we pull apart, my hands automatically on her face as I look down at her. And as she looks up at me, I think, for a moment, she wants to kiss me. So I let my hands go to her shoulders instead, back up a step.

"If I need anything," she finishes for me, "I'll call you."

EDEN

The second week of January comes faster than I thought it would. It's the same courtroom as before, except it feels even smaller now because they're so many more bodies in it. More people sitting in the gallery on each side. Extra reporters in the back. A jury now.

I take a sip of water and look out at Mara and Lane. Then my eyes set on CeCe, who's looking down at her notes.

Kevin is there at his table with his lawyers. The white-haired lawyer who loves to raise his hand and object and talk in circles until he makes us all dizzy asks me the same questions as last time, except in more confusing ways, trying to trip me up.

I'd been preparing myself for the past two weeks to be able to face the last question again. I studied the transcripts from the first hearing as if they were for another exam I was destined to ace. I practiced in my apartment, like I practiced the clarinet. Out loud, I practiced saying no in as many ways as I could imagine. I compared each one and ended up picking out my version of no just like I picked out my outfit. Business. Casual. Modest. *No*, I would say, simple and straightforward. Unemotional. Because anyone with half a brain or half a heart would understand that me verbally saying the word no was beside the point.

Last night, at two in the morning, I went into the kitchen to get some water, and when I leaned up against the sink, I remembered something. Something I thought should definitely be on this exam. I texted CeCe about how he assaulted me the next Christmas in our kitchen—I've had to practice using that word too, "assault." I never even mentioned it to anyone, not the detective or Lane or CeCe. It was something I thought didn't even matter before, wasn't bad enough to be worth mentioning. I sent her a text that took up the entire length of the screen on my phone. I told her how I'd remembered when I was in the kitchen just now getting water that he came in when no one was there and pinned me up against the sink from behind while he put his hands all over me, up my shirt and down my pants and wasn't it important to let them know how he kept managing to find these little pockets of terror? To remind me that he was there, to remind me that I'd promised not to tell? That he was holding me hostage for so long after that one night. Because I'd read that article—and even though Josh told me not to read the comments, I did—and I saw the one about five minutes. *Only* five minutes. And they needed to know it wasn't only five minutes that he had me.

CeCe texted back right away:

> Thank you, Eden. This is helpful. But please make sure you get some sleep before tomorrow.

But now that's what I'm thinking about as I sit here—wondering if I made my point earlier when CeCe had seamlessly slipped it into her questions that she somehow wove together to tell a story. And now I've missed the question White Hair has just asked me.

"Do you need me to repeat the question?" he asks.

"Yes," I say clearly into the microphone.

Except now I'm remembering that I forgot to say the part about how he smiled at me. I was supposed to tell them this time how he smiled at me before he left. Kissed. Smiled. Boxers. Door. How could I have forgotten? Stupid. We studied this!

"Can you please instruct the witness to answer the question?" White Hair is saying now.

The judge leans toward me and says, "Eden, please answer the question."

But wait, I missed it again. *Fuck.*

"Um," I begin, and the mic lets out a high-pitched note in place of my voice. "Can you repeat the question again?" I say, too far away from the microphone.

White Hair scoffs and says, "Again, at any point during this encounter, did you verbally say no?"

This is it. The last question. I have to get it right. I search my brain, but I can't find the no I'd memorized. It was supposed to be right there, waiting for me to scoop it up and throw it in his face, all business and casual. But what the fuck. I open my mouth and literally nothing comes out.

"Your Honor," he says.

"The witness will answer the question," the judge says.

I look down at my hands in my lap, and I see my dandelion sticking out from under the cuff of my shirt. "There was no question," I hear myself say, quietly, into the microphone.

"Please speak up," the judge says.

"There was no question," I repeat.

White Hair sighs and says, slowly, enunciating his words: "The question was, did you, at any point during the encounter, say no?"

"And my answer is, there was never a question." I hear my voice shaking. "He never asked."

The lawyer repeats himself, this time adding, "Just yes or no."

"There wasn't a question to answer," I say again, and I can see how mad I'm making him, his face turning red and his mouth going all rigid as he speaks.

"Yes or no," he says. "Did you tell him no?"

"I couldn't answer a question that was never asked."

"Did you ever say the word no?" he almost yells at me now.

I look down at my tattoo again. Then back up, except this time, instead of looking at White Hair or CeCe or Mara or Lane, I look at Kevin. He's watching me closely, that same knifelike stare he used to control me, all this time, up until now.

I lean into the microphone, even as my whole body is trembling, even as I feel the tears rushing to my face, and say with precision now, not breaking eye contact with him: "He. Never. Asked. The. Question." I bypass White Hair and look up at the judge, sitting there perched above my shoulder. "That's my answer."

The next thing I know, I'm busting out through the doors, racing down the hall, trying to remember if I'm headed in the right direction for the bathroom. Mara's running behind me, calling my name. But I don't stop until I make it. And then I push the door open and throw up. Everything.

Mara holds my hair back and keeps telling me how amazing I was.

I hear Lane's heels against the tiles. She says something like "Oh! Eden. Okay. It's okay." And then I'm sweating and freezing and laughing and crying all at the same time as I kneel on the floor next to the toilet. Mara flushes it for me, and Lane brings me some wet paper towels to wipe my mouth, and then even she kneels down on the floor next to me and Mara.

"You did it," Lane tells me with a big smile.

"She was awesome, right?" Mara asks Lane.

She nods, echoing, "Awesome."

When we finally get out to the car, Mara checks her phone. "It's Josh," she tells me as she reads the text.

"He's texting *you*?" I double-check.

She nods. "He didn't want to bother you. He's asking how it went. Is it okay if I tell him you kicked ass?"

I laugh but then say, "Okay."

Her phone dings immediately. "He says: 'I knew she would.'"

We sit there for a moment, and I can feel the effects of the midwinter heat wave that hit this week. Sunbeams catching dust motes in the stuffy car. The silence isn't uncomfortable, and it breaks when Mara leans forward to start the engine and rolls down all the windows, letting in the fresh air.

I realize there's a calmness inside me, for once nothing warring in my head. No fears or guilt or regret or even sadness, just a plain open quietness. I've done what I came to do, and I did it the very best way I knew how. I look at the courthouse, the massiveness of the building striking me as cruel and cold, as I think about Mandy and Gen still in there, waiting. And I wish I could somehow share just a little bit of this feeling with them.

I pull out my phone and find Amanda's number, adding Gen to a new group text. My fingers hover over the letters unsure of what words I can, or should, say. So instead, I send a heart. Just one. Purple. Amanda sends one back immediately, then Gen.

I look at our three hearts for a moment and remember, whatever happens, we did this *for us.*

"So, where to, Edy?" Mara revs the engine. "Food? Coffee? More tattoos?"

I put my phone away and look over at my friend who has become even more my friend over the past few months, who, after all these years, I finally feel like I understand. I'd always made it too complicated, but it was simple. She's Team Edy, as she calls it—and I don't doubt that anymore. I also think she might be the only person in the world I will let keep calling me by that name.

"I know exactly where I want to be."

JOSH

We've been on the roof all day, drinking sun tea Parker made in a big glass jar. "If it's gonna pretend to be spring in the winter, then I'm making some goddamned homestyle tea," she'd said before lugging it up to the roof yesterday.

Dominic and Luke had been doing a good job of keeping me distracted with stories about Luke's many band camp adventures while Parker added jabs and sarcastic comments here and there to keep things exciting. I'd barely been listening, my mind going back to Eden and the trial and what was happening hours away. The not knowing is eating a pit in my stomach, and the not being there was almost painful. I'd spent a good fifteen minutes on it last night at Al-Anon. Ida, a retired professor and our group's designated leader, went over how important it was to have self-care, reminding me to put my oxygen mask on first, even if the plane might be going down, and I try to keep doing that.

I run downstairs to grab sunscreen when Parker complains

she's lobstering, and as I open the door to the roof, I see her and Dominic huddled over my phone.

"What is it?" I ask, hearing the tremble of fear in my voice. "Is it guilty? Is it . . .?" I can't even say the other option.

"We've got good news and bad news," Parker starts.

"Parker—" Dominic cuts her off. "Don't say it like that."

Bad news. And good. There's no equation that works here for me, no way those two things can come together. It's either guilty and good or not guilty and bad. What happens if it's bad? How bad will it get if it's bad news?

"The jury's gonna be out for a while," Dominic explains, reading off my phone, likely noticing my freaked-out expression. "Eden's lawyer said it could be days."

"And that's the bad news?" I ask. It's not great but not that bad. I can deal with this. "What's the good?"

"Eden's on her way back right now," Parker says, a sly smile on her face as she hands me my phone. "And she wants to meet you at the fountain—whatever sinful place that is—at six tonight."

I get there early, and while I wait for her, I think about that day in the grass with the dandelions. I was watching her for a few minutes before I ever walked over, sitting there all quiet and intense. It was like she was the only thing in color to me, everything else in my life felt so gray. I don't know how I convinced myself to go sit down next to her. She was unlike anyone I'd ever known, and I was so intimidated by her—but I liked her. I wanted to know her, wanted her to know me. It was that simple. I was sure. She was worth whatever risk came with trying. Then and now.

EDEN

I get out of the shower and wipe the steam from the mirror. I look at myself for the first time in a long time. I'm almost surprised to see that it's still my face, my eyes, looking back at me. My hair, my body, my tattoo, my scars. "*This is you*," I whisper to myself.

I barely even pay attention as I get dressed; I'm so focused on getting there. I don't want to wait any longer.

I take the path he brought me on that night—our first real date—and I follow it past all the plants with names and the willow tree, and I pick up my pace when I see the clearing up ahead. This time, though, there's no water splashing, no lights, no sounds. Because it's still supposed to be winter, despite the unseasonably warm weather of the evening.

When I get there, I think I've arrived first. But then I see him sitting on the bench inside the alcove of the apple fountain, looking ahead. As I step closer, I see that he has something in his hand. I try to stay light on my feet. And it's only when I'm right behind him that I see what he has. It's a dandelion, and he's blowing on it, watching the little seeds fly off high into the air. I look around and see that dandelions have sprouted up all around the perimeter of the fountain, just over the past few days of sunny weather, just for us, it seems.

For this.

I walk up behind him, slide both of my hands onto his shoulders, and lean forward to kiss his cheek. "I hope you're making wishes when you do that."

He turns his head to look at me, already smiling.

"I was," he says. "Don't worry."

He takes my hand from his shoulder and brings my wrist to his mouth to kiss my tattoo. Then he leads me around to the front of the bench, where I take a seat next to him.

"Well, just one wish, actually," he adds.

"Do you think it'll come true?" I ask.

"It did. You appeared."

I have appeared, I think to myself, and smile as I interlace my arm with his, pulling him closer to me.

"This is a good place," I tell him.

"For what?"

"To be ready," I answer. And then I take his hand in mine. I squeeze once. He looks down at me and squeezes back, two light pulses. I repeat myself, clearly this time, no questions, no doubts. "I'm ready."

RESOURCES

Rape, Abuse & Incest National Network (RAINN): rainn.org

National Suicide Prevention Lifeline: 988lifeline.org

Al-Anon & Alateen: al-anon.org

Alcoholics Anonymous (AA): aa.org

Narcotics Anonymous (NA): na.org

Substance Abuse and Mental Health Services Administration (SAMHSA): samhsa.gov

National Alliance on Mental Illness (NAMI): nami.org

The Trevor Project: thetrevorproject.org

Planned Parenthood: plannedparenthood.org

ACKNOWLEDGMENTS

First and foremost, thank *you*, dear reader, for making space in your heart and mind for Eden's story. For all the kind words, posts, #BookTok edits . . . and your sometimes not-so-subtle requests for a book two! You made me believe another chapter for Eden was not only possible but needed. For that, I will be forever grateful.

My agent, Jess Regel, thank you for bearing with me through the literal years of fits and starts while I stumbled around in the dark trying to figure out what the heck this book was supposed to be. For always championing my writing and having my back through the ups and downs of this wild business over the past decade (*decade*, can you believe it!?). Sincerest thanks to Helm Literary and Jenny Meyer and Heidi Gall at Jenny Meyer Literary for bringing this story to readers far and wide.

Enormous heartfelt thanks are due to my editor, Nicole Fiorica, for your unwavering support of this book—even when it was only a paragraph of an idea. Thank you for understanding Eden and Josh so completely, and for being this book's advocate every step of the way. Your sharp insights and thoughtful guidance have been invaluable in shaping this story . . . and keeping me sane throughout its writing!

I'm also grateful to Justin Chanda, Anne Zafian, Karen Wojtyla, and the amazing team at McElderry Books. So many talented, creative, and dedicated people at Simon & Schuster had a hand in bringing this book to fruition. From its copyediting team, including Bridget Madsen and Penina Lopez, to its designers, Deb Sfetsios-Conover and Steve Gardner, to its production manager, Elizabeth Blake-Linn. And the publicity and marketing teams, with Nicole Valdez, Anna Elling, Antonella Colon, Emily Ritter, Ashley Mitchell, Amy Lavigne, Bezawit Yohannes, and Caitlin Sweeny. As well as Michelle Leo, Amy Beaudoin, Nicole Benevento, and the education and library team.

Additionally, I am thankful, as ever, to editor Ruta Rimas, without whom there would never have been a book called *The Way I Used to Be* and nothing that could be continued here in *The Way I Am Now*.

Endless thanks to my friends and family for putting up with all the canceled plans, missed calls, and unanswered texts while I was writing this book . . . and for still being there when I finished and crawled back out of my writer's cave. The love and inspiration you provide are unparalleled—I owe you big-time.

To my author friends, thank you for your solace at the low points and for celebrating in the highs—Cyndy Etler, Robin Roe, Kathleen Glasgow, Amy Reed, Jaye Robin Brown, Robin Constantine,

Rebecca Petruck, and the entire extended "Camp Nebo" crew—you are all the best of the best.

And last but never least, Sam. Your love has taught me "to wish, to hope, to heal" in ways I never dreamed possible. Thank you for allowing this book to infiltrate our daily lives for *so* long, for the countless conversations about Eden and Josh, for reading innumerable drafts . . . and for letting me borrow our little hand-squeeze-Morse-code thing. You inspire me at every turn.

READING GROUP GUIDE

THE WAY I AM NOW

By Amber Smith

ABOUT THIS BOOK

The unthinkable happened to Eden, and it came close to ruining her life. She'd been on a trajectory full of desperate decisions, self-destructive behavior, and unbearable pain. But now she has told others about what happened, and Kevin is going to have to face the consequences of what he did. So why isn't Eden's life back to normal? Her dad barely talks to her, and her brother's life has been turned upside down. Her friends don't know how to treat her, and Eden can't seem to move forward. She's tried everything she can think of—therapy, dating a "nice" guy, working hard at her schoolwork, and getting a job—but she feels like she's still in survival mode.

When she finds out that she's been admitted to Tucker Hill University, Eden can't wait to accept. In a new city and a new environment, she can start to rebuild her life without confronting a bad memory at every turn. And if she's able to reconnect with Josh in a meaningful way, all the better.

And at first it works. She and Josh pick up where they left off with one big difference—this time there are no secrets between them. But Eden has a lot of baggage, and Josh isn't always sure he's doing the right thing. Can they each put aside their pasts long enough to build a future together? And is their relationship built on trust or something altogether shakier?

DISCUSSION QUESTIONS

1. The book begins with Eden saying, "I'm disappearing again," which is a familiar feeling for her. (p. 3) What are some other times that Eden "disappears" or "slips away"? Why does she do it? Is it on purpose? Are there times when she is very present and not in danger of disappearing at all?
2. Why is Eden grateful to Cameron for not pretending to be nice to her? Are there other people who treat her normally? How does Cameron's attitude toward her change over the course of the book?
3. Eden's medication calms her panic attacks but also dulls her emotions. At one point, she says, "I'm suddenly unsure if I can trust myself to even know whether I'm safe or not with that part of me dormant." (p. 13) Do you think she can trust herself to recognize unsafe situations? Discuss your feelings about the costs and benefits of medications like the one Eden is taking.
4. When Eden sees Josh at the concert, she says, "There's nothing I needed more tonight than this, with Josh. And God, how I'm not used to getting what I need." (p. 26) Why do you think this is? Who is not giving Eden what she needs?
5. How does Kevin get a high-powered defense attorney? How does this make Eden feel? Why is Josh so bitter about it?
6. Why is Eden dating Steve? What effect does Eden's past have on their relationship? Why does she end it with him?
7. How has Eden's relationship with Mara changed since she told everyone about the rape? Before the trial, Mara says, "'You never gave me the chance to be a good friend to you.'" (p. 258)

Why did Eden do this? How does Eden change her relationship with Mara after this confession?

8. Why does Josh get drunk after the concert while hanging out with his high school friends? What are the repercussions for his drunken evening? Is it fair to Josh that his parents put so much pressure on him to remain sober?
9. When thinking about their high school relationship, Josh says, "Eden was angry and I was sad, and we shouldn't have worked but we did." (p. 115) Do you think this is true? How do these roles shift throughout the novel? How does this past relationship affect Josh's dealings with Bella?
10. Why is it so important to Eden that she leave home and go away to school? What aspects of her life, both positive and negative, is she leaving behind? Why do you think Caelin makes the opposite decision and stays home instead of going back to school?
11. Why is Josh so worried about his behavior toward Eden during high school? What about Eden's behavior back then might make him think that he might have pressured her?
12. What qualities make Parker a good friend for Eden and Josh? What about Dominic? How do they support the couple, and what do they get from the friendship?
13. When Josh and Eden have sex again for the first time since high school, she says, "I've never been so present. . . . I realize, I'm crying. Crying because I've never felt this way before. About him, about myself. I don't even know what *it* is, but I feel it in my body, my heart, my mind, everywhere—it's everything. And then I know, all at once: This feeling is freedom." (p. 205) Why didn't she have this feeling any of

the other times she had sex, even with Josh? What makes this time different? Why do you think she calls it "freedom"?

14. Why doesn't Eden want Josh to attend the hearing with her? How does Josh feel about this?
15. Who or what made Eden feel like a jack-o'-lantern? (p. 295) How do you feel about her metaphor? How does she find her way to feeling human again?
16. Why is Eden's nightmare so traumatic for Josh? For Eden? How does it change their relationship?
17. How did Eden respond to Josh's strong reaction about her slip-up with her birth control pills? Was it fair of her to put him in this position? Why did he react the way he does? What did he mean when he said, "'This is you'"? Why was this statement so triggering for Eden? (p. 337)
18. Why does Josh play basketball? What does it mean to him? Why has he grown to resent it so much? Why does his playing improve after he and Eden break up?
19. It is very important to Eden that she make people understand why she didn't say no to Kevin when he was raping her. Why does her answer make the defense attorney so angry?
20. The format of *The Way I Am Now* is very different than that of *The Way I Used to Be*, with Josh and Eden narrating alternate chapters. Why do you think the author chose to make this change? Why was it important that both their voices be heard?

TURN THE PAGE FOR A SNEAK PEEK AT

SOMETHING LIKE GRAVITY.

EIGHT MINUTES. THAT'S HOW LONG IT TAKES LIGHT from the Sun to reach Earth. That means every time we look up at the sky, we can only ever see the Sun as it was eight minutes ago, never how it is right in this moment.

The next closest star to our Sun is Proxima Centauri, at 4.2 light-years away. That's 25 trillion miles. It would take tens of thousands of years to get there. And the farthest stars are millions of light-years away. Far enough that so many of the stars we see don't even exist anymore; they've died in the time it took for their light to reach us. All we can see is the past, but only so far—13 billion light-years. Anything beyond that is simply too distant, and the light hasn't had enough time to reach us yet.

There's something about that. Something fascinating. Terrifying. Beautiful.

But sometimes I wish that for just once I could see into the future, not on an astronomical scale, maybe just two or three years into my own life. If I could know ahead of time how this will all turn out, whether I'll be okay or not, then maybe I'd be a lot less scared, a lot less angry, right now.

That's what I was thinking about in the backseat, as I stared out the window, watching the scenery on the I-90 turn like seasons, from suburbs to city to suburbs to country and back again. Until now, my parents had only spoken once in two and a half hours, and that was to tell me to turn my music down.

"Chris?" I pretended not to hear. *"Chris,"* Mom repeated, louder, twisting around in her seat.

My dad's eyes ticked up to meet mine in the rearview mirror.

I pulled my headphones down around my neck. That was all the response I'd give her.

She stared at me like she was trying really hard to see something in me, see some*one* in me. "Is this punishment?" she asked. "You're trying to punish me by doing this?"

"Sure," I muttered.

Monosyllabic. I learned that word when I was seven, as in Mom hated when I would give her monosyllabic answers instead of full sentences, which is why I used them strategically.

"I said I was sorry, Chris." *She hadn't, actually.* "You hate me that much?" she asked, and I could tell by the sharp edges of her words that I was making her angry. *Good.*

"Whate'er," I mumbled, smashing the word down to a single, compact sound. I hadn't spoken more than one-syllable words to Mom in two days, and I sure as hell wasn't about to start now.

"I—you—" she began, but stopped herself, realizing we'd had this fight a million times already, not only over the last two days, but the whole past year, and no one ever ended up winning. She turned to Dad instead. "A little help, Joe? I mean, really. God, she just—"

"He," Dad interrupted. "Okay? Can we just let it be?" He cut his eyes to her, not quite raising his voice. It takes a lot for him to actually get angry, but lately that quality has only seemed to enrage my mom.

"Let it be?" she repeated, this bitter laugh vibrating under her words. "Fine." She jerked herself around in the seat, crossing her arms and making a point to stare straight ahead, without a sound. But I could see her working the muscles of her jaws, clenching her teeth like she was chewing up whatever words were left over in her mouth.

Dad watched me in the rearview again, his eyes wanting to tell me something I don't think he knew how to say with his voice. That he was trying. That maybe part of him understood part of me. That he was on my side. Sometimes.

He looked forward again, rolled his head from side to side, and then readjusted his grip on the steering wheel, accelerating to just above the speed limit. I put my headphones back on and closed my eyes.

All I'd done was dare to leave my house. All I wanted was a little freedom, just a tiny amount of control over my own life.

Two days ago I woke up early, before my parents. The house was quiet and the day was perfect. I started getting dressed, laced up my running shoes. I was planning on heading down to the basement to use Mom's old treadmill, like I did most mornings.

But somehow, I walked out of the front door instead.

I took three easy steps down our porch stairs, then into the driveway, and then down the sidewalk. First I just jogged. Past our neighbor's house, then up to the stop sign at the corner. I was going to turn around.

But as my feet hit the pavement, falling into that old familiar rhythm, I ran. Ran the way I used to before school, back when they still let me go to school. I didn't mean to be gone for so long. Maybe I knew they'd be worrying, but I just couldn't care anymore. I couldn't keep living inside their fear, because, as much as I hated to admit it, their fear was contagious and it was beginning to become mine too.

Yes, I forgot to bring my phone, but that was an accident.

When I got back, they were waiting for me in the living room. They'd even called Coleton, my only remaining real-life, flesh-and-blood friend, who was sitting on the couch looking like he'd just rolled out of bed. I walked through the door, and Dad stopped, midpace, stood very still, and yelled, really yelled, "Where the hell have you been?" in a voice that sounded like a stranger's. Coleton stood quickly, and I distinctly remember the look on his face as he approached me. He came so close, I actually thought he was going to hit me, but instead he just stood in front of me and said, "You're good." I couldn't tell if it was a question or a statement, but I didn't have time to respond because he shook his head and elbowed past me, slamming the door behind him on his way out.

Mom didn't say anything.

She marched up to me with yesterday's mascara streaked in angry black lines across her cheeks, and pushed me. Shoved me, hard, against the door. And then she took a step back, and I remember it happening almost in slow motion. I heard it before I felt it. Like that sharp crack of the door slamming shut again. Except it took me a second to realize that sound was her hand against my cheek. A slap. The feeling spread like a million tiny needles piercing the side of my face one after the other. She had never hit me before; neither of my parents had ever hit me, not so much as a single spanking as a child. I don't remember if anyone said anything; I just remember Mom backing up slowly, looking at me as if *I* was the one who'd hit *her*.

I stormed up the stairs to my bedroom, grabbed my phone, and saw that I had forty-seven missed calls, eighteen voice mails, and twenty-nine text messages from the three of them.

That was when I called Isobel. Because she had promised me she'd be there if I ever needed anything. And I desperately did.

The chirping of the turn signal woke me. Then the rumble of loose gravel under the tires made me sit up. I looked around as we were finally pulling into the driveway that led up to Aunt Isobel's house, which used to be my mom's house too; it was the house they grew up in.

After ten hours of sitting in the four-door pressure cooker that was our family car, I jumped out the instant Dad shifted into park.

"Holy shit," I mumbled under my breath. This was really, truly the middle of nowhere. People say that, but I always thought it was an exaggeration. Not this time. Nothing but farms and fields and woods as far as I could see. I'd only ever seen this place in old photographs; it felt strange to be here in person. Exactly what I was expecting, yet nothing like it at all. The only thing that resembled civilization was the old, dilapidated house that stood in front of me, the place that would be home for the next two and a half months.

I had the urge to run again—to run and keep on running forever. But just then, I caught sight of Isobel on the front porch. She was wearing her nurse's scrubs and leaning up against a post that also leaned, supporting an awning that sloped too far downward to be structurally sound. Her feet were bare as she descended the steps, and as she came closer I could tell from her heavy eyelids and her casual smile that she was tired. She must've just gotten off work. But something changed in her face when our eyes met, like we were coconspirators and this whole mess, this whole fucked-up year, was all part of some elaborate plan that was working out perfectly because it had brought us together, right here, right now.

Isobel could make me believe in a lot of things.

She was holding her arms open, and as I walked toward her I remembered everything I loved about her all at once. And I felt less like running away. Isobel is older than Mom by three years, but still, I've always thought of her as the cool, young aunt. She's brave. Does her own thing and doesn't care what people think—like last year, how she streaked her hair electric blue, just because. Or when she got that bird tattoo when my grandma died.

I usually only get to see her once or twice a year. Thanksgiving and Christmas, or sometimes she'll make the trip for a special birthday or anniversary.

She'll come for bad things too. Like Grandma's funeral. Or like last fall, when I was beaten so bad that I was in the hospital—she was there then. She was also there when I got out, and she stayed with us for the six weeks it took for me to get better. She forced me to do all the painful physical therapy, and even let me hate her for pushing me so hard. She wouldn't let me give up. She made me strong again, even stronger than I was before.

"Chris, my goodness! Look at you, come here." She gave me a quick, firm hug. Not a long, drawn-out pity hug, for which I was thankful. When she pulled away, she shielded her eyes from the sun as she looked up at me, then took my chin in her other hand and said, like it was no big deal, "So handsome."

But before I could respond, Mom appeared right next to me, saying, "Hello, Isobel," her voice all tight and annoyed and disapproving.

"Sheila, good to see you." Isobel flashed a smile that was so much warmer than my mom deserved, but then she gave me a wink when Mom wasn't looking.

The three of us stood there, silent, as we waited for Dad to trudge up from the car, struggling to carry four of my bags at once. As he set them down on the ground and looked at Isobel, he smiled—a real smile—for the first time in a long time.

Isobel pulled him into a hug that lasted just a few seconds too long. Definitely a pity hug—poor old Joe and his nasty wife and his screwed-up kid that he doesn't know what to do with anymore.

Mom looked down at the ground and cleared her throat. As my dad and Isobel pulled apart, Isobel said, "How you doing, Joey?"

"Joey?" He scoffed. "Please, you make it sound like I'm twelve years old."

"What can I say? In my mind you'll always be a twelve-year-old." She clapped him on the shoulder and reached over to mess up his thinning hair, but he ducked away quickly.

Dad and Isobel graduated high school the same year. They used to date when they were my age, and that's how my mom and dad first met: Mom was Dad's girlfriend's little sister. It's hard to imagine any of them being my age. It's hard to imagine Dad with Isobel.

Isobel always said they were better as friends. And Dad never said much about it at all. They still had this sibling-like banter that always seemed to make Mom so jealous. All my life, she had made these little comments about it, jokes usually. But there was no humor in Mom's face now, as she leveled the two of them with her eyes.

Sometimes I wonder if my parents were ever really happy, if it was me who did this to them. Maybe there's something like the speed of light when it comes to love, too. Like they were doomed before they ever started, but it's just taken seventeen years for them to be able to see it.

conditions
of a
heart
BETHANY MANGLE